# KESTREL'S DANCE

Also by Misty Massey:

# MAD KESTREL

# Kestrel's Dance

## Misty Massey

LORE
SEEKERS
PRESS

KESTREL'S DANCE
ISBN 978-1-62268-137-2

Copyright © 2022 by Misty Massey

This book is a work of fiction. Names, characters, places and incidents are products of the author's imagination or are used fictitiously. Any resemblance to actual events, locales, or persons, living or dead, is entirely coincidental.

Poem excerpts from the collection "Salt-Water Poems and Ballads" by John Masefield, Published 1913, The MacMillan Company.

Also available in e-book form: ISBN 978-1-62268-138-9

Cover illustration by Susan Roddey.

Lore Seekers Press is an imprint of Bella Rosa Books.
Lore Seekers Press and logo are trademarks of Bella Rosa Books.

10   9   8   7   6   5   4   3   2   1

*For Bleys, who sprinted with me all the way to the last page.*
*Love you, Beetle.*

# Kestrel's Dance

# PROLOGUE

*I saw her at the sea-line's smoky rim*
*Grow swiftly vaguer . . .*
—JOHN MASEFIELD, *The Wanderer*

Silver winked at the edges of the man's sleeve. He ran a long fingernail across the smooth wooden counter, turning his finger to produce a high-pitched scraping sound that sent shivers down the bookseller's back. "The pirate. She was here?"

"Yes, my lord."

"You sold her a book?"

The bookseller swallowed the lump that had arisen in his throat. "Two."

"And those would be?"

"An atlas of our fine islands, and a flapbook detailing the exploits of Flingo Naile."

"Nothing else?" The hand lifted from the counter, the finger pointing at the bookseller's face. "You needn't answer. I'll save us both some time."

The bookseller's heart thudded against his ribs. He wanted to close his eyes, but something forced his lids to stay open. He stared into the watery blue eyes shadowed within the hood. Something tickled at the back of his neck, as if an insect was crawling into the short hairs there. The tickle grew into a stinging, then a stabbing pain at the base of his skull. His sight blurred, the blue eyes expanding into blue sky, then light, vicious burning light. The bookseller's teeth ached, and his skull pulsed as if it was about to explode. The bookseller's legs failed him, and he crumpled to the floor of his shop.

"One more book she took. One you had no right to own, much less to sell. Your life should be forfeit, but I am a merciful man." The Danisoban's footsteps echoed through the empty shop, ending with the slamming of the door.

Soft hands stroked the bookseller's face, wiping away the sweat of his agony. His wife helped him sit up, but he couldn't see her. Everything was a blur of gray. "I can't see. Gods help me." He laughed without humor. "I'm blind."

"Are you out of your mind? Why didn't you just tell him?"

He dropped his chin to his chest. "Would it have ended any differently?"

# CHAPTER 1

*Oh some are sad and wretched folks that go in silken suits*
*And there's a mort of wicked rogues that live in good reputes*
*But I'm for drinking honestly and dying in my boots . . .*
— JOHN MASEFIELD, *Captain Stratton's Fancy*

The pub wasn't crowded. She hadn't expected it to be, not yet. The afternoon was only half-gone, but there were more than enough patrons already seated and drinking to suit her purposes. Sunbeams pierced the grubby windows wherever a clean spot allowed for it, sending spears of light over the worn wooden floor. One salt-stained table ran the length of the room, with benches on either side. Smaller tables of various sizes and styles filled in the rest of the space. The bar itself held court at the back. Fanciful creatures were carved into the dark hardwood, and the smooth edge looked like the railing from a rich man's stairway. It was much nicer than anything else in the place, and Kestrel had a feeling it had been salvaged from some shipwreck long ago. The ever-present stink of marsh mud wafted through the room every time someone opened the door, but she hardly minded. She found a seat at one of the smaller tables close to the bar. She'd have preferred sitting near the door, but her instructions gave her little choice. Over in the corner, half a dozen men were gathered around a table, playing a rousing game of hounscozza with some tumbling cubes that had seen better days. Now and then she'd hear hollow rattling followed by cheers or groans. She wished she could join in the game.

"What'll it be, dearie?" The serving wench swung by, two empty pitchers dangling from one hand.

Kestrel shook her head. "Nothing, thanks. I won't be here long."

"Not even long enough for a drink?"

"I'm meeting someone."

A sparkle leapt into the wench's eye. "A romantic tryst is it? Here in the middle of the day. You're a saucy one, you!"

Kestrel's throat tightened with revulsion at the thought of sharing anything that could be called "romantic" with the man she'd agreed to meet. "Business. Sorry to disappoint you."

"Isn't me who's disappointed, I reckon," the wench laughed, flitting away toward the bar.

Kestrel crossed both arms on the leather-bound book in front of her, and dropped her head, her braids tumbling down around her head. The wench was closer to right than she knew. A rendezvous in the warmth of the afternoon would be a pleasant diversion. It had been so long.

There'd been opportunities aplenty, especially since she'd become captain of the *Thanos*. Men approached her in every port the ship visited. Pirates, sailors, sun-browned Doanan farmers come to market, even land-bound merchants passing through — they'd all heard about the magic wielding pirate woman. Some wanted to convince themselves her reputation wasn't a tall tale. Others were determined to add her to their own stories, a shining bauble that they couldn't own, but could perhaps borrow for a night. And more than a few of them had been attractive enough to light a fire in her body. She hadn't needed to pay for her own ale in a very long time.

But none of the attention was ever any good. As soon as she let a man buy her a drink, sing her a song, even steal a furtive kiss, an image of honey-gold hair and a mischievous grin would float into her awareness. Flames of need would blaze with the memory of McAvery's kiss, only to crumble into ash at the touch of any other man's hand.

She reached up to the open neck of her shirt and fingered the red stone that hung there. Warm. As warm as his lips against hers, that day on the docks. She might be able to whistle a waterspout into existence, or sing a breeze to fill her sails, but she didn't know how to make the one man she wanted stay by her side. Damn McAvery. He'd flashed into her life sharp as lightning, and disappeared as quickly.

Tightening her fist, she flexed her arm. Maybe it was time to yank the last trace of him off her neck, throw it away. Free herself of him at last. She drew the lanyard tight, intending to pull it off, but something made her relax her grip and drop the jewel back under her shirt. She couldn't do it, couldn't take it off. Not yet. Not until she'd seen him once more.

"Drinking alone, sweeting?"

One of the hounscozza players stood, hip-shot, next to her table, two mugs of ale in his hands. Decent looking, with the bleached hair and ruddy tan achieved by a life spent under the sun. His hands were strong, the skin marred by tiny white scars along his knuckles and wrists. Sailor, she decided, maybe drummed out of the service for knife fighting, to judge by his hands. He grinned, revealing unappealing yellow teeth. "A woman as beautiful as you should never be alone."

*Bloody Grace and all her besotted nephews*, she thought, her mood sinking even further. Not another one. Not now. "I'm waiting for someone."

The man pulled out a chair with his foot, and seated himself, pushing a mug to her. "I'll wait with you, then. Name's Tooley."

Direct, this one. No flowery poetry to try and sweep her off her feet. He probably didn't know enough words to call a pup to heel, much less to romance a woman. Back at the table, several of his fellows were smirking and nudging each other. One fellow reached into his jerkin, pulled out a paper bill and laid it on top of a growing stack. A betting stack, but no one was tossing the cubes. There was only one other chance they might be betting on. If there was a wager on his success, someone was about to be disappointed.

Kestrel watched the foam in the mug dissipate in slow, languid pops. "Best if you press on now, lad."

He cleared his throat. "There's a right lot of wicked fellows about. What kind of gentleman would I be if I left a lady undefended?"

She leaned back in her chair, and laid her hand on the leather dagger scabbard strapped to her thigh. "A lady I'm not."

He waggled his eyebrows in a way that he must have thought was appealing, but only reminded Kestrel of wooly worms writhing in the sun. "You're going to be more of a challenge than I thought, Captain."

"You know me."

Tooley scooted his chair closer, and took a swig from his mug. "Aye, sweeting. I'm the man what'll be winning you."

The others were huddling closer to each other, their laughter now unmistakable. She wondered whether he was the best they had, or whether they were hoping to embarrass their companion by watching him fail so publicly. It didn't matter much either way. Kestrel pushed the ale back toward her suitor. "You've lost your bet. I'm not interested. If I was, I wouldn't choose a man who'd lay money on my knees parting."

Guffaws exploded from the crowd behind him, and money began changing hands. Kestrel didn't join in. She kept her gaze fixed on Tooley. Color drained from his face. His jaw tightened. Slowly, he rose to his feet, took another swallow of ale, and set his mug down on the table. "No woman tells me what I can bet on," he said, his voice measured. "Think you're above me, do you?" Reaching down, he grabbed his mug and flung the contents in her direction. Ale splashed across the table, filling the air with its pungent tang.

Kestrel rolled out of her chair, drew her dagger and dropped into a fighting crouch. There was nothing for it now. "You've spilled your beer," she said.

Tooley growled, low in his throat. He drew his own weapon. A knife, with a wicked serrated blade. She'd read the signs aright. And now he was between her and the door.

He launched himself across the short distance, swiping the vicious knife in a tight arc toward her belly. Kestrel hopped back, vaguely noticing people yelling around her. Could be the bar wench screaming, or the onlookers laying new wagers. She didn't have the luxury of looking around.

He was bigger than she was by a good margin. She'd have to come in close to do him any real damage, but he'd bury his knife between her ribs before then. He had the advantage. And he knew it.

Tooley rocked side to side, deftly tossing the knife from one hand to the other, grinning. "Come on, woman. Let's see how much better you are," he said, amusement tinging his words. "Or are you scared of a real man?"

His knife flashed, catching glints of afternoon sun as it passed back and forth. For the briefest second, every time he tossed it, the weapon was free. A childhood filled with running and hiding left her uncomfortable with using her talent in front of people, but sometimes it became necessary. If she could whistle that knife the second it was in midair, she could slam it into the ceiling, out of his reach. Maybe make up the difference, and give herself a little leverage in this fight. Kestrel licked her lips, and started to blow.

Tooley leaped for her. Driving his shoulder into her midsection, he knocked the breath from her. She spun to the floor. Tooley flung himself onto her, pinning her in place.

Stars danced before her eyes. She'd landed on her belly, her chest paralyzed from his blow, her lungs like stone. She opened her mouth wide. Her throat was tight as dried leather. Kestrel thrashed, tried to throw off the weight. Air. She needed air.

"Now who's better?" Tooley pulled her braided hair, lifting her head away from the floor. Blackness was seeping into her vision. She wanted to hold still, but her body spasmed, strain-ing for a breath.

"If I won't be winning you," he said, his voice echoing in her pounding ears, "I'll have to be satisfied with killing you." He shifted his weight and pulled her hair harder. A cold sliver of steel pressed against her taut throat.

Her vision was closing into a tunnel of darkness, ending at his face. Thunder pounded from inside her head. Not like this, she thought. I can't die like this. She scrabbled her fingers against the wooden floor.

As suddenly as her throat had closed, it opened again. *Sweet Grace,* but it felt wonderful to breathe. Her abdomen cramped with the effort. She didn't care, as long as she could finally pull air into her lungs. An oily voice insinuated itself into the rum-bling behind her eyes. "Forgive my intrusion, but your disagree-ment with the captain will have to wait." She blinked, cleared her eyes and rolled over.

Tooley still straddled her, but he'd risen to his feet. His atten-tion was on his raised knife arm; it was trembling violently. He grimaced. His hand opened, as if some invisible person had taken hold and was prying his fingers apart. The knife clattered to the wood floor inches from Kestrel's head.

Now his free arm was moving as well, both hands jerking together over his head. His back twisted, bending far too sharply backward with an alarming bone-on-bone crunch. Tooley wailed. "Stop, please . . ." he gasped.

Kestrel struggled to sit up, her hand landing on the hilt of Tooley's wicked knife. She felt a sticky wetness, and turned her palm to look. Spots of blood dotted her skin. But she bore no cut, and the knife blade was clean — Tooley hadn't landed a strike. The blood couldn't be hers. She pressed on her ribs, but felt no wound. And now that she looked more carefully, there were other, tiny spots of blood on the floor around her.

With another hideous crack, Tooley's body tipped over. He landed hard, and rolled onto his side. Two of the hounscozza players rushed over, and grabbed him by the arms. "My legs! I can't move," he groaned. They hustled Tooley out the door, his legs dragging behind him, followed by most of the patrons. Even though the fight was over, no one in the harborside taverns liked to stick around in case tensions erupted again. An unconscious man in the opposite corner and the last two hounscozza players were all that remained. The gamblers turned away to their game.

"Well met, Captain! I trust I have not kept you waiting over-long." The voice was icy water on the back of her neck, making the hairs on her arms prickle uncomfortably.

Menja Lig stood over her. The King's Danisoban, counselor and right hand. A man with eyes in every port of the Nine Islands. Who had already made it clear the Brotherhood wanted her as one of their own, and would take her however it could. Her old captain, Binns, may have felt comfortable with him, safe even. She could never, would never trust a mage. Lig had his own agenda, and she knew better than to believe he would keep his distance. No, if she was going to let herself get that close, she was doing it with several dozen witnesses at hand. Lig wasn't a tall man, but his gaunt frame gave him the illusion of towering height. His face was hidden within the deep recesses of his hood, his features shadowed. He corked a tiny glass vial before slipping it into the folds of his sleeve.

Breathing and talking still took effort. "What'd you do to him?"

"It seemed you needed help. I was only too happy to lend my assistance."

"Help like yours I can do without."

He chuckled. "You're most welcome, Captain."

As an orphan child, she'd feared the Brethren. Maybe it was the way they seemed to glide when they walked, as if their feet didn't touch the earth. Their cagey habit of covering themselves head to toe inside black robes, with only their bony hands poking out, the glint of silver at the wrists as a warning. Even now she was an adult, the apprehension never left her.

Sitting on the floor looking up at Lig wasn't helping her feel any stronger. Her dagger lay under the table, not far from Tooley's knife. Kestrel grabbed both weapons and got to her feet, brushing her free hand on her breeches. She sheathed her blade, and laid Tooley's knife on the table.

The wench approached. "Care for anything to drink, my lord?" Her flirtatious manner had disappeared. Everyone knew better than to irritate a Danisoban.

"Melan Gold," said Lig, taking a seat. "Two glasses."

"One glass," Kestrel said, knowing she sounded petulant and not caring. "I'm not drinking."

Skeletal hands, pale even in the dimness of the tavern, reached up and pushed the voluminous hood away from his face. "A sailor who doesn't drink. Isn't that what started the trouble before?" Lig flicked his hand at the wench. "Away with you."

He looked like nothing more than a friendly old uncle, grizzled and smiling, with blue eyes that in any other face might have been charming. That was how he, and all the others like him, had managed their atrocities. Pretending to be harmless and gentle, offering sweets and warmth to the street urchins of Eldraga. No one ever missed the lost children when they disappeared. No one except their own.

She no longer feared him, not as she once had. He was a man, skillful and possessed of power she couldn't dream of, but mortal just the same. He could be stopped. He could be killed. No, the fear had faded away, but the disquiet and contempt never would. The Danisobans had murdered her parents. If the chance presented itself, she would destroy him.

Unfortunately, it wouldn't be today. The two of them worked for the same man. It wouldn't be smart of her to anger him now. The least she could do was behave like a civilized person. Taking the job of Royal Privateer had seemed like such a good idea when it fell into her lap months ago. Standing in the opulent royal garden of the palace on Pecheta, dressed in silk and linen and being waited on as if she was royalty herself, the anticipation of being the *Thanos'* captain had been a heady thrill. She'd stood next to her retiring captain, smiling vaguely as the king dug a hole, and planted the sanguina shrub she rescued for him only a few days before. Kneeling in front of the plant, he bent forward and consumed the youth-restoring fruit that hung from it in a few quick bites. The gathered nobility fell into a hush, waiting to see what would happen to their king. Kestrel herself wasn't sure what to expect. A flash of light, perhaps, or a sudden change. The transformation from old man to young happened gradually, the lines in the king's face softening, his skin tightening, the silver of his hair darkening to a rich brown, all over the course of a few minutes. Before she knew it, the king looked like a man of thirty. No one could keep their eyes off him. No one but his Daniso-ban. While everyone else marveled over the king's restored beauty, Menja Lig had kept his gaze firmly fixed on Kestrel. His terrifying attention had reminded her of the danger he posed, even while she served the King.

She took her seat at the table. "I have work to do," Kestrel said. "Let's get this over with."

He sighed, as if the weight of the world lay on his shoulders. "Captain, I assure you, there are other places I'd choose to be. We all serve as we must."

He was right, as much as she despised admitting it. Arguments won her nothing. It would only extend the time she had to spend in his company. Make the trade and get out; wasn't that the way Binns had always done it? Planting both hands on the salt-stained leather of the log book, she shoved it across the table to Lig. And waited.

He glanced down, and back at her, his face unreadable. "You've checked the figures twice?"

"If there's a discrepancy, you know where to find me."

His tone was ice. "Always, Captain."

It took every ounce of control not to grab the book and slam it against his smirking face. "Are we finished?"

He leaned to his right, and came up with another log book,

clean and new. He laid it gently on top of the one Kestrel had given him. "Before I send you on your way, there is just one other thing."

"No." She surprised herself with the suddenness of her response. "It's no use starting this again."

"Starting what again?"

"My answer hasn't changed. I won't join the Brotherhood."

"What led you to think I'd ask?"

"Don't play the innocent, old man," Kestrel snapped. "You lot've been chasing me since I can remember."

Lig widened his eyes. "My dear captain, it is our duty to seek and claim those who exhibit ability. You eluded us as a child — you're very likely too old for training now. It would be counter to our purposes to take you on as a student."

She shook her head. "We both know that's not what you're after. It's what I already know how to do that interests your kind."

"I can't deny that, Captain. Still, if your family hadn't resisted . . ."

"What choice did they have? You steal children from their homes!"

"We're hardly thieves. The families are well-compensated. As yours would have been."

"My parents were murdered," she snarled.

Lig dropped his gaze, spreading his hands in front of him. "Unfortunate, that business. But look how you've turned out. Royal Privateer, captain of a crew that would follow you anywhere. And you not only young, but a woman as well."

Fury rushed through Kestrel's veins like a storm swell. He sat across from her, knowing what his kind had done to her, yet he had the gall to imply she should feel grateful.

Lig leaned forward, his breath ruffling the loose hairs at her temples. "Have I upset you?" he whispered. "I hear whistling can cure a foul mood."

Tooley's knife was so close. Her fingers itched to spill the bastard's life on the pub's dusty floor. It would be so easy. One little whistle, and she could drive the blade into Lig's eye.

"Curious." His smile was a predator's grin, his eyes intent. "You think you could do me harm. I find myself intrigued."

Kestrel drew a breath, and sat back on her chair. He was trying to push her into losing her temper, get a look at what she was capable of. For an instant, she wondered if he knew about her morning shopping, but no. He couldn't have found out so soon. The bookseller hardly wanted to admit it to her, and he'd owned the book for years. If Lig knew, he'd have confiscated it long ago. Well, damn his eyes, let him bait her — she could resist for now. They'd face each other eventually, but not until she was ready.

"Alas, as much as I would love to explore your abilities," he said, "I'm here on His Majesty's business, not that of the Brotherhood. I've given my word of honor not to pursue my own interests in this case until such time as His Majesty has released you from service."

Kestrel barked a laugh. "I wasn't aware someone like you had honor."

Cold fire burned in his gaze. "Captain, my word is the only thing that does bind me."

Damn him for the truth. It was the day he'd take his word back that she needed to fear. Until then, they were locked in a bizarre arms-length dance. She wanted to get back to her ship, to the safe whoosh of water splashing against the hull.

"What's your one thing, then?"

A tight smile creased Lig's face. "His Majesty wishes you to sail to the seas around the Children. There you are to capture and bring back a most unusual creature, of which His Majesty has heard tales. He would like very much to add this animal to his menagerie."

The Children. If the reef known as the Children had ever been an island, it was destroyed in the far distant past, leaving nothing but huge water-smoothed stones rising from the ocean like ancient gods. The currents in the area were capricious as a teenaged queen, liable to send a ship rocking too far in one direction and crashing into a Child. Sailing through the Children was dangerous on the best of days, and deadly on the worst. Was Lig joking? Was a Danisoban even possessed of a sense of humor? Other than the smile on his face, Lig seemed as serious as she'd ever seen him.

"Aren't there folk who do this sort of thing for him already?" she asked.

Lig tilted his head, but said nothing. With one long-fingered hand, he opened the cover of the book. A thick parchment packet lay within, the royal seal stamped in red wax. Lig handed it across the table to her. Kestrel eyed the packet, reluctant to touch it, as if the very paper would sting her.

"What's this?"

"Your orders. Including a detailed description and sketch of the creature you're to capture, along with care and feeding instructions. His Majesty wishes the animal delivered healthy." He let the packet fall gently to the tabletop. "Read them, and carry them out with all due promptness."

"We're to go on a fishing trip?"

"If His Majesty had any further instructions for you, he did not see fit to share them with me, Captain," he said. "It isn't my place to break His Majesty's seal, once set."

Was there the slightest chance he hadn't read the orders? Or was this distrust merely a symptom of her childhood fear? Not in her mind, but in the last few months, so many things she believed to be truths were turned upside-down. Trust had become a luxury she could ill afford.

"Of course," he continued, smooth as a serpent in sand, "you could ignore His Majesty's orders, and leave royal service. Attempt to make your own way, as it were."

Her own way. Right into the waiting jaws of the Danisobans. "Is that a threat?"

Lig raised his eyebrows. "Captain, a Danisoban doesn't have to threaten. Perhaps one day, you'll wish to learn why that is. The choice is, as always, yours." He tapped the packet with one long fingernail. "Read the orders, Captain. I'm certain His Majesty was most specific." Lig rose, took the old log book out from under the newer one, and bowed. "Be seeing you." Standing, he slid his hands into the sleeves in front of him, and moved toward the door. Not a footfall echoed as he went, his gait as smooth and silent as a current in the ocean.

She stared after him. Her gut tightened, trembling with leftover tension. Pressing her hands against her temples, she sat for a moment, trying to force herself to calm enough that she could walk the streets without being distracted. She could face a heavily armed ship, outmanned two to one, and attack without a second thought, but sitting two feet from a mage, made her skin crawl.

One of the hounscozza players sauntered to her table. A tall man, almost the same size as Tooley. She pushed back and stood to face him, ready to warn him off. He wore a dark hood that shadowed his face, but there was something familiar about the way he moved. Not the silken motion of a Danisoban, thank goodness. She couldn't quite put a finger on it. Had they perhaps met in the past? Before she could figure out how, or even if, she knew him, he reached out and tossed a gold octavo onto the table.

"I'm not interested in a drink," she said.

He leaned both hands on the table, turning his face away just enough that she couldn't get a good look. "It's a bet."

"Sorry, mate, I'm out of patience. Take your coin and spend it on something more certain." She pushed the gold coin toward him, but the man reared back as if she'd thrown fire his way.

"This bet will be settled down the line," he said. "When you admit that not all your fish stay netted."

Kestrel stared at him. Was this another of the king's men, trying to deliver a message in code? But he said nothing more, straightening and striding out of the pub, leaving the gold octavo gleaming on the table. Kestrel picked it up, and turned it in her fingers. An ordinary coin, with the face of the former crown prince, worn down a bit from its travels through the markets. Whatever it meant, it was still money. She slipped it into her pocket, and made her way to the door.

# CHAPTER 2

*. . . the wheel's kick and the wind's song and the white sail's shaking,*
*And a gray mist on the sea's face and a gray dawn breaking,*
— JOHN MASEFIELD, *Sea-Fever*

"Wingspan as wide as a deep water fishin' vessel. Black body, although it can appear a dark red if seen under bright sunshine. Eats fresh fish. Since when are we bloody fishermen?" Shadd growled. He shook the rattling parchment. "This ain't our responsibility." Her quartermaster had demanded to know all the details of her meeting almost before her feet were off the boarding plank. Instead of explaining, Kestrel shoved the orders into his hands, watching his eyes widening as he read.

"Stow your objections, lad. Deal's done." She walked to the water barrel, and thumped it. "Water's low. Get someone to fill it up, aye? We'll need to replenish the food. How's the rum holding out?"

"Sendin' us out to fetch him a pet, here on the edge of spin-storm season."

Kestrel leaned back to gaze at her sails far above. "Sails look good. Angus finish mending the tears?"

"We oughta be settlin' in for the summer, not chasin' off after a trophy for the king's menagerie."

Ignore him all she would, he never gave up his grumbling unless she forced him. It wasn't what she hoped to be doing with her afternoon, but Shadd had that bull-headed look in his eye. "Why are you still arguing?"

He crossed his arms across his burly chest. "I didn't like ye takin' up with royalty from the start, and this here's precisely why. How many men do ye think are goin' to agree to this fool's mission? Especially with nothin' to show at the end."

Back in the old days on board the sloop *Wolfshead*, when she was a mere swabbie and Shadd served as Binns' master gunner, he took her under his wing. Protected her from the unwelcome attentions of the crew, taught her to fight, and acted as the brother she always wished for. After becoming captain of the *Thanos*, she immediately promoted Shadd to be her right hand. Who better to serve as her second than the man who'd always been closer than blood to her? But that kind of relationship bore a price. He told her when he thought she was making a mistake. Every time. There were times she wished he wasn't quite so ready to speak his mind.

"I'll ask none to remain who don't wish it," she said. "Any man of the crew who takes the release does so without any bitterness from me. Put the word out, and let me know who signs on." Snatching the pages from his grip, Kestrel marched to her cabin.

Shadd followed her inside, shutting the door behind him. "Oh, that's a fine thought," he said. "Ye'd sail us into the most dangerous seas in the Nine Islands with less than a full crew?"

Kestrel tucked the folded parchments into the cover of her new log book, and crossed to the bookcase. "We've done it before. The *Thanos* can be handled, for a short time, with a minimum complement. And if we manage to catch this beast, the pay won't have to be shared among so many — bigger reward to match the danger." She slid the book into its place on the shelf. "We'll anchor well clear of the Children and their shoals, take the hackney boats down for the fishing."

"Fishin'? What, ye think we're goin' to go toss in a line and the beastie'll take a nibble at a worm?"

"We'll go for a baby. Flip of a bozorgi's tail and we'll be done." She tried to grin. "You'll only be a week or so late for your leave time, and with extra coin in your pocket. Olympia won't mind that."

Shadd poked his lower lip out, fretful as a spoiled child. "Somethin' doesn't feel right about this, Kes," he muttered.

She nodded. "I know. It feels suspicious to me, too. But we have our orders, and until things change, we have to carry them out."

He ran one meaty hand through his shaggy mop of blond hair. "It peeves me mind why the king has to have his prize now. Why couldn't he wait 'til the storms is all died down?"

"Good question," Kestrel walked to the sideboard, opened the little door and took out a bottle of black rum and two tin cups. She plunked the cups down on the table, splashed rum into both, then handed one to her quartermaster. "He's the king, and used to getting what he wants when he wants it." She sat down and leaned on her elbows, breathing deep the hot-sugar scent of the liquor.

Shadd tossed back his rum, and wiped his mouth with the back of his hand. "Kes, we're pirates, ain't we? What's to stop us takin' the ship and makin' our own way?"

Her own way. She'd heard those words twice now in one day. She swirled the black rum in the bottom of her cup, watching a tiny whirlpool form and subside. Shadd knew, better than almost anyone, how she felt about Danisobans. Glistening obsidian nightmares, razor-sharp and cold but only half-remembered in the morning light. The way she sometimes couldn't catch her breath at the sight of a silver bracelet. Sailing under the auspices, if not the colors, of the king of the Nine Islands offered her a measure of security from the Brotherhood. Especially now that they knew how very unusual her magic was.

Shadd pushed his cup forward, a grin on his face. "I thought as much. Ye've been thinkin' the same thing, ain't ye? Who needs the King watchin' over ye when ye got the wide, wild ocean to keep the magi away? Ain't as if His High-and-Mightiness could stop old Lig, not like the water would." He raised his cup. "Dip a wizard in the drink, watch him bubble, thrash and sink."

Kestrel raised her cup to the old children's rhyme, and tapped it against Shadd's before tossing back the contents. The one thing that weakened a Danisoban mage was salt water. They took great pains to avoid contact with the ocean. But Kestrel was very, very different. Proximity to the water strengthened her. She'd be worth more to the Danisoban Brotherhood than any gold or jewels. If they could study her, figure out how her power functioned, it was possible they could make it so for themselves. And not only the Brotherhood, but the mysterious Eusebians as well. They worked for the Danisobans as bounty hunters, but they had a plan for her, if they could lay hands on her. There'd been no sign of them since that fateful day on the palace turret, when she defeated their man, but that didn't mean they weren't still waiting, somewhere.

She uncorked the rum bottle again, and poured her quarter-master another shot. "Aye, Shadd, I've considered it. Been thinking about it ever since Binns retired."

"Long enough, to my mind." He rolled the cup between his palms. "Think too long and ye grow roots out of yer feet."

"When this job fell in my lap, I felt as if fortune was finally smiling on me. I should have guessed it wouldn't be simple. It never is." Kestrel shoved her chair back and started pacing. "Bloody Grace defend me, I never wanted anything so much as a life on the sea."

"Ye've got one, lass. Or didn't ye notice?"

"No, I had one." She leaned on one arm against the window-sill. "What I've got now is eyes on my back and a leash around my neck. Every night I have to spend hours writing nonsense in that bloody book, and I never know whether I'm getting it right. Hell, a few days back, I was trying to scribe *ten bales of linen flax* in that daft code of theirs, but next morning when I was checking my figures, I realized I'd written *tin balls of lemon figs*. I didn't sign on to be a squint-eyed clerk, for Grace's sake."

Straightening, she returned to her chair and sank wearily into it. "I've been imagining how much better freedom would be. Real freedom. But right behind those thoughts come the ones in which I'm queen of the hempen ball and the rest of you waiting your turn to dance at the end of the same rope. Because you know as well as I do how quickly he'd send ships out to find us, once he knew we'd turned outlaw."

"Ye ain't just a pirate, though. Whistle up a wave and sink the whole fleet, ye could."

Once upon a time, she feared telling him about herself, about her magic. She thought sure he'd want to kill her. How wrong she'd been not to trust him. "A man jumped me in the pub today while I was waiting for the mage. Very nearly slit my throat. And all because the wind was knocked out of me. My magic isn't much good if I can't breathe."

"Too bad McAvery couldn't have stuck around, then. He seemed to know an awful lot about such things. Could've trained ye in the ways t' use yer skills."

He hadn't stayed. He wasn't the staying kind. He'd kissed her and left her, without even a glance behind. McAvery was the king's man, never hers. That was a subject she was glad to avoid. "Wouldn't it be wonderful to be on the *Wolfshead* again, Shadd? Chasing rich merchants, just taking enough to live comfortably? Nobody particularly important paying us any attention, nor caring at all where we are from day to night."

"That it would, Kes. But the *Wolfie*'s sunk, and the world's turned to a different spot for us."

"That it has." She tipped her cup, watching the dark liquor within roll against the sides like a tiny ocean. "Time to stop dreaming. Work awaits."

"No fear, Captain," he said. "I'll lay in more food. Plenty of salted fish. That sound good to ye?"

Kestrel grimaced. Just the thought of salted fish turned her stomach, and he knew it. "Anything else, please. Even hard tack's better."

He laughed, rising to his feet. "No worries. There'll be a scrap o' pork for ye. And I'll alert the crew. See who's willin' to stay on a wee bit longer. Mayhap we can get home afore the first storm presents herself."

Home. The word hung in the air after Shadd was gone. Her truest home stood under her feet, rocking slowly with the movement of the tides. Kestrel retrieved her cup and tipped the last swallow of rum into her mouth. The familiar heat of it slinking down her throat was comforting. Not so much as the thought of a home, a ship, of her own. In the months since signing on with the king, she'd managed to put aside enough money to afford a small sloop. Pure freedom was at the tips of her fingers.

Except that she'd fallen in love with the *Thanos*. The ship was a living, breathing being. The snap and flutter of her sails was blessed music; the wooden creaking of her hull like the low humming of a mother to her child. Kestrel's heart was hopelessly lost to her. No other ship would do but the one she could never truly possess.

She leaned back in her chair again, and noticed the gentle weight of McAvery's jewel against her breastbone. Damn it, no man would do but the one she couldn't keep, either. Was that her fate — to be always wanting, never having?

She reached into her backpack, and slowly withdrew her

morning's purchases. An atlas of the Nine Islands, and a small paper flapbook filled with fanciful tales and colorful drawings of the legendary pirate Flingo Naile. A gift for Binns, who claimed to have sailed with the man. And one more book, the leather thick and smooth, the paper musty, with an aura of power she couldn't quite wrap her mind around. Spending even the short time with Lig had worried her, for fear he'd know, somehow.

Her friend Olympia put her on the trail the last time she docked on Eldraga. No one could ferret out secret information the way Olympia could, so when Kestrel told her she wished for some way to even the playing field between herself and Lig, it took Olympia only a few days to come up with a suggestion. She warned her that the rumor might be false, but Kestrel was willing to try.

At first, the bookseller didn't want to admit the book existed, and even after she convinced him of her seriousness, by counting gold octavos onto the table, he didn't want to sell it to her. He kept it in a locked box in his storeroom for fear of the Brethren detecting its presence. Too dangerous, he called it, even as he unwrapped it from its silken covering. Maybe the information in the book was dangerous or maybe it was all a lie, invented secrets to thrill the dilettantes. For her, the danger was necessary. She stroked the cover. *The Source of Conjurr* was printed in faded silver letters on the well-handled leather. The primary book of instruction in the Danisoban School. Removing even one copy of the book from the enclave was a crime punishable by memory cleansing, leaving the unfortunate criminal with no more intellect than an infant. How the bookseller had gotten his hands on it, she couldn't guess. For him to sell it to her... she didn't even want to think what might have happened if anyone walked in on their transaction. It had taken three times the asking price to convince him, octavos she paid willingly. All she needed now was time, time to read and understand.

The sun was dropping below the horizon, flashing fire along the edge of the Pechetan Arch in the harbor, by the time the *Thanos* was ready to sail. The enormous ivory structure soared above the water, erected there long ago for the royal guard to keep watch over all ships coming in and leaving. Its whiteness reflected the glow of the setting sun, warm and inviting. Kestrel stood on the quarterdeck of her ship, gazing out at her men working on the main deck below her. The ocean beyond the Arch's shadow called to her.

"We've kept twenty-eight of the men. They're all aboard and the articles signed. If we lengthen the watches, everyone'll get a chance to sleep. Food stores weren't low, but I've laid in extra biscuit, salt fish and water, enough for thirty days, just for safety's sake," Shadd said. "And topped off the rum, like ye asked."

"Rum. Good." She ran her hands over the spokes of the *Thanos'* wheel, relishing the soft vibration from the wood. The tug of the tide changing. Too bad for the sentries; it was time to put Pecheta to her rudder, and sail into the sun.

"Are ye well, Kes?" he asked. "Most times ye give me grief about the salt fish."

"Sorry." She tore her eyes from the horizon, focusing on Shadd as well as she could manage. "Let's get under way."

"Bring up the plank," Shadd bellowed. "Full sails, heave 'er up." Men sprang to action, scrambling into the rigging. A half dozen grabbed the spokes of the windlass and began turning it, winding the dripping anchor chain up and around. Shadd grinned at Kestrel. "Waitin' on yer whistle, Captain."

Kestrel pursed her lips and blew, a gentle quaver that wrapped itself around her in silken threads, lifting the loose hairs near her temple and tickling her skin. She took another breath. The softly moving air strengthened with her renewed whistling, building from a breeze to a wind. The *Thanos'* sails billowed, supple as birds wings above her head. It was her favorite sound, the thudding snap of canvas filling with air. No music in the world was as sweet.

Kestrel maintained her tune, providing a steady wind, and kept a firm hand on the *Thanos'* mighty wheel, guiding the vessel under the great ivory arch and into the open water. Once they were clear of the harbor, Kestrel stopped whistling. Natural breezes caught the *Thanos'* sails. The ship seemed to leap over the waves, as if it, too, was eager to be moving. The sun was a warm orange sliver peeking above the edge of the world. On the main deck, men were securing the rigging, their bodies glowing gold in the waning light. Shadd turned around and gave a hearty wave.

"Can't tell ye how much I enjoy seein' that island behind us," he said.

"Couldn't agree more," she answered. Her stomach rumbled suddenly. She hadn't eaten anything since sun up. "Did the cook stay on?"

"Aye. He's puttin' a meal together now. Could be a bit. Want somethin' to tide ye over?"

"Please." She grinned at her quartermaster. "Don't bring me salt fish."

He laughed, and headed for the main hatch amidships.

The rhythmic creaking of the ship rising and falling over the water was hypnotic. For now, she could forget her worries and just sail, the wheel under her hands and the wind keening through the lines.

"Captain!" The cry startled her from her reverie. Shadd was running toward her as if his life depended on it. "Get down!"

"Are we under attack?" She scanned the water. No ships were in sight, at least not within the range of her naked eye.

He flung himself up the quarterdeck steps, yanking his scarf from around his neck. "Ye're on fire!"

"What?"

"Yer shirt's on bloody fire!" Shadd nearly knocked her off her feet, patting at her chest with his scarf.

Fire? Kestrel pushed Shadd away, and glanced down at her body. Redness was beaming from under her shirt, flickering like an ember. But no heat, no burning. If it wasn't fire . . . Slowly she pulled open the neck of her shirt, and drew out McAvery's amulet.

A light was shining from deep inside it, casting scarlet onto Shadd's surprised face.

"Why's it doin' that?" he asked, dropping his scarf and backing away.

"I don't know," she said. She lifted the gem up higher. The light inside it danced off the facets, glittering. Kestrel tilted her head. A dark spot moved in the heart of the gem. A flaw, perhaps. But it moved. Of all the jewels she'd ever seen, not a one had moving parts inside it. She brought it closer to her face, staring intently.

The spot grew, changed shape. A fuzzy star. No, a person. Arms, legs and head. As she watched, the figure became more distinct; a man, handsome, with a face she knew all too well.

"What're ye lookin' at?" Shadd's voice seemed to be coming from far away.

As she watched, the scene expanded. Behind McAvery, the railing of a ship appeared, then the deck. An armed ship; the edge of a brass monkey loaded with cannon shot was visible to McAvery's left, a soot-blackened swivel gun on the railing close by. An edge of striped sail snapped over his shoulder. Behind him other men emerged, holding his arms. They were dressed in plain clothing, so they weren't royal navy. Pirates, or merchants, perhaps.

Not a one of them looked at all happy about whatever situation this was. The man on McAvery's right nodded, and slipped out of view behind him. A second later he reappeared, and clamped an iron shackle around McAvery's neck.

McAvery struggled, and his mouth moved. Kestrel couldn't hear anything, but it almost seemed that he was saying her name. Did he know she was watching? The scene vanished.

The lanyard in her fist snapped, and the gem tumbled to the deck. It lay at her feet, lightless as any stone on a street. She bent and picked it up. As she watched, its color faded, the rich red replaced by a dusty dried blood hue.

"Captain?" Shadd looked genuinely worried. "Kes?" He gulped. "Are ye with us? Ye ain't possessed?"

"Don't be absurd." She held the darkened gem up between the two of them. "Did you see that?" she asked.

"I saw ye staring at the light for a minute, holding the lanyard so tight ye should've choked yerself. Then ye threw the bloody thing on the deck."

Kestrel shook her head. "McAvery's in trouble. I saw him."

"In the dangle?" She nodded, and Shadd visibly relaxed. "Should've guessed it'd be one of McAvery magical trinkets. So we're off to a fight, then?" Shadd rubbed his hands together. "I love a good tussle."

Kestrel retied the cord and hung the gem on a wheel spoke. It bumped against the wood, sounding hollow and lonely. "I don't know where he is."

Shadd's face fell. "Ye can't locate him through yer little necklace?"

"I wouldn't know how to try, but even so, I think the gem's used up. McAvery's the one knows how to play with these baubles, not me. It's all I can do to make the whistling work." She squinted at the horizon. "We have a job to finish."

"His Majesty's zoo won't mind a few days' delay."

"Maybe not. But what if it's not really McAvery? What if it's an illusion, designed to pull my strings in just the right way? Doesn't it strike you as convenient, happening just now while we're still in range of Pecheta?"

Shadd screwed his face up, wrinkling his forehead. "Didn't McAvery give ye that trinket? It ain't been off yer neck in all that time."

"That doesn't mean it's not an illusion. I have no idea how much control the Brethren have over objects they've spelled. And if it is real, Lig could have arranged McAvery's capture, knowing I'd be watching."

"And ye're willin' to take the chance he'll be killed while ye run off to go fishin'? That ain't right, Kes. Ye know it ain't."

"If Lig could prove I delayed the king's orders by rushing off to rescue a friend, he could convince the king to release me from service. I'd be playing right into his hands."

"Ye couldn't have saved Binns without McAvery's help," Shadd reminded her. "Seems like we owe him a bit, don't ye think?"

Binns. Her first captain, the man who'd given her a chance at being a sailor when no one else would. The closest thing she'd had to a father. McAvery had been a valuable asset when the king's son kidnapped Binns. Her heart thumped miserably. Shadd was right about that. Bad enough that she wanted so much to see him again, but she owed him as well. That debt made the situation worse. The shadow of Lig weighed on her. She couldn't take the chance. "Don't you think I want to rush off to McAvery's aid? The way things stand, it's simply too risky. Lig is watching everything I do, looking for a reason to snatch me up and study me. I can't afford a misstep. We finish this job first."

Silence dropped between them. Kestrel stared at the horizon, feeling Shadd's disapproval like a rain-soaked cloak on her shoulders. "McAvery's a big boy," she said finally. "He's been getting out of scrapes for years all by himself. And if Lig's got him," she paused, hating herself for even saying the words out loud. "We have to hope McAvery's more valuable to him alive."

She lifted the dark, dead gem from where it hung, and held it near her eye. Nothing now but reddish gray shadows. She slipped it back over her head, and tucked it inside her shirt again. She didn't look at her quartermaster until his thudding footsteps receded down the ladder. The look in his eye would have been harder than her last glimpse of McAvery, clapped in chains and begging for her help.

# CHAPTER 3

*... To a windy, tossing anchorage where yawls and ketches ride,*
*Oh I'll be going, going until I meet the tide.*
—JOHN MASEFIELD, *A Wanderer's Song*

A dull thud exploded from belowdecks. "Again, ye bloody scalawags! 'Twas ten seconds longer than the last time! Yer enemy ain't goin' to wait for ye to be ready afore he strikes!"

Shadd had been running gundeck drills for the last three days since their argument, much to the chagrin of his exhausted gun crew. Storm drills would have been more appropriate, considering the time of year, but Kestrel didn't bother to suggest it.

They hadn't spoken of McAvery again. Shadd stomped away belowdecks while Kestrel remained on the quarterdeck, forcing herself not to stare at the horizon. If she saw another ship, she didn't know if she could hold to her own bidding. Any ship she spotted might be the one holding McAvery hostage. Every mile closer to the Children was another mile distant from him.

Another explosion sent ripples through the sails above her head. "And that one was short by a ship's length. Ye think the enemy's plannin' on waitin' for ye to come closer?"

She needed to order him to stop for the night, just so the day watch could sleep for a few hours. She didn't look forward to the conversation. For the last three days, Shadd avoided any but the most necessary contact with her. He wasn't angry, as far as she could tell. The cursing was just his usual way. But a gray sadness filled his eyes on the rare occasion she actually met his gaze, and it cut into her soul. He was disappointed in her.

She wasn't sure what he expected her to do. Defy the King and his Danisoban? Walk away from a job that ensured her safety to go rescue one man who might not even remember her name? And how did he think she could even find McAvery in the wide ocean?

Of course that's what he expected. And he was right to assume so. She was Kestrel, the only female pirate captain in the Nine Islands, the woman who could whistle a hundred swords to her hand if she chose. Why should she care about an old king who'd far outlived his usefulness? Where had His Majesty been when the Danisobans murdered her parents?

When it all came down, she owed the Ageless King very little. Much less than this job was worth. In fact, it was he who owed her. Without her intervention, his crown would be on his only son's head now, and he'd be a shambling wreck, dying under the weight of years he borrowed. Thanks to her, the king remained on his throne and his deceitful son was locked away for good. She ran her hands over the smooth wood of the wheel. All of Binns' talk of duty and honor had been just that. Talk. The only thing keeping her in this situation was the *Thanos*. Hers only by stewardship. If she quit the king's service, she gave up the *Thanos* as well. Unless she didn't have to. The dangerous thought leaped to the forefront of her mind as it often did, even while she insisted to Shadd that such a course was impossible. Did she possess the strength of will to run off with the ship? She'd been a pirate most of her adult life, and pirates took ships. How would it be any different if she laid claim to the *Thanos*? Painted its hull, changed its name, prowled the waters far from Eldraga and the King's reach?

Kestrel shook her head, as if she might toss the thought of running away out of her mind. Binns wouldn't run. He had served the king for years, even admired the man. If she kept at it, she might find a way to respect the king herself. Every new life had its unpleasant points. Perhaps she only considered running away because she hadn't settled into the rhythm of the job yet. She should give it more time, find a way to make herself and her crew indispensable to the king in such a way that he'd never allow Menja Lig anywhere near her.

To do that, they had a job to finish. Better to concentrate on catching the King's latest fancy, and think about the future later. She still didn't know how she was going to lure and capture the animal. Merely line fishing wasn't likely to result in anything but a dead animal or a pirate dragged overboard. A net might be better, although they'd bring up all sorts of other creatures along the way.

She blew out a dispirited breath, watching the waves in the distance toss and glitter in the waning light. Was there anything her magic could do? Not for the first time, she almost wished the Danisobans had taken her. At least then she'd understand her power. Almost, but not quite. The vague memory of her mother's eyes and voice reminded her that such a price was too high for what the mages promised.

Still, it was worth a try. Licking her lips, she began to whistle, a gentle tune she knew from listening to the men singing at night. The song begged a sailor to return from his long voyage away from his lover. *Come to me,* she sang in her head as she whistled out loud. *I dream of thee, love, come to me.* The tingle of magic crept over her skin. She imagined the animal they sought sweeping up to the ship, swimming alongside willingly all the way back to Pecheta. Never happen, she knew, but the thought was charming, and she smiled, nearly ruining her whistle.

Eventually she reached the end of the song, and let her whistle blow away on the breeze. Nothing happened. The sea rolled along as it always did, looking no different. The snap of sail and the soft whine of the breeze in the rigging sang as they always did. Ah well, she thought. It was a long shot. The animals had only been sighted around the cruel shoals of the Children. The ship might still be too far for one even to hear her call. At least she tried. Learning how to handle the ship had been simple compared to learning magic. At least a ship's workings made sense. Magic, not so much.

A rumbling shook all around her, shaking her out of her musing. Tomorrow she'd put her foot down, tell Shadd to stop drilling the men and wasting supplies. Whether or not he wanted to talk to her. For now, it was time to send the day watch to bed, let the dark watch take over. The scent of food being prepared below wafted close. Stew, probably, cooking all day so the meat would be tender. It smelled appetizing. The dark watch would already be eating, preparing for the call to duty. The gun crew needed their rest. If she let him, Shadd would probably keep at the drills all night, and run her out of black powder in the process. She turned toward the quarterdeck stairs, taking two steps down when another rumble followed, and she realized it wasn't coming from the gundeck. No cursing, for one thing.

Could it be thunder? Stars were twinkling in the sky, but storm season loomed, and squalls were known to sweep over the sea in an instant. "Damn," she muttered, rubbing the itchy corners of her eyes. There'd be no sleeping yet. If a storm was really on the way, there was work to see to. "All hands, look lively," she called. "Secure the deck! Shorten sail!" She crossed to the hatch, and called down. "Ahoy, the gun deck! Put your ladies to bed, Shadd. There's weather coming in."

Men scrambled into the rigging, furling the sails. Others tied down the deck guns with thick rope. The water and rum barrels were rolled close to the mainmast and also bound with rope in hope of keeping them from tipping and crushing someone if the seas tossed the ship too hard.

The noise came again, a rolling, belly-rumbling snarl that didn't end even after she couldn't hear it anymore. It wasn't com-ing from the distant horizon, though — this time she could have sworn it was coming from underneath her feet. As if something was thundering beneath the ship.

Shadd climbed up from the lower deck hatch. His shaggy hair was more disheveled than usual, soot stained his cheeks and his homespun tunic was hanging loose. "What the hell's happening?" she bellowed, not waiting for him to come any closer.

"I thought you said a storm's comin', but there ain't no wind nor chop." He shoved the ends of his tunic into his breeches.

"Gundeck secure?"

"As the Mayor of Pecheta's strongbox, Captain, aye."

The sudden moaning was long, and loud, an eerie wail raising gooseflesh on her arms. It shuddered up through the decks and vibrated her very bones. No way this was thunder. At the same instant, the ship's timbers groaned in wooden agony. The *Thanos* began shaking. Mildly at first, increasing in intensity until the barrels tied to the mast rattled against the wooden deck. The ship tilted, and Kestrel skipped a few steps, fighting to maintain her balance. Oil splashed out of the lanterns on that side, throwing the deck into heavier shadow. She grabbed onto Shadd's shirt, trying to keep from tumbling to the deck. Men in the rigging cried out at the unexpected lurch. The ship righted itself, and

Kestrel let her quartermaster go.

"Earthquake?" she asked.

"At this depth?" He frowned, clearly puzzled. "Most we'd feel would be a heavier roll."

"If that's not it—" she stopped, confused. They stared at each other helplessly.

Deafening clanking exploded over the thunder. The capstan, the huge spool on which the messenger rope was wound, began to spin, slowly at first, then building up speed. It unwound its long rope, the anchor chain to which the rope was attached banging against the hull loud enough to be heard on deck. Two men were standing nearby, watching helplessly as the spokes shot past in a blur. The rope whined dangerously. Kestrel took the ladder two steps at a time, sprinting across the deck toward the capstan.

"Why's it playing out so fast?"

"Don't know, Captain," David DeadEye cried. "The bight slipped right off, and around she went."

"Like a fish with a hook," yelled Hudee.

Shadd caught up to her, panting. "What's happenin'?"

"We have to stop the anchor!" She tipped into the railing with another round of shaking, grabbing at the smooth wood for purchase. Her feet barely stayed under her.

"How?"

Even if it hadn't been unwinding too fast for her to cut, the capstan rope was thick as a small child's waist, and humming under the strain. A day's worth of sawing wouldn't have made a dent in it. When it played out, it could snap, and lose her the anchor. If it didn't snap, if for some reason the rope was tough enough to hold fast, the whole capstan might tear loose, taking a hefty chunk of her deck with it.

The ship jerked under her feet again. A scream from above drew her eyes up. One of the men had fallen. His leg had tangled in the rigging and kept him from crashing to his death on the wooden deck. He swung upside down, crying out for help. Kestrel wondered how long their luck would hold. The next yank from below could spell death for one or more of the crew. The ship righted itself, rocking side to side as it settled into plumb. This couldn't go on. She had to try something. Anything to save her ship. Commanding the *Thanos* had been her dream for too long to let it sink in the middle of the ocean with no one to ever know what had happened. Licking her lips, she pressed them together and whistled.

She could barely hear herself — she wasn't even sure she was following any kind of tune. There wasn't time to worry about it. The tingle of magic rose around her in the familiar way, warm pinpricks tickling all over, forcing gooseflesh to rise on her exposed skin. Despite working her magic for months, the sensation remained strange and unsettling.

The anchor chain squealed, and she focused her attention on the spinning capstan. The only way she knew to stop a wheel was to grab its spokes. If she attempted to lay hands on the spokes, at the rate they were spinning, she'd probably break both arms. But the magic . . . she stretched out the fingers of both hands toward the wheel, then closed her fists tightly.

The pull nearly yanked her off her feet. The wheel's momentum was heavy as an anchor itself, pulling against her efforts. She tightened her fists, and drew out her tune, careful to make her notes slow and long, all the while concentrating on the idea of grasping, stopping. She locked her legs against the capstan's pull. Her body rocked forward, and she struggled to keep in place. If she fell into the spinning spokes now, the best she could hope for would be broken bones. The worst . . . better not to think of it. Slow, she thought, fighting the rising panic in her throat. Slow. Stop.

A pair of hands gripped her waist. She didn't have to look to know who it was. Now that Shadd had grabbed on, he surely could feel the weight of the capstan pulling against her. His strength was enough, though, to keep them both safe. She concentrated on the capstan again, and whistled even harder. Hard enough, she hoped, to make that anchor stop dead.

Suddenly whatever was pulling against her gave way. The capstan wheezed as it slowed, and Kestrel fell against Shadd, both of them tumbling backward, heels over heads, as the line slackened. They struggled to untangle themselves.

"That's my arm you're stepping on," she said, breathless, her heart still pounding from her efforts. She needed to come up with some way to make the magic work without leaving herself breathless in the process. McAvery could probably teach her. If she ever found him.

The anchor was no longer moving. The capstan ground to a halt with an exhausted groan. Pirates hung in the rigging, staring at each other. Kestrel didn't want to move, for fear of breaking whatever spell had fallen over everyone and everything, and seeing the capstan start to move again. When a minute passed without incident, she nodded. "Alright men. Bring it up," she said, hoping her voice sounded calm.

As if they'd been waiting on her, men leaped to the capstan braces, and began winding the thick anchor rope back into place.

Kestrel rose to her feet, and leaned over the rail to watch the anchor being pulled into place. The ocean below was black now that the sun had completely fallen, the surface gently broken by glittering reflections of the lanterns on her deck. All was peaceful. A quiet night to sail. As if nothing had happened.

Her heart slowed, her breath easing back to a normal rate. She probably could have whistled now without a problem. Not that she wanted to.

A splash caught her attention. From the west, it was. And whatever made it must have been big, because the ripples were rolling toward the *Thanos*, and they were impressive. Damn near the size of coastal waves. She squinted into the distance.

Something crested the water. Something dark, and gleaming, and huge. Its hide glistened briefly in the lights of the *Thanos'* lanterns before it slid below the water, out of sight. Kestrel's breath caught again. Whatever the creature was, it was enormous, and alive.

"Kes?" Shadd was standing next to her.

"What?" she managed.

"Did ye see that?"

"Uh huh." How could she have missed it? It was the size of a fishing boat.

"So what was it?"

"I can guess."

"Ye don't think that was what we're s'posed to catch, do ye?" He shook his head. "Even if we go for a baby, it could be big as a hackney boat. How'll we get it aboard without killin' it?"

"And where do we keep it if we do catch it? The orders didn't mention it needed water to live." The worry had already crossed her mind. The orders were for a live animal. If it died, they might as well eat the meat and make boots from the skin for all the good its carcass would do them. And what would the king have to say if she returned empty-handed?

The anchor chain clanked, drawing Kestrel's attention back down. The massive iron anchor was breaking the surface, drawing back up to its usual spot. But something was wrong. The tines on the anchor's ends were bent inward, as if something huge had grabbed and squeezed them, forced them flat against the ends.

Kestrel strode to the mainmast, grabbed one of the still-lit lanterns from its place and shoved it at her quartermaster. "Tie a rope on this, and hang it over the side." She continued on to the railing amidships, and swung a leg over, touching the first rung of the ladder with her toe.

"What are ye doin'?" Shadd asked.

"Something's wrong with the anchor." Kestrel set her foot securely, then threw her other leg over the rail. "I'm going down to see what's what."

"Ye think that's safe? With that monster out there? Ye'd be nothin' but a mouthful to a beastie like that."

"Did I mention I wanted you to shut up?"

He threw his hands up. "Fine. Kill yerself. See if I grieve over ye when ye're a bit o' bait."

Kestrel carefully began to climb down, the lantern following a few inches away. When she'd reached the halfway point, she stopped. Hooking her free arm into a rung, she reached out for the lantern and raised it to take a hard look at the anchor hanging just above the waterline. Cold ran through her veins. The tines weren't just bent. There were marks on the anchor — teeth marks. Something had bitten the anchor. Something with big teeth. It hadn't snapped it clean, but that wasn't much of a reassurance. She'd been sailing for years, but not only had she never seen a creature as big as the one that just swam by, she'd never heard of anything that would bite an anchor. What had one of the men said, about fishing? It was almost as if the anchor had acted as a baited line, and the creature a catch.

"Shadd," she called up. "I'm coming back. Tell Tom to work out our current bearings, if you please."

His shaggy head disappeared as he left to do her bidding.

Kestrel thought about the bent anchor as she hauled herself back up to the main deck. Fishing trip, Shadd had called this. She hadn't considered that her own ship might be the lure.

As soon as she reached the rail, men reached out and pulled her to safety. "Thanks, lads. Back to work. Give the ship a once-over, make sure nothing else is damaged."

"Aye, Captain!" they called, but she was already making her way up the stairs to the quarterdeck where Red Tom stood quietly by the binnacle lamp.

"So where've we ended, Tom?" Kestrel asked.

"We're a good ways off course. Looks like we were dragged during that bloody great shaking before."

"Like an angler with a fish on the line. One that's too big for his tools, so it's pulling him off his feet." She'd never experienced anything like that. Bloody Grace willing, she never would again. "And if that creature we saw was the thing on our anchor, we'd better be thanking the gods it decided to let go."

Tom's eyes widened. "Are you thinking it meant to let go? The beast was playing with us?"

She didn't know how to answer him without making him more frightened, but he'd hit the nail on its head. Whatever that thing was, it had known exactly what it was doing. Against it, her ship was no more than a toy.

# CHAPTER 4

*Called with their sirens, hooting their sea-speech;*
*Out of the dimness others made reply . . .*
—JOHN MASEFIELD, *The Wanderer*

One of the benefits of being captain was having a cabin to herself. The captain's cabin aboard the *Thanos* was luxurious. Highly polished dark wood furniture gleamed, and the wide, beveled glass windows reflected the light from the candle next to the comfortable bed. Kestrel hadn't wanted to claim the room at first; it had seemed too rich for her. That worry faded once she accepted that she was captain of the ship. Sliding the bolt to lock the door behind her, she walked over to the table and set down the bowl of stew and plate of hard tack the cook delivered to her. It smelled rich and meaty, and her belly grumbled with the need of it. Before sitting, she opened the cabinet where the fine black rum was kept, poured herself a slug and carried it to the map table as well. She broke the hard bread into the stew, letting it soak up the liquid until it was soft enough to chew. The stew tasted wonderful. Too soon she was scraping the bottom of the bowl with her spoon. A few crumbs remained on the table, but she didn't bother sweeping it away. She sat back in her chair, enjoying the momentary satisfaction of a full belly.

Pursing her lips, she blew a whisper of air. A tiny sound floated out, almost imperceptible, but just enough to flutter the velvet curtains. She barely understood the power she possessed. It wasn't all that uncommon — most families in the Nine Islands, noble or not, could claim magic-wielding relations. The rarity lay in her bond with water. There wasn't a Danisoban in the islands who could work magic in close proximity to the oceans.

But Kestrel could. She wondered sometimes if the water enhanced what she could do, but she never experimented. She avoided using the power for nearly twenty years, too afraid of herself and what she might become. Until a handsome man with mischievous eyes and his own agenda forced her hand. Reaching up to the open neck of her shirt, she drew out the red gem. After it showed her the image of McAvery in trouble, it seemed to be used up, its color faded and dull. She'd worn it so long, though, leaving it hanging on the wheel felt ungracious. Besides, maybe its power could recharge in some way. She had reknotted the broken lanyard and slipped it back onto her neck, where it felt most familiar. The faceted edges were still warm from lying next to her skin. He put it around her neck that day, on the docks of Pecheta, just before he disappeared into the crowds. "Wear this. For me," he whispered, the warmth of his breath sending tingles down her neck. She wondered where he was right now. He was the most irritating man she'd ever met. Gods, but she missed him.

"What should I do?" she asked, holding the gem in front of her eye. The room beyond was shadowed in red, and slightly warped, but it was nevertheless the same room. Same ship, same Kestrel. No men, no chains, no McAvery in trouble.

"Why didn't you tell me what you were hanging around my neck?" she muttered. "It might've helped me know what to do now." Her eyes were burning, and she took a sip of the rum in her cup. It wouldn't have mattered if he'd told her, she knew that. He likely assumed he'd be the one swooping in to save her.

She tucked the gem back into her shirt. What she'd told Shadd was true. McAvery had gotten himself out of far more scrapes than she could guess, and had been doing so long before they met. He couldn't expect her to come rushing to his aid when he could be anywhere in the wide seas.

Well and good. She didn't need him. She yawned, her jaw cracking with the effort. Sweet Grace, but she was tired. It was almost as if the bed was crooning a siren's song, and she wasn't in the mood to ignore it any longer.

Sleep . . . the sensuous temptation to sink back onto her pillows, relaxing until her body floated on a sea of softness. Kicking her boots off, Kestrel wiggled her toes. She unbuckled her belt, letting it fall to the floor, and unbuttoned her breeches. Shimmying them off, she crossed to the sideboard, where a china wash basin full of fresh water waited. She picked up the rag next to it, dipped it in the water and wrung it out, then wiped the sweat of the day off her face and neck. Dipping it again, she reached under her shirt to clean her armpits and under her breasts. The water was cool and relaxing, but she promised herself that she'd pay whatever some innkeeper asked for a long soak in a hot tub the next time she was in port. It would be so lovely to take down her braids and wash her hair, too. Finish this task, she told herself. Dropping the rag into the basin, she walked back over to the bed and slid her body between the smooth, cool sheets. Blissful velvet sleep, with no cares to disturb it. She let her eyelids slip down, and let out a deep, relaxed breath.

A low, unearthly moan shattered the silence all around her, jerking her out of near-sleep. Maybe she'd imagined it, in the halfway place between waking and sleeping. As if it had waited for her to think just that, the noise came again. She sat up, pushing the bed linens away. Was it the creature again? This sound wasn't as deep or bone shaking as the rumbling from before. Thank goodness. She wasn't sure the ship could bear another dragging like the first one. "Damn," she muttered, rubbing the itchy corners of her eyes. There'd be no sleeping yet. She'd have to take a look, make sure the dark watch was securing the deck guns, furling sails. Even though they'd just finished untying everything. Kestrel swung her legs over the side of the bed, jumping at the touch of the chilly wood on her bare toes.

It came again, a sharp wail, almost sad in its tone. This time she could have sworn it was coming from underneath her feet. As if something was groaning somewhere close by.

The candle's flame sputtered and went out, leaving her in darkness. Her heart slammed against her ribs. She held her breath, listening hard for a footfall, a rustle of clothing, anything to target whatever might be in the cabin with her. The warm night air was still, silent except for a gentle splashing of water against the hull far below.

Her eyes hadn't adjusted to the sudden darkness — the room was a cave. She snaked a hand down to her belt on the floor, to the long knife that hung from it. The smooth, wooden hilt was warm from her body, warm as a living thing. Wrapping her fingers around it, she drew it from the sheath and readied herself.

Whatever was in here, it wasn't getting her without a fight.

But she couldn't fight what she couldn't see. She forced herself to wait, still as a stone. With agonizing slowness, everything came into focus, the edges of all the furnishings blurred in the half-light from the beveled window. Shadows blanketed the cabin, but all seemed normal. The books stood, bindings out, along the wide shelves. The massive sideboard with its mirrored back, the great map table and comfortable leather-seated chairs were right where they were supposed to be. Even the shadows looked usual, safe and unthreatening. Nothing moved except the stray hairs from her braids fluttering in her breath.

Kestrel searched the room, looking under the bed, inside the wardrobe. Nothing was hiding anywhere in her cabin. Her door was secured by the bolt. Alone. She was completely alone.

She resheathed the knife. Her chest ached from the slamming of her heart and, the sweat on her brow cold and clammy. She wiped her sleeve over her face, and crossed to the door. It opened onto the main deck, and she expected to see men scurrying to and fro, but all seemed calm. Two men from the dark watch sat amidships, playing cards to keep awake. A soft light fell from the quarterdeck above — probably the binnacle Red Tom lit to read by when he had the wheel. Whatever she'd heard clearly hadn't alarmed anyone else. The noise must have been one of those illusions that happen on the edge of sleep. Good thing she hadn't gone running out on deck, gotten the men in a lather over nothing.

Reaching up to her left ear lobe, Kestrel fingered the slender silver hoop that hung there. Binns gave it to her after her first battle, as a badge of her courage. She'd only removed it once, when the need was great. Even though he was far away now, settled in his new life on Bix, the hoop was her link to him. She imagined she could feel his fatherly warmth from across the ocean. She closed her door quietly, and returned to the bed.

Outside the cabin window, the sky sparkled with twinkling stars. Morning was a long time yet to come. The dark watch manned the deck. The rest of the crew were rolled into their hammocks belowdecks, snoring. All was well. She yawned mightily. Time to grab a little shut-eye. She climbed into the bed, pulling the covers back up from where she'd left them. Perhaps if she tried, she could reclaim the dream of the other night, and find out what the honey-haired man had been about to say to her. She laid her head down on one of the fluffy pillows.

The sudden moaning was long, and loud, an eerie wail that raised gooseflesh on her arms. The sound vibrated up through the decks and shook her very bones. No way this was thunder or an illusion.

Kestrel shot out of the bed, grabbed her breeches from the floor and yanked them on without buttoning them tight. Holding them up with one hand, she slid the bolt aside and threw open her cabin door. Other men were clambering up from the hold, some pulling on their pants as they lurched across the rolling, slippery deck. Kestrel met Shadd stumbling across the deck. He'd apparently rolled straight out of his hammock.

"Well," she said, turning back to her assembled crew and trying to insert a lightness to her voice, "I s'pose it wasn't just my bad dream, eh?" She pointed toward Red Tom, her navigator and dark-watch helmsman. "You heard the noise, too?"

He nodded.

"Any guesses what it was?" The men shot glances at each other, but no one had an opinion to offer. "Alright, then. Pair up, men, and search the ship."

"What are we looking for, Captain?" David DeadEye asked.

Kestrel shrugged. "I don't know, lads. But anything you find that doesn't belong, you come tell me." With weary nods, the pirates moved off. Kestrel stopped Shadd with a hand.

"What do you think it is?"

"Somebody ate too much salt fish at supper?"

"Ho ho ho."

He grinned. "I take that to mean ye weren't whistling in yer sleep?"

Shadd was her oldest friend on board, and one of the only people she'd trusted with her secret. She shook her head. "It's hard enough to whistle while I'm awake. Anyway, I've never made a sound so loud as that. Not sure I could." She rubbed her eyes again. "Are we haunted, then? Or is it sea monsters come to visit again?"

"Ghost, or monster, makes little difference to me. I jes' want him to shut up. I'm too tired to be listenin' to somebody moanin' all night. Louder'n midnight in a brothel, that was." He snapped his fingers. "What if it's some sort of animal got on board by stealth?" he asked. "Surely it would've got hungry. Come out lookin' fer food, and cryin' its achin' belly."

"Have you ever heard an animal make a sound so loud?"

"I have. When I was a young'un, livin' out away from town. Ye'd hear hill dogs all the time, callin' to each other in the dead of night, keepin' track of their huntin'."

"I was a city child. Dogs that cried out at night usually ended up in someone's stew pot. Take a couple of men and search the lower decks."

He bopped his ear with the butt of his hand, as if knocking something out of it. "Ain't that what ye jes' ordered?"

"Yeah, but you know the men'll give no more than a quick look and skedaddle back to their hammocks." She lowered her voice. "You're looking for whatever made that noise. Look everywhere. And go to it armed. If you're right and we do have some sort of loudmouth stowaway, I want him found and quieted."

"And if we got somethin' else?"

She crossed her arms and scowled. "We'll deal with it." Kestrel looked at her master gunner. "I want it off my ship, right now."

# CHAPTER 5

*I looked with them towards the dimness; there*
*Gleamed like a spirit striding out of night*
— JOHN MASEFIELD, *The Wanderer*


Shadd and his party searched every inch of the *Thanos*, tipping crates, peering down gun barrels, hunting even in places too tight for a child to fit. And they found nothing. No ghosts, no demons, no Danisoban plotting insidious magic under her decks. Kestrel sent her men to their hammocks to finish out the sleep they'd missed.

The noise had to have a source. She was pretty sure it wasn't the animal that played with their anchor before. That call was deep, a gut-twisting rumble transformed by the water. This sound ranged higher to the ear, an almost anguished noise. If it was related to the first animal, she couldn't guess how. Although happening so soon after did make her wonder. Luckily, since the first time they heard it, other than the sounds of boots stumping against the wood of the deck, the night was quiet and undisturbed. So much so that she could almost believe she'd dreamed the whole incident.

Except that Shadd, and Tom and the rest of the crew had heard it too. It would make for the kind of story she'd love to hear in the taverns, if she weren't on the wrong end of it.

So what could it have been? The sleep she'd promised herself before all the chaos was a distant memory. She couldn't sleep now if she hit herself over the head with a belaying pin. She didn't bother lighting the candle that had blown out — the darkness was soothing. Pulling out the wooden chair, she sank into it and propped her chin in one hand.

As if she'd ever be able to do anything like what they'd felt tonight. Shadd was crazy to think for a second she could have been

responsible. Pursing her lips, she blew a whisper of air. A tiny
sound floated out, almost imperceptible, but just enough to flutter the velvet curtains on either side of the windows. It was good
enough for driving a ship along when the wind had died, but she
needed to learn control, and power. It was possible to perform
feats with her skill, she'd proved that the night Bardo tried take
the ship from her. She'd managed to lift every sword on the
deck, and drive them at her enemies. But surely there was more
she could learn. What good did a stiff breeze do when a blade
was at a friend's throat? What if she wanted to whistle up a wind
strong enough to pick up McAvery and whisk him to her? Across
the room, tucked on the bookcase next to the logbook, was the
Danisoban text. So many answers lay within its covers. No reason
she couldn't open it up, start reading. Start learning. Why was
she waiting?

She pushed back from the table, and walked over to the bookcase. Running a finger long the book's spine, she imagined she
felt a tingle of magic merely by touching the book. She pulled it
out, holding it before her, contemplating. And as suddenly as the
mood hit her, it left again. This wasn't the time. She was too distracted to pay attention to words in a book, and reading a book
like *The Source of Conjurr* without full concentration could end
up hurting someone.

Sitting in her cabin torturing herself wasn't doing her any
good, either. Her men hadn't found anything. That didn't mean
there was nothing to find. Besides, it wasn't as if she'd be sleeping
tonight. She slid the book back into its place. Strapping her
sword belt around her waist, strode, barefooted, out of her cabin
and across the deck to the hatch, grabbing a lighted lantern on
her way. The obvious place to start was the lower hold, and work
her way up. By the time she reached the main deck, she'd either
have found whatever was haunting her ship, or tired herself out
enough to tumble into bed.

The air was hot, thick with the stink of tar, and fish, and the animals they kept onboard. A half-dozen sonnies a few feet away noticed her presence, and made sure she heard their clucking pleas
for feed. Kestrel ignored them and stepped off the bottom rung

of the ladder. She held up the lantern and opened the shutters wider. Light spilled out, breaking the gloom for a few feet. The sonnies became even more excited, their noisy chatter echoing in the darkness. She walked slowly, from bow to stern, scanning the hull for any marks or drawings that might indicate magic being used against her. The walls, though smoky dark with tar, were clear.

Barrels of fresh water were lined against the hull, secured by ropes lashing them to iron rings, and nearly as many of rum stood along the opposite side. A number of empty crates were piled near the stern. Other than those, and despite the sonnies cackling, the hold echoed emptiness. Not a sound she ever liked to hear. In her mind's eye, she could see crates and boxes, full of spices and fabrics, jewels and octavos and treasures she couldn't even imagine but that she knew must be out there for the picking. As soon as this storm season is ended, she promised herself, I'm filling this hold to the beams.

She moved to the crates, and checked them one by one. Nothing there except a few unhappy roders who skittered back into the shadows, cheeping angrily. Behind the barrels was more evidence of the usual stowaways — bits of bone, and scattered pellets, but still, nothing that could have caused so much disturbance.

Kestrel stood back, free hand on her hip, and lantern held high. She took one more look around. "Gods, woman," she whispered. "You're hunting for shadows." She was so busy seeing ghosts behind her, the real dangers could be right in her lap and she'd miss them entirely. "Right then," she said, "nothing here. Up we go." She slipped the lantern's shutters nearly closed, looked up to grip the rung of the ladder. And stopped dead.

Tucked into a corner of the crossbeams, hidden deep in the shadows against the hull, two slitted eyes reflected her lantern light, glowing like dying embers. Kestrel tilted her head, trying to get a better vantage. It couldn't have been much bigger than a lap pup, to fit in such a tight space. Although how a pup would have managed the climb to the rafters was beyond her. Was it a kittle, then? "Here, you," she urged. "Come out and let's have a look at you."

She'd never declared any hard and fast rules against pets on her ship. Men were always adopting roders, wounded birds, even the occasional scaveroach. Pups and kittles were the sort of luxury few sailors could afford. They ate too much, and required far too much attention. Maybe one of the men she'd released days ago had left it behind. It could even have been hiding down here since before she took over the ship, scrounging for scraps of food. She wondered how long it had been since the poor thing saw daylight.

One thing was certain — it couldn't stay where it was. If she could coax it down from its hiding place, an excellent home awaited it. She knew just the place. Olympia Camberlin, madam of the most well-known pleasure house on Eldraga, was the closest thing the island had to nobility. Olympia wore the finest silks and brocades, all gifts from grateful patrons. She held court in her common room from a huge, hand carved wooden throne. Nothing would complement her better than a fluffy pup to pamper. Even if it was a kittle, she'd still be overjoyed.

"Hey, there, little one," Kestrel murmured. "You can't be happy hiding up there." She gnawed her lip. The problem now was how to get the creature down. Growing up in the alleys of Eldraga, she knew better than to grab at an animal. The embers of its eyes seemed more curious than fearful, but Kestrel was not about to risk her fingers in a hungry animal's jaws.

The little creature's body was shrouded in blackness, barely discernible from the darkness surrounding it. Kestrel lifted the lantern and carefully opened a shutter, pointing the light upward the rafter. The creature reacted to the light, shifting further back on the beam, enough that she still couldn't get a decent look.

Shadd was probably already tucked back into his hammock, snoring. She'd have liked his assistance, but yelling for him wouldn't wake him up. Nothing short of another earthquake would rouse the man once he was asleep. And she didn't want to leave the little animal, in case it changed its hiding place while she was gone. Only one option left. She glanced over her shoulder. The hatchway at the top of the ladder was empty and dark. No flickering light coming through. She had to be cautious.

She focused her gaze on the shadowed creature above her. "Sorry, little one, but you can't stay up there forever," she whispered. Drawing a deep breath, she pursed her lips and whistled, notes twinkling up and down on the unseen air. As she blew, the now-familiar fingers of power stretched out from behind Kestrel's eyes, strengthened by her lively whistle. As gently as she could, she sent the music up, to wrap itself in velvet caresses around the creature, and lift.

The little animal didn't struggle, much to Kestrel's surprise. It was lighter than she'd expected, hardly stretching against her power at all. It must have been starving, yet it neither growled nor whined. It remained curled tight, its head tucked into its breast. She brought it down slowly, then, with the last of her breath, set it carefully on a barrel top.

Now that it was out in the open, it was obviously not a pup. Not a kittle, either. She stood back and stared at it. Damned if she'd ever seen anything like this animal. Crouched on thick, muscled hind legs, its smaller front legs held tight against its body, the hairless animal stretched, glistening burgundy skin rolling like an ebbing wave across its ridged back. It raised a slender head, looking a little like the sand lizards she used to chase as a girl, with its graceful neck and long, pointed snout. It was far bigger than any she'd ever seen on Eldraga. The eyes, open wide now, were still glowing a fiery orange-red, two depthless pools of liquid fire. Intelligence shone from within them. It reached out its two skinny front legs.

Kestrel's breath caught in her throat. Beneath its front legs were draped folds of skin, the color of dried blood. As the creature arched its back, the folds opened, flattened, shimmering like fine silk even in the half-light of the hooded lantern. It opened its mouth in a huge yawn, tiny pointed teeth glistening. Suddenly its arms dropped again, the folds sliding out of view.

Wings. The bloody thing had wings. In all the years she'd lived near and on the sea, she'd seen enough strange animals to fill a storybook. But she'd never seen a lizard that could fly. Never even heard tales of one. Flaming snakes, giant bogorzi that spit acid, shellfish big enough to snap up a fishing boat — there were enough tavern stories of those to keep a body entertained for hours. This was new.

Kestrel dropped her head to the side, wondering. "I'll bet the Danisobans would pay a hefty ransom for you." The creature mimicked her movement, turning its head to one side as she had. She bent her head the other way, and again the creature mirrored her. She frowned. "Are you teasing me?" It only blinked its large eyes in an innocent fashion.

Pup or kittle she'd been prepared for, but this thing . . . it certainly didn't seem dangerous, but how was she to tell? It wasn't making any of the usual warning noises. Not that she could depend on that. This was the least ordinary creature she'd ever laid eyes on. Still, she couldn't leave it down here while a danger might exist. If she could get her hands on it, she'd sneak it into her cabin. Maybe bring Shadd in on the secret. He'd probably have a good idea what to do with it, if she could get past his superstitions.

"Little one, whatever you are," she said, "time to get you out of this smelly hold." She clucked softly, reaching out one hand, palm down, the way one approached a strange dog. The animal bent its sinuous neck, trying to peer under her hand, to see what she was holding. It nudged at her fingers with its snout, as if hunting for a treat.

The ruddy skin was warm and smooth. Kestrel wanted to stroke it, but she resisted the urge. She turned her hand over, and opened it, expecting the animal to sniff at her. It glanced at her empty hand, then up at her, with a look that was almost chagrin.

"Sorry, I don't have any food down here." She eyed it curiously. "We'll have to check with the cook. If you eat something too exotic, dinner may be a problem." She eyed the waiting animal, then tilted her chin. "I wish you could tell me what you're doing on my ship."

It reached forward, nudging her empty hand. Its long tongue flicked out, licking at her palm. Her skin tingled with the lizard's touch, as if sparks swam gently along her bones. It felt curiously close to the magic that bubbled within her when she whistled, but before she could think about it, the feeling faded. Kestrel looked at her unblemished palm, wondering what just happened. She saw no hint of injury, no mark at all. Her thoughts were clear, and the animal wasn't behaving in a threatening way.

"What do you like to eat?" Kestrel asked, then shook her head. She was talking to an animal as if it could answer.

The lizard scooted forward, close enough to reach its head up and rub against Kestrel's arm. The shadows around her faded into blue, the deep blue of the ocean. Beams of sunlight drove down from the surface in glittering falls. Silver shapes flashed past her vision. Fish. She stepped back, breaking the contact with the lizard, her heart pounding. What sort of animal was this? She swallowed hard. "You eat fish?"

The creature raised its brows.

She put her hands palms together and moved them back and forth like a fish through water. "Like this?"

It licked its mouth again.

# CHAPTER 6

*By dawn the gale had dwindled into flaw,*
*A glorious morning followed . . .*
— JOHN MASEFIELD, *The Wanderer*

All was dark and quiet when she reached the main deck. She hurried to her cabin, and closed the door behind her. Reaching in her shirt, she pulled the animal out and set it on top of the mirrored sideboard. It looked at her expectantly.

"Stop it," she muttered. "I'll find you some fish in the morning. But until then," she moved to her desk, and rummaged through the papers. A few broken bits of hardtack bread leftover from dinner lay next to the empty stew bowl. She picked up a fragment and offered it to the lizard. "This is sailor's nuts. Dried bread. Nowhere near as good as fish, but it'll fill your belly."

The lizard nosed the hard bread in her hand.

"Aye, that's right." She put it in her mouth. "You hold it," she mumbled, "until your spit softens it enough to chew." She began chewing, and rubbed her abdomen in mock appreciation. "Yum!"

The lizard didn't look convinced. It reached out, snagged a wedge with its long tongue and pulled it into its mouth. It held the dry bread for a few seconds, then opened its slender jaws and dropped the morsel back onto the plate.

"Aren't you hungry?" Kestrel asked.

Lifting one foot, it snatched another bit of biscuit in its claws and tossed it up, then caught the morsel on its nose. It took a few steps across the sideboard, keeping the bread on the tip of its snout.

Kestrel chuckled at the lizard's antics. Maybe it had been a performer in a travelling show, and gotten lost on the Pechetan docks. It jerked its head upward, sent the biscuit fragment tumbling through the air, and caught the crumb deftly on its nose.

"You're a funny one," Kestrel said.

There was a knock at the door. The lizard promptly dropped its plaything and hunched down, its nostrils flaring. It spread its wings, as if it intended to launch itself at the door. Kestrel put a finger to her lips, then leaned against the door. "Who's there?"

"Me, Captain." Shadd. He should have been long gone to his hammock, snoring away this last hour or so before sunrise. She wondered, for one panicky second, if he'd seen her crossing the deck with her lumpy burden. He wouldn't be pleased at all. If it had turned out to be a pup or kittle . . . but it wasn't. It was a strange thing, like nothing they'd seen before. No better gunner sailed the oceans, but Shadd was also one of the most superstitious men she'd ever met, including her old captain Binns. She'd watched Shadd once climb the rigging and crawl across a spar, just to avoid crossing a black bird's eye. What he might think of the lizard, only the gods could say.

"Can it wait until morning, Shadd?" she asked, trying to make her voice grainy as if she'd woken from a sound sleep.

"No, Kes. I found somethin' ye oughta see."

"I'll be right out." She eyed the lizard. It had relaxed, tucking its wings against its sides, and was nosing at the biscuit again. "You, behave yourself, and don't make a mess. I have to leave for a bit." It knocked the crumbly bread across the sideboard and romped across the table after it, nearly skidding off the edge.

"Careful, you." Kestrel picked up the lizard and placed it carefully on the floor, and laid the plate of biscuit beside it. "Have fun. And be quiet. I'll be back."

She opened the door and slipped out, closing it firmly behind her. Shadd was waiting in the passage.

"What're ye hidin' in there?" he asked.

"A pair of twin circus tumblers, and they're both unhappy you rousted me from their loving arms. What did you find that couldn't wait until the sun?" she asked.

"This way." He lumbered down the passage, leading her to the main deck. The half-moon hung low in the empty sky, spilling light on the sparkling ripples of their wake below. The ship rolled gently over the calm ocean, its quiet sway mesmerizing. Young Hudee strolled back and forth, from amidships to the poop deck, carrying on a conversation with the man in the crow's nest high above him. All was utterly peaceful. Red Tom stood near the binnacle, using its faint reddish light to read one of the books he'd claimed from the last round of plunder. She smiled at the sight. She'd never known he could read, much less that he enjoyed it, until they captured a ship whose captain was also a reader. Tom had claimed three fine leather books as his share, giving up any claim to gold. "What care I for gold?" he'd said. "I have all the food and drink I need aboard the *Thanos*. But a book is a rare treasure."

Shadd crossed to the windward railing. "I couldn't sleep, thinkin' of the quakin' from before. I came out for a walk 'round." His normal rumbling voice was low now, more like a growling animal. "So I'm runnin' me hands along the railin' when me fingers catch a roughish edge I ain't felt before. I peer over and — well, see fer yerself."

Kestrel leaned over the rail. There was a rough spot, just as he'd described, right under her hands. The usually silky wood had been splintered in a number of tiny places. It would be easy enough to sand down and polish over the damage. But she realized immediately that there was a different problem. Below, there were more torn places where the paint had been plucked away. Equal size, equal distance from each other, in a relatively straight line from the water to the railing. It resembled what happened when boarding spikes were jammed into the hull by a raiding party, but smaller. Much smaller. As if something had clawed its way up the side of her ship.

She'd assumed the poor little thing had flown out to the *Thanos* or stowed away while they were docked at Pecheta. Now it appeared to have dragged itself all the way up to the main deck from the water. A long climb. She'd done it herself once, and with an injured shoulder. No wonder the creature was hungry.

"I've got to get some fish," she murmured.

"Fish?" Shadd asked. "Kes, are ye sure ye're awake?"

"Sorry," she said, shaking her head, "I meant . . . hell, I don't know what I meant. So what do you think caused this damage?"

"Ain't it obvious? Somebody's boarded us. Maybe even them Danisobans, much as I hate to believe it."

"But you said it couldn't possibly be them," she said, unable to resist the chance to throw the big man's words back at him. "They're too smart for such tactics and we're much too far from land. Isn't that what you told me?"

He shrugged. "I've been wrong before."

"It would please my heart fine to blame the Danisobans, but they wouldn't sneak aboard like this. Too close to wild water."

He snapped his fingers. "Could be some assassin, sent from a rival captain to slit yer throat and steal yer ship out from under ye."

"Now you're talking like a schoolboy," she said. "If it was an assassin, wouldn't I be dead already?" She held up a hand before he could come up with another theory. "I don't think this is anything to worry about. But just to be on the safe side, post an extra two men to the watches, dark and day." Kestrel yawned, and had to grab the rail to keep from tipping over. "Whew! I know where I need to be." She made her way back across the deck and down the passage to her cabin door, Shadd following a step behind.

As she reached the door, there was a suspicious thump from inside the cabin. Shadd's eyes tightened.

"Assassins!" he growled. "I knew it!"

Kestrel grabbed for his meaty arm. She couldn't let him charge in and discover the lizard, not before she had a chance to explain. But he moved too fast, leaping forward and throwing open the door.

Her windows were shut. Broken biscuit lay scattered around the plate where she'd left it, and a book was open on the floor. The pages fluttered in the light breeze from the open door, but other than that, all was still. Shadd stomped inside, and looked behind the door. He dropped to his hands and knees, peering under the bed. Finding nothing, he rose, opened the armoire and began rifling through the hanging clothes.

"Enough!" Kestrel barked. She stepped between him and the armoire. "There's no one hiding in there, and if you don't stop, you're going to tear my best silk shirts." Shadd blew out a frustrated breath and stepped away so that Kestrel could close the door.

"You're acting like a spooked kittle," she said.

"Hell, Kes, I'm yer quarter. It's me job, in't it?"

He was right. When Binns retired and left her in charge,

she'd needed a man she could trust with her life as well as her confidences. There'd been no question who she'd choose. For the first four years of her life at sea, Shadd had been her best friend, her protector and brother. He'd taught her to fight and drink, and everything else she needed to know to get by on a ship full of randy men, and she owed him better.

But not until she found the lizard. Where could it have gone? Obviously not under the bed, nor in the armoire. Her windows were still pulled to, and she doubted it would have had the presence of mind to close them on its way out.

Shadd picked up the book. "One o' them old logs, eh? A little light readin' for bedtime?" He crossed to the shelf to slip the book into its place. "Ye shouldn't leave yer books on the floor. Ye'll trip on 'em and break yer leg."

The silly thing was hiding. But where? She scanned the room. There. Two shelves from the top, looking like nothing more than a dusty bookend without a match. It was hidden in the shadowed recesses, its eyes glowing dimly. A smile tweaked itself at Kestrel's lips.

"What're ye smilin' for?" Shadd rumbled. He turned his back to the shelf, and crossed his arms across his barrel chest.

"Nothing," she managed. "Just relieved there wasn't anything lying in wait for me." The lizard stretched its neck, and peered over the edge, its snout inches from Shadd's head. It pulled back out of sight, then peeked around the other side. It reached out and snagged one of Shadd's messy curls, releasing it to bounce near his ear, then ducked back like a shot.

Kestrel bit her lip nearly hard enough to draw blood. Her abdomen was shaking from holding in the laughter.

Shadd waved an absent hand at his hair. "Ye need to take this a wee bit more serious. Yer ship was dang near shook to bits, dragged across the sea, there could be raiders sneakin' about belowdecks, and ye're laughin'?"

Above Shadd's head, the lizard peeked again, then dropped down. Up, down. It was playing peeksie-boo, like a little child. It nipped another of Shadd's curls.

"Ow." He grabbed at the captive lock of hair, and turned around.

The big gunner and the lizard froze, face to face. Shadd's

mouth dropped open. The lizard tilted its head mischievously. The glow in its eyes brightened.

Kestrel stopped laughing. "No, don't," she began, but the lizard didn't wait. With a silken rustle, it spread its wings wide, and wailed.

Shadd stumbled backward, nearly toppling a chair in his haste and bumping against the round table. His eyes were wide as gold octavos, and his face had gone pale, a gleam of sweat shining on his brow. "What in Pantheus' belly is that thing?" he whispered. He fumbled at his waist as if trying to draw a blade.

"Calm down, Shadd." She touched him, but he jerked away as if burnt.

The lizard waved its wings. Shadd backed up another step and grabbed the brass candle snuffer from the table behind him. "Stay back," he warned, "I can get it." He swung the snuffer, making it sing with the force.

"Stop that right now!" Kestrel stepped between Shadd and the bookshelf. "You'll hurt it."

"I'll hurt it?" Confusion played over his face. "Kes, get out o' my way."

She held out a hand. "Give me the snuffer."

His gaze shifted from his captain to the lizard and back again. "Ye're sure it's harmless?" he asked, sounding plaintive. Kestrel nodded, fighting hard not to smile. The last thing Shadd needed was for her to laugh at his trepidation. After one more suspicious glance at the lizard, he relented, and laid the snuffer in Kestrel's hand.

"Thank you. Take a seat."

He did as she said, sinking into the chair closest to him. Kestrel crossed to the sideboard and opened the door, getting out a black bottle and two mugs. Popping the cork loose, she poured a generous cupful. Immediately the cabin filled with the rich scent of rum. She handed the mug to Shadd. "Drink."

The lizard folded its wings and was looking as innocent as a new lamb. Kestrel stuck out her finger and shook it at the little creature. "That," she scolded, "was not funny."

It drew its ruddy head back close to its shoulders, and flicked its tongue once.

Her second-in-command hadn't touched his rum. He was

sitting so stiffly a strong wind might break him, his eyes focused on the lizard. "I've heard of lizards growin' this big, over on t' Continent. Poisonous. Man eaters. But I never heard they had," he raised the cup and gulped a desperate swig, "wings."

"I'm pretty sure it isn't a man eater. I carried it up here in my shirt."

He tore his gaze from the lizard. "In yer shirt? Have ye taken leave of all yer senses? What if it's a fire-breathin' daga? It coulda burned a hole in yer middle faster'n a plate of Lidian peppers!" Shadd took another swallow from his cup, squinting suspiciously over the rim. "Was it this thing makin' all that racket?"

"Nonsense." She reached up and stroked the lizard's eye ridges. It closed its eyes and leaned into her hand. "Poor little thing. Does it look like it could make enough noise to even shake a wine glass?"

"Telgars like a bit o' scratch. Just like a kittle, purrin' and such. Until their bellies get to rumblin' and they recall as how the hand that's doin' the scratchin' is made of meat, too." He eyed the lizard. "What's to say it won't bite yer neck and suck out all yer blood while ye're sleeping? Then move on to the rest of us?"

"For one thing, it's nowhere near big enough to hold all the blood in me, much less you, so I'd say you're in no immediate danger." She balled a fist and punched him lightly on the shoulder. "Settle yourself, you lily-livered coward. As it happens, this little fellow likes fish. And it says—"

"What d'ye mean 'says'? The damned thing talks?"

Kestrel's breath caught in her throat. She hadn't intended to tell that part yet. "After a fashion," she said finally.

"What's that supposed to mean?"

"It doesn't talk, not with words. It's more as if I can—"

"Ye can what?"

She took a deep breath, blowing it out with the finality of a woman with nothing left to lose. "I can see what it's thinking. In my head."

Shadd stared at her. "In yer head." He rolled the words over thoughtfully, then began to chuckle, his cheeks reddening. He laughed harder, tears rolling down his face. Bending over to rest his hands on his knees, he sputtered, "In yer head!"

His laughter was infectious. Kestrel found herself joining him, the stress of the last few days spilling from her in gales of laughter. Shadd held his side, fighting to breathe. Kestrel sank onto her bed. The creature, still sitting on the sideboard, was watching them, turning its head first toward Shadd and then to Kestrel, back and forth as if it was utterly confused by their behavior. It finally stopped, its glowing eyes fixed on Kestrel. It whined softly, its voice sounding plaintive, a child lost in a foreign land. In her mind's eye, Kestrel saw blue softness, shot through with shimmering light in random patterns. Blue and warm, and comforting. Home. She drew a breath. "No fear, little one."

Shadd's guffaws subsided. He wiped his eyes with the tail of his shirt. "Bloody blazes," he muttered. "Is it communicatin' wi' ye now?"

Kestrel stroked the creature's eye ridges. "You're not seeing anything?" she asked, even though she was sure she knew the answer.

"What are ye plannin' to do with it?" Shadd asked.

His question stopped her cold. What could she do with such a pet? Running a ship wasn't so difficult that she couldn't take care of an animal, especially one that seemed able to entertain itself. The legendary pirate king Flingo Naile himself was rumored to have kept a brightly colored bird that sat on his shoulder, even during battles. The image of herself, the lizard gripping her shoulder as they sailed forth into battle, was compelling.

"I suppose he could stay aboard," she ventured.

Shadd nodded. "Could be a handy lookout. Flyin' ahead and scoutin' likely targets. Them wings o' his work?"

Kestrel eyed the little creature. The wings had been so impressive, it hadn't occurred to her to wonder if they worked. "What about it, little one? Can you fly? Use your wings," she ran one gentle finger from its shoulder joint down to its claws, "to move through the sky? Not touching the ground or the water. Can you do that?"

It spread its wings, beat them once, twice. They belled with air.

"That leaves us with another mystery. If you can fly," she mused, "then it wasn't you who left the gouges on the hull."

The lizard nudged her hand, and the blue of the earlier vision swept over her mind's eye. She rocked, as if floating in the ocean, and tried to move her arms, but the resistance defeated her. She wasn't strong enough to lift them free of the water. A wave tossed her against a huge, solid darkness above her, and she grabbed at it with her hands. Except they weren't human hands. They were long, slender, and tipped with sharp talons, which caught on the darkness. Slowly she pulled herself upward toward the sky, leaving scars in the wood as she climbed.

The vision broke. The lizard stared at her, and Kestrel nodded. "You couldn't launch yourself from the depths? You were too wet?"

It spread its wings again, sweeping them down hard enough to lift its body an inch or two in the air. "Enough! I understand." If she let him fly around in her cabin, he'd end up knocking everything on the floor and leaving a worse mess than she already had.

"Hey." Shadd thumped the table with a fist. "Where's that scroll Lig gave ye?"

Crossing to the bookshelf, Kestrel pulled out the new leather logbook, and showed him the parchment orders. He took it, and read it silently, his lips moving. "Ha!" he barked. He slapped the paper down on the table, pointing at the description passage with a triumphant finger. "I thought somethin' felt right familiar."

Kestrel leaned over and read aloud, "Black body with a red cast under the sun." She shrugged. "This one's red all over. And what about the wingspan? He's nowhere near as big as what's written here."

"Here, it says somethin' about touchin' it?" Shadd raised an eyebrow. "See here . . . 'Do not lay hands on the creature, for its skin is poison.' Ye carried it in yer hands, but ye're not dead."

Kestrel opened her palms. The skin was clear as always, except for the usual calluses from working. "I feel fine. A little tired, but I haven't slept, so I can't blame that on him."

"Mayhap it was to keep you from hearing it talk. Maybe touching it does the trick." Shadd continued his perusal of the scroll. "This part about what the creatures like to eat? Didn't ye say he was askin' for fish?" He grinned. "How's that for luck, aye? I'm bettin' ye got just what ye went fishin' for. We got us a baby." He laughed, slapping his knee with one hand.

A baby. It made sense. The lizard was playful and curious as a pup. There were all kinds of big animals that started out small.

Kestrel grabbed up the parchment, reading the rest of the description. Wings, claws on the feet . . . except for the size, everything fit. The ship hadn't reached the Children yet, but that meant little. Animals were always moving, following food or running from predators. Maybe the food supply had dwindled, forcing these lizards further afield.

The lizard whined, and Kestrel reached over to comfort it. A vision bloomed behind her eyes, the surrounding blue of the lizard's home. But this time, a sound swept through, a high-pitched tone that moved up and down the scale in a pattern. It called, insistent, pleading, and familiar. The blue lightened, and suddenly Kestrel saw the black sides of her ship, as if from the water's surface. The tone cleared, became obvious. It was her whistling. The song she sent out across the water.

Kestrel dropped her hand, staring at the little lizard. "Shadd," she said finally, "I think I did this."

He laughed again. "Aye, this'un ain't as big as the orders asked for, but the king ought to like it better. Nice and trainable. It'll be doin' tricks for the court this time next year."

He didn't understand. He thought she meant they'd been successful. And they had, so for the moment, she was inclined to leave him to his satisfaction. "Wonder why he wanted a big one in the first place? Seems as if a baby would be a better choice, to train before it learns to hate captivity." She reached out to the lizard. It raised its head to meet her hand, rubbing its jaw against her fingers and making a pleasured sound not unlike the purr of a satisfied kittle. "Sure would be nice to keep him, though."

"Kes." He gripped her shoulder, forcing her to turn and look at him. His usually jovial face was grave, sending a slender bolt of cold shock into her heart. "We can come fishing for another little fella next year."

"I know, I know. You're right." An opportunity like this one didn't pop up every day. She'd be a fool to ignore it. Still, something about the mission was bothering her. Maybe it was just how tired she was. "Go and change our course, then get a bit of sleep."

He grinned. "Back to Pecheta?"

"Back to Pecheta." Kestrel shooed her quartermaster out the door, and turned to the lizard. She yawned, her eyes itching with fatigue. "Find yourself a little spot to lay down, and we'll think some more in the morning."

The lizard crawled back into its hiding space on the book-shelf, its wings folded tight against its body. Its eyes glowed softly red in the shadowed nook, but now the sight was vaguely reassuring. Kestrel kicked her boots off, sat down on her bed and blew out her candle.

Their job had just become easier than breathing. The lizard was damn near tame, and willing to go along with them. She'd sail back to Pecheta, her prize in hand. With the assignment completed, Lig would be off her back for a while. She'd be free to go after McAvery. She lay back against the pillows, and closed her eyes.

Sleep refused to come. Her legs jerked restlessly, as twitchy as the thoughts that swept through her mind at top speed. Why did the king need the lizard at all? Where was McAvery now? The questions began running into each other, making her dizzy. She tossed, trying to find a position that might attract sleep.

A beam of moonlight cast a soft light against her bookcase. *The Source of Conjurr* was sitting on the bookcase, right where she'd slipped it. The idea of owning a tome full of Danisoban secrets had been intoxicating at the time she purchased it. Being different as she was, there was no one to teach her how to use her innate power, and even though she didn't want to join the Brethren, their knowledge surely could prove useful. She'd only intended to study the basics, just enough to move forward on her own. Now that she knew her magic could do more than move objects around, she wanted even more to learn how to use it.

What else was she to do? Reaching out toward her table, she opened her tinder box and sparked a flame to relight her candle, then walked to the bookcase. The lizard seemed to be asleep, tucked in between the books. Ever so carefully, Kestrel lifted the book from its place, and tiptoed back to the bed.

The warm light flickered over the worn cover. This was dangerous, playing with magic she barely understood. The only way to learn it, short of throwing in her lot with the Brethren, was to take the chance on the words inside. Taking a deep breath, she lifted the cover.

The crackling paper was covered in the strange, wiggly script she'd been required to learn for her position in the king's employ. So it was a Danisoban code. Lig probably didn't like her knowing even that, but it wasn't up to him. She smiled. If he knew she had the tome, and could read it, he'd likely have come to sea himself, to pry it out of her hands.

The first few pages were an introduction to the life of the Brotherhood, spelling out what was expected of the new conscripts, and moving on to the daily schedule of life in the school. Dull stuff, that. Kestrel flipped past that section, coming to a list of specialties the student would study as time went by. "This is more like it," she murmured, bending closer to the pages.

McAvery had mentioned different disciplines of Danisoban magic, not that Kestrel had bothered keeping them all in mind. At the time, she'd hoped to never need the information. That was before she'd accepted her own power, before she'd entered royal employ and put herself directly in the eye of the King's own Danisoban.

The book was divided according to the uses desired. "A course to heal injury, sickness and death," she read out loud. "A course to achieve wealth." Page after page of courses — what Danisobans called spells or workings. Some were only a few paragraphs, others much longer. Despite herself, Kestrel was impressed. She'd grown up learning about the Danisobans, known since childhood they were dangerous, but she'd had no idea magic could be used for so many purposes. She turned another page, and gasped. "A course to find what was lost." Could this be what she needed? Could she use the words on the page to tell her where McAvery was being held?

"More likely I'll look over the side and find someone's half-rotted glove floating along," she muttered. And that was the least of what could go wrong. She had no real idea what she was doing, and it would be so easy to make a mistake that might burn her ship down around her ears. But then again, if it did work . . . she grinned at the notion of McAvery owing her a favor of this magnitude.

Some of the courses required dried herbs and rare oils she'd never heard of, but one ingredient appeared in every course. Whether a drop or a cupful, each course demanded blood. She remembered the spots of blood on the floor of the tavern after her fight with Tooley, and Lig tucking a glass vial into his sleeve. She'd never noticed it before, not that she'd paid close attention to Danisoban workings at all. It was a sure bet the mages weren't spilling so much as a drop of their own blood. Was this why they stole the street children? To drain them dry and toss them away? The idea chilled her to the bone. Someday she'd have to find out, but not while they knew more than she did.

The course for finding what was lost asked only for a bowl of water and a drop of blood. She could spare a drop, she told herself. She picked up the bowl from her sideboard. It still held the water she'd used to clean up earlier, which looked clear enough to see the bottom of the bowl at least. If the course required perfectly clean water, it didn't say. She placed the bowl on her table, and spared a glance toward the lizard. Sound asleep, as far as she could tell. She picked up the book, along with the candle, and took them both to the table to read.

*With the sharpest of blades, cut the third finger on the left hand, but let no drop fall. Gaze into the still surface of the water, and say the words Hesh fara menya. There shall be seven times seven utterances. As the final words are spoken, press the cut finger only until one drop appears, and let it fall to the water, keeping firmly in mind the object to be located.*

She grabbed her dagger from the sideboard where she'd left it and pressed the tip into the pad of her left ring finger, just hard enough to break the skin. Blood oozed from the cut, and Kestrel turned the finger upward to keep from dripping into the water too soon. She leaned over the bowl. "Hesh fara menya," she murmured. "Hesh fara menya."

At first, the strange words sounded like children's nonsense words, but she concentrated on the last image of McAvery she had, the vision from the red gem. His features were tinted red in her mind's eye. The chanting ceased to feel silly, now that she'd become used to the words, and seemed rhythmic. She caught herself nodding her head in time with the chant. Just as she noticed it, she also felt the stirrings of her magic, the tingling beginning at her feet and rising. Was it working? And how many times had she said the words? She couldn't stop too early, but would it fail if she chanted too long as well? She dragged her attention back to McAvery's face.

The magic was surrounding her in the familiar way, but pulled in close, sweeping past her face in ripples as if it was waiting for her to release it. Time for the blood. She held her finger over the bowl as she chanted the final time, squeezing the tiny cut. A single drop formed and fell, redness spreading across the surface.

Something in the water moved, swirled. Light shimmered from the surface, and in spite of herself, Kestrel raised her hands to cup the bowl. Her magic slid easily away; almost as if she could see it, a silver, silken flow pouring from all around her into the water. The soft light from the bowl snapped into intense brightness, nearly blinding her. Energy rushed at her, rocked her head back with its force, and suddenly she could see him.

He stood in a dark room, his hands bound before him, gazing out of a crack in the planking. Next to him was a person, smaller than he was by a few inches, swathed in a thick brown garment. They seemed to be speaking of whatever he saw outside. He stepped aside to let the person have a look. Kestrel strained to move closer, to see what they were seeing. It felt as if she was walking through marsh mud, her feet sticking as she struggled. She caught a glimpse through the crack. A dock. Not very busy, and seemingly peopled with hardbitten men loading baskets of fresh vegetables onto waiting vessels. And there, at the knee of one of the men, was a silky-haired animal, nipping at the man's breeches with its lip. An alfer, no older than a year. The man holding its lead held out his hand, accepted money from the second man, and handed over the alfer's lead. Kestrel grinned. He was on Doana.

The twin islands of Mela and Doana were the major sources of food for the Nine Islands. Mela had, in the last twenty years, become solely involved in raising fruit, particularly grapes for wine production, leaving Doana to handle the farming of other crops. In addition to raising root vegetables and harvesting kelp grains, the Doanan farmers kept herds of alfers, small hooved creatures with long silky hair that provided meat for the markets of the Nine Islands. Common superstition barred the farmers from doing any butchering on Doana itself. They believed the rich soil would stop producing food if it absorbed blood. Alfers were sold alive. Which meant McAvery was in the hold of a ship at the docks on Doana. She was as certain as if she had suddenly become the needle of a compass.

The magic had worked. Not only that, but Doana was between their current position and Pecheta. After a fashion. It was only a day off course, but not so far as to be suspicious. She could plausibly argue that it had been on their way back, if Lig dared to question her. They could rescue McAvery and still complete their task.

The image was fading. Her vision of the docks pulled back, returning to McAvery. He had raised his bound hands, and seemed to be comforting the person next to him, his hand touching the person's face under the hood. The gesture sent a strange twist through Kestrel's belly. It seemed such an intimate touch. It didn't last long. Another person stepped into view, shoving the two of them apart and pushing McAvery to the deck. This figure was hooded too, and as tall as McAvery. Who was this? If she could only see the face, know who had taken McAvery, she might be able to formulate a better plan. "Turn around," Kestrel whispered, but the image in the water vanished. She leaned on the table, her heart pounding.

Her head ached as if she'd fallen into a vise and someone was turning the handle. The pain was incredible. She bent forward, holding on to the table's edge to keep from falling, and laid her head against the wood with a tiny moan. Nausea cramped her belly. Her chest tightened and she feared she was about to vomit up her dinner. The weight of the air around her was too much to bear. Holding the table's edge as tightly as she could, she let herself sink down to the floor, curling into a ball. She kept her eyes tightly shut, breathing as lightly as she could manage, until the aching and nausea began to subside. Her skin itself ached. If her hair could have felt pain, she was certain she'd have known every strand's agony. Using magic had never hurt like this before. Her own magic left her breathless, and a bit dizzy, nothing more. Of course, her own magic couldn't achieve what she'd just done. If this was what Danisoban initiates went through to learn, it was no wonder they were all ill-tempered. Eventually, the pain faded, and she let herself relax onto her back. She opened her eyes, staring at the ceiling above her.

Magic, real magic, and she had done it. All by herself, with no help from the Danisobans. So many things she'd be able to do, with a little practice. Maybe she could even become strong enough to defeat Lig himself, freeing herself and those like her from Danisoban domination. She rolled over and picked up the book, hugging it tight. She'd never had even the chance of real freedom before, and now it lay in the pages of a book. Rising, she crossed to the bookcase, slid the *Source* back into the space, gently so as to avoid waking the lizard, then headed out onto the deck.

Tom glanced up at her reappearance, his eyebrows raised in silent question. "I need you to change course, Tom," Kestrel said, barely able to keep the delight from her voice. "Plot us a course to Pecheta by way of Doana, aye?"

"Doana?" he asked. "Aye, Captain." He cocked his head at her. "Are you feeling well?"

"I think I may know where they've taken McAvery," she said, enjoying the look of surprise on his face. "Figured we'd swing by, rescue the blackguard on our way to Pecheta."

"That's fine, that is. But Captain?" he said, as she turned to leave. "What's wrong with your eyes?"

She lifted a hand to her face. "My eyes?"

"Looks like you've been in a scrap. Two black eyes you're sporting. I can call Jaques for you, if you're hurting."

Jaques grew up in service to a doctor on Eldraga. He took to sea after the man died, leaving him without a patron and no way to become a doctor himself. Pirate he might be, but the skills from his childhood served them all well whenever someone suffered an illness or injury. "No, Tom, I'm fine. I'll put a cool cloth on them, be good as new in the morning."

She didn't wait for his response, but strode back to her cabin. Her mind spun with ideas and plans, and she feared she wouldn't sleep at all. Peering into the small mirror on the sideboard, she saw what Tom had noticed. Holding her black braids away from her face, she drew the mirror closer. Charcoal bruises marred the brown skin around her dark eyes, red streaks running through the whites. Tom had called it — even she thought she looked liked she'd lost a fight. She let her braids fall, the weight of them brushing her neck. She didn't think about her looks often. She didn't live the kind of life that required she care for cosmetics and primping, but she still didn't want to look this badly used all the time. The Danisobans didn't walk around bruised, so clearly there was more to learning magic. She pressed the skin gently, feeling a slight stinging at the pressure. Something else her own brand of magic had never done. She hunted through the drawers of the sideboard until she located some linen napkins. Dipping one into the bowl of water, she wrung it out and laid down in bed, placing the wet napkin over her eyes. She hoped the bruising would clear as quickly as the headache had. If she was still bruised in the morning, she'd talk to Jaques about one of his remedies.

# Chapter 7

*A wind's in the heart of me, a fire's in my heels . . .*
— JOHN MASEFIELD, *A Wanderer's Song*

It seemed she'd only just closed her eyes when the sun's light stabbed her back into wakefulness. There was a weight on her chest, making it hard to breathe. Kestrel blinked. Two red eyes stared into hers from about an inch away.

Kestrel groaned, and rolled over, burying her face in the huge pillow. The lizard quick-stepped across her body, keeping in place as she moved, and settled on her back, plucking at the ends of her hair. She'd had so little sleep because of the night's excitement. Their new direction was set, and she'd hoped to keep to her bed a bit longer.

"Stop that," she grumbled. She pushed away from the bed, shrugging the lizard off as she rose. "I'm up." She picked up her breeches from the floor, pulling them on and buttoning them, then wrapping her belt tight around her waist.

The lizard folded its wings and stared at her intently. It opened its mouth and clacked its teeth together.

"You act like someone has fed you before. Didn't you learn to catch your own food?"

The lizard extended its arms and swept its wings down, catching air in their folds and lifting itself off its feet. Tucking its feet close to its body, it flew across the room, its tail acting as a balance. Kestrel laid a hand against her mouth to stop from crying out in surprise. Years at sea, but she'd never seen such a creature as this. It slapped the door knob with one wing, then settled on the floor and looked back at her expectantly. She'd seen birds fly before, and never thought much of it. Such strength and grace in so vulnerable an animal. She wanted to stroke the smooth leather of its wings, feel the dainty bones underneath. It was a miracle, this creature. No wonder His Majesty desired to own it. But why had they never seen them flying over the waters? No sailor worth his salt would have kept a wonder like the flying lizard a secret. They'd have found a place in stories and songs long before now.

The lizard whined, snapping her out of her thoughts. Kestrel padded over to the door, and laid a hand on the knob. She paused. If she let the lizard out, it might not come back, and she'd be forced to take her crew out fishing all over again.

She caught her own reflection in the mirror, and stopped to inspect her wounded eyes. The bruising was gone, as if it had never been there. That was a relief. "On second thought," she said, letting her hand drop, "maybe I'd better fetch you a bit of breakfast myself. Where are my boots?"

An image of flickering silver bodies appeared behind her eyes, hundreds of glistening fish schooling and darting so quickly Kestrel almost felt sick from the motion. "Yes, fish, of course. I'll drop a line."

Another image . . . fish suddenly swimming away, only to be caught in strong jaws, and gulped down.

"I know, you can catch your own breakfast. But what if there's something else swimming around that thinks you'd be a tasty morsel?" She pulled one boot onto her foot, and picked up the other. "I can't afford to let you loose, little one."

The lizard launched itself again, flying back to the bed and landing on the window ledge. It nosed the beveled pane with a small tick, then cocked its head and stared at her. Suddenly the cabin around her faded. Instead of the room, she saw an endless horizon, the sea going on forever below it, and herself watching, watching for something that would never return.

Kestrel's boot slipped from her suddenly nerveless hand, and thudded to the floor. It was a lizard, gods be damned. How could it possibly understand her worries? Questions rattled through her mind like bones in a fate-teller's bowl, yet she couldn't think of one thing to say. It heard her thinking. She felt her eyes widening, stretching with disbelief. Being able to understand the lizard had seemed a gift, a delightful game. She'd not dreamed that it was hearing her thoughts, too. As an orphan child, she'd grown up with stories of the Danisobans who could find hiding children by listening for their panicked thoughts. Maybe the lizards were the key to that ability.

And if they were, the King was probably not adding to his menagerie as she'd been told, but assisting the Danisobans instead. She could strike a blow by not delivering this one. But that would be the thing Lig had waited for — blatant disobedience to the crown. Her success with the spell book the night before had been a first step, but she was nowhere near good enough to take him on. Damn his eyes, Lig had her no matter which way she turned.

The dangerous thought crept into her mind again, as it so often did. She feared the Danisoban, with some good reasons, but what if he wasn't planning her doom with nearly the energy as she granted him in her imagination? What if she kept the lizard, kept the ship, ran off and somehow he had not expected it? She allowed him far too much control over her, control he hadn't even demanded from her.

The lizard nosed her hand, and with its touch, Kestrel saw the same horizon, but this time, with a lizard leaping from the water, flying toward her. It was trying to promise it would come back.

"Why would you?" she asked, surprised at herself for asking.

Spreading its wings, the lizard rose in the air. It flew once around the room, and landed on her shoulder, gripping with its talons just hard enough to hold its body in place. The sudden weight startled Kestrel, but the lizard didn't fall. It raised its head and let loose with a piercingly high call, very near to a squeal, and stretched its long neck to reach up toward her face. It bumped its nose against her lips, then sat back, as if waiting for her to understand.

It liked her whistling. A smile teased at the corners of her lips. But it could read her thoughts, and that was a little too unnerving.

"I can't." She reached a hand to the lizard and stroked its head. Its eyes closed, and it shivered at her touch. "When I whistle, things happen." Not always bad things, of course. Her ability had even saved her life once or twice. "I don't like to make the sound unless I have to."

A gentle rumbling shook the lizard's body. It opened its mouth in a yawn, and flew over to the window.

"Promise you'll return?" she asked. What a stupid thought, asking a wild thing like this to make a promise.

The lizard bobbed its head.

"I hope I don't regret this later," Kestrel muttered. She leaned on the bed, staring at the window latch. Flip it open, and let the little creature go. All it would take was a quick movement. What would she tell Shadd if the lizard never came back? Heaving a sigh, she flipped the latch. The window creaked as it swung into the room, pushed by the fresh morning breeze. "I'll prop it open, so you can come back here when you're finished."

The lizard rubbed its head against her hand, then slipped through the open window. In an instant, it was gone.

Kestrel sank onto the bed. Shadd would hang her by her toes if that little creature had played her for a fool. She scooted to the edge of the bed, retrieved her boot from the floor and pulled it on. Breakfast suddenly seemed like an excellent idea for her, too. If she sat here waiting, she'd drive herself mad.

Her deck bustled with men hard at work. Cheerful men, singing as they dangled in the rigging, men who knew they were finally at the end of a season, and on their way to shore for a nice, long chance to spend their money. She wondered who put the word around when they changed course for Pecheta. A smile tickled at the corners of her mouth, so she ducked her head until she could get control of her expression again. The whole ship probably knew before sunup. Knew about the course change, even if they didn't know why. Shadd stood on the quarterdeck, staring through the telescope intently. He glanced toward her cabin, and noticed her. He waved excitedly.

"Captain!"

Kestrel took the quarterdeck steps two at a time, grabbing her scope from Shadd as she skidded to the railing. "What'd you see?"

"A merket, I reckon."

Merkets were small ships, with fairly limited cargo space. They'd been popular long ago, but when shipbuilders learned to build bigger vessels with more efficient cargo holds, the merkets had become pleasure boats for rich nobles, who tended to stick close to the seas around Pecheta and Eldraga. This far out to sea, a merket was an odd sight.

"You're not sure it's a merket? Or is there something else that befuddles you?"

"Look for yerself."

A second later, she knew. She peered through the glass, focusing on the ship where it sat on the horizon. "By Grace's nephews," she said. Fortune seemed to be smiling on her. She lowered the telescope. "What's our position?"

"Half a day out from Doana, on the course you recommended last night," he said. "Why'd ye do that, if'n I could be so bold?"

As badly as she wanted to tell Shadd what she'd accomplished, it wasn't the right time. Last night's working could have been a fluke. Or the other chapters of the book could ask more of her than she was willing to sacrifice. One drop of blood was no great loss, but what if another spell required she drain the life from a pup? Or even a child? There was still so much to learn. When she'd read more, practiced more and had a better handle on what she was capable of, maybe she'd admit it then. For now, a lie would have to do. "I had a dream."

"I had a dream, too, about a night on Eldraga at Camberlin's. What's that prove?"

"Mine was about McAvery."

Shadd grinned. "Was he on Doana?"

"On a ship docked there."

"Is it the same ship?" His voice was calm, but she could feel the excitement he tried to hide. He wanted to change course, and bring battle to the merket. So did she. She couldn't be certain, because she hadn't seen the ship full on. It was the sails.

Striped. Just like she'd seen in McAvery's jewel. Just like she'd told Shadd afterward. He thought this might be the ship that bore Philip McAvery. Damn her own eyes, she was hoping the very same thing. They had their prize, and they were pointed in the right direction. If this was that very ship, right here under their noses, no one could claim she was shirking her duty to the crown if they attacked and took it. Not to mention the great weight that would be lifted from her shoulders if she was able to rescue McAvery. Any debt she felt would be paid, and maybe she'd finally stop dreaming of him at night. If it wasn't the same ship, they'd plunder it and add some coin to their current haul. Either way, the situation seemed destined to work in their favor.

Kestrel slammed the telescope closed, and turned to her quartermaster. He was grinning, and she couldn't help matching it with her own. "Shadd," she said, "We've been idle too long."

"Couldn't agree more, Captain. What's your pleasure?"

She looked out to sea at the striped sails snapping in the wind. "Yonder merket may have something that belongs to me. Bring us about. And see to your gun crew, if you'd be so kind. I find myself itching for the scent of black powder on the air."

# CHAPTER 8

*Roared like a battle, snapping like a shark*
*and drunken seamen struggled with the sail*
—JOHN MASEFIELD, *The Wanderer*

Shadd began barking orders to the men on deck, who leaped to obey, and Kestrel returned to her cabin. The merket appearing like that was a convenient happenstance. She closed the door, crossed to the still-open casement and leaned out, searching the tossing waves below for the lizard. It must have had enough time to catch a fish by now, and she needed to have it securely aboard before she went chasing a quarry.

She drew in a breath and licked her lips. Maybe once or twice would be enough. Two quick bursts, not in any sort of rhythm. For a second, she envied the people who could whistle without a thought. Some nights, when the men were happily in their cups and singing some bawdy tune or other, she found herself wishing she could join in. If she'd joined the Brotherhood, she probably would have learned how to control her magic. But she'd also have been sequestered in some dank and miserable dungeon, us-ing orphaned children and stray animals in her learning. She was no stranger to violence, but the only men she'd ever killed had been able to defend themselves. She wouldn't hurt innocents. And besides that, the Brethren would never have allowed her anywhere near the sea again. This way, with all its limitations and secrets, was still better.

Kestrel leaned far out of the window, pursed her lips and blew a short, sharp note. Far below, a tongue of water leaped up, as if in answer to her call, and slapped against the hull, spraying her with drops. Had the lizard heard?

A familiar whistling cry sounded from behind her. Kestrel spun. The lizard was curled up in her bookshelf, in the little niche it had used to hide from Shadd the night before. Its heavy-lidded eyes glittered with satisfaction, and its belly bulged.

It had returned, just as it promised it would. What sort of creature was this? A wild thing that kept promises. She cast her questions aside for another time, her relief making her feel slightly dizzy. "Good," Kestrel said. She pulled the window closed, and latched it. "We're about to enjoy a little tussle, and I wanted to make sure you were safe aboard."

It stretched its neck and yawned, its mouth opening wide enough to let Kestrel see all its tiny, sharp teeth. She reached out to stroke its smooth skin. It felt like living, breathing silk under her fingertips.

"You know, it'd be helpful if I knew what to call you," Kestrel said. "Do you have a name?"

The lizard cocked its head, opened its mouth and let loose a high-pitched warbling. The cry lasted for several seconds, and ended in a sound like a gulping swallow. The lizard blinked its eyes.

"Nice name. Even if I could learn it, I'd be passed-out by the time I finished saying that once," Kestrel laughed. She took the Danisoban book from the shelf and laid it open on the table. The spell had shown her what she sought once. Now that she knew what to expect, maybe she could try again, make sure the merket was the vessel they were after. She took up the bowl she'd used the night before, and stopped. Would the same water do? The drop of blood from last night's course wasn't noticeable, but maybe it was enough to ruin a new working.

The lizard shook its body, casting a few stray drops of glistening water toward the window. Kestrel licked her lips. The water had responded just a minute ago, when she was calling the creature. She lifted the latch and let the window swing open, leaning out to pour out the old water, and whistled a series of low, smooth notes. A wave tossed, halfway as high as she needed. She tried again, this time a half-remembered tune she'd heard in some pub long ago. Waves swept higher up the hull, closer to her hand with every swell. She held the bowl out, and whistled just a little louder. Water splashed up into the bowl, soaking her arm and face. She drew the bowl back and closed the window again.

She set the dripping bowl on the table, and flipped through the book until she found the page again. "*Hesh fara menya*," she whispered, staring into the water. "*Hesh fara menya.*" She said it again and again, willing herself to concentrate on what she wanted and forget the thudding of her heart. Is this the boat I'm looking for, she thought, as she chanted the Danisoban words.

As before, the power swept in close, velvet waves stroking her face. Light built in the bowl as she chanted. Her breath came faster, the chants more immediate. The cut from the night before was barely closed. Running a thumbnail over the wound, she opened it again, ignoring the spark of pain and let a drop fall. Let me see, she thought. Brightness popped from the water, then cleared, showing her the merket raising anchor in the Doanan harbor. It was the same ship they chased now. She relaxed, letting the magic fade, and leaned on the table. Her head ached again, worse this time. Her stomach clenched suddenly in sharp nausea, and she heaved forward for the bowl. She misjudged the distance, splashing her face into the salty water that remained, and inhaled a small amount. It burned all the way behind her eyes. She gripped the edge of the table, holding herself upright, coughing to clear her passages. It was so much worse than the last time.

Noise exploded around her. A sound she knew well. Someone had fired at them. The floor shifted under her feet, throwing Kestrel sideways. She toppled to the ground. The lizard spread its wings, squealing.

Kestrel dragged herself to her feet, holding on to the furniture for support. Her cabin door had sprung open. Beyond it, men were running. She took the quarterdeck steps slowly, pulling herself along the railing, and grabbed her telescope from its place next to the wheel. They'd caught up to the merket. As far as she could see from here, the merket had only two swivel guns on deck. The owner must have given up the gun deck to make room for more cargo. It was a gamble, and not a wise one.

The merket was trying to maneuver itself into position for the morning sun to blind the warship. A good strategy when used against a ship equal in size, but the *Thanos* was twice as big. And turning that direction only put them both in line with a stiff breeze. The merket might be more sprightly, but it wasn't going to outrun the *Thanos*. Kestrel wouldn't give it the chance.

"They fired on us." David DeadEye, his hands straining on the wheel, had relieved Red Tom for the day watch. "Bastards thought they could cause this ship any sort of hurt."

"Which side?" Her jaw cramped. It hurt to talk. Cack, it hurt to be awake, but she didn't have any choice.

"Port."

"Bring us along her port side. I'm going to give us a bit more of an edge, but I'll likely be dizzy when I'm done." DeadEye nodded. Kestrel leaned over the railing, and shouted for her quartermaster. Shadd was crouched at the midship hatch, with his eye turned toward the quarterdeck. "Are the guns ready?" Kestrel yelled.

"Aye, Captain." He squinted up at her. "Kes, how'd ye get yer eyes so blackened?"

"Ran into a door."

"Ye're bleedin!"

She looked down. Blood was running between her fingers and dripping to the deck. She wiped the blood off on her breeches.

"Cut my finger. It's nothing." The last thing she needed was him worrying about her. "When we're in position, fire. Only two. I don't want her sunk, just affrighted. And when we come alongside, be ready to board her."

Kestrel tucked the scope into her belt. The pain in her head was clearing. She pressed the heel of her hand against her achy jaw. For an instant, she wondered if she'd do herself real harm by trying more magic so soon. Only for an instant, then the thought was banished. She had work to do. She strode across the quarterdeck, pressing her back against the stern railing, and wrapped her hands around the staves. She licked her lips and began to whistle, gazing at the sails.

The now-familiar tingling crept along her skin, beginning at her chest and moving out and down, spreading across her like a fall of silken thread. Staring at the sails, she imagined them full and creaking. The breeze behind her head strengthened, whipping her braids around her face. The wind ripped the sound from her lips.The ship responded with a leap, driving hard over the waves. The big ship's shadow fell over the merket's deck as the *Thanos* came alongside. They were so close now she could see the crew running frantically toward the port gun. Too late.

She released the whistling, her head spinning. Damn magic — either she ended up bruised and bloody or gasping. "Fire!" she yelled, with the last of her breath.

"Aye!" Shadd turned his face to the hatch, and bellowed the order.

A bone-rattling thump rocked the deck below her feet as the *Thanos'* guns spoke. The cannonball flew true, bursting a vicious hole in the merket's hull just above the waterline. White smoke belched from the *Thanos'* gunports again, rolling up and over her deck. The second shot struck higher, snapping the merket's mainmast. Broken wood shrieked as it fell, crashing to the deck and leaving the merket dead in the water.

"Secure!" Kestrel ordered. A good dozen of her men stood ready with grappling lines at hand. They flung their grapples over the space between the two ships, catching and holding the disabled merket. Drawing the lines tight, they twisted them to make them fast under the belaying pins.

"Board!"

Men hauled themselves up on the waiting lines and swung across the distance between, howling like banshees as they flew. DeadEye glanced over his shoulder. "Your men are leaving you behind, Captain."

"By Grace's whips, they're not!" Running down the quarterdeck stairs, Kestrel grabbed a line and joined her boarders.

The merket crew put up a valiant effort, for all that they were outnumbered. Two men were down, either dead or unconscious. Another had thrown himself onto the port cannon, and was holding on for dear life, screaming at anyone who tried to pry him loose. Shadd and Jaques, swords drawn, circled a fourth. The man was turning left, then right, then left again, keeping his eye on both pirates as best he could, holding his battered sword at the ready. Kestrel's heart gave a hard thump against her ribs — this was the same man she'd seen putting McAvery in chains. No question. The gods must have been smiling on her. First she'd found the lizard, and now she caught McAvery's abductors. Kestrel pressed her lips together, and blew a sharp note, her gaze firmly on the sailor's sword. The weapon jerked out of his hand, spinning in the air.

"Look out!" Shadd yelled. The sword sliced down, landing point-on into the wood of the deck. Two men jumped aside as it landed, the metal singing from the shock of its strike.

She approached the disarmed man. "On your knees," she snarled, and he was quick to comply.

"Don't kill me," he said, his arms shaking as he raised them behind his head. "We don't have any treasure."

"That'll be for us to determine. Jaques, tie his hands. Shadd," she turned to her quartermaster. "Search the ship. If our man is here, bring him out. Any treasure they find, that can come above-deck, too."

"What man?" He winced as Jaques drew his arms tight behind his back. "We're sailing empty."

Kestrel crouched down in front of him, and tilted her head. "Tall man, long hair, well-dressed. Name of McAvery."

"Don't know him." The sailor turned away, refusing to look in her eyes. She took his chin and pulled his face back forward.

"You do know him. I saw you with my own eyes, slapping chains on his arms."

"Couldn't have. I ain't ever seen you before today."

She grinned evilly at him. "Don't you know me? I'm the pirate witch." The fellow paled at her words. "I'd better find what I seek below, in good health, if you want to keep your ship."

"There's nothing below," he muttered, jerking out of her hand. He sat sideways onto the deck, and scooted himself against the bow railing. She'd get no more talk out of him for now. As long as they brought McAvery up, she didn't need to hear anything else.

# CHAPTER 9

*Come as of old a queen, untouched by Time,*
*Resting the beauty that no seas could tire*
—JOHN MASEFIELD, *The Wanderer*


Shadd lumbered across the deck to where Kestrel waited. The merket's crew, seeing they had no alternative, had dropped to the deck to wait for the pirates to leave. Their leader glared up at the pirates.

"Didn't find any coin, did you?"

Shadd turned his face away, speaking close to Kestrel's ear. "He ain't lyin'. McAvery ain't here, and they claim they never saw 'im. Nor have they got so much as an extra crate of biscuit. There was an old book behind the wheel, so I grabbed it up for Tom. She's takin' on water awful fast from that hit amidships, so it's just as well we ain't stayin' long."

Kestrel turned to the kneeling man. "You expect me to believe you're out for a pleasure cruise? Why are you sailing empty?"

"We deliver the goods. One way only. We get paid when we return to the dock." The man smirked. "That way pirates can't steal our hard-earned cash."

Kestrel wasn't sure what to think. This was the ship, no question. They might already have transferred McAvery to another ship. Or worse, tossed him overboard. "If their hold's empty, there's nothing for us here."

"I never said the hold was empty." Shadd waved a hand toward the hatch. Jaques emerged, toting a large wooden chest on one shoulder, and carrying a bundle tied with gold-colored twine on the other. He stepped clear of the hatch. A figure was climbing slowly up from below, head and shoulders wrapped in a dull fabric. The figure stepped onto the deck, and allowed the fabric to fall back. Black curls tumbled free of the wrappings. A woman, with enigmatic eyes deep as night, onyx jewels against skin the color of ancient gold. She smiled at Kestrel as if they were old friends.

"You're sure McAvery's not down there, too?"

"Aye." A grin was pulling at the corners of Shadd's lips. "Pretty, ain't she? Says she's a dancer from the Continent."

Kestrel turned to the merket's captain. "You're transporting passengers? Seems a long way for such a tiny vessel."

"Passengers." He stared at the woman, his eyes wide with fear. "How are you still here? We delivered you to the market!" The woman returned his gaze with a blank expression, then twisted one nonchalant finger through the curl hanging over her shoulder.

"Who's this?" Kestrel asked. The man seemed mesmerized by the woman, his face twisted with worry.

Kestrel threw a glance at Shadd, raising her eyebrows in a silent question. He drew his sword, pressing the point against the soft skin below the man's ear. "Ye'll answer me captain, and quick."

"We collected her on Lidias." His voice shook. "I don't know who brought her over from the Continent. We get paid to deliver, that's all."

"You talk as if she's cargo."

"She is. Was. I could have sworn we left her behind with the rest." He winced as Shadd pressed the sword harder against his neck. "Can you pull that back a bit, mate?"

Kestrel nodded, and Shadd sheathed his weapon. She squatted down to look in the man's face. "What do you mean?"

"Bought and paid for, she was."

"You mean she's a slave?"

Slavery had been outlawed in the Islands years ago, at least as far as the ordinary folk were concerned. Some said it was the goodness of the king's heart, that he wouldn't allow people to be mistreated so. Others called it a tactic to keep the nobility from building households large enough to function as armies. Either way, slavery had been against the law since long before Kestrel's birth. Not that there weren't people kept in service by those with wealth, but if they'd been bought for cash, no proof of their captivity would exist, at least not on paper.

"I don't deal in names, just coin. But whatever she is, she shouldn't be here."

"You said you came from Lidias?" she asked.

The sailor nodded.

"The man I'm looking for was on Lidias."

His eyes widened. Before he could speak, the woman crossed to Shadd's side. The slaver shrank back at her approach, but the woman paid him no notice. She laid a graceful hand on Shadd's elbow. "I beg your notice, *korsan.*"

"Ah, lass, my name ain't Korsan, but it's for sure ye have every bit o' my notice," he said, smiling in the flirtatious way he used when he was trying to impress a woman.

"*Korsan* . . . man of the sea?"

"Sailor, I think ye mean."

"Of course, sailor. Forgive me. Would this, by chance, be your *rais?*" she asked, extending her hand in Kestrel's direction.

A lump rose in Kestrel's throat. It was impossible. This dancer, this slave, from a world away . . . if she hadn't been using her eyes, Kestrel could have sworn it was her own lost mother's voice. The smooth accent, the quiet strength, all reminded her uncomfortably of the parent she lost. She blinked to clear her vision, not wanting this woman to see the grief in her eyes, and perhaps think it something else.

"My what?" Shadd asked.

"*Rais.* Your . . ." The woman tapped a finger against her lower lip, then pointed at Kestrel. "Your leader."

"I'm the captain," Kestrel said.

"Captain, that is the word, yes." She faced Kestrel, and inclined her head respectfully. "In my home, women are allowed such freedom to lead men, but I thought the custom was different here."

"Far as I know, I'm the only one." Kestrel turned to Shadd. "Gather the men. Since our quarry's not here, we need to keep moving. We're awaited on Pecheta."

"You are looking for Philip?"

The woman's voice was low, but her words rolled over Kestrel like thunder. Staring at her, Kestrel imagined the drape of the hood over the dancer's head. Suddenly she felt sick. She had seen this woman before. In the vision, standing next to McAvery. His hand touching her face under the hood. McAvery had been here, and this woman had met him. "What do you know about it?"

"She don't know anything!" The man had scooted his body as far from the two women as he could, his back pressed against the ship's railing.

"You are the Mad Kestrel." She smiled, an enigmatic expression that made Kestrel uncomfortable, though for reasons she couldn't quite name. "He said you might come looking. He described you accurately, although he did not tell me you were the *rais*."

McAvery'd described her. Well enough that the woman knew her. And he'd used that damnable nickname he'd tried to give her on the docks. Smart of him. Details like those could have come from no one else. She forced away the thought that made her want to know what he'd said, how he'd spoken of her. What other things he and this woman might have talked of together. "You know where he is?"

"The man who paid for his capture disembarked with him, and the others, at the market. Philip goes on the block later today. Once he is sold, it will be much harder to locate him." The woman tilted her head. "What battle caused you such wounds?" she asked, peering curiously at Kestrel's magic-blackened eyes.

Kestrel flinched away. "Who's this man? Where's the market?"

"I am told it is never held in the same place twice. If the authorities cannot find it, they cannot shut it down." She shrugged. "The man I do not know. He never said a name."

Kestrel couldn't help a suspicious little thought that perhaps the authorities weren't looking very diligently. The king could make all the proclamations against slavery he wanted, and still turn a blind eye if it suited him. Or perhaps he truly didn't know, and this was going on under his nose. Philip McAvery was the king's Knave, the left hand that accomplished what the right hand couldn't admit. His Majesty would be annoyed to discover his own man had been caught in that very trap. Whether or not he'd take pains to punish the slavers responsible was anyone's guess.

"I take it you know where the market's being held today."

The woman nodded.

"I'll also venture a guess that you'll tell me the location, even lead me there, once you're safely aboard my ship and away from these men."

She smiled again. "Philip said you were clever. I am pleased to see he was correct in that, too."

Kestrel looked around for Shadd. "Quarter!" she called. "Please assist this lady in boarding with us, and make us ready." Taking the woman's elbow, she led the dancer to the railing. "A question, then. Whose wrath am I incurring by taking you with me?"

"I do not understand."

Kestrel smiled. "Yonder fellow. All he really cares for is payment. I think you were intended for a specific buyer, or else you'd still be on that island. Which means that someone has already paid at least a portion of the asking price for you, if not all. So who might that be?"

"I cannot say. The *rais* told the men to stay away from me, not to speak. He believed I might enchant them."

"Will you?"

She brushed a lock of hair behind her ear, and smiled. "Do not most men fall victim to the enchantments of women?"

Kestrel realized she'd been holding a breath, waiting for the woman to speak. Silly of her. This woman was a dancer; her livelihood depended on being attractive to her audience. Most likely, the contract required the woman to arrive unsullied, and using the threat of magic to scare his men off was quicker than the threat of the lash. Still, this left the question of whose coin was in jeopardy if the woman did not arrive at her destination. Kestrel ran the risk of someone else joining the chase for her.

David DeadEye waited on the rail, one hand gripping a rope, and a huge smile on his face. "Her trunk and bag are already aboard, Captain," he called, as if he'd guessed Kestrel's decision before she even knew herself. He'd earn free drinks in the pub with this story, and he knew it. Kestrel offered her hand to the woman, and helped her step onto the rail beside the pirate. "Take hold of David here, and he'll swing you across. But hold on tight — we can't be fishing you out of the sea if you fall."

The woman stepped close to David, and twined her arms sinuously around his neck. "Shall I also curl my leg around your waist, to be certain?"

David seemed to choke on his own breath, and even Kestrel couldn't help a laugh. "As you see fit, lady. Just be sure I still have my man in able condition when you reach the other side."

"I am no lady, but a free woman who hopes to be free once more," she said, lifting her knee to the level of David's midsection. Her skirt fell back, revealing a smooth, brown leg, which she curled tightly around his body. She wrapped her arms around his neck. "My name is Nasrin."

With an idiotic grin, David launched from the rail, swinging with his burden across the expanse to the *Thanos'* deck. All the pirates, save the three guarding the slavers, had already returned to the ship.

The slaver regained his insolent manner now that the slave woman was gone from his ship. "Good riddance, and may you enjoy the sort of luck she'll bring you!" he snarled.

The merket lurched, and Kestrel threw out a hand to balance herself. The ship was headed for the bottom, going down fast, and they didn't have much time. Kestrel took a knee in front of the leader. "The woman," she said. "Who was she bound for?"

The leader snorted, and turned his head away. "Take our ship and toss us to the sea, but soon you'll be regretting ever running into us."

"Your ship's headed to the deeps," she said, rising. "If you don't want to tell, that's your choice. In any event, the plunder we've taken will have to do." She hoped the cheated slave owner wasn't too high in the nobility. Being rich offered chances to redress wrongs that the courts could not, and she didn't want to have some noble playing pirate and getting in her way.

"We'll be leaving you to it. I suggest you lower a hackney and start rowing for Doana. If your buyer wants to protest, tell him he shouldn't be buying and selling people. In the meantime, if this trade's leaving you without coin in your pocket, I recommend you engage in another line of work. Piracy, for instance." She bowed low, quirked a finger to her remaining men, and together they swung across to the *Thanos.*

Shadd was barking orders to get them under way. Nasrin sat curled on the quarterdeck stair, her trunk and bag on the step below her. The pirates released the grappling lines freeing the sinking merket to its fate. Its crew had abandoned the doomed ship for their tiny hackney and were already rowing away, yelling obscenities at the pirates as they went.

"What's our heading, Captain?" DeadEye called from the wheel.

"Shortly," she called back. "Nasrin," she said, "I'll arrange for quarters for you. Before I do, you will direct my navigator as to the location of the market." The dancer rose from the stair. Before she could take a step, Kestrel waved a hand upward. "That way, please." Nasrin began climbing the steps, Kestrel following.

This woman couldn't be gone from her ship soon enough. Men were easy to lead. Promise them money and a decent amount of ale, and they'd follow without argument. A woman like this could be much more of a job to handle, especially surrounded by the men. Slave she might be, but not the sort who was used to hard work. Her soft hands and delicately painted nails told the tale, as did her attitude. As soon as they found McAvery, Kestrel would find a way to be rid of her. Perhaps the king would hire her to entertain at his court. Or maybe Olympia Camberlin would take the woman in. The memory of seeing McAvery touch her so tenderly intruded, unwanted. It wasn't the dancer's fault, but right now, she could wander the streets of Eldraga, as far as Kestrel was concerned.

Kestrel climbed the steps to join Nasrin near the wheel. The dancer had let her hood fall back, and the wind tossed her hair in silken waves. She smiled at Kestrel's approach. "It has become a lovely day, has it not?"

"You claimed to have information of use to me."

"More than you know."

"A heading will suit me fine."

Nasrin tilted her head curiously. "What do you intend to do with me, once I have assisted you?"

"Bloody Grace! You're aboard a few minutes and already you're trying to negotiate with me?"

"Not at all, *rais*. Is it not a fair question?"

Kestrel stalked to the railing, and slapped it. It was a fair question. It just bothered her to have to answer. "How's this — you tell me what I want to know, and I won't put you overboard?"

She surprised herself with the empty threat. She'd never felt jealous before, and she wasn't proud of how it made her sound. She took a deep breath to steady herself, and raised her eyes to meet the dancer's gaze. "I'm sorry I spoke to you like that. I had very little sleep."

"Philip said you were impetuous."

Kestrel gripped the railing, ice rushing through her limbs. It shouldn't matter to her that he'd said such a thing. Nor should it matter that the dancer called him Philip. After all this time with no news, no sight of him at all, none of his words should mean anything to her. But they did, damn them. Not a day went by that McAvery didn't wander through her thoughts. Knowing he'd been able to describe her well enough that a stranger would recognize her meant he hadn't forgotten her. At the same time, she was disheartened that she'd had to hear of his words from this woman, this beautiful woman who used his given name as if he and she were friends.

The dancer glided across the deck, and leaned on the rail next to Kestrel. "I will tell you how to find him, and I will assist you in retrieving him from his captivity. In return, you will take me home."

That was all? She almost sagged with relief. She'd have the dancer out of her hair as soon as they reached one of the major islands. "You're from the Continent, aye? I can arrange passage on another vessel once we're docked on Pecheta."

"Your ship. You. No other will do."

"Are you mad?" Kestrel couldn't help a laugh. "That's the better part of a year away."

"Very well." Nasrin stood up and walked toward the stairs. She stopped halfway, and glanced over her shoulder. "Philip was sure you would come for him. I admit I thought you would, as well."

She was going to let him be sold into slavery. Knowing what he faced, and knowing she could help him with a word. Most of the pirates Kestrel knew had a warmer heart than this slave woman. Then again, wasn't Kestrel doing the same thing, by stubbornly refusing the woman's request? Which of them was the crueler? "It's just that such a journey is daunting, to say the least. We'd have to lay in extra food, and there's no telling if plunder awaits.

My old captain often spoke of the waters between here and the Continent. He said you might sail for days and see no other ship at all. These men follow me because I pay them. If I can't guarantee cash in their pockets at the end, they'll vote someone else to take command." Kestrel shook her head. "I want to help you, for McAvery's sake, but your demand is impossible."

Nasrin turned back, facing Kestrel. Her dark eyes had lost their languid calm, and now seemed to burn into her. "It is not impossible at all. You'll promise to take me home, and you'll save your Philip."

"I can't take you out of the Nine Islands." She pressed the heels of her hands against her temples, trying to rid herself of the subtle ache. "Even if I could convince enough of the men to sail there, the king would never allow it. It would take too long, leave him without his proper share for too many months. Should I choose to defy him, I'd lose what protection I have against the Danisobans. If that's your price, I can't meet it." She swallowed hard. "Even if it means leaving McAvery — Philip — on his own."

"It would not take as long as you imagine." Nasrin reached out one graceful hand, and laid it on Kestrel's shoulder. "There is something else, something I have not mentioned until now. Something I can use to," she halted, as if searching for the words, then smiled. "To make the arrangement more attractive." She reached for Kestrel, gentle fingers caressing the air inches from her bruised face. As if stroking her wounded skin. "I can show you a better way to accomplish what you wish. To use your inborn talent. A way that is better than this."

Kestrel stared at her, eyes wide. She knew. It wasn't possible, but this dainty woman knew what she'd done to herself. If she recognized what caused Kestrel's injury, it could only mean she knew how to use magic. And was willing to teach her.

A sudden beam of sunlight, glinting off the water, caught her eye. Nothing was more like home than this wide, wild ocean. She'd taken this position in the king's service to please her old captain, and to keep herself protected. In the months since, she'd found herself confined by the world she'd entered, locked down to requirements and commitments she'd never imagined. And she felt no safer for any of it. Why shouldn't she run off half a world away? How far would any of her pursuers follow? Her heart seemed to leap at the thought. Freedom, real freedom, waited over the horizon and all she had to do was sail toward it.

She needed to hear the words, to know the woman said what Kestrel suspected. "What do you think you can show me?" she murmured.

Nasrin spread her arms wide, letting her wrap slither to the deck. She wore a tight-fitting, intricately stitched chemise that ended just above her belly button. It tied around her neck, leaving her back and arms bare. Her brightly-colored skirt rode low on her full hips, and a fringed scarf that seemed to match the chemise was wrapped over it. She lifted her skirt a few inches, so that Kestrel could see her smooth, unshod feet and the glittering gold anklets that adorned her legs, and Nasrin began to dance.

Slowly at first, she reached out one leg, then snapped it back, tapping her heel on the deck, the anklets chiming. She crossed one foot over the other, and stepped aside, then repeated the movement in the opposite direction, over and again. The anklets chimed prettily, creating their own gentle music. Her arms rose and fell, graceful as two snakes, sweeping the skirt back and forth in flowing waves. Her belly muscles rolling beneath her skin in time with the movement of her arms. Rising on her toes, she began to spin, letting go of the skirt so that it could fly out on its own, and kicking with every other turn. Suddenly she stopped. The skirt's material swung around her legs and she flung one arm up in a proud pose, pointing past Kestrel with the other.

"Captain!"

David DeadEye's cry broke Kestrel's attention. He was floating, off his feet, hanging on to the ship's wheel with a desperate grip. Nasrin dropped her arms, and DeadEye thudded to the deck. He landed on his back. Slowly, he pushed himself up to a sitting position, staring at the two women.

For an instant, Kestrel couldn't move. She'd never imagined magic like that. Magic that depended on rhythm, and didn't require blood to accomplish. Magic that perhaps she herself could learn. The woman smiled, and Kestrel shook her head, crossing to DeadEye and offering him a hand up.

"You did that?" she asked the woman.

Nasrin bent her head, then turned her eye to DeadEye. "I apologize for startling you, *korsan*. It was necessary." She retrieved her wrap and covered her bright clothing. "*Rais*, do you understand what I am offering you?"

She was a mage. Not a Danisoban. And if Kestrel was understanding, this dancer was trying to point out that she made magic in the same way Kestrel did, using the patterns of music — and over the salt sea. Except that she wasn't at all out of breath from her effort. Another thought struck her — the slaver hadn't been lying. He did believe he'd been rid of the dancer at the market. Somehow she'd hidden herself from view, to reboard his ship. But why?

"Now that you have seen, I can teach you what you need to know. It will take time, time we'll have if you agree to the journey I propose. My way will not leave you bruised, suffering and near death." She smiled. "And if you choose to rob ships on our way, I'm sure your men would be pleased."

Kestrel considered the dancer's words. A real mage, who might be able to answer her questions, teach her how to use what she had. A mage who wouldn't demand lifelong servitude, who wouldn't lock her away from the sea. She could train with the dancer in the daytime, and learn from the book at night. Not to mention the possibility of plunder they needn't share with the king. How could she say no? It would cost her the safety of the king's protection, but if Nasrin could do what she claimed, Kestrel wouldn't need the king any longer. She'd be able to take care of herself, for the first time in her life. She'd never have to worry about the Danisobans again. "How do you manage, so close to the water?"

"I am not Danisoban. The water does not impair me, as it does not impair you."

"But how . . ." Questions babbled in her mind, almost making her dizzy.

"Have you never looked into a mirror?" Nasrin reached out and took up one of Kestrel's braids in her graceful hand. "You are not a child of the Nine Islands, despite being born there. You are black of hair and eye. You are brown from spending days in the sun, but far darker than your men, who spend an equal time on the deck as you. I imagine your skin's color does not fade during your time ashore." She took Kestrel's hand, holding her own arm close to it. "I would hazard a guess that your mother or father is a cousin to my people."

Kestrel pulled her hand free. "I don't look like you at all." But it was a hollow protest. Especially with the way Nasrin's voice sounded so like Mama's.

"More than you think, *rais*. And there is no question that the sea does not weaken either of us."

That, at least, was true. And a subject Kestrel was far more comfortable discussing than her parents. "What makes you sure I can be taught?"

"The bruises on your eyes tell a clear story. You have already attempted to learn a different way, and you are not dead." She pointed an elegant finger down. "Tap your toe."

Kestrel looked around, but only DeadEye was watching. He seemed curious instead of afraid. The rest of her men were going about their work. She should take Nasrin to her cabin, where no one would see, but suddenly even walking that far seemed like too much. She reached out a toe, and tapped three times. The familiar tingle of magic sparked along the bones of her foot. Barely discernible, but it was there. And she hadn't made a sound. She'd always been careful to walk in a stilted fashion, just in case her magic should bubble up and cause objects to move from their resting places while people could see. And she'd certainly never danced. Could it be? Could Nasrin teach her a way to use her power without becoming breathless, and without having to depend on the strange words and rituals of the Brethren? Could there be another way for her? Kestrel raised her eyes to the dancer. "Show me something else."

"Very well." Nasrin lifted her skirt high enough that her feet were easily visible. "Follow my steps." She pointed her right toe, tapped it three times then skipped to the right.

Kestrel never learned to dance. Street children weren't ordinarily taught the gentle art of dancing anyway. Quick on her feet she was, but only while fighting. She reached out a toe, and did her best to mimic what Nasrin had done. She felt slow and clumsy, but Nasrin was smiling encouragement.

"Now do the same thing, but moving to the left." Before Kestrel knew it, she was following Nasrin around the deck, tapping and skipping in a childlike dance. Energy flickered up her legs, in a way it never had before. Stronger, moving like silken ribbons over her skin, instead of the usual pins-and-needles, and building like a slow fire in the muscles of her arms.

"Spin!" Nasrin ordered, and Kestrel complied, spinning until she should have been nauseous. But she wasn't sick at all. No ill feeling, no pain. Instead, the power was balancing, filling the empty spaces of her body. So much energy, so much strength. Nothing she had attempted before had reached so deeply within her. She felt that she could lift the ship itself from the water, and make it fly.

Kestrel stopped short, both hands held out to the sky. Fountains of silent light burst forth, coloring the air above her head and sending poor DeadEye diving to the deck, with his head under his arms. The light dissipated. Kestrel let her arms drop to her sides, but this time, she could feel that power remained within her, ready for her to draw upon it when needed, if she only knew how. When the Danisoban magic left her, she felt nauseated, almost to the edges of death. This magic burned like pure, gleaming life. "Is this how it always is?" she panted.

Nasrin smiled. "Patience, my *rais*. This is but a taste. There is so much more I can teach you."

Less than an hour ago, Kestrel had been ready to deliver Nasrin to the king for his entertainment, and never look back. Now she wanted to know everything, to learn everything. She had the chance to stand against the Danisobans without the shield of a king or a captain. If this woman taught her more.

"Who were you intended to serve?"

"My truth, *rais*, I do not know. I was hired to dance for a court that does not exist. My *girifta* would be very angry if she knew what had happened to me. I think the person responsible was hoping the news would only reach her after it was too late for her to take steps."

Kestrel nodded. Distance and time were powerful weapons. Expensive weapons, too, but there were a number of nobles in the Nine Islands who could afford such a luxury. "Let's say, for the sake of argument," Kestrel said, fighting to keep her voice steady, "I do as you ask. I'd need some time to prepare. Buy food, water, all the supplies we usually lay in for a season. I'd force none of my men to go along who didn't wish it. And McAvery'd want to be let off on Pecheta, once we've found him."

"I can wait a little longer. I would not be so sure about Philip's desires."

"He's the king's man." That day on the docks played through her memory again. A kiss, and then he was gone. He had his loyalties, and she wasn't high on the list.

Nasrin smiled, that same mysterious smile that had so unnerved Kestrel before. "Offer him the choice. You may be surprised."

With a flash, it came to her. The familiar use of his first name, the concern for him . . . she wasn't saying he would change his mind for Kestrel. He and Nasrin had spent time on the slave ship together. All this time she'd wondered, and now she knew. He'd fallen in love with the beautiful dancer who could make magic. And who'd be surprised? Half of her own men were furtively glancing up at Nasrin, the other half openly staring. He'd moved on, before she ever had a chance to decide how she felt. That was good, she told herself. It saved her the trouble of letting him down. She'd never really wanted him, after all. A man like that was only a burden. If letting him go to someone else was the price of learning what Nasrin could teach, she would pay it.

Even if the thought left her chest suddenly heavy with grief.

# CHAPTER 10

*Life's battle is a conquest for the strong;*
*The meaning shows in the defeated thing.*
—JOHN MASEFIELD, *The Wanderer*

Once Kestrel assented to the trip, Nasrin provided DeadEye a description of the islet on which the slave market was being held, their heads bent close together, both of them smiling while they determined the location. As DeadEye handled the change in course, Kestrel climbed down to Shadd's gun deck to give him the news and make a plan.

"It's nigh time!" he bellowed. "We'll set their slavin' ships afire and laugh while they burn!"

"Exciting as that might be," she said, enjoying the surprise on his face, "I'd prefer to do this quietly. The islet we're sailing for lies off the west shore of Doana. I'll take a hackney boat, and sneak onto the island from the lee side. We'll need to rig it with a sail so I can use the wind to escape later. I'll take money and try to buy him. He'll hate it, but he doesn't get a choice today."

Shadd chuckled. "Mayhap he'll like bein' bought by you right well."

She ignored his comment. "However, if it all goes wrong for any reason, I'll need you to cause commotion and cover our getaway. You, my lad, will watch for my signal."

"What signal's that?"

She pulled a square of bright red silk from her pocket. It fell open, draping over her hand and showing itself to be a veil of impressive size. Nasrin had offered it up from her colorful belongings. "I'll whistle this into the air as soon as I'm in a position to free McAvery. You set David in the crow's nest to watch for it. When you see this floating in the sky above the trees, you'll sail around to their anchorage, and attack. I'll need noise and terror to keep everyone's attention while I collect our quarry and run for the boat. I'm sorry, but this won't be a plundering raid. We can't risk splitting the crew if we have to run. Do all the damage you can, sink them if it suits you, but everyone stays aboard the *Thanos.*"

Shadd rubbed his hands together. "Ye want us to attack while ye're still ashore?"

"If I haven't managed to extricate McAvery by then, the distraction will be just what I need. And if I have got my hands on him, we'll want the slavers delayed from pursuing us. Why chase one escaped slave when pirates are wreaking havoc on their ships?"

"How'm I to find ye later?"

"I'll steer us toward Bix. If we don't meet you on the way, we'll meet up with you at Binns' pub. Will that do?"

Shadd looked at her skeptically. "That's a right hefty distance."

"I'll be fine. A boat that small won't attract a lot of attention. I'll look like a fisherman. And if I do run into trouble, I'll be armed well enough."

"Speakin' of that . . . ye sure it's safe carrying a blade with ye?"

"Why?"

"Ye sure ye won't kill McAvery afore we can catch up to ye?"

She searched his face, and for the space of a breath, he looked dead serious. He laughed as she stared at him, and she couldn't help a smile herself. "Nothing's certain."

He stalked away to pass the word to the crew.

It had been a fair question. What would she do, alone in the boat with McAvery for that long? He inspired such fury in her. Other feelings, as well. He could easily annoy her until she drew a blade on him, if left to his own devices. And if he tried to kiss her again . . . she shook her head, as if to dislodge the idea from her thoughts. He wouldn't see her romantically, of course. If he ever really had. Not when he had Nasrin to return to. The dancer might claim she and Kestrel looked alike, but Kestrel knew better. Nasrin's hands were smooth, hers rough from work. Nasrin's sleek hair glistened in the sunlight, while Kestrel's stayed braided tight for utility's sake. Given the choice, any man would choose Nasrin. It wasn't a surprise to her. Still, how could she want something so much, and despise it, too?

Shadd's men rigged the spare sail well enough that she'd be able to whistle up a breeze to drive the small boat along, and carefully lowered it to ride next to the *Thanos* until she was ready. Jaques packed two filled water skins and a parcel of bread and hard cheese in a small wooden box, tucking it securely into a space under the bow. She'd raided the wardrobe in her cabin for clothing of a richer cut, something that would allow her to blend in with the moneyed clientele at the market. She settled on a pair of doeskin breeches, a linen shirt and a brocade frock coat that fit a little big. Room enough underneath for a couple of hidden blades, without bringing attention to her more feminine attributes. She tied her braids back and planted a trader's wide-brimmed hat on her head. Nasrin had brought cosmetics to disguise the bruises on her eyes. Kestrel wouldn't have cared normally, but she had to admit two blackened eyes did make her noticeable. But when the dancer put away her powders and brought out a jar of lip colors, Kestrel ordered her out of the cabin.

A rustling from behind her caught Kestrel's attention, and she turned to look. The lizard was nestled in the pillows on her bed, looking like a tiny potentate of some strange country. Kestrel felt a tickle of shame — she'd forgotten all about it. If Nasrin noticed, she hadn't said a word. Kestrel walked to the bed, sat down on the edge and reached out a hand to stroke the lizard. It preened under her touch, its eyes closed.

"I'm sorry, but I have to leave for a while." She smiled. "Nothing to be concerned about."

The lizard drew its head away from her hand, raising its eye ridges in a clearly questioning look.

"There's a man. A friend." The word felt strange in her mouth. "He's in trouble, and I have to help him. I'll only be as long as I have to be." She looked over at the casement, which was still propped open a bit. "Should I leave that open, in case you get hungry?"

A vision swept into her mind, one she'd seen before. The sea, stretching out forever, but this time it was the lizard staring off at the horizon. It was worried that she wouldn't return. Kestrel grinned. Communicating with the creature was becoming easier with every attempt. It was almost like talking.

"If I don't come back, slip out that window and return to the ocean. My crew won't wait forever. If they think I'm gone for good, the last thing on their minds will be the king and his menagerie. Best if you go." She scratched the creature's neck affectionately. "This is all silly. I'll be back by nightfall, and everything will be well." She rose and walked to the door. Behind her, the little lizard let out a quiet sound, something like a yawn, but Kestrel didn't look back.

"All's ready, Captain," Shadd said. He swept a hand toward the opening to the ship's ladder. "Boat's waitin', and we're set."

The plan was in place, and there was nothing more to be said. Or perhaps just one thing. Kestrel gripped Shadd's meaty shoulder and looked into his face. "Remember, if this all goes to hell, we meet up on Bix." She didn't wait for him to answer. Turning to face the deck, she started the long climb down to the boat. Once she boarded, she released the lines holding it fast, and whistled a breeze to drive her toward the islet and the man who wouldn't leave her dreams alone.

Kestrel stumbled forward, narrowly avoiding crashing into the trees on either side of her. She stopped to tie a length of red thread onto a nearby branch, as she'd done several times on her long walk. Insects buzzed past her ears, biting her neck and cheeks, delighted by the unexpected meal. *I wonder what they eat on the days I'm not here*, she thought, raising a hand to scratch, and using her hat to fan the tiny bloodsuckers away. The muggy air smelled of mud and greenery the farther she walked into the depths of the forest. The sun hung past midday when she started her walk, and beams of light stabbed through breaks in the trees above her. Sweat rolled down her forehead, dripped into the open collar of her shirt and stung her eyes, and the bag of coins she brought along bumped against her leg with every step. The rigged hackney boat sat hidden in a cove. She left Shadd in command of the *Thanos*, waiting hidden on the far side of the islet until she sent up the signal to sweep around and commit mayhem. Pressing her lips together, she whistled softly, pushing the air into movement. The breeze rattled the leaves around her, and cooled her sweat-glazed skin. The insects didn't seem much discouraged, but before she could whistle again, the path opened into a clearing crowded with people. Kestrel tied one last thread, and stepped out of the trees.

Well-dressed merchants, holding dainty crystal glasses of sparkling liquid, greeted each other like guests at a garden party. Smartly appointed servants wandered about, offering trays of rich sweets, or the occasional whiff of purple smoke from small silver boxes. Seamen, dressed in motley finery and walking with the odd, rolling gait of men without landlegs, squinted suspiciously at anyone who came close. A few noble women accompanied by hulking bodyguards, wore bulging purses at their waists and jeweled masks covering their faces for propriety. Even two Danisobans stood apart from each other at either side of the clearing, their hoods pulled down.

The sight of them caused her to stop short. Danisobans didn't use slaves. No, she corrected herself, they don't purchase slaves. Magi were, for the most part, content to abduct street children and beggars, the sort that were expendable and never missed. And they never took sea journeys if they could be avoided. Why would Danisobans have taken such a dangerous chance, crossing the ocean for a slave auction? She swallowed hard. What if they knew McAvery was in chains, and had shown up to reclaim him themselves and escort him back to Pecheta safely? Rescuing the King's Knave would please His Majesty, she had no doubt. As the Knave, McAvery provided information the King needed, so anyone who enslaved him risked royal wrath, and anyone who delivered him from bondage would earn royal gratitude. These mages would only have come at the direction of someone important, like Menja Lig. If that was indeed the case, her plan was unnecessary. She could sail back to the *Thanos* and be on her way, knowing McAvery was travelling safely home.

A twinge of apprehension tugged at her thoughts. How did Lig know McAvery needed help in time to send his mages? Was it possible he orchestrated McAvery's abduction, hoping she might show up here and attempt a rescue? An exploit he would somehow use to discredit her in the king's eyes? There wasn't a reason that sounded plausible, but the mages' presence worried her. She clenched her fists in frustration.

The odd assortment of people were gathered in expectant clumps around a wooden platform a couple of feet off the ground. It stood in the center of the sandy clearing, a set of steps on opposite sides. Five posts rose from the floor of the platform, dull iron shackles dangling from each.

"So this is the Market," she said under her breath. A noble-woman to her right inclined her head toward Kestrel.

"Indeed," she said, looking Kestrel up and down with an imperious expression. "As the invitation said. Didn't you read it? Or do you work for someone more important?"

"I represent a very rich man on Pecheta," Kestrel said, trying to affect the same haughty tone. The noblewoman sniffed and turned away. A tickle of disgust rolled in Kestrel's gut. She was no bastion of moral behavior, but at least she'd never forced anyone to become property.

"Your first time?"

A portly man stood on her other side, sweat rolling down his face. He mopped it with a square of cloth. "What sort of labor are you shopping for today?"

"Pickers, for my employer's fields on Doana," Kestrel said. "You?"

"I sell to the salt miners on the Continent." He rubbed the fingers of his right hand together, grinning. "Good money, that."

"I thought they only took prisoners," she said.

"Prisoners cost them less, naturally. But they don't survive as long. These folks are usually in better health. Takes them longer to die in the mines." He rubbed his pudgy hands together, as if expecting a delicious meal. "I sold seven men last month, made me enough to install my mistress into better apartments.

Kestrel turned away in disgust. Before the man could speak again, a voice cried out.

"Make way! Merchandise to the Market!" Buyers moved aside, forming a rough path through the middle, but only far enough out of the way to allow one body at a time. The spectators all seemed curious as children, craning their necks for glances at the bound men and women stumbling toward the platform. Most of the slaves were dressed poorly, with the tanned skin of farmers and field workers. They moved slowly, their ankles shackled close enough for small steps, each one with head down, watching the path. All but one. Near the end of the line, one man was standing tall. Kestrel's heart skipped at the sight of him. His golden hair was tied back with a rag, his clothes were filthy and he sported an ugly scrape on his right cheekbone, but somehow he looked as handsome as he ever had. She dropped her eyes before he could see and recognize her.

One at a time, the slave herders unbound each of the unfortunate people from the line, and shackled them, two at a time to posts along the back of the platform. When they reached Mc-Avery, Kestrel watched the slave herder take hold of the rope wrapped around McAvery's hands and yank him off to one side. Another man stood there, a rag wrapped around his mouth and nose. He held a wooden box, from which tendrils of smoke curled. He flipped open the lid, and in a swift movement, the herder forced McAvery's head down toward the box. It was so quick that McAvery didn't struggle at first, until his face was wreathed in the lavender smoke.

Kestrel leaned closer to the noblewoman who spoke to her before. "That smoke isn't likely to damage the merchandise, is it?"

"Don't be ridiculous," she sniffed. "It's just to keep them peaceful. They call it Solace. I use it on the kitchen girls."

"You benumb your servants?" Kestrel asked. "Doesn't that interfere with their work?"

"Just at night. So they don't sneak out to misbehave with local men. If I didn't do something, they'd all be round-bellied and weeping." She waved a hand in the air. "It lasts a few hours. In this case, long enough for the sale to end and the merchandise to be loaded."

The herder was smiling, holding McAvery's head in both hands. McAvery struggled at first, then relaxed visibly, his shoulders drooping. Eventually the herder let go, and McAvery straightened. His normal expression had been replaced with a vacuous grin. The herder led McAvery back to the last empty post, and shackled him. He and the boxman moved on to the other slaves, doing the same to each one that they'd done to McAvery.

Kestrel drew the brim of her hat down level with her brow, and settled herself into the middle of the crowd. The chatter quieted; bidding would begin soon. The noblewoman near her was untying her bulging purse from her waist. She noticed Kestrel watching, and flashed her a predatory smile. "Did you remember to bring your coin when you happened to land here? The verifier will want to count it before you receive a bidding token."

Her bag was full of octavos, which she hated to part with. She didn't know how much slaves might cost, but one thousand octavos was all she could fit into the bag and still pull the drawstring closed. If only she'd known how to disguise worthless bits of slag to resemble gold. Perhaps such a trick might be hidden in the Danisoban book.

A gray-haired man with sun-darkened skin and a slateboard under his arm approached, followed by a shorter fellow carrying a collapsible wooden table and a clay bowl in his hands. The verifier, Kestrel thought. He stopped in front of the noblewoman. His assistant snapped the table open and set the bowl upon it while the verifier took the slateboard from under his arm. He slid a writing stylus from behind one ear. "Name," he said.

"Jane Duke." The woman glanced over her shoulder at Kestrel, crinkling her nose and smiling tightly. The name seemed overly simple for someone as noble as this woman, and Kestrel wondered if she'd just been included in some sort of subterfuge she had no awareness of.

The verifier wrote the name on his board. Was that it? Was the name false? It would make sense for these rich people to keep their identities hidden if the slavers were determined to keep records. Perhaps she assumed Kestrel wouldn't know to say anything but her actual name, and felt even more superior because of it. "And how much coin have you brought with you today?"

"Five thousand octavos," the noblewoman said, opening her bag and handing it to the assistant. He set it on the table, reached in and withdrew a handful of coins. He slid them with his thumb one at a time into the waiting bowl, until the bag was empty. He nodded at the verifier, who wrote a figure on his board. The assistant poured the shining coins back into the woman's bag and returned it to her. "Thank you," she said.

The verifier took no notice, having stepped in front of Kestrel. The assistant picked up the table and bowl and moved next to his master. "Name?"

"Thiabrad Nesbit." Her old captain, Binns, long ago insisted on her adopting an alias for just such occasions as this, when she might need to grift her way out of some situation. This was the first time she'd ever needed to use it. The noble woman watched out of the corner of her eye, so Kestrel gave her a smile. She blew out an annoyed breath and turned away. The verifier wrote the name on his board.

"And how much coin have you brought today?" Kestrel handed her bag to the assistant, the mouth pulled wide. "One thousand," she said. The assistant counted her coins into the bowl quickly, nodded, and gave her bag back. The two men moved on.

One step down. She tied the bag back onto her belt. All that was left was to win the auction and get McAvery out on the open water before the Danisobans could stop her. A few buyers stepped forward to inspect the slaves, so Kestrel joined them. Arms were squeezed, mouths were forced open. The treatment of these people turned her stomach. Worse, though, was the effect of the Solace smoke. None of the slaves fought the inspections. Some even laughed, as if they enjoyed the attention. The two Danisobans lurked next to McAvery. Kestrel edged closer to try and hear their conversation, but they spoke too softly to be heard over the women admiring McAvery from the crowd.

"That one's fine," said a well-dressed woman. "I could use another bath slave, and he certainly looks capable."

"I heard he was a pirate's consort once. Can you imagine? A dirty, nasty pirate forcing himself on that pretty man?" her companion said. "I wonder if he knows how to please women, too."

Kestrel ground her teeth, but kept silent. No need to start an argument with two silly women with no idea of the real world around them. The Danisobans stepped away, and McAvery glanced out at the crowd. At her. His eyes caught her, held her. His smile became real, just for an instant.

"Oh, what a cheeky thing!" The women were giggling. "Looked right at me as if he wasn't a slave!"

"Attend me, ladies and gentlemen! Attend! Gather round for the bidding, if you please!" A plainly-dressed man had climbed the steps of the platform, and waved a hand at the waiting crowd.

"Tide will be turning, and many of you have far to go. Attend, please!"

The crowd quieted and tightened on itself, noble and merchant class pressing shoulders with no concern at all. The closeness was uncomfortable, but Kestrel didn't have any choice now. She put all her attention on the slave broker. He walked to the first slave in line, a huge man with a vacant expression. He wore only a pair of pants, their hems ragged and short. His broad chest rippled with muscle, as did his thick arms. The broker slapped him on the back with a short riding crop, and the poor fellow straightened immediately.

"First up, a strong fellow from Doana. Trained in all forms of farm labor, and I dare to guess he'd be a sturdy back for mine work as well. No skill at thinking, but his strength more than suffices."

Kestrel found the process sickening. Whether the poor man had been born lacking this way or suffered some illness or injury to leave his wits impaired, he didn't deserve a life as property. What had happened to his family? Where were friends to protect him? She drew a slow breath to calm herself, and to remind herself of what was at stake. She couldn't save everyone.

The bidding was quick and lighthearted, and when a winner was decided, the man seemed almost happy. Herders unshackled him and led him away to his new owner, and the broker moved on to the next unfortunate in line. It seemed to take forever to reach McAvery.

Two herders unshackled him and brought him forward to stand next to the broker. They stepped back, just far enough to avoid obstructing any buyer's view, but kept their eyes fixed on McAvery's back. The broker laid a hand on McAvery's shoulder, and smiled at the waiting crowd.

"A special treat, my lords and ladies! This fellow is fit and strong, has all his teeth. A fine addition to your stable of workers." The broker paused, and the crowd seemed to hold its breath, waiting for his next words. "He's educated. Reads and writes like a gentleman! You don't run across a specimen like this every day, no indeed. What am I bid for this excellent fellow?"

Voices shouted, and the broker began taking the bids as fast as he could. "Five octavos! Thank you, lady! Ah, seven! Very good, sir!" The Danisobans were standing apart from the main crowd, their heads close together, conferring. It was likely that they'd wait until things slowed down before making their bid, in the hope the others had reached their limit.

"Fourteen octavos!" cried the woman in front of Kestrel. McAvery spared a glance in the bidder's direction, his lips tipping into a half smile. The woman squeaked and fanned herself with a handkerchief. He was enjoying this, the blackguard. Kestrel had the briefest desire to walk away, leave him to his fate as some simpering noble's bath slave. She raised a hand to bid. "Twenty," she called. The broker acknowledged her. The woman threw a withering look back before bidding again.

"Thirty!"

"Fifty." A big leap in price, she knew, but the sun was setting, and Kestrel didn't want to wait any longer. It was time to see what the Danisobans had in mind.

The noblewoman snorted. "Pirate's consort, indeed. Probably only likes a dangler anyway." She took her companion's arm and stalked out of the bidding arena. The broker grabbed McAvery by the shoulders, and turned him in a circle.

"Look at this, lords and ladies! A good strong back to lift and carry for you, and a full head of learning to go along with it! Are you going to let him go for fifty octavos?"

The remaining bidders seemed reluctant to go any higher. Not a surprise, since Kestrel's bid had been an exorbitant amount for a slave. No one raised a hand to outbid her. Even the usual low chatter fell silent. The broker nodded his head. "Fifty, one call. Two calls. And three . . ."

"One hundred."

Heads swung at the sudden bid, and the broker's face lit like an evening star. He was about to make more on one man than on all the rest of his stock combined. "Yes, of course, one hundred. I have one hundred. Are there any further bids?"

The crowd's attention turned to Kestrel again. She made a show of searching her bag, then said, "Five hundred."

The crowd gasped. Five hundred was an astronomical price. Several of the merchants in the crowd were eyeing Kestrel curiously. The two brethren leaned close to each other, whispering. Everyone waited, and the broker coughed delicately. "We have five hundred. One call, two calls . . ." He raised a foot to stomp the platform and end the bidding.

A robed head lifted. "One thousand and ten."

A chill ran down Kestrel's back. The mages had been far away from her when the verifier counted her money, and couldn't possibly have heard her limit. How did they know by how much to outbid her? She gritted her teeth together. Buying McAvery would have been so much easier, but the hard way it would have to be.

McAvery was staring at her. The whole crowd was, in fact. Kestrel gazed at him, then shook her head. The bidding was over.

The Danisobans stepped forward to claim their purchase.

# CHAPTER 11

*Mocked and deserted by the common man,*
*Made half divine to me for having failed.*
—JOHN MASEFIELD, *The Wanderer*

Kestrel ducked into the thickness of the trees as the rest of the crowd made its way to the beach. Winning the bid would have been easiest. Walking away with McAvery, no one chasing, and she'd looked forward to tormenting the man with her ownership of him. Barring that course, she had another plan. Even though her second choice involved noise and exertion, it would have to do. She had no intention of leaving the island without McAvery in tow.

The Danisobans were settling their purchase with the slaver, and if it was anything like the other purchases she'd watched, she had only minutes. She slid out of sight of the crowd and drew the red silk veil from her pocket. The trees above her bore a canopy of thick green vines and leaves, but not so much that she couldn't see sky. She licked her lips and started to whistle, feeling the sharp tickle of power running along her skin. Balling the silk into her fist, she tossed it into the air. The red fabric slithered toward the ground, but she directed the air to move, felt it swirling around her head, teasing at the stray hairs falling loose from under her hat. She focused on the silk, driving the breeze under it, lifting it, pushing it up toward the sky between the trees.

After about a minute, she was running out of air, so she stopped to take another breath, her heart thumping painfully from the strain. The silk dropped, until she could whistle again. If only she knew how to make the air keep going after she stopped. Sometimes it did, sometimes not, and the inconsistency of her power was infuriating. She didn't know enough of Nasrin's way to dance for the power, not yet, and she worried that people would notice her flailing about if she tried. When she was back aboard the ship, she'd devote a week to training with the dancer and reading that bloody Danisoban book.

Slowly, carefully, she used her power to lift the red silk up above the treeline, up to where Shadd could see. It floated in the blue sky, rippling in the higher breezes. She held it there for as long as she was able, blowing the air to the limits of her strength until she had no breath left, and her jaw burned. She stopped whistling, letting the silk fall. It snagged in the branches, fluttering gently in the natural breeze.

She panted, breathless. Had Shadd seen? She'd know before long. Her chest ached from the exertion, and her head spun. She rested her hands against her knees, head down and eyes closed for a time to regain her strength. Shadd would be on his way. She'd need to be as close to McAvery as possible. She'd have to strike during the panic if she hoped to have the slightest chance of taking him from the Danisobans.

McAvery walked between the two robed mages, his hands tied but feet unshackled. They were leading him toward a short hackney boat drawn much farther onto shore than was usual, well clear of the reach of the tide. Two sailors stood beside the boat, ready to push it into the water and row it back to whatever ship had carried them here. The boat was wide, with shoulder-high barriers forming a three-sided cubicle in the center. A long waxed tarp hung off the back of the cubicle, like a curtained entrance. The mages would sit inside, and cover themselves with the tarp for the trip back. A fleeting notion to whistle up a wind and capsize their boat crossed Kestrel's mind, but she banished it. McAvery was strong, but with his hands tied and a head full of Solace, swimming could be too dangerous. One mage threw a leg over the gunwale of the boat, and disappeared inside the cubicle.

"Hurry up, Shadd," she whispered.

As if in answer, the *Thanos* hove into view, sweeping toward the tiny bay like an avenging juggernaut. The mighty ship bore down on the smaller merchant vessels, and let loose a thundering volley. People panicked, some running for the trees, others for hackney boats. The air in the bay soon clouded with steam and smoke. Screams of "Pirates!" echoed over the beach.

Kestrel dashed across the sand toward McAvery, still standing next to the Danisoban boat. The remaining mage faced away from her, waving his hands in a complicated dance, flicking drops of blood from a tiny vial, his sleeves bunched near his shoulders, his bare arms pale in the sunlight. Kestrel drove a shoulder into his unprotected back, knocking him face first into the sand. She hopped back, regaining her stance. The other mage climbed out of the cubicle, his robe hanging open, and charged at Kestrel with a sword in hand.

Kestrel drew her own weapon to meet his assault. Despite his bravado, the mage wasn't much of a sword fighter. His robe hung loose at the neck, displaying a purplish stain along his collarbone. Lunging over and over, Kestrel forced him back toward the boat and the waves, until his feet were being splashed. He glanced down. Kestrel leaped at the chance, lifted one foot and kicked him square in the chest, knocking him backward into the water. He fell, sputtering and cursing.

The first mage had risen, and waved his hands in some arcane fashion, the silver bracelets glinting in the sun. She rushed him, brandishing her sword. He flinched, letting his hands fall. "Mercy!" he cried.

She drew up short, her feet sliding on the sand. Had she heard right? A Danisoban crying for mercy?

The mage flashed out with his fists, slamming into Kestrel's midsection. Something crunched and a sharp pain stabbed her. Kestrel gasped for breath, hoping the sound wasn't a cracked rib. Raising her blade, she straightened, bringing her sword arm up to strike his temple with her hilt. He dropped to the sand. She grabbed McAvery's arm. "Come on!"

"Where are we going?"

"Move!"

McAvery laughed out loud, and took to his heels beside her. Together they made for the path back to the market clearing, pushing their way through frightened nobles going the same direction. A crowd milled around the platform, some crying, others screaming for someone, anyone, to take them to safety. Kestrel grabbed McAvery's hand, dragging him along as she pressed through the panicked people and into the thick brush of the forest. She spotted the tiny red thread she'd left there to mark her path. They were headed in the right direction. The voices of the frightened merchants faded the deeper she and McAvery ran into the trees, but Kestrel didn't slow. The Danisobans wouldn't be delayed long by the confusion.

Her side ached from fatigue or injury, she wasn't sure which. They moved as quickly as the forest would allow, keeping an eye out for the tiny red threads she'd tied to branches to mark her path on the way in. Trees bent low, the long fronds slapping her face. It was nearly impossible to see more than a few feet ahead. Her lungs burned with the moist air, but she didn't dare take the time to whistle up a breeze. She also didn't dare release her grip on McAvery. He laughed and sang bits of songs in turn, and she suspected if she let go, he'd turn back to look for a pub that didn't exist. How long would the effect of the smoke last?

Soon the trees began to thin, and the air to lighten. Kestrel launched herself through the last stand of trees, McAvery stumbling behind her, to find the strip of sand on which she'd beached the boat. She'd feared it would be gone, stolen or washed away, leaving her stranded. The boat was there, its sail furled against the makeshift mast. Sweat tickled its way down her back. Wind off the water lifted and tossed the free hairs around her face, and she couldn't help closing her eyes and enjoying the feel of the air on her sticky skin. But they weren't safe yet. Time enough for breezes later, when they were out to sea and away from their pursuers. She let go of McAvery's arm, took hold of the mooring line and began pulling the small craft toward the water. McAvery reached out with his bound hands, and tapped her on the back.

"What?" Kestrel said, not bothering to look over.

"Look, Kes, no hands!"

She spared him a glance. His bare chest glistened with sweat, droplets still slipping from under his hair. Bits of leaves and brush stuck to his body from their careening run through the trees. And his hands were still tied together. He couldn't help her in that state. She took a breath, pursed her dry, aching lips and whistled a sharp, pulsing tune directed at the ends of the knotted twine. They lifted on a gentle cushion of air, and began sliding slowly apart, until the knot was loose enough to let him shake it off. He rubbed his hands, smiling. "Thank you." He reached out again, and tapped her.

"Make yourself useful," she said.

His eyes shifted to a spot behind her. His mouth widened into a grin. "Better run!" he said. Kestrel looked back.

At first, everything seemed as it had been. The white sand beach was smooth except for their footprints and the long ditch left by the boat's hull, shadows of ancient trees overhanging the water's edge. Birds chortled. Water lapped softly at the shore. And then she heard it. Crashing, in the distance. Branches snapping, and the low hum of men's voices calling back and forth to each other, urging each other to hurry, to catch up. Kestrel took up the mooring line again. "Push!" she yelled.

McAvery put both hands on the bow and heaved. The boat slid down the soft sand of the beach and splashed into the water. Grabbing the gunwales, Kestrel swung one leg up and over, flopping like a caught fish into the bottom of the boat. As soon as she was safely aboard, she scrambled to her feet. McAvery flung himself over the side as well, settling himself onto one of the seats. He reached down for one of the oars, but didn't bother trying to slide it into the oarlock. Instead, he dropped it into the water and started paddling with all his strength.

She yanked loose the simple knot that held the sail. The stiff fabric fell with a hollow, satisfying thud, snapping under the breeze in miniature complement to her own mighty *Thanos*. "It's a fine wind," she cried. "We'll be at sea in a trice."

No sooner had she spoken than the breeze that had been tickling her face all afternoon died. Leaving both her hopes and their little boat's sail flat.

Back on shore, the trees were rocking as the owners of the voices came closer. Kestrel pressed her lips together, and began whistling. Her lips were sore and dry, and the best sound she could make was raw and halting. She stopped, and rubbed her mouth with the back of her hand, then tried again.

A little better this time. Her tune was slow, but the air began moving again, enough to catch the sail and bell it into driving along. The boat moved away from the shore, helped along by McAvery's furious rowing.

"Stop, thief!" The brush parted, revealing the two Danisobans and a tall man wearing a dark hood. The mages stopped short, skidding to avoid tripping into the water. The hooded man ran into the water up to his knees, shouting after the boat. "You can't run for long!" That voice . . . she frowned. It was so familiar.

McAvery stood, his sudden movement rocking the boat dangerously. He turned his backside toward the men on shore, shaking his hips back and forth. "Land and sea, can't catch me!" he cried, waving his arms. The oar slid from his hand, splashing into the water.

"Sit down, you fool!" Kestrel cried. She wondered if he behaved this nonsensically drunk on ale as he did from the smoke. Kestrel whistled harder. I'll whistle up a spinstorm if I have to, she thought desperately. The wind strengthened, pushing the boat further out of the slaver's reach. He'd waded out until he was nearly chest deep now. Back on the shore, one of the Danisobans was twining his hands together, and muttering something she couldn't hear. What could they possibly be sending her way? She didn't want to find out. She diverted her focus from the air around her to the air nearer the surface of the water. With a deep breath, she whistled a sharp note, forcing the water into a wave. It rose, driven by the air, and approached the Danisobans. Just before it crashed to shore, the one who'd been casting his spell noticed, and ran, shrieking, into the safety of the trees. The other one remained, letting the water splash him. The hooded fellow was trudging back to the shore, but he turned to watch her go, the weight of his eyes pressing like stones even from the distance. Kestrel fell back onto the bench, her head spinning. But she couldn't rest. Gripping the gunwale with one hand, she resumed her whistling, driving a breeze into the sail to push them farther.

The boat moved out of the protected cove, seeming to take forever to reach the open water where the natural wind could have its way. The sail puffed out mightily, and the little boat began dancing over the waves. McAvery sat down and leaned back. He shoved his sleeves up to his elbows. The flesh of his wrists was inflamed and torn in places from the abuse of the twine that had bound him. He inspected them both with a rueful expression, and looked up at Kestrel. "Ow," he said.

"We still have a long way to go. And since I'm not entirely sure why I rescued you, I'd prefer you sit quiet until we reach the ship."

McAvery frowned. "You don't have to yell at me."

Kestrel opened her mouth to snap at him, then stopped. She wasn't sure what had changed, but she knew she had no interest in exchanging barbs with him any longer. "You needed help. Now you've had it. I'll return you to Pecheta, and we'll be done. Move over and let me take the rudder."

"Why don't you come sit on my lap and take my rudder?" He grinned at her, crooking one finger at her.

"I'll do no such thing," she said. Worse things had passed her ears in pubs all over the Islands, but never from such as him. He was a quick hand with a teasing jest, yes, but this was far and away from his style. It was as if he was drunk.

Which of course, he was. The lavender smoke he'd breathed before the auction began. The rich woman had said it lasted hours. Kestrel never expected him to be quite so brash under its effects. "Bloody Grace and all her nephews," she muttered. She was trapped in this tiny boat with an intoxicated McAvery until she found the *Thanos.*

"We're all alone," he purred. "And I won't tell." He leaned over, placing his hands palm down on either side of her hips, his face close enough to share breath. "Give us a kiss, sweeting."

She pressed him back into his seat, and turned her head away. "Nasrin is waiting for you, you silly sod."

"Who?"

Kestrel bit her lip. The smoke muddled his brain. He'd be terribly embarrassed when the stuff wore off, and once she could have looked forward to torturing him with stories of his behavior. But things were different now. She didn't dare let him go as far as he seemed to want. They weren't out of danger. His passion was due to the smoke. It had to be.

He was pouting at her lack of enthusiasm for him. She waved a hand at his injured wrists. "Dangle your hands over the side. The salt will draw out any infection."

Without a word, he dipped both hands into the water, complaining as it splashed over his wounds. Kestrel settled herself in the stern of the boat, and reached into her frock coat for the compass. Something sharp stabbed into the tender pads of her fingers. "Oh bloody hell," she murmured, withdrawing her hand. On her palm lay the compass, its glass smashed and the needle waving like sea grass in a breeze. Now at least she knew what the mage had broken when he hit her. Turning her hand over, she let the ruined compass fall into the water, and washed off one hand, then the other. She'd have to hope she was headed in the correct direction until dark, then see if the stars agreed with her. She laid a hand on the rudder and concentrated on putting them on a course to intercept the *Thanos*.

The sky was a velvet riot of flame, with pink and orange threads of cloud interweaving on the face of the darkening blue. High overhead, a single star winked, heralding the approaching night.

"Someone kicked me in the head," McAvery groaned, stretching into wakefulness. He picked himself up and slid onto the bench opposite Kestrel.

After Kestrel rebuffed him, he had curled up in the bottom of the boat and dropped off to sleep, gently snoring. Extending a grateful prayer to Bloody Grace and whichever of her divine nephews watched over intoxicated fools, Kestrel spent what remained of the afternoon holding the course she'd chosen and watching for the *Thanos*.

The wind filling her sail continued its work, and they'd left the little islet long behind. The *Thanos* had yet to make an appearance. If anything had happened to her ship, she didn't know what she'd do. *We'll meet on Bix,* she assured herself for the hundredth time. *They'll be waiting for me there.* Any other possibility was unthinkable.

"How long have we been out here?"

"Hours."

"Where are we going?"

"Bix, unless we meet the *Thanos* on the way." Kestrel pointed at his still-inflamed wrists. "You ought to wrap those."

McAvery inspected his arms. "Perhaps I should." He reached over to one shoulder. With a quick yank, he ripped the sleeve of his shirt away. He shucked it down his arm and over his hand, and tore the sleeve into two pieces. He dipped one strip, then the other, in the water, and wrapped each wrist, carefully tucking the loose ends under the wrapping. When he finished, he leaned forward, elbows on knees, pressing his temples and watching her as she watched the horizon. "If only I could wrap my head."

"What was in that smoke?" Kestrel asked.

"I don't know, but I could earn a lot of money selling it in the bars on Eldraga. At least until the buyer woke up the next day with this headache." He leaned back, stretching as well as he could in the confines of the small boat. "Is there any water?"

"In that box," she said, raising her chin in the direction of the bow. "And some fish, if you're hungry."

McAvery opened the box, withdrew a waterskin, and took a long draught. "That's perfect," he said. He picked up a strip of dried meat, and ate it in quick bites. "So good."

They fell into silence for a time. Water splashed against the hull and the soft breeze murmured, a gentle lullaby that tempted Kestrel to close her eyes and drift off. "This reminds me," McAvery said, "of the last time we two were in a boat alone."

"Don't. I'm not in a mood for games." It annoyed her that his attention made her want to smile. She reminded herself of Nasrin, waiting for McAvery on the *Thanos*.

He nodded, and stared out at the darkening sky. "You came for me."

"I did," she replied, not looking at him.

"I wasn't sure you would."

"You're welcome," she said, stopping him before he could express his gratitude. "But if you don't mind, I'd prefer not talking."

McAvery dropped his head, and Kestrel relaxed a little. It was easier to be with him when he wasn't staring at her.

"I owe you an apology." McAvery's voice was as serious as she'd ever heard it. "I do appreciate the risk you took to come for me. If I offended you with what I said or did while I was under the smoke's influence, I am heartily sorry."

Kestrel avoided his eyes.

"Talk to me, please."

She'd wanted to talk to him for months. Dreamed of it, wished for it. In her thoughts, she'd known exactly the words that would make his eyes soften with caring. Now that they were truly together and alone, she had no idea what to say. "What do you want to talk about?" she asked.

"You came for me when I needed you. Why would you do

that if we had nothing to say to each other?"

There was so much she wanted to say, but none of it mattered anymore. "You're going to tease and flirt, trying to get a rise out of me. We'll spend a ridiculous amount of time tossing harsh words back and forth until one of us loses her temper and tosses the other overboard. And I just don't have the energy for that, McAvery." She finally looked right into his eyes. She wondered what color they might be, if there'd been enough light for her to see.

"Why did you come for me?"

"You didn't leave me a choice, did you? Hanging that bauble around my neck, without a word as to its nature?"

"I'd have thought you'd suspect it was more than a token." His eyes flicked to her open shirt. "You're still wearing it."

She ignored the implied question. She wasn't sure herself why it still hung there, and she didn't want to think about her reasons here in the dark on the water. "You set it off while Shadd and the others were looking. Poor Shadd thought I'd been possessed by spirits. I could do nothing else but come to your rescue. I didn't want to come, you know." She eased the rudder left. "Shadd tried to talk me into it. Said you were a friend, that I owed you. Once we came across the slavers, and learned your location, I was roped for certain. If I didn't mount an attempt to fetch you out, the whole crew would have taken me down."

"The slavers told you where they'd left me? I didn't think that was part of their plan." His confusion seemed genuine.

"Plan?"

He shrugged. "I only overheard the occasional snatch of conversation. There was another ship coming. I had the impression it was coming for me, that I wasn't supposed to be sold on the regular block. Not once they'd lured you in as well."

Kestrel's chest tightened. Plans, plots, lures...did she even want to know what he was talking about? "The Danisobans thought they could use you as bait to catch me."

He met her eyes. No laughter now, only quiet determination. She'd have given anything for the joke in his eyes right then. Because plans and plots belonged to those with far more power than a lowly pirate, even one employed by the crown. "Not the Brethren. At least, not them alone."

"Who else then?" she asked. "Eusebians?" The Danisobans' bounty hunters. She should have guessed they wouldn't give up just because they lost one man. How stupid she'd been — the mage she'd drenched on the beach. The mark under his open robe must have been an edge of the red and purple tattoos the Eusabians wore. And now that things were calm, she realized he'd worn no bracers. No wonder he hadn't ducked away from the water. If she'd been paying attention, she'd have seen all this. "Cack me for an idiot," she groaned, running a hand over her hair. What was it about McAvery that narrowed her vision until she saw only him? She could end up dead at this rate.

"Possibly. One of them was Eusebian, for certain. But the big fellow," McAvery frowned. "He was working with them, but he seemed to have some other plan of his own. There was something about him, reminded me of someone. I can't quite recall who, though."

That voice . . . she'd recognized the man, too. Not enough to know who he was, nor why she should be wary of him. She opened her mouth, intending to tell McAvery she'd known him, too. McAvery was staring at her, and the look on his face made her heart thud against her chest. She frowned. He had no right to look at her that way. "Not surprising that you can't remember. You seem to forget most people as soon as you walk away from them."

He reached out to her. Kestrel jerked back, slapping his hand away.

"Ow! That stings!"

"Keep to your end. I have to watch for the *Thanos.*" Not that she'd likely miss it. The sea spread out, empty in every direction. The sun was gone. Stars glittered above. It would be a while before moonrise. McAvery was a shadow in the bow, head down and still. He might have gone to sleep again, but she doubted it. The silence became heavy, questions rising in her mind like bubbles from a drowning man, but she'd be damned if she asked him anything right now.

"Do we have a destination in mind?" His voice was subdued, strange in the dark. For the first time, that teasing note was missing. She wondered why that didn't satisfy her. As many times as she'd wanted to quiet him, all she wanted now was that insolence back.

"If I can't run up on the *Thanos*, we'll meet them on Bix." She wasn't going to mention the lack of a compass. It would only give him something to argue about.

"I wonder where they are. Basa isn't that big of an island."

"Basa?" she asked, immediately cursing herself for it.

"The little islet you rescued me from."

"I didn't know it had a name." Kestrel stretched her legs out before her, letting her tense muscles lengthen. She was being ridiculous, she knew. Her feelings were not his fault. And conversation would help the night pass more quickly. She took a deep breath, and released it. "How'd the slavers get their hands on you? Last I heard, you were on Lidias."

"I was. Stayed there for a good while, too. Lidias is so barren, ships don't dock there on a regular basis." He shifted on the bench. "Not that I was in much of a hurry. His Majesty wanted me to keep an eye on the Scion. He suspected a certain dissatisfaction in some of the Scion's letters."

"Our king is a suspicious bastard."

"How do you think he stays king?" McAvery shrugged. "As it turned out, the Scion's no traitor. He'd come into possession of some information, which he refused to share with me."

"He didn't trust you? Imagine."

"The Most Sober Scion of Lidias called me a lackey, and made certain disparaging comments concerning my level of intelligence and the legitimacy of my birth. He did, however, entrust me with a sealed letter to deliver."

"Which you read."

He shrugged. "Never got the chance. The slavers overtook the ship half a day after we left Lidias. I secreted the letter in my inner pocket, but their man searched me and took it. Took everything I had on me. My money, a few useful trinkets, my sword, all gone. I was lucky to keep my clothes. They threw me in the hold. Flung a handful of biscuit at me once a day, and the big one visited belowdecks occasionally to thump me, remind me who was boss, until we reached the slave market."

"In the hold. With the dancer."

"Nasrin, yes, and all the other slaves going to the block."

"All the other slaves whose names you don't remember."

His body was a dark shape opposite her, yet Kestrel was certain he was smiling. And why shouldn't he smile? The memory of meeting the lovely Nasrin, of finding love . . . it was something to smile about. There was no way he could see her face, for which Kestrel was grateful. "Nasrin will be so happy to see you." She looked away from him again, fixing instead on the waves. It would have been too much to see the joy in his eyes at Nasrin's name. After all this time, with only a kiss to remind her, knowing he wanted someone else, that the kiss had been nothing to him, was more than she wanted to bear.

"Aren't you happy to see me?"

*I missed you*, she wished she could tell him. *I didn't want to come for you because I was afraid to see you again. Afraid of being sure of my feelings. And I was right.* She ground her teeth together, fighting the tears that suddenly threatened.

"Kestrel."

He raised himself from the bow plank, moving to kneel in front of her. His hands moved into sight, his fingers falling gently over hers. His touch was so warm, and she caught the scent of his sun-baked skin.

"Don't touch me," she said.

"I missed you. More than you know." He reached up, taking her chin and turning her face towards his. "I am very grateful for what you've done," he murmured. "If I've guessed what you're thinking, I hope you'll allow me the chance to prove you so very wrong."

"No need for that." She pushed his hands away, and rose, rocking the boat precariously. "I was wrong to rescue you from slavery. I should have watched them cart you away."

McAvery was gripping the sides of the boat against its rocking. "Please sit down."

"How can you be tender with me, when she's waiting for you on the ship? Bloody Grace whip me, but you're a fickle beast!"

"Kestrel, stop. I have to explain, about Nasrin. You don't understand."

"No, I don't. Who could?"

"She's so much more than –"

"Shut your mouth!" Kestrel dropped to the plank with a thud that jarred her tailbone and shook the boat. "It's bad enough that you toy with every woman you meet, but to flaunt it in front of me is too much."

He didn't answer, but leaned back on his bow plank, crossed his arms and stared out at the ocean. His jaw was tight, as if he was holding in everything he wasn't saying. She'd had the last word. She wanted to be satisfied, but all she felt was embarrassed. Of all the things she'd feared she might do while alone with McAvery, throwing a tantrum hadn't been one of them. He'd been near to kissing her again. Kestrel wondered for an instant if his lips would have been as soft as she remembered. Had she stopped him for Nasrin's sake? Or for her own?

An unearthly howl split the quiet night, echoing over the waves. Kestrel gripped the plank seat. She knew that sound. The accompaniment to her ship being dragged nearly to the bottom of the ocean. So much louder, now she rode this close to the water. Compared to the *Thanos*, this little vessel was as fragile as an eggshell. Another howl roared out of the darkness, closer this time, slamming against her ears. The boat rocked hard to one side, water splashing over the gunwales and soaking her to the knees.

The black water reflected the night sky. Something rose from the blackness, arcing up a few feet then sliding beneath the waves again. Its wake tossed their boat, sending more water splashing over the side and throwing her off the plank. She fell forward to her knees, catching hold of the plank seat in front of her. McAvery flung himself to the bottom of the boat, too, clutching the gunwales to either side. The mysterious creature rose from the depths, closer this time, and as it passed by, she heard the now-familiar howl. The sound vibrated the boat, even as the wake caught them. The boat rose on the swell, and dropped sharply. "Bloody damn!" she cried.

As quickly as it began, the tossing stopped. There was one last howl, and the waves calmed. The rocking eased back to the normal way. Gazing out across the darkness, she saw nothing moving except the rolling of the water. It seemed they were alone. With a huff, Kestrel sat back, landing in the cold water pooled in the bottom of the boat. She struggled to seat herself on the plank. "Wonderful," she grumbled. "I might as well have swum the whole way."

"What was that?"

Kestrel shrugged, not looking away from the water. The animal must have been passing by, was all. Looking for another ship for its entertainment, perhaps? Luckily, her boat was too small to be a plaything. Slowly, she retrieved the dropped oar, raised herself back onto the plank, and settled the oar across her lap. "Help me bail this water," she said, cupping her hands and tossing as much water as she could lift over the side. McAvery knelt in the puddle and bailed in silence. She sent up a silent plea to Bloody Grace to make the *Thanos* appear, and soon.

# CHAPTER 12

*. . . the call of the running tide*
*Is a wild call and a clear call that may not be denied*
— JOHN MASEFIELD, *Sea Fever*

Silence reigned. Uncomfortable, surly silence. Kestrel alternated her attention between watching the stars and doing her best to navigate, and scanning the ocean for signs of the creature's return. McAvery either sulked or slept, she wasn't sure. He'd curled himself into the bow, occasionally helping himself to the waterskin but saying nothing since they'd nearly been swamped. At first Kestrel thought he was planning his counterattack, but as time passed and he made no attempt to further press his case, she knew she'd won this round.

In one fashion, she was relieved. She'd been too close to admitting her feelings, too close for her own safety. He'd moved to kiss her, even knowing she was aware of his woman on her ship. How could she trust a man who'd betray another with such ease? Better that she'd learned it now. She couldn't afford to love a thief and charlatan. He'd play her false at the first opportunity. She'd been dazzled by his charm once, but that was over. From now on, she would look at him no differently from any other crew member, and keep her heart safely tucked away.

From somewhere off to port, she heard a splash. There'd been more than a few since the huge creature passed them earlier, but no more howling. She leaned against the port gunwale, trying to see what might have made the noise.

"What's wrong?" McAvery asked, his voice rough.

She saw nothing in the water, but suddenly, in her mind's eye, Kestrel saw light, glimmering like bright sunbeams reaching just under the water. At the height of the beam, the keel of a small boat wobbled on the surface. The vision rose through the depths, until it vanished from her thoughts. She blinked, the world around her returning to normal. A tiny head she recognized broke from the water inches below the gunwale. She started, nearly dropping the oar, then laughed out loud. The lizard had found her. McAvery scrambled to straighten himself, but Kestrel held a palm out at him. "Be still."

Another splash swept cold water over the port gunwale and soaked Kestrel's shins. The little face was gone again. She raised the lantern high, and called out, "Come out, come out!"

Had the lizard run away from the *Thanos*? Or had something happened to force it away? She wasn't about to let McAvery scare the poor thing. She set the lantern down and leaned over the side. "It's safe. Come aboard."

It peeked its snout over the edge, but came no farther, glaring at McAvery.

"He's harmless."

"How do you know it's harmless?" McAvery edged himself closer to starboard, keeping a suspicious eye on the invader.

"Not it," Kestrel said. "It's you who's no threat." Before he could ask any more questions, she offered her hand to the lizard. It caught hold, gently, its claws pinching not quite hard enough to hurt, and let her pull it out of the water.

McAvery swore softly. "What is that thing?"

Kestrel sat down on her stern plank. The lizard shook itself as a dog might, sending drops of water sizzling against the lantern's sides. "This is . . ." she stopped. "Actually, I'm not sure what it is." She stroked its cool skin, and the lizard preened under her hand. "We were sent out to catch one for the king's menagerie." The lizard scooted closer to her leg and settled in tight for her warmth. She bent close, scratching its eye ridges. "You found me, you smart thing. Where's the ship?"

The lizard raised its head, staring into Kestrel's eyes. As she gazed, she saw the deck of her ship as she'd left it. Shadd stood on the quarterdeck with a telescope to his eye. "She's nowhere to be seen." He bent down, his shaggy hair falling around his face. "I wonder can ye fetch her, beastie?" His face faded, leaving the lizard staring up at her.

Kestrel smiled. She'd been afraid she'd gone too far off course. At least that was all that had happened. She hadn't wanted to think the *Thanos* was damaged or sunk. She couldn't think of a future without her ship. "Can you lead me back to the *Thanos*?"

It bobbed its head in assent, turned toward McAvery. It opened its mouth and cried softly. Kestrel touched its head, stroking to calm it.

"He is the friend I went to rescue. I don't think he's seen anything like you before, but I promise he won't hurt you."

"I beg both of your kind pardons," McAvery said. "Are you having an actual conversation, or are you, Captain, merely indulging yourself with your pet?"

"I'd have thought you'd know I'm not a sentimental woman," Kestrel said. "The creature talks to me. After a fashion."

"I thought you once told me you couldn't talk to animals."

"I can't," she said, then wrinkled her forehead. "I never could before. I thought it was the lizard's doing."

"Some Promises can, but they're rare. And I don't know of any Promises who can perform two kinds of magic at once."

"How many of us have you met?"

"Not many."

If only he knew what she could do, and what more she was learning. "I don't know why I can hear him. It's for sure no one else can. He scared Shadd half to death when they met, but apparently all's forgiven. Shadd sent this little one out after us."

The lizard angled its body to the north, and Kestrel made the appropriate adjustment, whistling a quick wind up to help them along. Soon they were tossing over the water at a steady clip. Kestrel's heart lightened, knowing that her friends were well and the ship would be in her sights before day broke.

McAvery had been studying the lizard while Kestrel worked, although the lizard was paying him no attention. He cleared his throat. Kestrel cocked an eye his way.

"Something to say?"

"As it happens. You said you were ordered to catch this little fellow for the king?"

"For his menagerie, yes. And here on the eve of spinstorm season, when we should have been careening the ship and enjoying a bit of rest. Shadd was furious."

"Rightly so. Didn't it seem strange to you"

"I just said it did." She frowned. "What do you know that I don't?"

"Probably less than you think, but in this case, I know for an absolute certainty that the King of the Nine Islands doesn't keep a menagerie."

Cold enveloped her, squeezing her heart. If the lizard wasn't for the king, there was only one answer. "The orders were sealed with the royal stamp."

"Who gave you the orders?"

She thought she'd been so wary. So cautious. Everyone knew Danisobans couldn't be trusted. Even so, she was sick with the realization that he'd managed to trick her with the merest effort.

"Kestrel, who put the orders in your hands?" McAvery's voice was remarkably gentle, as if he knew what she was going to say, and how much it was making her suffer.

"Lig," she whispered.

"Lig," he repeated.

"Why would Lig want him?"

"Who knows why the Brethren do anything?"

"By Grace's whips, if he intends to experiment on this little one. . ." she stopped, fury choking her. She reached out and stroked the lizard. "When we reach the *Thanos*, I'm setting it loose. After that, I'm going to Pecheta to find that cold-blooded mage and tear out his stone of a heart."

"You're not ready to best Lig on your own, Kestrel, and you know it. Don't let your anger rule you."

He was right. She barely knew what she could do, and seemed to be learning something new every time she turned around. She wouldn't know where to begin fighting a Danisoban child, much less a full-grown mage with the experience and cunning Lig had. Just one little seeing spell left her bruised and exhausted. How would she possibly manage magical combat?

"As for the lizard, I'm not sure it will leave you even if you do set it free."

The lizard raised its wings, allowing the night breezes to flutter them. It glanced at Kestrel and winked one eye. Where had it learned to do that?

"It's staying of its own accord, Captain. If it weren't, do you think it would have come searching across the waves to find you?"

It was a fair question, but the answer would have to wait. She was more concerned with Lig's motives. If the king hadn't sent them on this expedition, that meant Lig had some use for this creature that he didn't want to share with anyone. Some use important enough to steal the king's sigil for his own use. What could be important enough about it to risk an unpleasant death for treason? Even the Danisobans had to face justice if convicted, and Lig had left Kestrel with plenty of damning evidence to use against him.

"Why were the Danisobans using the Eusabians?" she mused.

"They take commissions from the Brethren all the time. They're the best bounty hunters in the business, and the magi have the money to buy them."

"This is different. They were using you as bait, to draw me in. Wouldn't that get the king's attention?"

"Not if Lig arranged it properly. I've never liked the man. Didn't matter, since we both worked for the king. I did my job, and left him to his. What I know about him could be written on a child's school slate. I know more about you."

Kestrel snapped her fingers. "Lidias!"

"What about Lidias?"

"You told me the Scion gave you a letter. Are you being truthful that you didn't read it?"

McAvery let a wry grin play at his lips. "I swear by any god you'd name that I did not lay eyes on the contents of that document."

"I'll wager Lig thinks you read it."

"How would he know?"

The memory of Lig tipping a hand to her as he bid her an ominous farewell on Pecheta danced through her mind's eye. "He can see you if he wants to."

"You think the Scion found out something about our friend Lig, something that would damage the mage's standing with the king?"

"At the very least." She slapped one hand against her thigh. "I let him deceive me, but there's still time to make it right."

"Assuming we figure out what it is that we're after."

The lizard spread its wings, warbling loud enough to wake the sea gods. Dead ahead, a dark shape against the star-studded sky, lay the *Thanos*, her lanterns welcoming. Kestrel called out to alert the watch. She'd never heard anything so wonderful as Shadd's answering bellow. She whistled the wind into a driving breeze, and within minutes, her little boat bumped against the hull of the mighty ship. Men swarmed the deck, letting down lines for her to tie up the boat. She was home.

"Captain! It's a pleasure to see ye!" Shadd grabbed her up in a bear hug that took her breath away. She laughed, and beat on his arms.

"Let me down, boyo! I'm fine."

He did as she said, but he kept the huge grin. "That wee lizard is a smart beastie. When ye didn't turn up, it came gallumphin' out of yer quarters. Scared some of the fellows near out of their wits, but it rambled right up to me, and stared at me with them goggle eyes until I told it to go find ye." He glanced over her shoulder, and laughed. "And lookie here who ye've brought to supper!"

McAvery stepped forward, offering a hand to the big man. "Well met, my friend. I'm in your debt for the rescue."

"T'was all the captain's idea," Shadd said. "She wouldn't sit still 'til we went after ye." Kestrel glared at her quartermaster, who shot her a mischievous wink.

"I am happy to see you safely returned, *rais*." Nasrin stepped out of the shadows, moving with the grace Kestrel wished she could achieve. She nodded at the dancer, and waved a hand behind her. Nasrin smiled.

"Philip," she said, extending her hand. "You look well."

"Lady," he answered, bowing.

She moved past, but Kestrel didn't turn to watch their reunion. There was work to do. Plenty of work to fill up her mind and chase other thoughts and feelings out. She took Shadd's arm, drawing him off from the others. "Let's be on our way," she said. "Continue course for Bix."

"Aye, Captain. And not a minute too soon. Tom sighted some black clouds buildin' off to the east."

"Spinstorm?"

"No way to tell yet, but the sooner we're off the water, the better. We could do worse than spendin' a season with old Binns."

Kestrel shook her head. "We won't be staying."

"Ye're set on deliverin' the wee beastie?" Shadd's face fell.
"Of course ye are. I'd clean forgot about the orders. And here I
was getting' used to havin' him about."

No, she thought, I'd rather swim to Bix than turn the lizard
over to Lig. "We need to talk about that," she said. "I'm not sure
turning it over to the king is the best idea. It's possible we've been
hoodwinked by a master player. If it's true, we have to come up
with a course of action before we return to Pecheta." Shadd widened his eyes, and opened his mouth, but she waved him off. "I
promise, I'll share all that's in my mind. Later, when we reach
Bix." She patted her leg, and the lizard hopped to stand closer.
"Nasrin," she called behind her. "I'll want to meet with you in the
morning. We have work to do."

The dancer bowed. McAvery took a step toward Kestrel, but
she put up a hand to hold him off. "I'm tired. Hudee, fetch me
some fresh water, please. Shadd, see our guest to a hammock,
and get a bit of sleep yourself." She walked to her cabin, the lizard at her heels, and firmly closed the door on McAvery's questioning face.

Kestrel kicked off her boots and shed the sweat-stiffened brocade coat, dropping it on the floor and kicking it away from her.
It needed a real cleaning before she returned it to the wardrobe
else it would ruin the rest of the clothes near it. Shucking off the
vest, she unbuttoned two of the buttons on her shirt, shaking the
lapels to create a little air between the fabric and her skin. A
knock at her door turned out to be Hudee, bearing a small pail
of fresh water and a clean rag. He held it out to her, and she
smiled her thanks, closing the door again and throwing the bolt.
She hated to waste drinking water on washing, but her headlong
escape from the islet and the subsequent hours in the boat left
her skin itchy and in need of a wash. Sea water wouldn't be good
enough for this.

She poured the water into her porcelain bowl, enjoying the
sparkles of reflected lantern light. Squeezing the rag under the
water's surface, she raised it to her face and scrubbed, imagining
as she did so a steaming bath in some island inn. Hot water and

scented oils, a hairdresser to take her braids down for a good wash, and then an hour to soak . . . it sounded like bliss.

Alas, her dream would stay a dream until they figured out their current problem. She slid the filthy shirt off, scrubbed her body with the wet cloth, and retrieved another shirt from the wardrobe, slipping it on and doing up most of the buttons. Finally she skinned the breeches off, tossed them into the growing pile of dirty clothing to be dealt with some other time, and wiped down her legs. Not perfect, but it would have to do.

Tossing the rag into the bowl, she extinguished the lantern's flame and threw herself onto the bed, her mind racing. Lig wasn't waiting, wasn't holding back for the king's sake. He'd likely started planning her doom as soon as she turned him away on the palace turret a year ago. She was foolish to have assumed he'd play by anyone's rules except his own. He didn't care whether she accepted what he offered or not. Her acceptance would merely have made things easier. No, he was using all the resources at his disposal to slip under her defenses. While she'd been at sea, thinking herself safe, Lig had been quietly setting his dogs on her. He didn't have to come to sea to put hands on her. All he had to do was assign someone else to do it. She wasn't free. She'd fooled herself by accepting the job of Privateer. Lig wouldn't stop. Even if the king suspected something, Lig would find a way to make it look as if she'd joined the Danisobans voluntarily.

And what had that long-lost letter said? What did the Scion know that would make Lig react so? The slavers likely burned it in their galley stove, if they hadn't tossed it into the wind. Despite there being no way now to discover it, she'd pay good money for that information. Any secret about Lig would be welcome. If the Scion had evidence against the Danisoban, it could only help Kestrel. And if he was in league with the mage, that would have been good to know, too.

The lizard lay curled up on the bookshelf in the spot it liked. In the dark, Kestrel could see its eyes glowing softly, watching her. Shadd was right; it was nice having the little thing around. She couldn't deny the value of such a creature. It found her on the wide ocean, and led her back to the ship. As it grew older, it might be able to accomplish even more wonders. Assuming it decided to stay with her once it reached adulthood. If it grew to the size the king's orders had described — Lig's orders, she reminded herself — it would have to swim away one day, and there'd be nothing she could do to prevent it. That's good, she chastised herself. Make yourself feel even worse than you already do. There's a way to bring on sleep.

She threw her legs over the side of the bed, and rose. Opening the lantern's shutters, she looked around for her tinder box. Damn, it was nowhere in sight. She wondered where she'd left it this time. Maybe on the quarterdeck. She was ready to go searching, when a thought occurred to her. McAvery had said earlier that no Promise had more than one ability, yet here she was, able to whistle the wind and talk to the lizard. He might be on to something. Fire was a dangerous thing, especially on board ship. If she experimented and failed, she could cause the deaths of her entire crew. She'd be no better than the Danisobans she hated. But the sparks of power she'd created with Nasrin, sparks that exploded from her body like lit gunpowder . . . she was nothing like any Danisoban.

"I'll just try something small," she told herself. She took a deep breath, reached out a toe, and tapped it on the deck in the rhythm of a song she'd heard the men singing many times. The familiar tingle began, ever so gently, tickling up her leg. This time, she concentrated on forming the magic into a stream of flame, running from her tapping toe up through her leg and body, down her arm to spill from her finger. At first, she wasn't sure it would work, until she noticed a reddening on her fingertip. She tapped a little harder, then shuffled her foot over the deck. She liked the sound of that — soft but insistent. She shuffled again, and brought her heel down with a snap.

A tongue of fire burst forth from the end of her finger, comfortably warm but not hurting her. Fire, created by her own hand. She marveled at it, turning her hand over and back. Moving slowly, she reached out to the lantern's wick and touched the flame to it. The cabin filled with soft light. She wiggled her fingers in front of her face, delighted at her own success, then blew at it. The fire flickered out.

She sat down on her bed, staring at her hand. The redness on her skin faded quickly, the lit lantern the only evidence that anything had happened. She'd done it. She'd created fire. What else could she do? And how would she ever learn it all? Nasrin's request to be taken to the Continent was starting to feel less like a demand and more like an opportunity. One Bloody Grace herself must have dropped in front of Kestrel.

Talking to animals, moving the air and creating fire were all valuable skills, but there must be more. If Lig knew what she was truly capable of, he might be thinking twice about making his plans against her. Unless he did know, and hoped to get his hands on her before she fully recognized and controlled her own power. She had to learn more of the spells in the book. The more options she gave herself, the better.

She took the *Source* down from the shelf and crawled back onto her bed. She'd ignored the opening chapters before, but now she thought it might be better to know everything, even the boring bits. She forced herself to read from the beginning. The first pages consisted of a description of Danisoban philosophy, claiming their devotion to learning and wisdom, page after page of praise and glorification of the Brethren, without the slightest mention of their cruelty toward the less fortunate. After that came a chapter detailing Danisoban history. According to the book, the Brethren themselves had settled the Nine Islands, and instituted civilized behavior to the savages living there. Kestrel couldn't help a disgusted snort at what they must have done to the poor natives. There was no mention of the wizards' war of so long ago, the one that had placed the Ageless King's family in power. On the contrary, the book implied the king sat the throne only at the Danisobans' pleasure.

"Arrogant bastards," she grumbled, letting it fall closed onto the bed. If only she could learn from Nasrin everything she needed to know. She knew she didn't want to do things the Danisoban way, that she couldn't beat them at their own game when they'd played it for centuries and she still didn't know all the rules. Yes, trying to perform their magic left her with a vicious headache and might very well drain the blood from her very bones, but the chance to know how they thought, how they saw the world and their place in it, was too valuable to discard. Reading the book offered the easiest route to knowing their motivations. She'd balance what Nasrin taught her with the Danisoban teachings, and possibly earn herself an advantage.

This is the hard part, she reminded herself. You have to know how they think, what they know. Even if you can't do what they do yet. Maybe a drink would help settle her mind. She fetched the rum from her sideboard, poured herself a mug and crawled back onto the bed with the book. The rum slid down her throat like liquid sunlight, drifting through her body and bringing on the familiar relaxation. She rubbed her eyes clear, and set the mug on the floor next to the bed. Either she'd learn something, or she'd drop off to sleep over the pages.

The section that had put her off earlier, now that she was looking at it with more patient eyes, seemed to be related to casting magic. She turned pages, noting where the chapters ended or the subjects seemed to change. Halfway through, pictures started turning up. Portraits of famous Danisobans from years past and the ruling family, landscapes of all the Nine Islands, with descriptions of their coastlines and inhabitants, and animals. Land and sea animals. She yawned, but she wasn't ready to stop. There might be something useful, some answer to why Lig would create fraudulent orders sending her out on a fishing trip here at the beginning of storm season. And one that looked suspiciously familiar.

According to the book, the lizards were known as depwals. The young ones, like her little friend, began life no bigger than human infants, growing wings that allowed them to fly above the water, presumably to escape predators. By the time they reached adulthood, they were enormous, living only in the ocean, their wings having developed into mighty fins that allowed them to speed through the depths. As sweet as the little one was, the big one might have capsized her ship and drowned them all. Did she dare hope it had only acted from playfulness? Or was there a chance it might attack again, to retrieve its young? She glanced at the sleeping lizard, curled up so small. It was hard to believe it might grow as big as this book claimed. Details about the lizard's appearance, feeding choices and general habitat, all of which she'd seen in the scroll Lig gave her. No mention of the skin being poisonous, though. At the bottom of the entry, smaller symbols indicated that there was another mention further on in the book. She flipped through, leaving the pictures behind, and finally found the page she wanted — a drawing of a man clothed head to toe in a suit that seemed to be made of one continuous piece of fabric. A glass mask attached to his face, somehow flush with the edges of the suit. She wondered how he managed to breathe for long in such a thing. The symbols along the edges of the page were cribbed and harder to read, and didn't quite make sense. She picked out the symbol for the depwal, but nothing else was clear. Maybe this was the way the old Danisobans had found the depwals in the first place, by wearing the suit to swim in the ocean. However they had managed before, the knowledge was long gone now. No Danisoban could immerse himself in water, no matter how thickly armored. Everyone knew that.

The realization hit her like a sudden cold wave to the face. They didn't wear suits to hunt for depwals. The mages created the suits *from* depwals. If she delivered the little depwal lizard to the king, he might keep it for a time, until it grew too big to keep feeding. Lig would step in, offer to help, and take it to the Danisoban enclave, where they'd skin it and create suits. She felt sick. Lig had used her to help him work around the limitations salt water meant for him, and it meant the gruesome death of an innocent creature.

# CHAPTER 13

*. . . we watched in awe,*
*Wondering what bloody act her beauty planned,*
*What evil lurked behind the thing we saw*
—JOHN MASEFIELD, *The Wanderer*

At some point, she fell asleep, the book laying on her chest. The lantern had consumed the last of the oil and burnt out, and the sun was peeking at the edges of the sky. The lizard remained curled into a tight ball on the bookshelf, apparently deep in slumber. Kestrel rose and stretched. She pulled on a pair of clean breeches, buttoned them tight and padded out of the cabin to the deck.

Chilly morning air raised goosebumps on her exposed skin. She wrapped her arms across her body. Red Tom stood at the wheel, his eyes puffy from sleep. He raised his chin in greeting. Kestrel returned the nod. Too bad all men weren't as taciturn as her helmsman. He was poking at the lantern's wick with a length of rolled up paper. Paper with a bit of red wax on it. Red wax like the king used to seal letters.

"Tom!" she called. "What's that you're using?"

He blew the flame out, and held it toward her. The parchment was crumpled from being rolled up then flattened, and the edge was burnt away, but when she spread it out against her leg, she realized what she held. Her stomach tightened. Were the gods so kind? "Where'd you find it?"

"Stuck in that book Shadd gave me. Looked like scribbles to me."

"Looks like scribbles to me, too," she said, controlling her voice against the excitement she was feeling. The scribbles were similar to the symbols she'd been reading the night before, the symbols she used to keep her accounting. There were only two

people on the ship who could read this writing, and she wasn't
sure enough of her own skill.

"Good morning, Captain. Sleep well?"

She spun, holding the paper out. McAvery's damp hair was
pulled back into a slick queue, tied off with a bit of leather cord,
and the smudges of dirt washed away from his skin. He must
have asked for a wash, and borrowed fresh clothing from the
crew — a linen shirt over breeches, with a soft leather vest over
that. His feet were bare. The scrape on his face had faded a little,
giving him a rawboned cast that wasn't entirely unattractive. His
eyes, now that she could see them in the light, were a golden
brown.

"How do you do that?" she murmured.

"Do what?" he asked, and she realized she'd spoken aloud.

"Nothing," she said. "See this?"

He looked at the paper in her hand, surprise crossing his face.
He took it and turned it over, inspecting the broken fragment of
wax on the back. "That's the Scion's seal," he said. "You found
the letter?"

She smiled, tension releasing from her shoulders. She'd assumed the slavers threw it overboard. Who'd have known they'd
use it as a bookmark? And thank Grace for the chill in the air,
otherwise Tom wouldn't have used it to light his coals. "We need
to read it."

"In your cabin?"

Heat rose in her body, against her better sense. A mutinous
voice whispered in her head, telling her she wanted nothing more
than an hour alone, undisturbed, with this man. A good tumble
might get it all out of her system, let her think clearly again. If she
was careful, didn't make a show of it in front of them, the men
certainly wouldn't begrudge her a bit of pleasure. Nasrin need
never know.

But louder than that was another voice inside her, screaming
for her to use her common sense, tell him no, lock him away in
the hold and out of her sight, until they made land and she could
unload him into someone else's custody. She didn't know what
to do. She remembered the stone, still around her neck, its color
dull, its weight cold against her breastbone. The stone she never
removed. She hadn't allowed herself to wonder why she still

wore it, why she couldn't yank it from her neck and drop it over
the side. Now she knew. She hadn't removed it because it connected her to him. The only tangible thing, a symbol of what
she'd hoped for. And lost.

He was standing, waiting, a half-smile playing at his lips. Kestrel wondered if him falling into her path was all some godly joke
Bloody Grace decided to play on her. Sending this man, who was
somehow all Kestrel might want, then putting him a fingertip out
of her reach. Grace was a capricious deity; it wouldn't surprise
Kestrel at all. Or maybe Grace was attempting to make a point,
that Kestrel was better off alone. No matter how this man might
fuel her desire, he was the king's man first, and another woman's
second. If he wanted Nasrin, she wouldn't stand in the way.
She'd find out what he knew, deliver him to Pecheta and sail
away. Men might come and go, but she always had the sea.

"After you, sir," she said, waving a hand toward her cabin. Mc-
Avery walked in and stopped next to her table, waiting. Staring at
her. Damn it, she hated when he did that. Closing the door behind herself, she sat, propping one leg over the arm of the chair.
She wrinkled her nose against the faint reek of the filthy clothes
she'd piled in the corner. If she'd thought McAvery would be in
here, she'd have rinsed them out. Or at least hidden them in a
drawer. He said nothing about it, though, leaning forward and
spreading the letter open on the table.

"It's burnt," he said, flicking the charred bits away.

"Tom was using it to light his lantern. Another ten seconds
and you'd be trying to read ash." Finally, possible proof against
Lig that she could take to the king, use to bring him down. She
dragged it from under his hand, and concentrated on the script.
"Starts out with the usual flowery greeting." She peered at the
lacy script, running a finger along the line to keep her place. "*To
his most awesome Majesty, greetings. The Scion of the Austeric
Order of Lidias regrets to inform his Majesty of a threat to his
most gentle kingdom,*" she shook her head. "Burned part there."
She brushed the burnt edge away, and continued. "*The fish has
slipped from its net. We called upon the power of mighty
Desertus for aid in defending his Majesty's most shining interests
but even He was unable . . .* burned again." She slapped the
table. "They'd call on their god? As if the gods care what goes on

here."

"If only you could have found this before Tom did."

"Clearly I need to start reading on a regular basis." She frowned. "So an island full of monks think the king should hear about the loss of a fish. But what fish? Not the one we were sent to find, of that I'm almost certain. And what good can they do, besides praying? They're usually busy starving and sewing themselves uncomfortable shirts out of palm fibers."

"Can you imagine a more determined fighter than someone who'd suffered so long? Look at this bit. *The Scion recommends his Majesty not speak to his Danisoban, but keep the council the Scion most graciously has provided.*" McAvery raised his eyebrows. "I can't believe they mean a real net and fish. And why shouldn't he speak to his mage?"

Kestrel sat back in her chair, staring across at McAvery. "Wait. I've heard something like this before."

"Heard the bit about the net and the fish? Is it some old sailor's story?"

"No, it's . . ." She stopped, raised both hands and let them fall again. "I'd gone to meet Lig, to hand off the last year's logbook. There was a little trouble in the pub, and a man was injured."

"By you?"

"By the mage. When he left, another man walked up to me, and said, 'Not all your fish stay netted.' At the time, I thought he was a friend of the injured man. I assumed he was threatening me for what happened. But what if he wasn't?" She slammed both hands flat against the wood. "I could have gone after him, forced him to tell me what's going on."

"You didn't know, at the time."

The creature extended its sinuous tail, and opened its mouth in a huge yawn before leaping onto the bed and gallumphing to the window. It propped itself on the sill, staring out of the glass at the brightening day. She'd been sent on this mission under forged orders. It wasn't a fish, though a net could have captured it easily enough. But the lizard was safely in her hands, with no sign of wanting to leave her. And all the talk of nets had begun long before she'd found it.

"The fish is something else. A man, maybe? But who? We don't know anything more than we did."

"We know for certain that Lig's a villain." Kestrel raised an eyebrow, and McAvery shook his head. "Fine, you're right, we've always thought it. Now we know. And if the Scion is working against the Danisobans, what kind of trouble can we expect? From either side?"

She wondered if she could learn more by using the Danisoban book. So far it had led her straight to what she asked. The physical toll had been hard the first time, and harder the second. Nasrin implied that it might only get worse, and Kestrel didn't look forward to learning what "worse" could mean. She wasn't even sure she wanted McAvery to know she owned the book. It was a crime just to possess such a thing. Then again, her entire life had been a crime. The book was just one more mark against her.

McAvery broke the silence. "Until we know more, that line of conversation seems to be ended. Let me move on to another." He fixed his gaze on her, his eyes dark with an emotion she couldn't identify. "I am firmly in your debt." Kestrel opened her mouth, ready to deny any obligation, but he raised a warning hand. "You risked your own freedom, in the face of Danisobans ready to lay hands on you. Whether or not you agree that I owe you, I do."

Kestrel didn't know what to say. As much as she wanted to deny it, as much as she'd tried to convince herself that she only rescued him in order to have something to hold over his head, she knew it wasn't true. She'd wanted to run to him since the jewel glowed red. She would always want to run to him. But things were different now that the dancer had caught McAvery's eye. He wasn't saying what she wished he would. "You want to go to Pecheta." She wondered if she sounded as petulant to him as she did to herself.

"Don't you?"

"Pecheta," she said, "is the last place I want to go. And yet fate keeps driving me in that direction. If it was my choice, I'd leave everything and everyone behind, sail into the sun and take my chances on the high sea."

"Everyone?" he asked.

"Who have I to stay here for?"

McAvery smiled humorlessly. He rose, crossing to the window, running one long finger along the bevels. "You and I are laboring under a misunderstanding."

She watched him without speaking. He tipped the window open, letting a breeze in. It tickled the stray hairs that always escaped from her braids. She passed a hand over her face, trying to smooth the tendrils away. It was a little too intimate, as if the breeze was an extension of McAvery's hand.

"When we met, I knew Binns was grooming you to succeed him. He asked me to take a hand, to train you in the intrigues you'd need to understand for dealing with kings and courts and Danisobans. Once I saw you, I was delighted to assist him. Who wouldn't enjoy working with a lovely young woman for a few weeks?"

Kestrel snorted. Lovely, indeed. McAvery turned, facing her again. "Why do you laugh?"

"I'm not an addlebrain. Calling me 'lovely' as if you think it will turn my head. I'm short-legged and plain. I have scars no woman should have. My fingers are callused and I don't paint my face or dress my hair as a lady should. I am well aware of how I look."

"I don't think you are." He stepped forward, stopping at the edge of the table. "But it wasn't only your looks that fascinated me. I enjoyed our talks, and your magical ability astounds me. Eventually, I found myself in a position unsuitable for training."

"First I'm some great beauty, now I know everything you could teach me?"

"Hardly." McAvery moved slowly around the table, stalking her, holding her with his gaze. His eyes seemed to darken as she watched, but she couldn't look away. "There's much I have to show you. And I intend to, given the chance. It was my feelings that made the situation complicated."

His feelings. She swallowed against the lump that rose in her throat. He was inches from her now. "Complicated how?"

"You became the Privateer."

Her eyes widened. "You think I had a choice? Perhaps you weren't listening right then, but it was either take the job or submit to the Danisobans."

"You underestimate yourself. It was fear that made you think so."

"You're calling me a coward?"

"Hardly. But the king named you Privateer, awarded you a ship. The Danisobans couldn't lay hands on you if you stayed at sea. You were delighted to sail away from me."

"Delighted?" She rose, closing the distance between them. "You walked away! Hung this bloody bauble on my neck and disappeared into the crowd. You say you had feelings — well, cack you and your feelings. You turned from me without a backward glance. Or was I supposed to put on a dress and follow you, like some proper little wife?"

"As if you could be such a thing," he said.

Kestrel swung a fist at McAvery's face. With snakelike quickness, he grabbed her arm. "I meant no insult. You have to stop believing the worst in me."

She stared at him, so close. Slowly he pulled her up tight against him, one hand sliding behind her head, and kissed her. His lips weren't soft this time, but desperate and burning. The warning voice in her head whispered something about pushing him away, refusing him. But she didn't listen. Didn't want to. She'd waited too long for this to happen. She wrapped her hands in his hair, slipping it out of its queue. She pressed herself against him, relishing the feel of his body so close.

He raised his head, his breath coming hard. His cheeks were flushed, his eyes fervent as he gazed at her. "Have me flogged if you must, Captain, but I won't apologize for that."

Should she strike him or bed him? Her head was spinning. She stepped back, breaking the closeness of his embrace. He let her slip free, his hands falling to his sides.

"I need a drink." She stepped to her sideboard and withdrew the rum jug. Where the hell had her mug gone to? She glanced around the room, but didn't see it. Ah well, she'd hunt for it later. Pulling out the stopper, she slugged a swallow, then offered McAvery the jug.

"We could have saved ourselves so much time," he said, tilting the jug.

She'd been ready to throw caution to the wind for him. Ready to spill her secret longing, ready to steal him from under the dancer's eye. Suddenly, with one kiss, she was back to where she'd been. She still wanted him. Gods, how she wanted him but not at another's expense. All her life, there'd been so little she could call her own. Growing up in the alleys of Eldraga, even the food she found was only hers if she could wolf it down before someone else grabbed it from her hand. Anything else she wanted she took, but something inside was stopping her from taking this man. "Do I strike you as the kind of woman who shares?"

He cocked an eyebrow, frowning. "What would you be sharing?"

"Nasrin talked of you as if the two of you were . . ." Kestrel took the jug, stoppered it and put it back into the sideboard, staring at the wood surface as if the answers might magically appear there.

"Why should Nasrin have anything to do with what you and I might feel?"

"Oh. I see. I'm to be a dalliance, after which you'll vanish into a crowd, same as you did before?" She wanted to be angry, to keep him at a distance the way she had before. The heat of her anger had burned itself out, leaving her belly full of cold ashes. The very breath in her lungs was shaking from the chill. She'd dreamed of him for a year, and now that he was here, she was about to let him go. Her hands trembled. It was the right thing to do. She wasn't meant to have happiness. "You can't toy with me right under her nose. It isn't fair to either of us." She laid her hands flat, not wanting to look at him now that she'd brought it up. "I understand why you would want her. She's beautiful and graceful. She knows so much more about her power than I'll ever be able to learn about mine. The things she can do, I could never hope to achieve." She couldn't look at him, not if she wanted to finish what she was saying. "I thought I felt something for you, but I will not entangle myself in a fight over you with another woman. Especially one who can set my bones on fire by tapping her toes on the deck," she finished wryly.

"It's not like that."

"Don't lie to me," she snapped. "I saw you together, in the slaver's hold at Doana. The way you stood, the way you held her."

"What are you talking about?"

She took a deep breath. There'd never be a better time to say what she needed to. "I did miss you, damn your eyes. I thought about you every day since the day you left. I wondered what might have been. You should be pleased with yourself. One kiss and I was enthralled." Her cheeks were flaming "After your gem scared us all half to death, I tried a bit of magic, to see if I could locate you. To come to your rescue. But when the vision appeared in the water," the words caught in her throat. She had to force herself to keep speaking. "I saw you comforting Nasrin, touching her as a lover would."

"Still you came for me."

His voice was low and close, close enough to tickle the flesh of her neck. His nearness left her dizzy and hot. This conversation wasn't going at all the way she intended. They'd come in to figure out the Scion's letter, nothing more. Ducking away, she walked around McAvery to the table, and bent over the letter again. "We need to keep our minds on this problem."

"If I'd been touching her as a lover would," he said, running his fingers down her arm. He took Kestrel's hand. She found herself fascinated by the paleness of his skin against the darkness of hers. Drawing her hand to his lips, he turned it slowly, gently, and placed a kiss on her wrist. Her heart thudded in her chest, but she couldn't move. He grazed his teeth over her cool skin, sending chill bumps up her arm and making her knees weaken. "You would have known," he murmured, his words warm against the racing pulse in her wrist. Slowly, letting his fingers trace over her open palm, he released her hand. Reaching up, he slid his thumb along her jaw, cupping her face in his hand. "There is a woman I've wished to touch in such a way, but I promise you, it isn't Nasrin."

"Who?" She surprised herself with the question. He bent and kissed her, this time with the tenderness she remembered. The inner voice that had tortured her for so long fell blissfully silent.

McAvery raised his mouth from hers and gazed into her eyes. "Does that answer your question?"

Kestrel shook her head. "No." McAvery lowered his lips toward hers again, but she pressed the flat of her hand against his breastbone, drawing her head back. "Say it."

He brushed his fingers softly across her cheek. "I find myself utterly captive to you. I would cross the ocean to answer your call. If you told me—"

"Stop." Kestrel stepped back, just far enough to let his hands rest on her hips. "You have a trove of words to draw upon to keep from answering an honest question. I'm used to plain speaking. If you feel something for me, say it."

He stared into her eyes. Neither of them moved. Whether he was trying to think of a lie she'd accept or a way to let her down gently, she had no way of knowing, but it didn't matter. She was lost in his gaze, floating in the heat he always sparked in her. She remembered another time, when they'd first met, when she'd found herself trapped in his eyes like this. Then she'd believed it to be magic, but now she knew differently. She loved him. Whatever his next words were, would change nothing. Her feelings were her own.

Slowly, he slid his hands up, from her hips along her ribs, over her arms and down, taking her hands in his. He raised them to his lips, kissing one, then the other. "The hardest thing I ever did was to walk away from you. And the most foolish," he said, his voice soft as a caress. "I love you."

Fire exploded in her belly. Pulling one hand free, she twined her fingers into his golden hair and drew him close, capturing his mouth with hers. The months of denial, of wishing to know his touch, all rushed in on her. She tore at his shirt, sliding it up and over his head, letting it fall to the floor. His body was hard against her. He yanked her shirt free from her breeches, slipping a hand under to stroke her bare skin. Tingles ran across her body, similar to the onset of her magic. She raised her arms, letting him take her shirt as she had his. He bent his head to nuzzle at her throat, and she let her arms sink down around his head. Lost in the sensation, she barely noticed his hands working at the buttons of her breeches. A random thought leapt into her awareness . . . if rhythm caused her magic to manifest, what would happen once she joined with McAvery? She laughed, and McAvery lifted his head. "Should I stop?" he asked, breathless.

She didn't speak, reaching instead for the buttons of his breeches for answer.

"Your men will start to wonder."

"Let them," she said. "Shadd's probably outside with one ear against the door."

"Your pet is watching."

They lay together in the twisted sheets of her bed, sweat drying on their skin. McAvery was propped on an elbow, tracing the
lines of her body with his fingers. His hair had come loose from
its binding, and fell in a silken wave across his shoulders to tickle
wherever it touched her. The dull red gem she'd worn so long lay
stuck to her damp chest. McAvery hooked the lanyard with one
finger and held it up to dangle between them. "You know this
was only meant for one use? Why did you keep it?"

"Why do you think?" she said.

He smiled, and laid it back on her body. "Thank you for coming to rescue me."

A high-pitched yawn broke the quiet. McAvery inclined his
head toward the bookcase. "There's a spy yonder. Do you think
it'll report on our behavior to your men?"

Kestrel glanced up to the bookshelves, where the lizard
curled in the recesses of an empty space. Its eyes glowed in the
darkness, but closed once it noticed her watching.

"It won't be telling anyone." She slid one foot up and down
McAvery's leg, enjoying the softness of the golden hairs. He
leaned down and nipped at her neck, and she laughed. It had
been so long since she'd laughed this way.

"So Captain, about that question. Have I answered plainly
enough for you?"

She smiled. "I'm not sure," she said. "I may require more
proof e'er this voyage is done."

He chuckled, the sound low in his throat, and bent to kiss her
again. A knock sounded on her door, saving her from saying anything further. She scrambled free of his arms and rolled out of
the bed. Their clothing had fallen into a confused heap on the
floor. "Wait!" she called, hopping on one leg to drag the breeches on. Donning her shirt, she turned to see how far along Mc-
Avery was. He had covered himself with the sheets. He grinned
at her glare. She picked up his clothing and threw it at his head.
"Dress yourself!"

The knock sounded again. "Captain, are ye well?"

Kestrel finished tucking her shirt in. McAvery had pulled on
his breeches, and was buttoning them as slowly as he could man-

age. Whatever the crew thought, this delay had probably cemented their thoughts, regardless of McAvery's state of undress. She opened the door.

Shadd was outside, wearing a sheepish grin. "Sorry to interrupt ye, Captain, Phil," he said, nodding to McAvery behind her, "but there's a ship looks familiar, and she's gainin' on us."

"Show me," she said. At least this would put off any talk of her promise to Nasrin for a time. She padded, barefoot, up the quarterdeck steps, and took up her telescope.

Striped sails . . . exactly like those on the little merket. Except this ship was bigger, and to the eye, better armed. Eight guns on deck, with another eight closed gun ports. It flew no flag to indicate its owner. Its crew, from a distance, appeared hearty enough. They were running about on deck, seeing to their work, but gunners were standing by with lit punks. And she was moving toward the *Thanos*, no question.

"Shadd, wake the ladies. Looks like they're being asked to dance."

He flashed her a huge grin. "Aye, Captain!"

McAvery swung himself up the steps to join her, his shirt hanging loose. "Who's chasing us?"

Kestrel handed him the scope, which he raised to his eye. "Looks like your friends went and found help. Any chance you have that tuning fork that hides us?"

The first time Kestrel had been aboard ship with McAvery, he'd been armed with a number of magical objects that turned out to be useful, including a silver tuning fork that, when struck, provided a magical curtain to hide behind. If he'd found a way to hide his trinkets from his captors, they could prove helpful again. He shook his head. "I have nothing but what you found me wearing. The slavers took everything before they tossed me in their hold."

She cocked an eyebrow. "You managed to hide a few playthings from me when I had you in chains on the *Wolfshead*."

"You didn't search me as thoroughly then." He smiled. "Do you really think you wouldn't have found anything by now?"

She didn't rise to his bait. "We found nothing of value on the merket. And I've never heard of slavers attacking other ships. What's brought them after you? And how did they even find you here? Could there be something else you saw, some wayward conversation you heard? Something you haven't considered, but they think is worth killing you for?"

"Kestrel, I swear. It's my job to notice things like that. If I'd heard or seen something . . ." He let the scope fall against his leg. "I don't know what they're looking for." He pounded the flat of his other hand against the railing, cursing under his breath.

This was a new side to McAvery. He'd always been so confident; to see him like this, without some idea hiding up his sleeve, was unnerving. Nasrin stepped to the foot of the quarterdeck stairs, wrapped in plain scarves as if against the cold. Her face was serious. "*Rais*, is there something wrong?"

Kestrel spared her an irritated glance. She'd ordered the dancer to see her, but the situation wasn't safe for her to be abovedeck. "You'd best find a sheltered spot, somewhere off the deck."

"*Rais.*"

Kestrel took the telescope from McAvery and raised it again, peering at the ship coming closer. "We've sighted a ship that may be pursuing us."

"I see." Nasrin turned away, drawing the wrap tight around her face.

As Kestrel watched, a man stepped to the railing of the other ship and waved. Not especially tall or thick of body, and his hair was scattered with gray. He wore plain clothes, his shirt open at the neck, revealing some sort of discoloration on his skin. She couldn't be sure if it was a birthmark or a tattoo, but there was a familiarity to it. Despite appearing unimpressive, he was clearly in charge. He held up a large speaking tube, a cone-shaped device sailors used to speak from ship to ship.

"Shadd! Get the tube!"

"Aye, Captain." He returned with a tube like the other, and Kestrel held it high so the man could see she was ready. She handed the telescope to her second.

"Shadd, watch him while we speak. If anything looks amiss, tell me." He nodded. Kestrel turned to McAvery.

She could just make out the other man with her naked eyes. She didn't like such proximity, but her curiosity was getting the better of her. That mark on his neck still tugged at her thoughts.

The man didn't look like anyone she knew, but she must have seen him somewhere. She raised the tube to her mouth. "Speak your piece," she called out. Her voice echoed over the water.

"You've nowhere to run. Drop anchor and wait to be boarded," he bellowed.

Kestrel laughed, and her men joined in. "Are you spoiling for a fight, or are you just a fool?"

"He don't look happy, Kes," Shadd muttered. "His face is all manner of red, and he's fussin' at someone behind him. Their gunports are open." He peered again "Here's a thing. The fella behind him's wearin' a black robe. He's standin' in a box, and I think he might have a bit of the shine on his wrists."

Ice swept over Kestrel in a sharp wave. Bloody Grace's nephews, he was armed with a mage. Danisobans rarely went to sea, and when they did, they had to take along a crate of soil to protect themselves from the ocean's effects. Who was this man, who was important enough to warrant a mage on board? Not some ordinary sailor.

"What's wrong, *rais?*"

Of course, the dancer remained when she'd been told to hide. "Yonder captain has a pet Danisoban. Unless the mage is a rank child, I can't defend you. Likely not even then."

"Do you not have weapons aboard this ship?" Nasrin waved a hand toward the deck guns. "Surely those?"

Kestrel stared at Nasrin before answering. How could the dancer not understand the level of danger facing them? "Yes, I have weapons. And against any other ship, I'd have the advantage. With a mage aboard? He could sail over here, while his Danisoban holds all of us paralyzed. He and his men could board us, toss us all into the ocean, and take the *Thanos* without us being able to lift a finger against him."

A thump sounded from across the waves, and a cloud of black smoke spilled out of the other ship. "Captain!" Shadd yelled. A second later, the *Thanos* rocked under the sickening impact of a cannon strike. Their pursuers weren't waiting.

"Open fire!" Kestrel cried. Shadd tossed her the telescope and leaped down the quarterdeck stairs, bellowing orders to the men on deck. Her guns spoke, belching white clouds that billowed up, filling the sky. Kestrel raised the scope, peering through the rapidly-dissipating smoke between them. On the deck of the other ship, the black-robed mage was curling his hands together, and his lips were moving. Glittering light poured forth from his fingers, flying up and over the sails, creating a shining veil between his ship and hers.

"He's raising some sort of shield," she yelled. "Fire again!"

Shadd relayed the order. The *Thanos'* cannons fired, but this time, the cannon balls bounced off the glistening curtain surrounding the other ship, sparks flashing, and fell into the ocean. Kestrel could barely make out individuals through the sparkling magic and smoke, but the Danisoban was easy to find. He dropped his hands, miming the act of pulling something up from the ground. The veil he'd cast rose with his movement, stopping just above the open gun ports.

"Hard to port!" she yelled. DeadEye swung the wheel. The ship responded, veering away from the attacking ship with a groan. Water swept up along the side and splashed across the deck. Men stumbled at the sudden change in attitude, slipping on the wet wood and grabbing at lines and railings to keep from tumbling over the side. Kestrel pressed her lips together, and blew a sharp tone. Wind snapped at the sails, driving the *Thanos* to leap forward.

Cannons roared from across the water. A deafening thud slammed against the hull, followed by two mighty splashes to stern. Splinters of wood exploded across the deck, ripping into one unlucky fellow's cheek. He ducked down, blood dripping onto his shirt, and scrambled toward the hatch.

It wasn't right. She couldn't damage the other ship, not as long as that Danisoban was raising and dropping the magical shield. He could fire at her from behind that curtain until her ship shattered into so much flotsam. The only way to fight magic was with more magic, something she didn't have.

A flutter of color caught her eye, and Kestrel looked down. Nasrin stood at the bottom of the quarterdeck stairs, one end of her colorful head scarf loose and blowing in the breeze. She gripped the banisters tightly, keeping her body against the wooden underpinning of the stairs. *Magic*, Kestrel thought. *I may not have enough to help, but she does.* Taking the quarterdeck steps two at a time, she ran down and grabbed Nasrin's shoulder. "I need your help."

"I am no warrior, *rais*."

Kestrel waved a hand toward the approaching ship. "No, you're not. You're better. You can dance a turn and throw half those men into the water. You could light their sails on fire."

Nasrin's eyes tightened. "What makes you think I can make fire?"

"Can't you?" Nothing bad had happened when she'd experimented with the power, but suddenly Kestrel felt like a child lying to her mother. The dancer shook her head.

"*Rais*, you must not play with your power as if it is a child's game. You could set your own ship ablaze."

Another ugly roar heralded another cannon volley. One ball fell short, but the other slammed into the bow railing, snapping it and sending shards flying.

"Exactly why you need to teach me. For now, though," Kestrel jerked her chin toward the approaching enemy. "Show me what you can do to that ship yonder."

"A spell strong enough to damage an entire ship has dangerous, deadly consequences. For the target and the wielder."

"Dangerous and deadly is what I want."

"Even if I am able to destroy your enemy, the question of leverage remains. If I give you what you want now. I will have nothing with which to bargain. You will be free to abandon me in your islands, and I will never see my home again."

Kestrel curled her hands into fists, and squeezed. "I'm not asking you to teach me now. I want you to help us escape this attack. Besides, where is your home, exactly? How far along the journey were we going to be before you decided we'd gone far enough? All the way to the Continent? I could make a similar claim against you. That you might insist on waiting until we reach your home before training me. Only one night you would vanish into a city I don't know, and I'd be left with nothing for my trouble."

Nasrin tilted her head thoughtfully. "You have a point, *rais*."

"Under normal circumstances, there was no reason I couldn't blow that ship out of the water with cannons alone. This isn't normal. The Danisoban shield swings the balance too far in the wrong direction." she said. Kestrel took the dancer by an elbow, drawing her away from her hiding spot and toward the lowest stair. "You weren't afraid to board my ship, and you took the chance of showing me your skill. In front of DeadEye, no less. You're no coward." Slipping behind her, Kestrel pressed Nasrin to climb up. The dancer placed both hands on the railings, hesitating. She clearly wanted to return to the relative safety belowdecks, but with Kestrel behind her, she was trapped.

Nasrin climbed slowly, stopping at the top and turning to look at Kestrel. "You have no understanding of what I can do, *rais*."

"If you think I don't know how valuable you are, you haven't been paying attention." She leaned forward, both hands flat on the stair railing, and stared into Nasrin's face. "Becoming captain of this ship nearly killed me, and it's no less difficult remaining captain. I can't afford to drop my guard with my men watching. So if this reluctance is your attempt to make me feel subordinate to you, as part of my training," she emphasized the word, making it sound cheap, "I'll not only fail to cooperate, but I'll put you in a hackney boat and let you become someone else's problem."

Color drained from Nasrin's face, and she sent a worried glance toward the ship.

Kestrel drew back. Why hadn't she seen it before? So obvious, but she'd been so occupied, she'd missed the signs. "They're not after McAvery at all, are they?"

Silence hung in the air between them, until Nasrin crossed her hands before her. "No. They are not."

# CHAPTER 14

*Over the water came the lifted song—*
*Blind pieces in a mighty game we sing.*
—JOHN MASEFIELD, *The Wanderer*

"I thought you didn't know who you'd been bought for."

The dancer raised her chin. "They are not slave traders, in the usual sense. In my land, these men are called *esaba adlan*. It means hunters of blood."

Blood hunters, indeed. In the Nine Islands, they were called Eusebians, and the last thing she needed right now. Of course. The marks on the captain's neck were Eusebian tattoos, red and purple symbols that looked like writhing serpents. She should have remembered as soon as she saw them. The Eusebian Jaeger abducted her a year before when Binns was being threatened. He hadn't managed to hold her for long, but while she was in his control, he'd told her they wanted her for her strength around water, that they wanted to breed her, to develop magic users that could defeat the Danisobans.

She scowled at Nasrin. "You're going to tell me what they want with you later. You're going to answer a great many questions, assuming we survive. Right now we have more urgent concerns. They're blowing pieces off my ship and I can't return the favor. If they win this battle they *will* take you back. You could help protect this ship, protect yourself. Everyone on my ship, woman, has a job to do. Either do it yourself or show me how."

"The danger . . . I cannot teach under these conditions. You are a child." She shook her head helplessly. "There's too much to learn before you could safely protect your ship this way."

"You have the control, yes?"

"I've never opposed a ship. I don't know. I could kill you without meaning to."

Kestrel's heart thumped. Of course she didn't want to die, but she couldn't see any better way out of their current dilemma. Nasrin possessed the skill to face down a Danisoban, and Kestrel needed it. She pointed across the water. "And they will kill us on purpose."

Nasrin clenched her jaw and cast a despairing glance at McAvery. He shook his head. "Can't help you, lady. She's the captain."

She dropped her lovely head and released an audible breath. "What shall I do?"

Now that she'd bullied the dancer into obedience, Kestrel wasn't sure what to ask for. She knew little about her own magic, and even less about Nasrin's. Should she ask for a cloak, to cover the ship escaping, as they'd been able to do with McAvery's trinket? Perhaps Nasrin could construct a shield of power to keep the other ship's projectiles from doing any damage. Combined with her own whistling to add speed to their escape, that would be enough. "A shield. Like his. Can you do that?" The deck under their feet trembled as another cannon ball slammed into its hull. "And soon?" Nasrin let her wraps fall to the deck, and lifted her skirt an inch or two above her feet. "Very well, *rais*, But watch me only. Do not attempt to match me."

The *Thanos'* guns bellowed beneath their feet. Shadd was still trying to blast his way through the magic. She couldn't blame him. He wouldn't give up, and nor would she. Kestrel positioned herself behind the dancer. Nasrin pointed her right toe, then shifted her weight and stepped out to the side. She slid her left foot to join the right. Kestrel watched her movements, studying her feet closely.

"I begin slowly," Nasrin said, "allowing the power to build from a place of balance and strength. Too fast, and I will cause my body to catch fire from within." She pivoted, letting her skirt swing out in a spill of color. "I see the power as a substance I can hold, something I can touch. It is not solid, nor is it air. It is something in between."

Kestrel nodded. She understood fire's hunger. Fire from within, as she'd experienced when she created the tongue of flame in her cabin, was new to her.

Nasrin skipped three times to the left, and three times back to the right, ending where she began. Crossing her right foot in front of her left leg, she pulled herself into a slow spin, bending her knees and raising her arms above her head to end the movement.

The dance was mesmerizing, but Kestrel's attention was briefly shaken when she noticed Shadd yelling. They'd been hit again. She was a big ship, but even the *Thanos* couldn't last forever.

The dancer clasped her hands together and swung them up and overhead, twisting herself under them. She turned her back to Kestrel and began to repeat the steps she'd already danced, in the opposite direction this time. "The power is awake," she said, her breath coming a little harder with the effort, "so now I must decide what it is I am asking. Escape? Attack? Which one is it, *rais?*"

"Shield," Kestrel said. Her own breath came fast as if she'd been dancing, too. She pressed one hand against her chest, feeling her heartbeat like a drum. All her life, she'd kept away from dancing and song. Out of fear. She was sick of being afraid. She could master the power, with Nasrin's help. At last, she could face the Danisobans with weapons they couldn't ignore. The potential made her head spin with excitement.

"Very well. I will keep dancing, and as I do, I will let the power fill me, but only as much as I allow. I will not try to make it obey. Instead, I will ask of it what I desire. Beg it to answer my entreaties."

She danced without music, stepping and leaping, her arms rising and flowing like ribbons. Kestrel imagined she could hear the tune that matched her steps. As the music in her mind lilted and rolled, Kestrel couldn't help an intense desire to join in. It pulled at her soul, whispering without words, cajoling her to fling herself into the dance. And why shouldn't she? Magic was a part of her, same as her hair color or her agility. She'd locked it away for too long. Nasrin told her to watch, but the longing surrounded her. She let herself meld into the beat, tapping her bare foot against the dampness of the deck.

Bright needles of energy bloomed on her skin, the tingling she knew so well. Her own power was responding. Kestrel shuffled her foot in imitation of Nasrin's own steps, and raised one arm to follow along. This dance didn't look so complicated, a few steps left and right, a spin or two and a pattern with the arms. Why shouldn't she try? Surely her own power would add to Nasrin's, and help defeat the other ship more quickly. She glanced around the quarterdeck. DeadEye gripped the wheel, turning it to change the *Thanos'* aspect and avoid the other ship's assault. McAvery watched the battle through the telescope. Nasrin danced, facing away from Kestrel. Not a one of them looking at her. Never a better time than now to try.

Somewhere in the back of her mind, her own voice cried out in warning, but Kestrel smothered it under the swelling music she imagined. She watched Nasrin's back, the dancer's body lithe and graceful, and began to match her step for step. The sharp thorns of her magic softened, thickened into molten silver coating her limbs in brightness. Step, step, turn . . . dancing wasn't difficult at all. Light grew all around her. Whether she was the source, or merely reflecting the sun above, Kestrel didn't know. It made no difference. She swept her right arm in a full circle, repeating with the left, and spun her body. Drops of silver energy flew off the ends of her braids, disappearing before they struck the deck. The gleaming power crept over her chest and neck in filaments of coolness sliding across her skin.

Nasrin had not turned toward her, but she was saying something. Kestrel concentrated on her words. ". . . ask the power to form itself into a shield. I ask it to wrap your ship in protection."

Ask the power? Kestrel tapped her toe twice, marveling at the mirror she had become. Power grew within her, not the familiar tingle along her limbs but a bubbling rumble shaking her very bones, a weightless wall of fire coating her very heart and demanding to be released to the sky. It roared in her head, burned under her skin. Kestrel thought she might be able to see sparks spitting from her pores. Her eyes watered from the heat, her vision darkening. Blood boiled in her veins, blisters rising on her flesh as the moisture within her steamed away. Cracks in her skin broke open along her limbs. She shrieked when the air pressed its fingers into her raw wounds, a bright, searing pain she couldn't have imagined. The power threatened to burst from the confines of her body. She couldn't hold it any longer, she had to empty herself. She abandoned her careful mimicking of Nasrin's movements, and when she did, her body started to spin of its own accord. Faster and faster, her braided hair slapping against her face, her feet crossing each other so quickly she dared not think of it, for fear she'd crash to the deck.

"Stop, *rais*!" Who was calling? Her hair whipped past her face. Her feet no longer touched the deck. She was rising. No! This couldn't happen. She was no longer dancing, but she was still going around and around. She reached down with her toes, frantically kicking for the deck. White flame wreathed her, Her braids swept out away from her scalp like a strange crown. She hung in midair, spinning in a tornado of white fire, her arms pressed against her midsection. She fought to keep her head up, but the speed forced it back. With her last breath, she shrieked, throwing her arms wide.

Light exploded from her mouth, her eyes, the palms of her hands. White flame flowed, like a river of molten silver, over the deck and down to the sea. Instead of hissing in the cold water, it ran over the waves, chasing the Eusebian ship. It swept up the enemy's hull, engulfing the deck and men. Somewhere in the distance, she could hear screaming, the voices of pain and despair, but the sound was far away. Then there was nothing else — no ship, no screams, no ocean. Only darkness.


"Kestrel?"

Someone was calling her name, from very far away. She tried to open her eyes, but they felt sticky, as if old honey had been spilled on her face and dried in the sun. She tried to lift a hand to rub the stickiness away, but someone took gentle hold of her wrist and laid her arm down. Something cool and wet touched her forehead.

"Kestrel, can you hear me?"

The voice again, closer now. A familiar voice, one she'd wanted to hear.

"Can you open your eyes?"

"No," she groaned.

"Let her be." Soft hands touched her cheeks, her throat. Cool wetness again, this time over her eyes. "She may have burned them out."

Kestrel turned her head side to side, trying to wake up completely. What was burned? Why couldn't they clean the mess off her eyes and let her see?

"You must rest, *rais*."

"What happened . . . to me?" she asked. Her throat stung, sore and gritty.

An arm slid around her back, supporting and lifting her head. Pain swept over her skin, and she cried out. A cup touched her lips.

"Drink this. It'll help."

She opened her mouth, smelling the welcome fumes of rum, mixed with something she didn't recognize. Sweet and warm, it slid down her aching throat and she gulped gratefully. "More."

"Easy, now. You'll make yourself sick."

The cup was pulled away, and she let her head fall back. The cool weight returned, and she realized it was a damp rag. She reached up, tugging it away from whoever held it, and rubbed her eyes. The skin of her lids stung against the rough fibers of the rag. She touched her lids with her fingertips. They were smooth and clean, hot under her touch. Yet still they felt caked with filth. The gentle hands from before pulled her hands away from her face.

"It is best you keep your eyes closed, *rais*," Nasrin said. "I do not know how much light they can stand. Wait until darkness, so you do not cause any more harm than has already been done."

Wait for the night? Harm? Kestrel snorted, and blinked her eyes open.

The room seemed choked with a fog. Dark shapes filled the space around her, moving eerily. People, she assumed, but she couldn't tell who was who. It was as if someone had laid a thick silken drape over her face. Someone gasped. "Look at that!" One of the ghostly figures leaned in close, and Kestrel flinched.

"Changed, yes, but at least her eyes are still intact."

Kestrel reached out a tentative hand, connecting with skin-warmed fabric. "If that's you, Nasrin" she rasped, "you're a bit mushy 'round the edges."

"I feared there would be nothing but empty sockets," Nasrin said, her voice grateful.

"Why are you talking about my eyes? What happened with the battle? Did we defeat them? Is the *Thanos* hale?"

"*Rais*, you have been injured. Please keep your hands down. Jaques is preparing a salve for the burns on your skin, but your eyes will have to recover in their own time. You are very lucky."

Kestrel looked down at her body, seeing nothing but gray. She balled her hands into fists, cursing at the bright shock of pain. Spreading her fingers out, she blew on her smarting palms, then ran her hands gently over her arms, and down her torso. Something wasn't right. Her skin radiated heat like an oven, and even the gentlest pressure resulted in sharp tingles like needles poking into her. Her linen shirt was torn, with strange rigid edges to the tears. The sleeves were missing entirely.

"Here we go, Captain, let's have your hands." Jaques' voice, calming. He took her right hand carefully, and started smearing something thick and cool on her inflamed skin. "This'll cool you off before long. I'm surprised you're not hurt worse than you are. You should've been crisped, with all the fire around you."

"What happened to me?" Kestrel's throat tightened, and for an instant, she worried that she might begin screaming if someone didn't tell her the truth.

"I brought you to your cabin." McAvery said, "There was damage from the battle and from your . . ." he stopped, as if unsure of his next words. It made her uncomfortable to hear the tone in his voice. McAvery was never unsure of anything. "Nothing that can't be fixed." His words were quiet, steady.

Her eyes watered, making the fog thicken. Blind. She was blind. They were all treating her like some cub who'd lost an arm during his first sea battle. "Where's Shadd?"

Jaques finished applying his salve to her right arm, and moved to the left one. The thick cream soothed the stinging of her skin. "Shadd's on the quarterdeck, Captain, just where you'd want him to be. We practically had to tie him to the railing to keep him out there, even after we proved to him that you weren't dead. We've caught a good wind, and we should land on Bix by sunset tomorrow."

Bix. They'd been headed for Bix when the Eusebian ship crossed their path. They must have won. Her magic had done the trick. Jaques released her arms and moved to her legs, working skillfully. She hadn't realized her breeches were off, but her undergarments remained, and as much as her skin stung, she hardly cared about her flesh being seen by anyone. "Aren't you going to put your medicine on my eyes?" she asked when he seemed to be finished.

There was a brief silence, before Jaques answered. "No, Captain, it ain't made for that. Sting right hearty, it would, and it sure wouldn't do you no good."

"So what will do me good?" This time, the silence was deafening. She swallowed, afraid to know, but even more afraid not to. "McAvery . . . Philip," she pleaded, her voice rising in a panic. "Why can't I see?"

"Can she sit up now?" he asked, and she heard Nasrin murmur an acknowledgement. Tightening his arm around her shoulders, he helped her rise, and let her legs swing over the side of her bed. Sitting up was better, even if every inch of her stung furiously. She blinked, trying to clear her eyes. Moisture rolled down her cheeks, but her vision didn't improve. The world remained a gray haze filled with shadows. Her skin pulled tight around her bones, as if it had shrunk a size too small, and she almost expected it to creak like old leather when she moved. The insides of her nose and mouth stung with every breath she took.

"Kes, you tried too much too fast," he said softly.

Too much what? She wanted to change her shirt and get back on the deck, check the damage he'd mentioned, and make sure their enemy was long gone. But in this condition, she could tip right over the railing and break her neck on the way down to the unforgiving water. She balled up a fist again, crying out at the pain of it even beneath the slick salve.

"The power you created, Kes," he said. "You couldn't focus it, and it had to escape. It flashed out of your eyes, your mouth, your hands. Gods, woman, you looked like a statue of lightning!"

"I burned myself?" She brushed her arm again. The salve left her skin slick, but there were no blisters or tears she could feel. It didn't make sense. Last thing she remembered, she was mimicking Nasrin's dance, learning to draw on the magic with her body. "Bloody Grace keep me," she whispered.

"I thought you were being roasted alive." His voice caught, as if he had something in his throat. "I don't know why you're not a charred wreck."

"I am so sorry, *rais*. I should have stopped as soon as I realized what you were doing. I did not know how little you understood about the power," Nasrin said sorrowfully.

The stinging pain on her skin, her lost sight, she'd done it to herself. All their concern was painful to hear. It was all her fault. The magic had never behaved like that before. Her eyes welled with tears. She shouldn't have tried to change who she was. She should have stuck with the whistling. Hell, she should have kept to sailing and forgotten all about magic. Nothing good ever came of it.

"Is the *Thanos* safe?" she whispered.

"The ship sustained several bad hits, but nothing below the waterline. Shadd sent men to patch them until we can dock and make proper repair. There's a good deal of scorching on the deck from what you did. Like I told you, nothing that can't be repaired. Some of your men were injured, but none died."

"And the Eusebian ship?"

"Kes, please." McAvery stroked her hair.

She pushed at his hands, noticing for the first time that her braids weren't touching her shoulders. Using her fingertips, she reached for her hair. Dry, brittle, and much shorter than it had been. Had she burned off her hair? "Tell me what happened!"

Nasrin murmured, "Tell her."

She heard him draw a shuddering breath. "They were destroyed."

"We sunk her?" Kestrel nodded. "Worth it, then. How'd you get past their shield?"

"It was you. You threw everything you had directly at them. All the fire that was in you. Kes, it swept over the water and slammed into their ship like a river made of flame. It exploded over the hull, covered the decks. You collapsed to the deck, looking for all the world like a burnt ember, and while their ship burned, you healed. Men were jumping overboard, but the fire," he stopped, drawing a deep breath. "It reached out like the tentacles of some huge beast, and wrapped around them." He stopped, his breath catching. "They burned, Kestrel. Even after they fell into the water. Burned until there was nothing but ash floating on the surface. And your wounds disappeared. Most of them."

Her stomach twisted with nausea. "But the mage . . ."

There was silence. Then McAvery said, "He tried. Gods help him, he waved his hands, casting spells even while the fire melted his skin away. At the last, he managed to send a messenger spell."

Cold swept through her, and she felt dizzy. She'd destroyed a ship and killed its crew. Nothing she hadn't been part of before, as a pirate. If that had been all, she could have sailed away, pretending she knew nothing, and spent a week drinking the image out of her mind. Except this time she'd used her magic and killed a Danisoban. A Danisoban who sent a magical message detailing what happened. A messenger spell looked like a great white bird, one that never stopped for food or rest until it reached its destination. It would recreate the sender's final minutes, in all their hideous detail, as soon as it reached its recipient. She could sail anywhere, but the word had gotten out, the word of what her magic was, and she had no way to intercept it. She couldn't even make up a lie good enough to save her. She'd been the ruin of the breeder ship and crew, but add to that the Danisoban's death, and that was all Lig would need. In the eyes of the king, he'd look like the kind master, taking her into his custody so that she might avoid hanging with the rest of her men. He'd probably claim to be reforming her from her wild and wicked ways, but all the while, he'd be using her to further his own ends. And there wouldn't be a thing she could do to stop him. Her stomach cramped, and she grabbed out at the shadows around her. "I need a bucket."

Someone shoved one under her chin, just in time. She heaved, vomiting foulness from her belly, feeling like her body was turning itself inside out. Her ship, her crew, all would be taken from her. She heaved again. They'd fear her power, but that wouldn't stop them from hanging her men and making her watch. After which she'd be turned over to the Danisobans for whatever justice they decided to inflict.

"What have I done?" she groaned. Gods, but she was tired. She'd been so stupid. "Leave me alone."

"We can't Kes," McAvery murmured. "Until you can see again, it isn't safe to leave you like this. You'll feel better tomorrow. Let the salve take effect."

"I won't feel better ever. I'm dead no matter how you look at it."

He ran a hand over her back, almost too gently to notice. But even that careful touch brought pain. She winced and drew away from his hand. How could he stand to be close to her? How could any of them even look at her? Blindness was a blessing in that way at least; if she had to look at herself, she'd probably want to tear her eyes out.

McAvery rose from beside her. She dropped her head to the bucket again, but the shapes she could barely discern as people began moving away from her. She heard the door open, steps shuffling out. It closed with a thump, and she let herself dissolve into sobs. All those times she'd wondered how she'd die, whether in pitched battle, or in bed surrounded by weeping grandchildren. Either way was preferable to being captive to the Danisobans. She set the bucket on the floor, felt around for the wet rag, and found it in its bowl of water. Wringing it out, she wiped off her mouth and lay down again, throwing one arm over her face.

Something nudged her elbow. The lizard. In all the excitement, she hadn't given it any thought. Whatever reason Lig had for wanting the little creature, it was almost guaranteed to end in death to the lizard. She didn't know how she'd make this right for her men, but she could release the lizard. This, at least, she could do. "You need to go. They'll be coming for us."

It pushed at her again, obviously refusing to move away.

"You have to. I'll be locked away, and the men will hang. Lig wants to cut you up, make some kind of magic suit from your hide. I couldn't stand that." Tears rolled down her cheeks. "Please leave me. Let me die with one good thing on my conscience."

The lizard nosed at her arm until she lifted it, let the creature lay against her side. She curled herself around its warm little body, and dropped into sleep.

# CHAPTER 15

*. . . like a swan that died,*
*But altogether ruined she was still a queen*
—JOHN MASEFIELD, *The Wanderer*

*Fire, silver molten flames rolling over the sea, covering the is-*
*lands . . . Binns' pub filled with bubbling ale, exploding from the*
*kegs behind the bar. Binns burned, spinning in helpless panic,*
*his very skin melting while his house crumbled around him . . .*
*she screamed, but instead of sound, flames leaped from her*
*mouth. Death, she was death, the destruction of them all . . .*

"Kes! Wake up!"

She struggled against the hands at her shoulders, her burned
skin stinging with the contact. "Let me go!"

McAvery's strong arms wrapped around her, drawing her
close but holding her as gently as possible. "You're safe. Just
dreaming," he said.

She stopped fighting as she came to full wakefulness, and relaxed against him, beginning to weep. Sobs wracked her. She
reached up to his shirt, gripping it tightly as the tears fell. It was
so good to let go, to cry like a child. She always had to keep
strong in front of the men. Thinking of the men sparked another
thought. There could be ten of them standing around, watching
her break down, and wondering why they'd signed on with her in
the first place. She gulped a breath, trying to calm herself, and
wiped her wet face on McAvery's convenient shirt.

"Better?" he asked softly. Trying to comfort her. Just the way
the lizard had. Where was it? She drew away, feeling around the
bed for the smooth body of the little creature. Her hands met
cool skin. It was still here. She'd wanted it to go, to run away, but
it wouldn't. Ridiculous little animal, yet its loyalty meant so
much. She'd waked in the darkness once, wondering if it even

was night. The lizard had reached out its flickering tongue, touched her cheek, then purred a tuneless melody that eased her back into sleep.

"McAvery?"

"Right here," he said. "Are you all right?"

"No better, no worse," she said, scooting her body back to better sit up straight. But that wasn't right. Now that she noticed, her skin didn't ache as much as before. She stroked one hand over her arm, feeling no blisters. The heat seemed to have dissipated as well. Either Jaques had an exceptional skill with his healing salves, or magic wounds behaved in ways she couldn't fathom. She blinked, but the world before her remained cloudy and gray. Her stomach growled. "I think I'm hungry," she said.

"I hoped you might be." He took her hand, and guided it to a plate. "I've brought bread and hard cheese, and Jaques made a drink for you," he said, letting her fingers touch each item as he listed it. He set the plate carefully on her lap. "Eat."

She wondered how she could possibly want food, with everything that had happened. Her men, or even McAvery himself could have thrown her in chains and dropped her overboard. But she was still in her cabin. Still being cared for. She took a chunk of bread, but instead of eating it, she began tearing it to small bits.

"Are we alone?" she asked.

"Except for your lizard, yes." He put a mug in her hand. "You shouldn't leave your mug on the floor. I practically had to crawl under the bed to find it. Now drink."

She took a swallow, expecting rum. The liquid was sweet, with a spicy bite. The same thing she drank before, when she first woke. "What the hell is this?" she asked.

"Wine, along with some herbs Jaques mixed into it. And a bit of honey. He says you should drink it all." The mug shifted in her hand — he must have pushed it closer to her. "Finish it."

She drank, tilted it to get the last drops, and handed the mug back. She tucked a bit of the bread in her mouth. It tasted like ash. "You don't have to tend me."

"Who would you prefer?" he asked, humor tinging his voice. "I'm sure Shadd would be happy to come and play nursemaid."

"Don't joke." She let the bread fall, and lay back against her pillows. "The Danisobans were right. I'm a danger on my own."

His fingers brushed her damaged hair, sending a shiver down her back. "I rather enjoy your dangerous streak," he said.

Hours ago his touch was all she could think about. She couldn't bear the thought of what might have been. Especially since he didn't seem to be understanding the danger she'd placed him in with her madness. "You can't think that way. Not now."

"There's nothing you can do to stop me."

"You're the Knave, you idiot."

He didn't answer at first, so quiet she only knew he remained by the soft rhythm of his breathing. "I was yesterday."

"You expect me to believe you're willing to throw your position away for a dalliance?"

"Is that what you thought I was doing? Dallying with you? Even now you think so little of me? Of yourself?"

Kestrel turned into her pillows. "Gods, McAvery, don't you know? I've doomed my crew and you. It'll take every word from your silver tongue to keep your neck unstretched. I can't bear the thought of you dying, too."

She felt McAvery shift position, move closer to her. The heat from his body radiated across the distance between them. Two days ago, she was miserable with thinking he loved someone else. Knowing that he loved her was the only thing she had wanted, then. Now she wanted him to go away, to leave her in the darkness.

"What makes you sure? The king's the final arbiter, after all."

"It isn't up to him, is it? My crime is against the Danisobans. This is the kind of flop-headed thing Lig's been dreaming I'd do." She pushed the plate away, turning on her side to rest against the pillows. "I couldn't have walked into his hands better if I'd done it on purpose. I've been the death of a Danisoban and I'm blind because of it." Sitting back up, she threw her legs over the side of the bed. She heard the plate clatter off the bed. Planting her feet flat on the deck, she rose. The wood was cold under her feet, and they felt strange, as if they'd forgotten how to carry her weight. She took two steps and stumbled into the table, catching herself with a grunt.

McAvery's hands were on her in an instant, steadying, but she pushed them away. "Don't bother. I might as well fall over the rail, as much good as I am now." She stood again. Her bare feet crushed torn bread as she walked unsteadily around her cabin, hands stretched out before her to feel the way. She stubbed her small toe on something in the way. It throbbed with the shock — was she bleeding? She didn't know. Cursing, she dropped to the floor and rubbed her toe. "I'm no leader any longer, not like this. I can't even find my way across the room."

"You'd better find a way to lead," he said. "Those men believe in you."

"Shadd can run things. Grace's deeps, he's been here longer than me. They all look to him. He's strong enough to take the helm, and he can bloody see." She let her face fall into her hands, elbows digging into her knees. "Maybe if you hang me, sail into port with my body dangling from the bowsprit, they'll let you all live."

"If you've made up your mind," he said. She heard the bed creak, and suddenly he was beside her, pulling her up from the floor. "Death it is." She swung a fist wildly, but he was quicker. He wrapped both arms around hers, trapping them against her body. The sting from before had dulled into a throbbing ache all over. Hours ago he'd held her tight, close against his body. She'd dreamed of his arms around her, but not like this. How fast things could change. She kicked back, and connected with his shin, but he didn't release her.

"What are you fighting for?" he growled, his breath hot against her ear. "I thought you wanted me to hang you. Or is it just that you want to sit here and pity yourself until there's no other option?"

"Leave me be," she cried, embarrassed by the childish tone in her voice.

"When you stop feeling sorry for yourself, and start behaving like the captain I've become accustomed to," he said.

She stomped down, hoping to catch his toes, crying out when her bare instep connected with the hard leather of his boots. He laughed, a harsh edge in his tone.

"You took this job, and you'll see it through to the end, whatever that end might be."

Kestrel threw herself forward, but McAvery's grip was solid. She turned her head, trying to reach his shoulder with her teeth.

She caught only fabric, but the ripping sound was strangely satisfying. She spat out the torn cloth, threads sticking to her lips.

"Enjoying yourself?"

She let herself droop. Usually that move resulted in the captor
relaxing his grip, but McAvery wasn't budging. He tightened his
hold on her, making it harder for her to breathe.

"I can stay like this for a long time, you know." He lifted her
off the floor an inch or two. She groaned, and kicked out again.
This time she connected with the bed, or possibly the table — she
was no longer sure which direction she was facing. It didn't matter, because whatever she'd hit, now her toes were throbbing too
much to try again. She threw her weight to one side, then the
other, trying to knock McAvery off balance. He was breathing
harder, working to keep her pinned. She worked an arm free.
Cocking it, she heaved her elbow back, striking something solid.
He jerked with a yell, and she was free. She tumbled to the deck,
rose to her hands and knees and scrabbled across the room.
Where was her sword? It had to be here, at hand. But without
her eyes, she didn't know where to feel. She crawled, one hand
out, reaching, and slammed her shoulder hard into the bookshelf. Books rained down on top of her, their edges and corners
striking like missiles. She ducked her head for protection, both
hands over the back of her neck.

A hand wrapped around her wrist, yanking her up from the
floor. She rose in spite of herself, and he swung her around,
dragging her left arm up behind her back. Her free arm snapped
out and stopped suddenly against his side, sending a shooting
pain through her elbow. She cried out, but he pulled her arm a
little tighter, and slid his other arm against her chest, pressing her
to him. "Thought you said you wanted to die?" McAvery snarled.

"I don't!" she gasped.

"Then listen to me." He took a ragged breath. "No doubt
you're in a troubling situation. Every one of your men knows it.
And every one of your men is ready to stand by you. That kind
of loyalty is hard-won, but easily lost. If they see you giving up
like some coward . . . or was that your plan? Let the crew kill
you, so you didn't have to face what's happened? I might have
expected that from a mere quartermaster, but not from a captain
like you." He tightened the pull on her left arm. "Or have I been

deceived?"

"I'm blind!" she cried, hating the tears that threatened to fall.

"Yes, you are. At present."

"What's that mean?"

"I've seen men injured far worse than this recover, given time. I have every faith you will, too."

She wanted to hope, but how could she? She'd been at sea long enough to see men lose their arms, their legs, their eyes. It didn't seemed possible that this condition could repair itself. Even if she could somehow regain her eyes, that sort of recovery took time. Time she didn't have. Lig would sail in and take her before she could even see him coming. McAvery might believe, but she'd be dead or locked away long before his faith could prove itself. "There's just not enough time," she said.

"Yes, there is." He let his grip relax, let her arm fall back to her side. With his hands on her shoulders, he led her to sit on the bed again. "Nasrin believes this is only temporary. A few days' rest away from the sun's light will see you hale and fit. We're mere hours from Bix. Even if the magical message the dead Danisoban sent arrived instantly at its destination, it will take time for a ship to carry anyone from Eldraga. Binns will grant us sanctuary." He brushed the hair away from her face. "You are much too stubborn to let this temporary situation ruin you."

She might yet hang for the Danisoban's murder, but by Bloody Grace's capricious hand, she could die with her eyes open and seeing. Damn McAvery for being right again. A few days in Binns' pub, drinking his decent Bixian ale, would do them all good.

The lizard nudged her left arm. She raised her elbow and the creature slid beneath. Poor thing. It was so vulnerable on its own. It needed her, and here she sat, acting like a helpless fool. They all needed her. And she needed them. She reached out with her foot, but her bare skin slid on the smooth floor and connected painfully with a chair that hadn't been there yesterday.

With the suddenness of lightning it hit her. With all the people coming in and out of the cabin, the furniture wasn't in its usual place. But the lizard could see it all. It could tell her what was coming, without anyone hearing. Reasons it wouldn't work fluttered through her mind, but she cast them away. If the lizard was able to do what she was going to ask of it, this might be a very good idea.

"Climb up on my shoulder, little one," she said, excited to try.

"What are you doing?" McAvery asked.

"I think I'm learning to walk," she said.

The lizard set its claws into the fabric of her shirt, and gently pulled itself up and onto her shoulder. Its tail wrapped across her back and curled under her right arm. She pressed her hands against the bed, squaring her shoulders, scooted herself to the edge, and rose. Her knees twinged from falling earlier, but she ignored the pain.

"When I'm on my feet, I want you to show me what's in front of me. Be my guide."

The lizard tightened its grip on her shoulder. At first, the world remained the gray fog it had been since yesterday. Slowly, the mists cleared, revealing her cabin. The table was pushed against a wall, and all the chairs randomly set in the space where the table had been. Books were tumbled on the floor, and she smiled. "Now, look toward the door." The vision changed, blending like a painting dipped in water, then clearing to show the door. Kestrel took a tentative step, stretching out with her bare toes. She connected with nothing except the floor. Another step, then another. She reached toward the door in her mind's eye, and was rewarded by the feel of the cool metal knob at her hand. She wanted to laugh at the relief of what was happening. The lizard would be her eyes, until her own were recovered. She couldn't fight or even move quickly, but at least she wasn't trapped in this room any longer. Gripping the knob, she turned it and felt the latch give. "McAvery?"

"I'm here," he said, his voice close to her, his hand cupping her elbow.

"Let go." She shook her arm gently. "I can do this."

"Nasrin insisted you have to stay away from bright light until your eyes heal. You can't go out on deck."

He was right. If she had any chance of healing her eyes, she would do what the dancer said. But she wanted to try this new idea she'd had. She waved a hand toward her wardrobe. "Open the left door. There are some scarves hanging on it."

"You want me to blindfold you?"

"Do you have a better idea?"

McAvery's smile was infectious. "No, indeed I don't." He retrieved a scarf and gently wrapped it around Kestrel's head, tying a knot. "I suppose that will have to do."

"That's fine." It felt very strange knowing her eyes were covered, yet being able to see.

"Would you like pants, too?" he asked.

She'd forgotten her barely-clothed state. "Yes, please."

McAvery pulled a pair of breeches and a silk shirt from the wardrobe, and helped her dress. The linen pants lay uncomfortably against her abused skin, but the silk shirt felt weightless. "Stay close, please. Shut the door behind you, and follow us."

Slowly she made her way across the deck, sensing as the lizard directed her. The water splashing against the *Thanos'* hull was so loud — had it always been so? The wood of the deck below her feet, smooth and slightly sticky with soap and oil, creaked softly with each step, a sound she'd never paid attention to before. The men sang while they worked, one of those bawdy pub songs they loved, something about working girls walking along the riverside. The wind hummed a low, hollow music all its own, accompanied by the snap of the sails. The scent of salt on the air, mingled with tar and smoke, tickled her nose. So many sounds and smells she couldn't remember paying attention to before came at her at once, fighting for her to notice them all.

The singing drifted off. Murmurs of surprise wafted on the breeze, followed by laughter and a few cheers. "What the hell is that thing on her shoulder?" someone asked, but the voice sounded more curious than frightened. The lizard turned its head, letting her see her men gathered around, smiling. They were happy to see her. This was where she belonged.

"Kes?" Footsteps pounded toward her, footsteps so familiar she nearly wept. Shadd wrapped his huge arms around her, nearly dislodging the lizard. It hissed in protest, tightening its tail around her shoulder. "Yon dancer lady wouldn't let me come in, said I'd just be in the way. Why are yer eyes covered up? Are ye well, lass?"

Kestrel started to push him away. "Easy, lad, it still hurts like a flogging." He'd been worried, that was evident. And his affection wasn't entirely unwelcome. She wrapped her arms around him and squeezed, not minding the ache, then pushed him back gently. "I'm not full strength yet. It's going to take some time. My eyes were damaged, but I'm finding my way."

"Aye, ye've always been one to do that" he said. "It's good to see ye." He cleared his throat. "I mean, it's good that ye're up and about . . ."

Kestrel reached out and touched his arm. "It's fine, Shadd. My eyesight will return. And for now I've this wee lizard to help me see."

"Good to hear, Captain. We'll dock at Bix before the sun goes down, all safe and sound."

"Bix. That's perfect. When they come for me, I want them to find me alone."

"When who comes?" She could imagine the puzzled expression he was probably wearing, and she almost smiled.

"The Danisobans. They'll want to take me in for the death of one of their own, but they don't have to catch the rest of you. You'll leave me behind with Binns, and he can turn me in. The king still trusts him, so it would make sense."

"Did the magic burn yer brains out along wi' yer eyes? We're not leavin' ye anywhere. And even if we did, ye know good and well Binns wouldn't do any such thing."

As much as she wanted to argue the point, she couldn't. Artemus Binns, the only father she'd ever known, would no more turn her in to the authorities than she would him. And with that thought, she realized that none of her men were any less loyal. She could protest all she wanted, but they'd follow her into a maelstrom of fire if she led the way. Trying to convince them to save themselves by abandoning her probably insulted them all. She couldn't deny their friendship like that. It wasn't fair to any of them.

She reached forward, and thumped her fist against Shadd's broad chest. "You're a good man, Shadd. If any of the men want to leave service, let them know I won't hold it against them. But if they choose to follow me, I'll do whatever I must to bring them through alive."

"That's my captain!" he said, patting her shoulder.

"Lead me to the quarterdeck," she said softly to the lizard. "I want to feel the wheel under my hands."

The lizard looked forward and aft, and Kestrel understood it had no idea what the quarterdeck was. She reached up to the lizard's head, and turned it until the quarterdeck steps entered her view. "Those steps, little one. Watch those for me."

Slowly, following the lizard's sendings, she made her way across the deck and up the quarterdeck stairs. The men had returned to their work while she talked to Shadd, but when she began moving, she heard the whispers again. Some were marveling at the creature on her shoulder, others at her ease of movement. She let herself smile a little. If she had to sacrifice herself to save the men, at least the stories about Mad Kestrel would live forever.

# CHAPTER 16

*A wild bird that misfortune had made tame . . .*
—JOHN MASEFIELD, *The Wanderer*

Kestrel made her slow way all over, down to the bilges and back up again, McAvery at her elbow every step. She didn't need him. With the lizard's vision in her mind, she could find her way without injuring herself against a barrel. She wouldn't stand a chance in a fight. At her fastest pace, a very old woman could easily outrun her. But at least she could move around the ship without feeling her way. She returned to the main deck and ran her hands over the rigging, wondering how complicated climbing would be, when Nasrin approached her.

"Your *korsan* tells me we will dock in a very short time. You should rest before you attempt to walk across this island to your friend."

Kestrel searched for Shadd, and called out to him. "Is that right, quarter?"

"Aye, Captain. We'll be docked just as the sun's settin'."

Now that she was paying attention, she did feel a bit tired, and despite the blindfold keeping the sun out, her eyes stung. A rest wouldn't be such a bad idea. She walked to her cabin and let herself in, McAvery and Nasrin following. The dancer murmured something Kestrel couldn't hear, and soon she heard McAvery's footsteps thumping away.

"Where is he going?" Kestrel asked. She stopped by the bed, leaned over to let the lizard jump from her shoulder, then eased herself down. "Thank you, little one," she said, running a thumb over its back. Sometimes, while she'd been strolling around the deck, the lizard's gaze would swing to the left or right, looking at some glittering object that had distracted it. Now that it was off her shoulder, looking straight at her, seeing herself through its eyes was disconcerting. Her normally brown skin now bore light marks of silver ash, which ached if she rubbed at them. Her black braids were half the length they'd been, ending in frizzy flares of burnt hair. She wondered what her eyes looked like under the blindfold. Scorched? Blackened? Both? She reached up to the blindfold, but just as suddenly she didn't want to look. Seeing herself this way reminded her of her present helplessness, something she didn't want to remember at all. "You can stop now," she said to the lizard. Once it no longer sent her its vision, she pulled off the blindfold and fluttered her eyes open. The familiar gray fog filled her sight. A darker shape moved through the fog, stopping in front of her.

"What can you see, *rais*?" Nasrin murmured.

"I suppose it's you, but only if you've turned into a thunder cloud," Kestrel said, propping her head on her arms.

"An improvement on this morning. Very good. At this rate, you'll recover within days. Lie back." A cool cloth was laid on her head, and Kestrel relaxed into the bedding. Death waited just beyond the horizon, a death she couldn't even see coming. Her men might have to run, or face death themselves. Lig would claim the lizard if he managed to lay hands on it. All these thoughts should have been crushing her. But somehow the cool dampness against her brow forced her to relax.

"What do my eyes look like?" she asked lazily.

"Pretty, after a fashion. They are covered over with a glaze. If you could keep them this way and still be able to see, the effect would be most attractive."

Kestrel reached under the bandage, pressing gently. The skin below her eyes stung, and she gasped. "I suppose the blindfold was a good idea for more than just protection."

Nasrin tsked, pulling her hands away. "In what way, *rais*?"

"Half the men on deck are mighty superstitious. They're used to watching me whistle up a breeze, and most of them know I'd never hurt them, but seeing my eyes looking like mirrors could have shocked them into leaping overboard."

Nasrin chuckled. "For now, all seems well. Perhaps I could read to you." Nasrin walked to the bookcase, and Kestrel heard the soft shush of Nasrin's hand passing over the books' spines.

"Why are you doing this?" Kestrel asked. "Jaques could have

bandaged me just fine, and since there's nothing anyone can do for my eyes but wait . . ."

"I am sorry for my part in your injury," Nasrin said. "My *girifta* would be ashamed of my weakness."

"You said that word before. What's a *girifta*?"

The gray cloud that was Nasrin moved out of Kestrel's sight. "I haven't the word in your language, but I suppose you could call her a teacher. Although she was so much more. My *girifta* recognized my potential and withdrew me from the women's school. She trained me in the taming of magic, and made a home for me."

"Sounds an awful lot like what the Danisobans do."

"I suppose it does. Although we are never kept from our families. My sister and brothers visited me often, and I them. And we're allowed to leave whenever we choose, to shop in the market or to take trips."

Not at all like the Danisobans. Kestrel wondered how differently the island dwellers would feel about the Brethren if they were less secretive. She let her hand fall back against the bedclothes. "Are you a *girifta* too?"

Nasrin laughed softly. "Oh no, not at all. I am called *giri*, leader of the dance. It takes many years to become *girifta*. And I would have to go home to be initiated into the mysteries." Her voice caught, and Kestrel realized how lonely for her own land she must be. "It was important that I make the journey to your lands, but I will be so happy to see the golden sand of my home." She stroked Kestrel's eyelids, her fingers as gentle as a mother's. "I intend to hold up my part of our bargain, *rais*. I will teach you what I know on the journey to my home."

Kestrel shook her head. "Clearly no one's told you. It's possible I won't live long enough to take you myself. I'll talk to Shadd. He'll do whatever he must to deliver you safely wherever you need to go."

"Why do you believe death is your only option?"

"There's no escaping the Danisobans, once they decide you belong to them."

"Did you not escape them already, when you were a mere child?"

Someone had been talking out of turn, telling her story to the dancer. Kestrel wouldn't have guessed any of her crew would bother talking about her to a stunning woman like Nasrin. More likely they'd want to regale her with stories of their personal prowess, in hopes of winning another minute of her attention. She wasn't sure how many of them even knew of her origins. It had to have been McAvery. Probably during their shared captivity on the slave ship.

"They didn't know what they sought, then. A lost Promise, no different from any other. Now they not only know me, but they have a reason beyond their own plans. The law allows them to hunt me for the crime of destroying one of their own. If the mages don't find me, the Eusebians will."

"Have you given any thought to what you accomplished? You destroyed an entire ship by yourself, without endangering your own. Once you're trained, the Danisobans will require a small army to lay claim to you."

"Still, the law stands on their side. And training requires time, time we don't have."

"If your king does not expect you to use the weapons at hand to defend your interests, he is a fool. Foolish kings find themselves unthroned quickly, therefore I would venture he is more cunning than you credit him." She stopped speaking, and Kestrel heard the sound of a book sliding out from its mates. "Ah, I've found some entertainment. A book of adventures, of a pirate called Naile. Have you already read it?"

Kestrel smiled. "That's a present for my friend, the one we're travelling to visit. He loves those old stories."

"Old stories often carry important truths, dear child." She sat down on the edge of the bed. Her soft hands touched the corners of Kestrel's eyes, pressing against the bone. She swept her thumbs across the lids, pressing lightly without hurting. Her fingers were warm and gentle. "Even if your king allows the Danisobans to lay charges against you, you should not remain in the Islands very much longer."

"I should seek out a career mining salt on the Continent, is that it?"

"More paths lie before you than you realize. But let us speak of this *korsan* Naile. Oh my, what an exciting story this seems to be."

"I don't want to hear stories." She turned on her side, curling into the pillows. "Where would I go, then, if I did choose to leave the Islands?"

"Many places. All places. Have you never dreamed of the world you've never seen, outside of these small islands?"

"There's nowhere else but the Continent." A thought teased at the edges of her mind. "Is there?"

Nasrin rose, stepping away from Kestrel's side. "Much has been hidden from you, and much will be revealed. For now, suffice to say that I have come to bring you out of the Islands. And the fish has slipped its net."

Kestrel sat up, startled. The words the stranger in the pub said to her on the day Lig sent her on this journey — how could Nasrin know them? What was the fish? The net? "What did you say?"

Before Nasrin could speak, Kestrel heard a familiar click as the door opened. "How is our patient feeling?" McAvery. Damn his eyes, his timing couldn't have been worse.

Nasrin's steps were light, and she was quickly out the door and out of Kestrel's hearing. What did she know, and why wouldn't she just come out and say it?

"Did I interrupt something?" He sat down on the edge of the bed, taking one of her hands in his.

"What have you told her about me?"

"I may have mentioned your limitless stubbornness."

"You told her about the magic."

"Yes, but only because I wanted her to help you."

"You told her about the Danisobans killing my family."

His hand tightened on hers. "Kestrel, I did tell her you were gifted, because I knew what she could teach you, if I could ever put the two of you together. By all the gods anyone prays to, I did not say a word about your childhood. I would never break the confidence we shared. Anything she knows didn't come from me."

He was a trickster, that she knew. But something in his tone rang too sincerely to be anything but truth. So if he didn't tell Nasrin, who had? "She said she'd come to take me away, that the fish had slipped its net."

"The net. Again."

"Everywhere I turn, someone is talking about this fish. A fish that's certainly not a fish. A fish that wants to do me harm. Or is this all a way of driving me to do her will? Frightening me with talk of this danger, when she really knows nothing about it. Might she have seen the letter on the slave ship?"

"I don't see how. She was confined, as I was."

"No, not the same. She was free to move as she liked, to make herself unnoticed and go where she liked." Kestrel looked up at him, worried. "She snuck back aboard the slave ship after being delivered to the market. Didn't you notice that she was gone from your company?"

"I assumed she'd been delivered to her buyer."

Thinking of Nasrin as a rescued slave was simple. Knowing she was something so much more shook Kestrel to the bone. So far the dancer hadn't done anything to hurt her, but what if that was all part of the game? What if she worked with the Danisobans? "Why would she return to the slavers? What had she to gain being there?"

"You think she knew you were coming."

Kestrel shook her head. "Me, yes, but who else?"

The words hung in the air between them, heavy with significance. Kestrel's heart thudded in her chest, loud enough that it seemed the men on deck could hear it. The dancer might have been waylaid, but she had a purpose. A purpose that focused on Kestrel. First the Danisobans, then the breeders, now Nasrin and whoever she represented. It was enough to make Kestrel want to throw herself into the sea and be done with all of them.

"What are you thinking?" McAvery asked.

She sat up, leaning her elbows on her knees. "My magic is different, but why is it so important to everyone? I'm just one woman. I have no interest in anyone's politics, and I wouldn't be any good at it if I did. Short of locking me away and taking notes on the methods I used to try to escape, I can't think what value I might have." She tried to look at McAvery's face, even though he was nothing but a shadowy shape before her. "Tell me."

"If I were a Danisoban, I would want to learn how you retain your power and your freedom of movement so close to the ocean. We already know the Eusebians want to use you to begin their own magical line."

Kestrel snorted. "Do they really? Or is that just an excuse for some other purpose? They had to know I'd never submit to such a thing."

"I daresay any of their people foolhardy enough to volunteer to impregnate you would come out of the encounter bruised and limping. You're right, it does seem as if you'd be more trouble than you're worth."

"Thank you."

He touched her hand again. "If there's something else they're after . . ."

"Nasrin knows. It's time we made her tell."

Most people in the Nine Islands gave their children over when the Danisoban Factors came knocking. They wept, and mourned, but they didn't resist. Kestrel's mother had kept Kestrel away from curious eyes most of the time, and when the Factors finally did arrive, she sacrificed her life to let Kestrel escape. What had she known? Cold began seeping into Kestrel's chest, the cold of panic. There was something they all knew, something about her that made her more than different. And if she was still in the Islands when the mysterious net fell, it might be that she had more to fear than mere execution.

"Yes. Bring her back in here. And before you go," Kestrel waved at the sideboard. "Hand me the small bag in that top drawer."

He did as she asked. "What's in the bag?"

She untied the drawstring and opened the bag, upending it to let the object inside roll out into her hand. A small gray stone, rounded and plain, like an ordinary stone a child might try to skip across a calm lake. Holding it on her flat palm, she showed it to McAvery.

"My surety stone. You kept it?" His voice was almost a whisper.

When they first met, before she learned to trust him, Mc-Avery used the little stone to prove he meant her no harm. It was magically enhanced to shine with a blue glow if the truth was spoken aloud in its presence. He left the stone with her that night, and never asked for it back. She hadn't had occasion to bring it out until now, but of course she had kept it. It belonged to him once. "We're not leaving this to fate."


A short time later, she heard them enter. McAvery's steps hard, Nasrin's soft and resistant. The door clicked shut behind them.

In her damaged eyesight, the two of them were shadows, one taller than the other. "Sit."

The smaller shadow sank down, not speaking.

"You're not who you claim to be, and your presence here is a danger to us all. Either you know something important you're not willing to tell me, or this is all a ruse to convince me to help you despite my obligation to my crew. You leave me in an awful dilemma, one in which I don't win no matter which way I choose to go."

Nasrin did not move, did not speak. If she was even breathing, it was so lightly and quietly Kestrel couldn't hear her. She was a cool one, this dancer.

"I find myself facing two evils. One that's familiar to me, and one I've never seen before. Since I have to choose, I'm leaning toward the one I know. I've murdered a Danisoban, that much is certain. But it occurs to me that if I turn myself in to the court, and produce the woman whose strange teachings led to my lapse in judgement, I might get out of this with my skin intact. I'll lose my position, of course, and the ship, and if the mages don't swallow me up, I'll be forced to beg on the streets to eat, but I'll be alive." Kestrel rose, keeping one leg against the bed's edge as she stepped cautiously around it to the window. "I have no idea what they'll do with you, but it won't be my concern any longer. I'll order the ship turned toward Pecheta immediately. Unless you'd like to tell me something to change my mind."

"You're not ready," Nasrin murmured, her voice cracking in a way Kestrel had never expected to hear from her.

"And I never will be." Kestrel sat down on the wide windowsill, fixing her damaged eyes in the direction of the woman in the chair. "If we wait to be ready for everything in life, we'll all die waiting."

No one spoke. No one moved. The air in the cabin thickened with the tension. It seemed they might remain this way, still as stone, forever. "That's it, then," Kestrel said. "McAvery, go and tell the helm to lay in a new course, straight for Pecheta."

"No." The dancer almost sounded as if she was moaning. "Please do not change your course."

Nasrin kept insisting she wasn't ready. For what, she didn't know. So far she'd done mighty damage to herself by pushing be-

yond her understanding. Would it be right to press the matter
this time? Or would she harm herself more? Her eyes watered
suddenly and she blinked the moisture away. She was blind, with
no guarantees of recovery. It was time to learn what Nasrin knew,
ready or not.

Tucking her tongue behind her teeth, Kestrel whistled a single
note, just enough to get the lizard's attention, but not to rouse a
breeze or knock anything on the floor. For this, she would need
to see. She heard a rustle, and felt the familiar nudge at her hand.
She stroked it, bringing it close enough to touch, and whispered,
"I want to see through your eyes, little one."

A vision swam before her eyes, a vision of the lizard curled up
and sleeping on the bookshelf. The warmth of sleep teased at the
edges of her mind, forcing a yawn from her. "I know you're
tired," she said, "I'm sorry."

"Let the creature be. It drains him greatly to be used so."

Kestrel started. "How do you know that?"

Nasrin released a long, defeated sigh. "If I tell you, I fear you
will wish you did not know even a small part of all that I do." She
clapped her hands. A long pause, three quick claps, another
pause, and two quick finger snaps. Heat built in the cabin, stifling
as a closed room in the dead of summer. Nasrin repeated the
sounds, again and again. The air became close, as if they tried to
breathe through water. Kestrel's lungs ached with the effort of
taking a breath, her throat burning from the heat. Her skin was
clammy with perspiration, sweat rolling into her eyes and stinging.

"It's too much," Kestrel whimpered, sagging against the chair.
The clapping stopped. The heat rushed past her head like a
storm's breeze, leaving behind fresh air that Kestrel gulped into
her lungs. Nasrin's hands pressed gently against Kestrel's eyes,
hot as bread fresh from the fire. The familiar prickling of magic
teased her skin. Her eyes warmed, soft at first as if the morning
sun shone on her closed lids. The heat grew, now roasting like
the flames of a cookfire, increasing to an almost unbearable level.
Kestrel groaned, pounding one foot against the deck, and leaned
away from Nasrin's touch, but the dancer followed with her
hands.

"Nearly finished, *rais,*" she said. With those words, the burning cooled. Nasrin took her hands away. "Open your eyes."

Kestrel blinked. The gray fog that had blocked her sight was gone, cleared as if a morning breeze had blown it away. McAvery was leaning against the doorjamb, his arms crossed and his face grim. Nasrin stood in front of her, looking smaller than she had before. Her head was bowed, her black hair a curtain hiding her face from view. Her hands were twisted, her fingers tangled and gripped so tightly the knuckles were white.

"I can see." Kestrel touched her face. All the stinging was gone. Her sight was as perfect as it had ever been. She laughed, turning toward McAvery. "I'm good as new!" He let his arms drop, his face betraying his surprise. But he wasn't smiling. Why wasn't he smiling?

Because he was as betrayed as she. How long had Nasrin planned to leave her blind? Leave her weak and vulnerable, at the mercy of anyone who decided to take the advantage. Nasrin reached out to touch Kestrel, but she slid sideways off the windowsill and avoided the dancer's hand. "You could have done this yesterday."

"Kes." McAvery said.

The dancer turned her palms up in surrender. "You needed to understand the danger. Magic is not to be used lightly. Misuse of the power can leave scars, even if it does not kill you."

"What care I about scars?" Kestrel shoved her sleeves up to her elbows, and presented her arms. A scattering of old scars stood out from her brown skin. "Scars I have a wealth of. One more will make no difference."

"The pain you suffered when you played with the Danisoban book was only a taste of what could happen. I hoped to take my time in explaining—"

Kestrel slapped at a pile of papers on the desk, sending them fluttering to the floor. "You left me blind to teach me a bleeding lesson?"

"Kestrel." McAvery grabbed her elbow. Kestrel cocked back her fist, and he stepped away, one hand raised in defense. "Look." He'd opened the wardrobe door. The one with a mirror inside. Kestrel glanced at her reflection.

Her cheekbones and chin sported ash-gray streaks from the magical burns she'd suffered. Her braids were half undone, leaving a halo of tight black curls framing her face. But her eyes. Her brown eyes were silvered over with a mirror glaze, reflecting her own face back to her. Silver, as cold and resolute as the silver wave McAvery had described flowing from her to destroy the other ship. She touched her fingers lightly to where the whites of her eyes should have been, and blinked at the irritation. They felt right, but they looked like something out of a horrifying tale told to scare people. Her knees buckled. She caught herself, unable to look away. "But I can see."

"I said there would be scars."

Kestrel's chest tightened, her breath as thick as honey to draw. Dizziness overwhelmed her, and she reached out for something to steady herself. Her hand met McAvery's shoulder. He slid an arm around her, and she allowed herself to fall against him. "Sit down," he said, steering her toward a chair. The wood of the chair was solid and reassuring against her back. She wrapped her fingers under the seat, to keep from falling.

"I am sorry, *rais*," Nasrin said, sinking into a chair of her own. "I had hoped to take a day or two, to give you time to become used to the change. You moved more quickly than I anticipated. How was I to guess you would be out of your sick bed so soon?"

Kes didn't speak right away, fearing that opening her mouth would only send her running for the bucket again. Once her stomach eased, she drew a deep breath. "I didn't have the time to spare. I killed people, including a Danisoban. Doesn't leave room for leisurely recuperation."

"Your determination is remarkable."

The last thing Kestrel wanted to hear was flattery. Especially coming from Nasrin. The dancer had managed to fool them all. "And speaking of time," she said, leaning back and letting her head rest on the wood, "You're out of it. I have questions and you're going to answer them."

The smooth, gray surety stone waited on the table. Not so long ago the thought of merely touching a magical object like the stone had been enough to send chills down her spine. How things did change. "The stone will flash blue if you speak the truth." Kestrel let her lip twitch into the tiniest of smiles. "It belonged to a friend. I never thought I'd have to use it myself. Pick it up."

KESTREL'S DANCE
179

Nasrin raised her head. Her face was expressionless, as blank as a new sail. She took a deep breath, and released it. As the breath whispered from her lips, a change swept over her. Silver strands began appearing within the inky blackness of her hair. Her smooth skin relaxed, tiny lines forming at her eyes and the corners of her mouth. The skin of her neck rippled, and her throat lost its firmness. Her eyes dulled, the deep brown of them fading into a gleaming silver that matched Kestrel's own.

The dancer stood, pushing up from the chair with a groan. The skin of her hands was loose now, showing every fragile bone beneath. She rose to the fullest height she could manage, reached out and took the stone in her hand. "It is tiring holding that form." She stretched her neck, bending her head to the left, then to the right, The crackling of her joints carried across the room. The stone flashed its blue light.

"I don't understand," Kestrel said, her throat tightening.

Nasrin sat again, laid her hands, palms up and holding the stone, in her lap. Her smile vanished. "It was necessary. A young dancer can move more freely. She is harmless, a stupid, pretty thing. No one suspects her of anything more dangerous than enticing other women's men. And silver eyes tend to draw the sort of attention I did not wish to experience. I had hoped to bring you to a safer place before revealing everything, somewhere that I could control your learning. The intensity of your power, child, awes me like nothing I have seen in many years."

Kestrel frowned. "What happened yesterday—"

"Was precisely what has now forced my hand. Someone as ordinary as you wish you were would never have been able to bring forth such a tempest, my *rais*. I am left with the unenviable task of teaching you while we are both in the land of our enemies."

"What enemies? This is my home." Kestrel wrapped her arms around her body, shivering despite the warm closeness of her cabin. "If you mean the Danisobans, I've always known about them. The threat of them is nothing new."

"Oh, but it is, very new and far more dangerous than the mere threat of being made one of them. The last message sent by the doomed ship is going to reach the highest levels of power, and they will know with certainty what you are." The stone flashed again.

"They already know what I am!" Kestrel protested, even while a quiet voice in her mind whispered that perhaps this wasn't quite true.

"The Brethren believed you were another lost Promise, someone like them, until they noticed you could move near the water unhindered. You have an ability they do not, something they want. They had the word of the blood hunter who abducted you to confirm it. The interesting problem was that he did not tell them the truth. He intended to claim you for his own interests, give you over to his superiors for breeding. It was easier to let the Danisobans take you and retrieve you from them later, before they had the time to learn the truth about you." Nasrin coughed, the sound rattling in her chest like dry leaves.

"How do you know about that? How do you know about me?"

"Because my own *girifta* hired the blood hunter to find you."

Blue light. Was this Kestrel's lot, to always be running from someone? "Why is anyone searching for me at all? You work for the Eusebians? I won't be a brood mare for them, or you."

Nasrin waved a dismissive hand. "No, she had no intention of allowing him to enslave you. She hired the blood hunter under the guise of working for the Brethren, of course. The last thing we wanted was to . . ." she stopped, her eyes rolling upward as if looking for something overhead. "Tip our hand?" she finished, her face questioning. She shrugged. "No matter. The time for subterfuge is over. Especially seeing that you have caught a *devwella*. Someday you must tell me how you managed that."

*Devwella.* Did she mean the lizard? The Danisoban book had called it a depwal. So Nasrin knew about the creature. She knew about so many things.

"What exactly," McAvery said, "is it you want with the captain?"

Nasrin leaned forward, reaching for Kestrel's hands. Her fingers were still warm as they'd been before, but now Kestrel's skin was ice. "She is the lost daughter for whom our hearts have grieved. The stolen child who haunts our dreams. She is the one born *giriftana*, the receptacle of power, she who will complete our circle."

"Your circle? Doesn't that just sound sisterly." Kestrel shook her head. "You keep talking but none of this makes sense. I was born on Eldraga. I can move a little air, create a flame in the palm of my hand and send a wave of destruction over the water if I happen to lose control. Granted the water doesn't bother me, but beyond that, I'm not much of a mage. I don't know what you think I can do, but you're wrong."

"It is not what I think, but what I know. You are the link in our chain. Deny the evidence of your own experience if you wish, but the fact remains that yours is the power that can defeat all others."

Laughter bubbled up from Kestrel's belly. Nasrin stared at her, her face dark with concern. Her worry only fueled Kestrel's irritation. What right did the dancer have feeling any sort of way? She'd caused all this. A few minutes of truth, and everything might have turned out so differently. "You think I'm some sort of savior, sent to deliver you? Lead you to a land of sunshine and glory?" She let herself fall onto the bed, ignoring the twinge of her still-tender skin protesting her sudden movement and nearly knocking the lizard off the side. It scrambled across the linens to a safer perch. "You'll have to get in line behind the rest. I have prior commitments, and it may take me some time to work my way around to your salvation."

"Kestrel," McAvery began, stepping toward her with a hand out. She slapped at him playfully.

"No touching the chosen one, mate!"

"Damn it, Kes, she's speaking the truth. Look."

She'd noticed the blue flash of the surety stone. She'd hoped no one else did. How could anyone see her as a champion of any sort? She had a good hand with a sword, a strong stomach for travel on the water and up to this point, she'd been able to convince a ship full of pirates to follow her lead, but none of that made her worthy of what Nasrin was saying. She shook her head. It had been so much simpler when she believed Nasrin a mere romantic rival. Having another person try to label her as something other than an ordinary pirate was more than she could handle. Nasrin had been right; she wasn't ready. For any of this. She needed to talk to Binns. He was always able to clear her head.

"*Rais*, I can prove what I claim."

"Can you now?" She wasn't sure she wanted proof. Right now living in ignorance seemed far more attractive.

A mighty hammering shook the door. "We're dockin', Captain," Shadd called from the other side.

Kestrel sat up. "I'll be out presently," she called back.

Nasrin laid a hand on Kestrel's arm. "You have already tasted the power of which you are capable. Power you should not be able to wield without Danisoban training. You can do these things because you are not one of them. Your heritage is much older and nobler."

"I don't want to hear this. I'm as noble as a stray pup."

"Your mother came from our shores."

Kestrel jerked her arm away. "I told you before, I was born on Eldraga."

"Her name was Eliana."

That name. She hadn't heard it spoken since she was a tiny girl. Her heart pounded in her ears like a drum. The stone flashed. She looked at McAvery, and she knew from the expression on his face that he saw the truth of it as well. Her parents were merchants, common folk. Not magic wielders at all. Weren't they? She was so young when they were killed, she knew nothing about their lives before her birth. If her mother was a native of the Continent, and had known Nasrin, she never told Kestrel. Never had the time to tell her. Kestrel swallowed back a lump forming in her throat. What if there was more to know about her parents?

Before Nasrin could say anything else, Shadd's voice thundered through the door. "We're ready to go ashore, with yer kind permission."

She was on the verge of answers, answers to the questions that had tortured her all her life. Going ashore seemed a waste now. But the men wouldn't leave unless she gave the order, and they needed the leave. Kestrel stood and retrieved the length of silk she'd used to cover her eyes before. She tied it around her head.

"What are you doing?" McAvery asked.

"I can't go out there looking like this. Not yet." She tightened the knot against her hair. "The men understand, but we can't know who we'll meet walking to the pub. If some islander sees my eyes silvered over like this, the worst that'll happen is them following me around making god signs behind my back. That sort of attention I don't need. I can see a little through the silk, and I'll just hold on to someone while we walk. All people will see is a poor, blind woman." She reached out a hand to the bed and clicked her tongue to the lizard. "Coming, little one?"

"*Rais*, the *devwella* has expended a great deal of energy helping you already this day. It may not show, but you are depleting him."

"Not to mention he's not an ordinary animal. He'll draw exactly the kind of attention you hope to avoid," McAvery said. Damn his eyes, he was right. She wasn't happy leaving the creature alone and undefended, but her cabin was probably the safest choice.

The familiar nudge of the lizard's nose against her hand was comforting. It reached out as if to climb onto her shoulder, but she pressed it gently back onto the bed. "No, dear one. They're right. You stay on the ship." She turned to Nasrin. "As do you, lady. You can keep an eye on our little friend. There'll be a few men aboard at all times, so don't go thinking you can slip away from me before I have the rest of your story." There probably wasn't anything the pirates could do to stop Nasrin if she did try to escape. Kestrel shook the thought away — there were more than enough worries without adding one to the pile. She straightened to rise from the bed, and the blindfold slid away from her face.

"Give me that!"

McAvery held the circle of silk dangling from a finger. "You need your own vision. What if the Danisobans are already on the island? Do you really believe you can move and fight effectively with a blindfold and a lizard doing your seeing for you?" He tossed the silk aside, and rummaged in the wardrobe. "Wear this." He held out a floppy straw hat. "It should shade your eyes enough that only those who stand close to you can see the change."

Kestrel snatched the hat from his hand and put it on. The brim fell low, just over her eyebrows, but low enough, as McAvery had guessed, to keep her eyes in shadow. And she admitted grudgingly that it would be easier to fight if she didn't have to depend on the lizard to help her.

"Nasrin," she said. "I'll have the rest of your story when I return. Whether or not you think me ready." She opened her door. Shadd waited outside, tapping one mighty foot as if he was ready to run down the plank into town. She let her lids fall half-closed, to further continue the ruse. "Have you set the watches?"

"Aye, Kes, I did." He peered curiously into the room. "Everythin' peaceful in here?"

"For now," she said. "Let's go see Binns." Taking his arm, she let him walk her onto the deck.

# CHAPTER 17

*It is herself; she cannot change her style;*
*She has the habit now of being foiled.*
—JOHN MASEFIELD, *The Wanderer*

Even with the hat shading her face, the sun tortured Kestrel's newly healed eyes, and she found she gripped Shadd's arm just a bit tighter than she might otherwise. He didn't think anything of it, fortunately, assuming she was unsure of her feet due to the blindness. McAvery walked in front of them, and Jaques behind, both watching out for the telltale black robes of the Danisobans. The men who hadn't drawn watch duty were scattering in different directions, some to shop the market, others searching for drinks, games and a night's true love. Nasrin and the lizard stayed behind on the *Thanos*. For their own safety. The kind of attention they'd have drawn in a place like this, no one needed. Kestrel kept her head tilted down as Shadd led her through the busy Bixian streets to Artemis Binns' pub.

The building was bigger than she'd expected, almost the size of Camberlin's back on Eldraga, although it wasn't crowded on either side by other business. It stood alone on the corner of the street. Above the doorway hung a sign that said "The Old Captain's Pub". Kestrel smiled. Her old captain, the Privateer before her, had retired and moved to Bix a year before. He'd chosen a perfect name for his place. Shadd walked her inside. The main room was shaded and cool. Kestrel blinked to adjust her vision. Men sat at round tables, some drinking, some throwing houn-scozza cubes, and one alone at a corner table, reading from a book. Binns' barmaids moved in and out of the crowd, dropping off pitchers of ale and picking up empty ones to refill. No different from any other pub in the world. Except that this one was owned by a man she trusted with her life. And if no other option

presented itself, she was going to trust him with her death. She
steeled herself for the conversation. He wasn't going to like this at
all.

"Artemus Binns!" Shadd yelled, loud enough to shake the
windows. "Get out here!"

"Who's makin' such a racket? I'm comin'." Binns appeared
from the kitchen and squinted toward the door. His usual grizzle
and ragged hair had been cleaned up by regular visits to the bar-
ber, and his clothes verged on finery. "My girl!" Tossing a rag
over his shoulder, the old man strode across the room and threw
his arms around Kestrel, squeezing her tight. "Shadd! Jaques!
And Master McAvery." He pumped each man's hand in turn,
before hugging Kestrel again. "I've missed you, I have. I want to
hear all your adventures. Startin' with, what's this hat you're wearin'? Some new fashion on Pecheta?" He reached to flick it back
from her face. She grabbed for it, but too late. His eyes widened.
"What in blazes have you done to your eyes, girl?"

"Artie, the land-bound life seems to suit you. I swear you look
ten years younger." She sank onto a bench and laid her head on
her folded arms, turning so he could still hear her. "I'm in a
world of trouble."

"I reckoned as much, seein' as you're here without notice and
at the wrong time of year. You ought to be careenin' that fine
mighty ship o' yours about now, scrapin' them barnacles off her
hull. And that silver in your eyes." He shook his head. "Let me
order you up a pint, and you can tell me what you're runnin'
from."

It took nearly the whole mug to get the story told, and Binns'
face grew grimmer with each word. She tilted the mug to finish
the last swallow, warm though it was by now. She usually hated
ale that wasn't cold, but this might very well be the last she'd
drink for a long time.

Binns shook his head. "I leave you alone for a year's time,
and look what you get up to." He peered closely at her damaged
eyes. "You're sure this won't go away?"

"I don't know what to be sure of anymore."

"I've never doubted anythin' you set your mind to, stubborn
as you are. The magi, they're stubborn, too. They don't take to
sea lightly, even to chase down someone who killed one of their

own. But," he shrugged. "I wouldn't put it past them to come after you."

She nodded. She'd thought the same thing. "I'm left with two choices. Run, and hope they can't catch me, or stay and take what's coming."

"Sounds to me as if you've already made your choice."

"I suppose I have." She turned around on the bench, leaning her elbows against the table now behind her. Binns always did have a way of reading her. "They'll be coming for me soon, so I can't spare even a minute. Just because I can fight them now doesn't mean it's the best idea. I'd probably end up burning down the whole island." She tried to tell herself she was surprised with the decision. But no — it had been simmering in the back of her mind ever since the battle, and her disastrous attempt at magic. There was so much she needed to know, so much Nasrin offered. Kestrel had known what she was doing before she let herself believe it. "Yes, I'm running. I need you to help me find berths for the men who don't choose to run with me."

"Easy enough, I reckon. What about the lady?"

The dancer didn't argue over being ordered to stay aboard, instead dancing a quick combination of moves to regain her youthful look before leaving Kestrel's cabin to return to her own, carrying the lizard with her. She hadn't said another word, but there'd be more than enough time on the journey. Kestrel had so many questions for Nasrin, about her mother most of all. She knew so little, only the faded memories of childhood. If the dancer had known her mother, Kestrel intended to find out every detail she could.

"She wants to go home, to the Continent, and since I'll have to run so far anyway, I might as well take her where she wants to go."

She wasn't entirely inclined to trust Nasrin, not yet, now that she knew she'd been deceived once. The things she'd said, the things she'd implied she knew . . . the dancer had offered the information as if it might sway Kestrel to believe anything she said. Too bad for them both that all the years of running from the Danisobans had trained Kestrel to avoid trusting anyone who seemed to know too much. The Brethren wanted her for being special. Nasrin wanted her for the same reason. The surety stone backed up everything Nasrin said. Deep inside, Kestrel wanted to believe in her. Then again, feelings were worth precisely what one paid for them. She could go 'round and 'round forever, never making a choice, but that way lay madness.

"And the Knave?"

McAvery was sitting at the table with Shadd, but his gaze had never left her. "He's still in the king's good grace. At least I'm guessing. He's insisting he won't leave me, but he's being an idiot. Tie him up in the cellar if you have to, but keep him from ruining his own standing, would you?" Her chest ached at the thought of leaving him when they'd only just found each other, but she couldn't drag him into the net she'd thrown over herself. Trickster he might be, but he didn't deserve that.

Binns had tried to push them together from their first real meeting, and the grin on his face showed that his opinion hadn't changed. "Look at you, my girl. Worryin' about him when it's your own neck needs savin'. Does my raggedy old heart good to see you like this." He shot a quick glance at McAvery, and patted Kestrel's hand. "The way he looks at you, I'm inclined to disobey you and let him do what he chooses. Ain't like you'll come back and fuss at me, aye?"

"I'd rather be the only one in jeopardy, Artie."

The men throwing hounscozza cubes erupted into cheers and raucous teasing. Their noise proved enough for the reader. Slamming his book closed, he tossed back his drink and stood. Now that she could see his face, Kestrel realized she'd seen him before. She pressed her hands flat on the table, letting the residual ache remind her to stay calm. On Eldraga, after her brawl with the knife-fighter. This was the strange man who stopped at her table and made the vague threat about the fish slipping its net, one she hadn't put any stock in at the time. Yet she'd heard the threat more and more, and now here he was. With all that had happened, she wasn't in a mind to think it was coincidence.

The man squinted at her. He smiled slowly, no trace of humor in his eyes. He rubbed his free hand over his belly, and marched out the door before she could say anything. The Islands weren't so big that a person wouldn't run into people this way, but something was wrong.

"Shadd," she said. When the big man glanced over, she beckoned him to her. "That man who was reading in the corner -- did you notice him leave just now?"

He furrowed his brow. "I think so, Captain. Is somethin' amiss?"

"Can you follow him a bit? And tell me where he stops?"

"On my way," he said. He stopped at his table and muttered something to McAvery, then sauntered out the door, as if he'd meant to go all along.

"What's wrong, my girl?" Binns asked.

"Did you know that man?"

"Can't say I do. He usually orders a drink and reads until his mug is empty. Hasn't given the barmaid any trouble."

Of course not. There'd have been no reason to draw attention to himself, not if he was waiting for someone. For her. "He approached me on Eldraga. Very mysterious. He said something strange to me about a fish not staying netted, then walked away."

Binns' eyes widened. "Did he say anythin' else?"

"No," she said. "Why?"

He drummed his fingers on the tabletop. "I had a network of informants, back in my day. You might recall one of 'em givin' you a message about roses and thorns one time."

She did remember. On Eldraga, the night before Binns was arrested and jailed, and his ship stolen from the harbor. She'd believed the messenger to be a drunken tramp at the time, talking nonsense. "You mean that was one of yours?"

"He wasn't. But that phrase, 'fish not staying netted'? That was one o' mine."

"What did it mean?"

He frowned. "It means someone you thought safely locked away may have gotten loose."

"Wonderful. All I need is another enemy I don't even know about." She picked up her mug, but only a drop remained. "I need another drink."

Binns turned and waved a hand for the barmaid. After she took their mugs to refill, he said, "Are you sure you can't present your case to the court? Sounds like you was defendin' yourself to me, and I imagine the king'll see it that way himself. His Majesty is a reasonable man."

"His Majesty's Danisoban is not, Artie, and that's where the trouble lies. You did this job a long time, I know, and you got along right well with Lig. Me he's been trying to catch out since the first day. All the care I took for the last year, only to ruin it for the sake of magic. I wouldn't put it past Lig to have sacrificed that mage of his on purpose."

"How could he have guessed what you'd do? A month ago you didn't know yourself."

No, she hadn't. She'd never have guessed.

A fresh mug appeared at her hand. "Here's a question to take your mind off your troubles, then," Binns said. "Your little lizard friend. What do you imagine Lig's wantin' with him?"

She shrugged, and took the mug in her hands, rolling it slowly back and forth and watching the foam spin. "He wants to make a suit out of the creature's hide."

"What in blazes for?"

"His endgame remains a mystery, but I fear such a suit allows a mage to travel on, or even in, the water without any detriment to his health. Or his magic."

Binns' eyes widened, and he gulped a swallow of ale. "They'd be free to move around the Islands as they liked."

"Exactly," she said. The idea of the Danisobans having no limitations on movement filled her with dread. "The lizard's called a depwal. The book said they grow to a hefty size. I don't know how much leather a full grown depwal can provide, but if the one I saw is any indication, Lig might be able to suit a dozen of his men or more. Even one Danisoban not locked to the land is more than anyone needs."

"What book is that?"

Kestrel dropped her voice to a murmur, leaning closer to her old captain. "I got my hands on one of their teaching books. Called *The Source of Conjurr*. It's supposed to be the main book they use inside the school."

Binns drew back, clearly shocked at her admission. "By Pantheus' third ridge, how much did that cost you? And where'd you even think to look for it?"

"Thirty octavos. Shadd would faint if he knew I spent so much on a book, even that one. It took some asking, but there was a bookseller on Eldraga. Rumor on the street said that his little brother had run away from the school, and gave him the book before—"

Binns raised his eyebrows. "Before what?"

"Before the magi struck him down in the street and left his body a pile of crackling ashes." She smiled humorlessly. "Bookseller felt no loyalty to them. It still took every bit of my persuasion and most of the coin in my purse to convince him."

"Be careful who you show that book to, my girl. Word gets out you have it, and you'll be the one who's cracklin'."

She barked a laugh. "As if I needed anything else to fear." She raised her mug and took a long swallow. Cold, just the way she preferred it.

A cheer rose up across the room. Shadd had returned. He grinned at his shipmates. "Be right with ye, lads!" he said as he passed their table. He sat down on the bench next to Kestrel. "I'm afraid I lost him, Captain," he said softly. "He headed toward the harbor, but somewhere between the harbormaster's office and the docks, he slipped away. Don't worry," he said, raising a hand as if taking a vow, "I checked on the *Thanos* soon as I knew the fella gave me the slip. Tom was readin', and all was quiet. I warned him to keep a weather eye peeled."

"Thanks for trying," she said. "Do me one last favor?"

"Anythin'," he said.

"Put the word out that I need to see the crew on the ship in half an hour. I won't keep them from their drinking long, I promise."

He frowned, but nodded. "I'll make sure they're on deck and waitin', Kes. Count on me."


Shadd was as good as his word. When Kestrel returned to the ship, her crew was gathered, in various states of intoxication. She climbed to the quarterdeck so everyone could see and hear her. "Listen up, men. I'm sorry to tell you all," she began, "but the last battle we engaged in—" she stopped, and plastered a grin she didn't feel on her face. "That battle we won!" Cheers erupted, as she'd expected they would. Good. She put up her hands to regain their attention. "That battle has left us in a predicament. There was a mage aboard, a mage that died in the conflagration. We had no way of guessing such a man sailed with them, but our ignorance makes no difference. If I'm any judge, there's likely to be a noose waiting for me and anyone who sails under my command, if we return to Pecheta."

Quiet swept over the deck. Kestrel let the news sink in. The men looked at each other, some whispering to each other, as she continued. "I intend to sail east, toward the Continent, to waters we've never dreamed of plundering, and no king to take a share off the top." She held still, letting the words drift on the wind. What she said was, strictly speaking, treason. No one spoke, although some of them were smiling, as if the idea appealed.

"Anyone who wants to come with me on this adventure should tell Shadd tonight. Understand, I don't know when I'll return. I have loved these islands as you do, but it may not be possible for me to ever come back. Therefore, I ask no one to come with me who doesn't wish it. Some of you have loved ones you can't leave behind, so arrangements are being made to sign you on to other crews right here on Bix. You'll be paid what you're owed before you go. Once you're not beholden to me, you won't be held responsible for the mage's death." Her heart beat so hard she felt sure they could all hear it. "You're a fine bunch, and it has been my honor to serve as your captain, whatever your choice."

She walked down the quarterdeck stairs, letting the men make their decisions without her staring down at them. As she guessed, a great many of the men chose to take the release, some trying to explain no matter how much Shadd told them no excuse was necessary. Shadd, of course, insisted on coming with her, as did Tom, Jaques, David DeadEye and a dozen others. That small a crew wasn't ideal for a ship the size of the *Thanos*, but it would be no great hardship either. When she offered to let the men leave, McAvery stepped next to Shadd, indicating his intent to stay at her side. She hadn't spoken at the time, waiting until the others had gone off to pack their sea chests.

"You don't have the luxury of a choice," she'd said to him when they were finally alone. "You stay here with Binns until you can arrange passage to Pecheta."

"You're not my captain," he said.

"No, I'm not. You answer to the king, and you'll return to him with your reputation clean."

He took her hand, raised it to his lips and kissed her palm. "It's for me to say whose man I am."

His tawny eyes reflected the lantern's light, and she felt as if she could stare into them forever. "Your eyes are gold," she murmured, raising a hand to stroke his cheek.

"And yours are silver. Together we're treasure."

She drew a ragged breath, tearing her gaze away. "If you stay with me, you become outlaw, too. They'll hang you if we're caught."

"You're assuming they can catch us."

"Cack you for a fool, McAvery," she said. "Philip, please. Don't ask me to let you throw your entire life into the sea on my account."

He tightened his hold on her hand, and pulled her closer. "You say I'm throwing away my life. I can't imagine being anywhere but next to you. No king, no flag, no island draws me as you do. I'd gladly leave it all behind, in order to be always at your side."

Her belly tightened. No one had ever spoken to her this way. Such words a woman could spend her youth dreaming about, and she was hearing them with the echo of barking dogs and the thud of a gallows pull. Bloody Grace, capricious goddess that she was, had dreadful timing. "You're a fool. You can do better for yourself. Return to court, find a rich woman who doesn't mind you being gone half the time. Live to be an old, fat man."

"I go where you go. Whatever the consequences."

"You could die." She hadn't intended to say what she was thinking, but somehow it slipped out. Before she could scramble to take back the words, he captured her mouth with his. For the space of a dozen heartbeats, there was nothing for her but the joy of his kiss. Tension flowed from her shoulders, and she relaxed into his warmth.

He lifted his lips away from hers, touching them to the tip of her nose, and then to her forehead. "That's what I thought."

There'd been no more time for argument. Men were coming abovedeck, carrying their belongings. A few stopped to bid her farewell, but most gave her a wide berth. Knowing she could perform a little magic to fill the sails had been fine, but roasting men in a magical fire was a different kind of magic, one they wanted to put themselves far away from. And then there was her eyes. She couldn't blame the men. Her magic frightened her as much as it did them, but at least they had the option of escaping.

Binns was as good as his word. He busied himself calling in every marker he held with the captains in dock. Every man who left her service found a berth. Once they'd safely gone, Binns turned up, accompanied by two young men dragging a cart. "I brought a feast," he announced, marching up the plank. "Anyone hungry?"

Shadd and Tom went below to bring up some lengths of wood suitable for makeshift tables. Kestrel took McAvery's arm. "Fetch Nasrin," she said. "She should enjoy a good meal, since it might be the last one for a while."

Binns hadn't exaggerated when he called it a feast. His cart held all sorts of delicious items — fresh ripe beryl fruits, their skins plump with the promise of sweetness, greens tossed in a light citrus dressing, freshly baked bread, rich cheeses, a roast still warm from the oven and of course a keg of his finest ale.

Kestrel was helping him lay the food on the tables when Binns stopped dead, staring over her shoulder. "Who on Pantheus' sea might that be?"

Kestrel followed his gaze. Nasrin, of course. She'd reinstated her youthful look, and wrapped herself modestly in a silk veil the color of a storm cloud. Kestrel took her old captain's hand and walked him across the deck. "Nasrin, may I introduce Captain Artemis Binns?"

Nasrin extended a graceful hand, which Binns took and raised to his lips. "My lady, I am honored to make your acquaintance."

"And I yours, Binns *rais*."

Binns raised his eyebrows in question. "It's the word for captain in her language," Kestrel explained. Binns smiled then, and offered Nasrin his arm. She took it, and together they strolled toward the waiting food. McAvery slipped next to Kestrel.

"A match made for the ages, do you think?"

She shook her head. "More of a star-crossed romance, I'd say. But they can spend the evening pretending." She looked at him, her heart twisting in her chest. "As are we all." He frowned, but Kestrel joined the others at the tables, stalling any attempt to argue. Soon the tiny crew and their friends were gathered on the deck, eating and drinking as if none of them had a care at all. In between plates of food, David DeadEye played rousing tunes on his mouth organ, accompanied by Jaques pounding a rhythm on a nearby barrel.

The party lasted well into the night, but when the food ran out, Binns dismissed his servers and walked with Kestrel onto the quarterdeck. He leaned over the railing, staring out at the darkening sky. "There are times when I miss this life, my girl. There surely are."

"Are you happy, Artie?"

"Aye, yonder inn of mine pleases me no end. Not to mention my joints are grateful for the easy life they lead now."

Kestrel laughed, and laid a hand against the old man's arm. "I'm sorry to involve you in my troubles. I couldn't leave the islands without saying goodbye."

"Right you are. I'd have had to search you out!" He turned around, perched himself on the railing and gave her a searching look. "It's strange to look at you with them eyes all flashin' silver."

"I know. It may not last," she said, but Binns was waving a hand.

"'Tisn't important. What is important," he said thoughtfully, "Is this for sure and certain the only way out of your troubles? The Continent is a long way, across seas you don't know. What if the journey's just as deadly as the mages?"

No, she wanted to say. I'd rather be forgiven by the king, have him send his mage on another errand and leave me to my ship. The *Thanos* wasn't her ship, not really. She had no other way to escape. Buying passage to the Continent was risky — any bounty the Danisobans might set on her head would be too high for most sailors to resist. She couldn't afford to purchase a ship with what money she had, especially after paying the men who left, and stealing another ship would be no different than taking the *Thanos*. So she'd be called murderer and thief for the rest of her days, however long they turned out to be. Let them call her names if they liked. At least she'd be alive and free.

"I'm sure," she answered.

Binns huffed, stood up and clapped a hand against her shoulder. "Well then, we need to provision you properly. If you'll stay 'til mornin', I can stock your holds for the journey west."

She nodded. Pecheta and Eldraga were days away. There was time to restock the supplies, and they'd certainly need it. All she knew of the Continent was that it had salt mines and was many months away. "What do you think I'll find?" she mused, not really expecting an answer. Binns patted her head in his fatherly way.

"A glorious sunset, and the new day that always follows, my lass. It always does."

The night passed by quickly, and Kestrel hardly knew she'd slept before the lizard was nudging her, showing her the fingers of light that were peeking over the horizon, signaling the dawn. She rose and dressed quickly. "Are you hungry?" she asked. The lizard scampered to the window and nudged it with its nose. "Well, then, go find yourself some breakfast," she said, opening the latch to let the window fall open. "But be back before the tide turns." It slid through the open window, and Kestrel heard a soft splash far below. She left the window open, and walked out of her cabin. Binns had been as good as his word. Men were hustling along the docks with crates and barrels of food and water for her holds.

"Shadd," she called. He popped his head out of the hatch. "See to the loading, would you?"

"Where are ye goin'?"

"Into town, to tell Binns goodbye." She dropped to her haunches, and lowered her voice. "Seen McAvery this morning?"

"I'm right here."

Kestrel jumped at the sudden voice behind her. "Ah well, I'd hoped we could raise anchor and leave him here."

Her quartermaster grinned. "I don't think he'll take kindly to that, Captain."

"Indeed I wouldn't." McAvery laid a hand on her shoulder. "Why don't I walk you to the inn? Just so I can be sure you aren't going to try anything tricky." He'd been determined to stay with her, and there wasn't much she could do to stop him being aboard when she raised anchor. Shadd wore a knowing look, though. He probably suspected what she was thinking. She rose to her feet, waved at her quartermaster and strode down the gangplank. "Be ready to raise anchor when I get back."

She and McAvery walked through the busy throngs at the docks, and found their way to the main street. The morning breeze swept in from the bay, bringing with it the salt smell of the ocean. It smelled like home to her. She tilted her face up to the sun's warmth, wishing she didn't have to leave these islands she'd always known. For the first time since the battle, her skin didn't sting at all.

"Missing the place already?"

"Not the place so much as the idea of it. It's home, you know. Does it show?"

McAvery's hand tightened on her elbow. "A bit. If there was another way . . ."

"There's not. Not for me." She stopped, forcing him to look at her. "You can still go back to your life."

"No, I can't." He took her hand in his, stroking it with his fingers. "I spent a year wondering what sort of idiot I'd been to walk away from you on the docks. Every day I woke, wondering how I'd find my way back to you. Either of us could have died in that time, leaving the other to wonder always what might have happened. Now that I have you at hand, I see no reason to tempt fate twice."

She could lose herself in his eyes. "I spent that same year, with you in my dreams. It wasn't any easier for me to be without you. All I want is to walk in the sun next to you. But the next best thing would be to know you are somewhere safe, even if it is somewhere without me. You'll be sailing into the unknown if you go with me, throwing off the protection of the crown." Tears welled in her eyes, tears she for once didn't bother to wipe away. "Over the course of the last year, I told myself you knew how to stay alive all on your own. But now I'd rather not have to see you die."

He wiped a drop from her cheek with his thumb, as gently as he would for a child. "We're both able to take care of ourselves. Why don't we take the chance on staying alive, together?"

She let herself fall against his body, resting her head against his chest and drawing on his warmth. He wrapped an arm around her and pulled her close. For a time, she stopped listening to the hustle of people around them, enjoying the peace she could only find within range of this man. "We're wasting time standing here, and the tide won't wait."

He lifted a strand of hair away from her face, smiling. "No, it won't."

She stuck out a finger. "I'm warning you, though. If you get yourself killed by coming with me, don't expect me to wear black and mourn you for a year. I'll give you a week, at most."

"I'll consider myself fortunate."

The door to Binns' pub stood open, taking advantage of the cool morning. A nearly transparent silken drape, hung to keep insects from flying into the room, fluttered in the breeze. She stared into the pub. A handful of men sat at a table talking quietly together. Binns was behind the bar, rubbing the worn wood and wearing a forlorn expression. She wished she could have had a real visit, time to talk and reminisce, time to say a proper good-bye. Lifting the curtain aside, she took a step forward. Binns' gaze shot up. He caught sight of her, and his eyes widened. He shook his head slightly, then reached back with an elbow, tipping a bottle off the shelf and sending it crashing to the floor. The men at the table rose, all staring at him, but he raised his hands. "Sorry, gentlemen, my clumsiness! Please don't run off." He stressed the word 'run', flicking his eyes toward Kestrel again.

Something was wrong. The men who'd risen were already turning toward the doorway. Men in black robes. One raised a hand, revealing a glint of silver in the dim light. Kestrel tensed. Run. Yes. There was no more time for anything but running. Before she could move, she heard a sickly smack, and McAvery's grip on her arm released suddenly, followed by a thud.

Danisobans. How could they have arrived so soon? There hadn't been a new ship in port since she arrived the day before. She stepped back to make her escape. Her heel caught on something heavy and she tripped, tumbling to the ground. McAvery. He lay slumped in the dust, unmoving. She straddled him, sweeping the hair off his face. He was still breathing, thank the gods, and his pulse throbbed in his neck. Standing behind him, smiling in a way that made her skin crawl, stood Menja Lig, the king's personal mage.

"What have you done to him?" she asked.

"Well met, Captain. Or should I call you miss?" He lifted a

hand to drop his hood back, his silver bracers winking in the morning sunlight. "What's this you've done to your eyes, my dear? They look a bit scarred." He took a step closer. Kestrel lifted her legs free of McAvery, scrambling to her feet. She bumped against someone, and suddenly her arms were gripped tight. Another mage, younger, but with a sour expression.

"You're going to regret putting your hands on me," Kestrel growled, but Lig laughed. Kes pressed her lips together to whistle.

In a flash, Lig cupped her jaw and pinched her mouth, forcing her to stop. "Not that I fear your paltry skill, but there are innocents present. We wouldn't want anyone else to be killed by your misuse of magic, would we?" Lig laughed softly. "In fact, perhaps we should secure you somewhere you can do no one any harm. *Hesh marrap me ah*," he whispered, waving his free hand in a complicated gesture. He pressed his palm against her forehead, and the world went black.

# CHAPTER 18

*And the gale's gathering made the darkness blind*
—JOHN MASEFIELD, *The Wanderer*

It was still light when she woke. That was the only thing she could be certain of. She wondered if McAvery lived. Everything around her had returned to the gray fog it had been after she injured her eyes. She squeezed her eyes tight, then blinked, but no. She was impaired again. No injury this time to blame it on. She'd been standing still when she lost consciousness, held tight by Lig's people. Her current blindness had to be caused by the Danisoban. For a second she wished she'd brought the lizard to town with her, then remembered it was safer where it was on the ship. She wasn't even sure their link would have worked against magical blindness, anyway. She lay on her side on what felt like a bed. Her wrists seemed locked in place, as if tied, except she couldn't feel any binding keeping them that way. She dug at the space between her wrists with the fingertips of one hand, trying to push them in between her wrists, but no matter how much she strained, she couldn't pull her hands away from each other. Her legs were drawn in tight like her wrists, from knees to ankles. She raised her hands, rubbing her wrists against her cheeks, but felt only skin. No rope held her. Even her lips were closed, leaving her silent and helpless. She couldn't stand, see, or make a sound. At least she wasn't dead. It wasn't much. She relaxed on the bed again, listening for noises, hoping to determine where they held her. Somewhere on land, that she knew. Everything was too solid, too still. Inside a building, since she heard no sounds of people or animals. The faint scent of beer made her wonder if she was still in Binns' pub. Then again, she could be smelling the ale on her breath from before.

A familiar click of a door opening, and footsteps thudding

across the floor alerted her to company. Vague dark shapes moved toward her, and hands grasped her body and yanked her upright. Someone murmured a phrase of the Danisoban language, and suddenly, her lips opened. She let out a breath, the air burning against their chapped surface. She was rewarded with a hard slap across the face. "None of your whistling, woman!"

"Please, Brother Tel. There's no need for violence. The captain," Lig stopped, and chuckled. "Sorry, old habits. I meant to say the woman knows better than to try anything foolish."

"Where am I?" she rasped.

"Your old friend kindly gave us the best room in the inn, my dear. So thoughtful of him, considering your helpless state."

*If I could only whistle,* she thought, *I'd show him how helpless I am.* Except she'd probably burn down the pub and her friends along with it. As she'd said not long ago, Lig seemed to be ahead of her at every turn. "Water?" she croaked.

"Of course. How rude of me!" A cup was pushed against her mouth. She gulped the water, grateful for the coolness in her parched throat. "Better?"

She nodded. A man-shaped figure settled directly in front of her. She kept her eyes open, hoping they'd at least make him uncomfortable. For now it was all she had.

"Things would have been simpler if you'd joined us when we met at court. For one thing, you'd still have lovely brown eyes. Instead of shiny silver ones that never work properly."

They'd been working fine before, something he obviously knew. "Blindness is a small price to pay, if it means I don't have to look at your face."

"Such a spitfire." He tsked. "You'll need lessons in etiquette, clearly. Perhaps if you knew the wonders we can offer." Something waved before her face. "*Hesh abranto kerra.*"

Her head spun. The gray fog vanished, as if it had never been. The room sprang into clarity, the light hitting her with almost physical force. Kestrel pressed her fingers against the fabric of her breeches and blinked, trying to keep from tipping over at the sudden dizziness she felt. Lig sat in a chair in front of her, dressed in ordinary workmen's clothing instead of his usual robes. He looked like a harmless Doanan farmer, his white hair contrasting with his ruddy skin. His blue eyes were as piercing as ever, giving the lie to his appearance.

"Yes, she who was blind can see. That was only a hint of what we can offer."

"You don't want to offer me anything," she said. "You fear me."

"I fear nothing, dear lady. I do, however, find your raw talent intriguing. I look forward to learning more about you."

"Release me, and you'll learn all you need to." She looked at her arms. Bright spots of red dotted her sleeves and breeches. Her hands were crossed at the wrist in front of her, palms down. She pulled, but they wouldn't come away from each other. She lifted her magically trapped feet onto their toes, and tried to tap her heels against the floor. The mage who'd slapped her reached over and pushed her, toppling her onto her side. She kicked out at him, and was rewarded with another slap.

"Are you finished?" Lig asked, his voice as dry as Lidian sand.

"Are you breathing?"

"Fight if it makes you happy. It hardly matters. I have the right to take you where I wish." From his sleeve he withdrew a rolled parchment. Sitting down on the edge of the bed, he unrolled it and held it open for her to see. "By order of the most gracious King of the Nine Islands, the pirate Kestrel is declared an enemy of the Crown. Her life and goods are forfeit, and any who sail with her or offer her aid are also declared enemies of the Crown." He rolled the parchment and returned it to his sleeve. "You see? Your only choice is to give yourself over to my protection."

Protection. An unusual way to name her enslavement. He probably even believed his lie. "How did you get here?" She hated herself for asking, but anything she could find out might be useful.

He smiled. "Don't you mean how did we arrive so quickly? Unlike you, we do not need ships to travel from one place to another." He brought his face close to hers, his words cutting into her like a knife. "I don't usually share our practices with the public, but since you'll be one of us soon, I'm inclined to generosity. We collect a child from the street, one of the many thrown aside to fend for themselves. In a lengthy, and judging by the screaming, painful ritual, we spill the child's blood while arranging the

entrails into a pleasing pattern and speaking the proper incantation. The gods, in gratitude for our thoughtful sacrifice, transport
us to the destination of our choosing. I'd be delighted to show
you. Unfortunately, the ship must also be transported. We'll be
taking the *Thanos* for our return trip. It must be returned to His
Majesty, of course. Besides, there just aren't enough spare children for our uses here." His breath was hot against her cheek.
"Isn't it lucky you were never chosen for our purposes?"

She'd never known for certain what happened to those poor
children who fell into the Danisoban clutches. She spent years
living in the alleys and hideaways with the other street children,
who told stories to each other about the atrocities the Danisoban
mages committed, but no one found proof. Not that city guards
would have acted if the orphans found bothered reporting what
they suspected. Any time a child disappeared, only the other urchins even cared. The few adults who noticed them would only
be relieved at one less thieving brat robbing their market stalls.
Now, so many years later, Kestrel heard an actual confession, but
she remained as powerless as the orphan child she'd been. All
that blood spilled, only to allow mages to commit their wicked-
ness. Their sort of magic demanded its due. Anger swept through
her, a wave of rage for all the death he must have left in his wake.
"One day, mage, I'll show you how lucky I feel."

"I look forward to it. Until then, you're mine."

Kestrel spat blood onto the bedclothes. Her lip must have
split under the mage's blows. She struggled to right herself. "I'll
take my chances on a trial before the king."

"The trial is being held as we speak. Your presence isn't necessary. We happen to have a messenger spell that displays your
treasonous actions, not to mention the evidence we found aboard
the *Thanos*. A book you had no right to own. We showed mercy
to the bookseller, by the way. He paid with his sight. You, by attempting to read our secret texts, are guilty of a greater crime. By
the time we arrive, they'll have found you guilty and decided your
sentence." He extended a finger and shook it at her. "Wicked
girl. As impertinent as you may be, I'd still rather take you to our
enclave. You have secrets to share, secrets I'm determined to pry
out of you one way or another. But if you'd prefer death, possession of that book is enough of a crime. Luckily we retrieved it.

You'll hang within an hour of your return, and your men will hang with you. Or, I can have sentence passed here. Save you the long wait. And I'll study your corpse instead."

He'd kill her on the spot, and carry her remains back to Eldraga without a backward glance. She should have guessed. Even if the king was a man of honor, as Binns had insisted, the Danisobans were the real power. If they could show what she'd done, her reasons wouldn't matter.

Lig was still talking. "His Majesty will be especially sorry to lose the Knave. The man was a skillful agent, but reading confidential correspondence cannot be condoned." He waved a battered piece of paper. The letter from the Scion. Her belly spasmed. That letter was safe in her cabin last night. Which meant Lig had been aboard the *Thanos*. Were her men still alive? She wouldn't have been surprised if Lig had killed them all, to save himself the trouble of a trial. "Clearly you've enticed the Knave into your web. A shame, really." He widened his eyes in mock innocence. "I exercise a bit of influence. If you want me to intercede with the royal decision, you have only to ask."

And there it was. "What's the price of my asking?" she asked, hating the tremor in her voice.

Lig sat back in his chair, and looked toward his man. "You see, Brother? She may be a pirate and a thief, but she can be reasoned with." He tilted his head. "The depwal you found. It's an excellent specimen, indeed. And already tame. I found it curled up sleeping in the captain's cabin. I admit I'm excited to learn how you caught and tamed it. It suits his Majesty's purposes nicely."

No. He had the lizard. Kestrel felt tears welling, and forced them back. She wouldn't cry in front of this man. "We both know this has nothing to do with the king."

"Indeed. And now it has nothing to do with you."

"What are you planning to do to it?" She couldn't keep herself from asking. The poor little beast didn't deserve the kind of fate she imagined Lig had in mind. No one did.

"You needn't concern yourself. It's just an animal, after all. I'm surprised you let it roam so freely, with that sting it has."

She'd spent enough time with the lizard to know it had no stinger. But the parchment had mentioned something about its skin being poisonous. Could that be what Lig meant? And if it was so poisonous, why hadn't she been injured? Yet another mystery about the difference between herself and the Danisobans, one she intended to keep tucked away for as long as possible. The less Lig knew about her, the better.

"We've secured it in a cage, nice and tight, where it cannot hurt anyone. Seeing as you did fulfill your last task, I could be persuaded to allow your men to slip away in the night. What few men you have left."

He had her men, he had McAvery and he had the lizard. Lig hadn't mentioned the dancer. She wondered if he even knew about her. Nasrin could make herself look younger, perhaps she could make herself look like someone else entirely. She could be hiding in plain sight aboard the ship, as a common deckhand. Until Kestrel was sure, she wouldn't say anything. "My men may already have gone."

"If they could lift the holdfast I placed around the *Thanos*, I'm sure they'd have flown like the savages they are. Their fate rests in your hands. They can't even jump the railing unless I allow it."

A holdfast. Damn him. An invisible wall that surrounded whatever structure on which it was cast. She'd heard of such a thing being used to protect homes from thieves but she hadn't thought it could stop a ship from sailing. But he didn't admit to killing her remaining crew. She tucked that small bit of good news away for later. "Binns?"

Lig cocked his head to one side and turned his eyes to the ceiling, as if pondering some knotty problem. "Artemus Binns is guilty of treason as much as you, since he provided assistance and aid while knowing what you had done. Under the law, he should be arrested and his holdings confiscated. However, seeing as he was a loyal servant to the crown for so long, he could, I suppose, be allowed to remain here. Once you're securely locked away, there's little trouble he could cause, at his age."

"So if I go with you willingly, you'll leave Binns and my men alone."

He tilted his head in assent.

It was the closest thing to an answer she was likely to get. "You haven't answered my question. What price do you ask of me?"

"I thought that was understood. You'll return to the Enclave with me, where you'll remain under our close supervision. You wanted to read the *Conjurr* badly enough to break the law. Now you can finish studying it while we study you. We're eager to know what makes you so special."

She'd had twenty years of freedom. Twenty years that should have belonged to the Danisobans already. If Lig wanted to study her, that meant she'd stay alive, even if it was a life of captivity. She'd die behind their walls, that she knew, but the wind off the water would bring her the scent of the tides changing, and the sky above would still be filled with clouds and sunshine. She'd have her memories of her life on the water and they would have to sustain her. Along with the knowledge that Binns and McAvery still lived, somewhere. If that was the price of keeping them alive, she'd pay it. "Fine. I'll go with you. You'll leave Binns and my men alone, and allow McAvery to return to his life."

Lig tapped one bony finger against his chin. "I did say that, yes. And His Majesty would accept my word in the matter. As he always does." He leaned close to her again, holding her gaze with his own. "Although it occurs to me that I spoke in haste. Your men are pirates. They'll be carousing in pubs an hour after you enter the Enclave, and will have forgotten your name within a week. But the Knave — I fear I'd have to waste time stopping him from climbing the walls and making rash attempts to rescue you. I shall have to consider the Knave's fate a little more carefully."

She glared at him. "If he dies, so do you. Even while I'm trapped with you, the day will come when you forget to watch me close, and that will be the day I cut your throat."

Lig leaned back in his chair. "You've such a delicious sense of humor, my dear. Please feel free to continue making jokes. We sail in the morning. Until then, you'll remain here, under our watch." He rose and crossed to the door. "Brother Tel has volunteered to stay by your side. I've arranged food for you. Eat." He waved a hand toward her. "*Hesh kerra abranto.*"

Her lips locked together, and the fog over her eyes returned, obliterating her sight.

"My magic is far greater than you know, Kestrel. And you have nowhere to run." The door slammed closed.

Kestrel cursed, the sound nothing but grunts in her current

state. She had to find a way to escape, to take back her ship and sail far away from Lig's influence. Nasrin would know a way to lift the holdfast course; she'd have to.

Footsteps approached in the hallway, and the door opened again. Rough hands sat her up straight, and a voice murmured the strange words again. Her lips opened, and this time she was careful not to give her captor a reason to believe she would try to spell him. "Eat," he said, "but make no attempt at your witchery, or we'll beat you senseless and let you starve."

Kestrel raised her joined wrists. "Am I allowed to use my hands, or must I lick the food off the floor?"

A shadow moved in front of her, and she flinched. "Nay, lass, 'tis only me. I'll feed you."

Binns. He was alive, and as far as she could tell from his voice, unharmed. She was so relieved, she nearly wept. But the mage was still in the room. She tilted her face up. "How do I rate having the innkeeper himself to wait on me?"

"Mages sent the barmaid home and locked my doors tight. I had to put this together myself." His hand laid gently on her shoulder as he settled himself on the bed next to her. "Your favorite. Salt fish in bread. And ale to wash it down."

Was he joking? He better than anyone knew how she hated salt fish. Or was this his way of telling her something? She wished she could see his face, read his eyes. "Ummm," she said, trying to insert a note of sarcasm in the sound. "Delicious. Leave it to you to remember, Artie."

He squeezed her shoulder again, and let go. "Right you are, my girl. You'll feel better after you eat."

The edge of a cup nudged at her lip, and she opened her mouth, catching the scent of ale. She gulped, only then noticing a stringent burn to the taste. She choked, and drew back.

"Sorry, lass, did I give you too much? This is our new Nazareen brew." The shadow that was Binns leaned closer. "Has a snap to it, guaranteed to fix you right up."

Nazareen . . . Nasrin. Binns wouldn't have said her name so transparently if it wasn't safe. So the Danisobans didn't know about the dancer. Kestrel wondered what Nasrin added to the ale to make it fix her right up, as Binns had said. What if she'd been waiting for a chance to poison Kestrel all along? Kestrel stopped herself, taking a slow breath to calm the panicked thoughts swirling into her mind. Binns wouldn't involve himself with a plot to kill her. She was letting her imagination run wild, and this wasn't the time for it.

"Here, lass, take a bite of the bread and fish, too."

She steeled herself for the acrid bite of salt fish, but she tasted something bitter along with it. A bitterness similar to the ale's. "Delicious," she said around the mouthful. Alternating between food and drink, she finished eating quickly. Even with the overly salty fish biting her tongue.

"There now, my girl. I know everythin' looks like rain right now, but you'll be starin' at blue skies soon. Remember what I told you, about every new day? This'll be yours, is all. Who knows, mayhap you'll like bein' a mage. Fixin' broken things, changin' the weather, all with a wave of your hand. Not that I ever doubted you could do that on your own. Shucks, soon I'll be readin' books about your accomplishments."

He was trying to tell her something, but what? She wished her mind was clearer, that she could puzzle out the clues he was tossing her way. Did he mean for her to remember something from the Danisoban book? Or perhaps she was reading too much into his words, hoping for a plan that didn't exist. "Artie, I'm sorry I pulled you into this mess."

"Shush, girl. It was my pleasure. One last adventure before I grow old and gray." He chuckled. "I'm no threat any longer. Lig himself said I could stay here until my inn fell down around my ears. I'll be watched for a time, I imagine, but what trouble can I cause once you've gone off?"

She let her body fall against him, wishing she could put her arms around him. "You've been good to me, Artie. Take care of yourself, please?"

"Always, my girl" He patted her cheek, and rose from the bed. His footsteps thumped across the room to the door. He stopped, she supposed to wait for someone to let him out. "Why don't you take a nap, Kes? You'll need your strength for the trainin' to come." The door opened and closed again. The mage spoke his words, closing off Kestrel's ability to speak, and she heard the creak of wood. He said nothing else to her, for which she was grateful. She needed to think.

Binns and Nasrin had cooked something up together. Whatever they'd just fed her, and now wanting her to sleep. It had to
mean something. She hardly dared to hope they'd found some
way to escape all this. But she had nothing better to do than wait.
She might as well do as her old captain suggested. Tipping herself sideways on the bed. she closed her damaged eyes against the
faint light. Now that she was awake, she feared she wouldn't be
able to pass out on her own, that she'd lie on the bed with her
mind careening in all different directions, but to her surprise, she
felt herself slipping down into the soft caverns of sleep.

A voice was calling to her, a voice she couldn't quite understand,
calling her from far away. She tried to look around, but the darkness was absolute. Nothing but shadows on shadows, veils of
night wrapped around her, keeping her separate from the world.
"Where are you?" she whispered. "What is this place?" She
reached out, and realized her arms were no longer bound together. Nor were her legs. She stood up, and tried to take a step forward. She wasn't awake. She wasn't asleep. But in this realm of
shadows, wherever it was, she was free. She walked slowly, her
hands stretched out in front of her, not sure if the next step
would send her falling into an unseen danger.

"Stop trying so hard," the voice murmured. "You might speak
aloud, and your guard will hear." The voice was faint, but it
seemed as if someone was yelling just to make that much sound.
Whoever it was must be very far away, indeed.

"Who are you?"

An image of eyes dark with wisdom shimmered into focus.
Nasrin.

"Who released me? Where's the mage who was watching
me?"

"You're not free, and he's in the room," the voice was a soft
breath now. "I'm speaking to you within a dream. Be still and
listen."

No dream ever felt as real as this. Kestrel let her hand fall to
her side. Everything about magic astounded her, and being
drawn into a waking dream was just the latest astonishment.
Questions crowded her thoughts, but they would have to wait.

The last thing she wanted was for the baleful Danisoban watching her sleeping self to notice anything happening. Kestrel focused on her breath, taking each more slowly than the last. She imagined the borders of her body softening, blending with the shadows, until she became as dark and silent as the space around her.

"Better." The voice was easier to hear now, and didn't seem to be straining. "Do not speak, only listen."

Kestrel nodded, not sure if Nasrin could see her. It wasn't as if she could do anything else in this place.

"The food contained a combination of herbs that together force your mind to open. It is not the method I would have chosen, but I can find no other way to reach you. Now that I have, I am going to work with you, show you how to undo what was done to you."

"I can't."

"You must. Your blindness is no longer due to injury, but artifice. Rest will not overcome it, and the luxury of time is not on our side. The mage intends to sail away on your ship in the morning. If you hope to make any kind of stand, it must be done tonight."

"What do I do?"

"You are going to dance from within."

Dance from within? What did that mean? She breathed out slowly, trying to rid herself of the worrisome thoughts pulling at her attention. Nasrin had tried to warn her about the danger of indiscriminate magic. Kestrel let the magic take control, and learned a hard lesson. This time, she had no choice but to hold herself together.

"Your body will remain asleep, but your soul will leap and turn in the steps of the dance." An image of Nasrin as Kestrel had first seen her shimmered into her mind. "Imagine yourself standing next to me."

Imagine herself . . . this was awfully similar to the shape-changing magic McAvery taught her on Eldraga when they first met. Was that the entire trick to magic, just imagining what you wanted? It couldn't be that simple. It couldn't. She focused her thoughts, remembering herself reflected in a mirror. Short of stature, and slender, with powerful legs and arms from working all her life. Black hair in many tight, long braids, all drawn into a thick queue by a strip of leather. Wide dark eyes, set in a brown face. She stopped. Her eyes had been brown once. She'd always thought they were a common color, but now that her eyes were glazed with silver, she missed the brown. Should she imagine the silver? She found that the new image didn't come, so she let the brown she knew have its place. She saw herself in her usual breeches and a red shirt, the color pleasing against her skin, and her feet bare. Last, she imagined the gem McAvery gave her, the one she wore always, on its leather lanyard around her neck. Slowly, once she thought she'd covered everything, she envisioned herself appearing next to the image of the dancer, transparent first, and finally solidifying. She smiled, and her double smiled back.

"Well done. Now, follow my steps. Dance only the steps I demonstrate to you. More important, do not leave me behind. Stay in control of your movements."

The dancer raised her right arm, letting it float down, elbow leading, in time with the music of Kestrel's heart beating. Kestrel matched her. Their right legs slid out, toes pointed, swept in a wide circle across their bodies, then finished with a stamp. They repeated the movements on the opposite side.

"Now, dance the combination of movements again, and again. While you are dancing, gently direct the power to lift the layers of darkness surrounding you. They represent the magic that has blinded, muted and trapped you. Your power is stronger. Believe what I tell you, and remove the spell."

Once such a ridiculous thought would have sent Kestrel snorting off to the quarterdeck. Not anymore. She continued the dance, moving in her mind the way Nasrin showed her. The tingle rose within her body, but instead of prickling at her skin in the usual way, it seemed to sparkle in her blood, bubbling like a fountain up her legs and into her chest. She'd never felt so glorious. This was what magic should feel like. No headaches or bruising, no effort. No wonder the mages guarded power so jealously. The potential before her was just as wild and maddening as the way she'd felt on the deck that day, but instead of fire, she became water. Cool white water crashing at the edge of the shore, smoothing the sand as it rolled back to its source, tiny diamonds of spray forming rainbows in the sun. Most of all, no pain. She wanted to throw her arms wide and spin with the joy of it, but Nasrin snorted, a disparaging sound that reminded Kestrel to stay in control.

The bubbling rose until it settled in her head, behind her forehead. Now she was a babbling brook, no wider than a handspan, sparkling water tumbling over waving plants beneath. She imagined the water eddying off the main stream, pouring over her eyes. Washing away the gray, the shadows. Healing her.

"Nicely done, *rais.*" Nasrin's voice was soft, as if she'd wandered further away.

Kestrel's movements faltered, and she stopped dancing. Her image slowed, stopped, slumped to the ground and curled into a ball before fading from view. Nasrin's image was fading as well. The image was no more than a wisp of light, and the voice was becoming almost impossible to hear. "You are in terrible danger." The voice was a whisper. "Wake."

With the last word, Kestrel snapped into awareness. The air around her was thick and hot, stinging down her throat and forcing her to cough. She struggled to sit up, expecting the attendant mage to push her over any second, only then realizing the dance worked — her hands and legs were free. She opened her eyes, blinking to clear them. Her sight was restored, her lips unclosed, just as Nasrin had said. The sky outside the windows was dark, the room swathed in shadow, but nothing like the darkness in her dream. Night had fallen. How long had she been asleep? The mage's chair lay tipped sideways on the floor near her bed. No wonder he wasn't striking her — her guard had vanished. She was alone in the room. Alone and free. Time to run.

Standing up slowly, she bent and slapped at her legs, to wake her muscles from their long reclining. Only then did she notice the smell on the air. Burning wood, as if the chimney in the common room had become blocked and was sending smoke back into the room and up the stairs. That, or something worse.

She crossed the room to the door. The iron latch was hot, hotter than the air, and she snatched her hand back. Holding her hand against her chest, she leaned an ear to the wood. It, too, felt hot against her skin. Outside the door, she could hear a roaring sound. Roaring and crackling. Fire. The inn was on fire.

# CHAPTER 19

*She has been gutted and has lost a man . . .*
— JOHN MASEFIELD, *The Wanderer*

Kestrel ran to the window. It wasn't designed to open, built right into the wall. She pressed her hands against the frame, hoping it would be loose from years of temperature changes making the wood swell and shrink, but nothing gave. The glass was spotted with grime and impossible to see through, but it was too thick to break with a fist. She'd avoid burning to death by bleeding to death instead. She stood back, lifted a foot and aimed her boot heel at the lower pane.

"Here we are, together again." The voice surprised her, nearly throwing her off balance. She hopped on one leg, trying to keep from falling, and winced at a twinge in her knee as she turned to look behind her.

A man stood in the open doorway. The man from Eldraga, who'd passed her in Binns' pub talking about nets and fish. Smoke billowed behind him, and heat from the fire pulsed into the room like blood from a mortal wound. He smiled, his face soot-smudged and his hair a scorched mess. Probably because he'd trapped Binns in front of him, holding him like a shield. The smile was so familiar. The man twisted one of Binns' arms behind him, and a long, vicious knife rested tight against the skin of the old man's throat.

Kestrel licked her lips, ready to whistle the knife out of his hand, but the air was so hot and dry she couldn't draw a breath without coughing. The man pressed the flat of the knife against Binns' neck. "No magic, there. I've got a good hold on my weapon. I turn it just right, and your friend's throat will be sliced open like a pig to the spit."

"Let him go," she growled.

"Not very original." He took another step into the room, pushing Binns ahead of him. "Funny how much this reminds me of the last time we met. It was warm then, as I recall."

"You have me. Just let her go, while she can still get out," Binns pleaded.

"We've met?" A thought rattled just beyond her memory's reach, something she knew she should be recalling, but she couldn't put a finger on it. Something about his eyes, perhaps. Or that smile. If she could only think.

"I'm hurt you don't remember. After all we shared." A loud crash broke her concentration, followed by an explosion of sparks outside the open door. She started, but the man laughed. "Ah, there go the stairs. The floor will follow before very long."

Binns' eyes were wild. "Run, girl," he said. The man turned the blade up to Binns' jaw, nicking the skin just enough to allow a trickle of blood to dribble down to his collar.

"Yes, run. Leave your friend to die, just as you should have done before. But you won't will you?" He stamped one foot, and sparks shot up from between the boards. "You bought yourself a year, at my expense. I hope you enjoyed it."

He expects me to remember him, she thought frantically. The only time she'd been facing someone threatening Binns this way was on a tower in the king's palace. None of those men survived. He had no markings on his chest like a Eusebian would, and he was clearly no Danisoban. Where were the mages anyway? One man couldn't possibly have defeated them. "What do you want?" Kestrel yelled.

"I want what you took from me. I want what was mine. But since that avenue is closed for now, I'll have to be satisfied with watching you both die."

Kestrel tapped her foot on the floor, hoping to bring up the magic. She'd sent swords flying across a dark ship's deck before — disarming one man shouldn't be too hard.

"Oh no, not this time. I won't be ruined twice by your tricks," he snarled. Raising his arm, he drove the knife point down in a swift stroke, burying it to the hilt into Binns' neck.

"Artie!" Kestrel rushed forward as the man pulled his knife free and stepped back, letting Binns slide to the floor. Kestrel flung herself to her knees to catch her friend. Blood pumped from his wound in great gouts. Kestrel bunched the ends of his shirt in her hands, shoving the fabric against the blood and pressing to staunch the bleeding.

The man backed away into the hallway, his features glistening from the flames. His hand and arm were stained with Binns' blood, and as she stared at him, he lifted his hand to his mouth, licking the blood off his thumb. Another crash shook the floor. "I'll have to be going now," he said, as if sorry to say it. He dashed out of her sight.

Binns lifted one hand and tried to wrap his fingers around Kestrel's arm. His grip was as weak as an infant's. "Lass," he whispered. "Save yourself."

"We'll go together," she whispered, swallowing back the lump that had formed in her throat. "I won't leave you here." She lifted her hand to check the wound. Blood soaked Binns' shirt, the hot metal smell surrounding her even against the burning wood. Kestrel pressed the fabric down again. The air was thick and hot, almost too hot to breathe. Smoke billowed above their heads.

Taking his hands in hers, she guided them to the makeshift bandage. "Hold this here," she said. "I'm going to see if we can still use the stairs." Crawling on hands and knees, she looked around the edge of the door. Heat washed over her, baking her tender skin and making her eyes water. She saw nothing but painfully bright light and vicious heat, flames filling the space everywhere she looked. Even if she could have navigated what was left of the stairs, she couldn't get to them through the inferno of the hallway. They'd have to go out the window.

A crumpled heap in a black robe lay a few feet from the door. A Danisoban, probably the one who'd been left to watch her. She reached out a toe, and nudged the body. It rolled, revealing a monstrous gash in his throat and a pool of congealing blood bubbling from the heat. Blood . . . Binns.

She rushed back to his side. His skin was pale, his lips white, and his hands had fallen away from the wound. Blood coursed more slowly now, but that didn't seem to be a good thing. "Artie," she gasped. "Can you hear me?" His dull eyes stared upward. "Artie, hang on. I'm going to break the window. Just keep breathing."

"Always proud," His words drifted from him like a breeze,

and she could hardly hear him over the roar of the flames around them.

"No, Artie, I'm breaking the window. I'll be right back."

"Knew you were special," His chest lifted and fell. Blood was pooling on the floor under Binns' neck, soaking into his shirt. "My girl," his eyes rolled upward, and his head lolled to one side.

"No, Artie!" Kestrel sobbed. "I'll get you out." She shook his shoulders. "Artie! Wake up!" She slapped his face. His mouth had gone slack, the meat of his plump jaw quivering under her assault. "Artie, you can't leave me!" She collapsed onto his bloody chest, weeping. No heartbeat sounded, no breathing at all. He was gone.

Kestrel wrapped her arms around his neck, hugging his lifeless body to her chest. "Artie!" she screamed. Rocking back and forth, she wept, her tears drying instantly on her cheeks. She should have followed the man, she should have paid more attention when she first caught sight of him. She'd been so involved in saving herself, she hadn't noticed the world ending around her.

Another crash from somewhere down the hallway shocked her back to her situation. The wooden floor under her knees was hot as shore sand on a summer's day. The flooring might collapse at any second. She had to escape before she burned with the building. Letting Artie down slowly, she took his hands, crossed them on his chest, and closed his eyes. "I'm so sorry, Artie," she whispered. She leaned forward to kiss his wrinkled brow, whispered a silent prayer for his forgiveness, and rose to her feet.

The hallway was too hot to approach. However the man had escaped, that way was closed to her. The window was all she had left. The air was so dry, she couldn't whistle. Cack this magic. It was never useful. She scrambled to her feet, looking wildly around for the chair. It lay on its side, where someone had knocked it. Taking it up, she slammed it onto the floor, splitting the pieces until she had one chair leg loose in her hand. Aiming for the lower panes, she ran at the window and battered the chair leg at the glass, striking it with all the anger and grief inside her. The glass cracked under her onslaught. She kept hitting, until the thick panes shattered.

Cool air rushed in. She gulped great lungfuls, the air almost chilly in her singed chest. Behind her, flames roared into the open door, licking at Binns' body and catching his hair. Her time had run out. She ran the chair leg around the window's edge to break off any remaining shards still attached to the wood. As soon as she'd cleared the opening, she leaned out of the window. A few feet below was the thatched rooftop of the shop across the alley between them. It was luck alone that the thatching wasn't blazing yet. She'd have to jump, and hope the thatching didn't give way with the impact.

Reaching up to grip the window from outside, she carefully eased her body out, sitting on the sill to ready herself. The breeze that heralded the change of the tides blew the smoke away even as it billowed past her. Her tongue stuck to the top of her mouth, but the air was thick with moisture. It might be enough. She parted her lips, and drew in the humid air, then licked her lips with what small amount of spit she could create. It would have to be enough. She whistled softly, as if calming a baby.

Her power responded, tickling up from the depths of her skin. She trilled, forming the air into a thick cushion between herself and the rooftop. Taking another breath, she continued the tune, and let herself slide forward from the windowsill.

The walls of the pub creaked behind her, and the floor inside collapsed. Fire billowed up from below and shot out the window. Kestrel cried out from the shock, but the cushion she'd created was a cloud around her, letting her fall as delicately as a feather toward the thatched roof. She landed on her back, bouncing on the hard straw. She blinked, staring up at the window from which she'd come. Fire belched through the opening she'd made. The whole building was an inferno. Artie's pub was gone. Artie was gone.

Sobs racked her body. She knew she needed to run, to get away from the fire, but she couldn't move. She rolled onto her side, like a child, and wept for what she'd lost.

When her tears ended, she didn't know how long she'd lain there, but suddenly water was dropping from the sky. Rain? Now that all was destroyed, the rains come? She shook her head and looked up, in time for another drenching, but saw only stars above her. Kestrel rolled to the edge of the roof and peered over.

A small crowd of islanders had gathered, forming a fire line to carry buckets of water from the market well to the building. The water she initially thought was rain splashed up from below. The building's owner was soaking his building, in hopes of saving it from the same fate Binns' pub was suffering. Several feet away, watching the pub burn, stood Lig and his magi. Lig was clearly angry at one of them, waving his hands at the pub and shouting, though between the roar of the fire and the cries of the islanders, Kestrel couldn't hear him at all. It appeared that the fire wasn't his doing. Why hadn't he used his power to stop it? Surely a Danisoban had the skill for something so simple. Unless he'd been distracted long enough, until the fire was too strong. But what could have distracted him?

She was free of him for the present. Groaning with the effort, Kestrel rose to her hands and knees and crawled to the back edge of the roof. The alley below was dark and empty of people. Rolling onto her belly, she slid her legs over the side and let herself hang, then dropped, landing easily on the dirt. Artie would have appreciated how often she seemed to jump out of windows, she thought. Wherever he was now.

She stood, trying to get her bearings. The harbor lay to the west, but unless Lig had raised his holdfast, she couldn't board the *Thanos*. Her own magic wasn't strong enough for such a thing, and she didn't dare attempt to dance again, for fear of causing more devastation. There might be a ship on which she could stow away, but the islands weren't big enough for her to stay hidden forever. She needed to put enough distance between herself and Lig that following her would be more trouble than it was worth. She laughed at the irony. At last she had a real reason to go where Nasrin wanted, and had no way to do so.

"*Rais*, you must be quiet."

Kestrel spun, flattening her back to the wall. From the shadows, the dancer emerged. She wore breeches and a shirt, her hair pulled away from her face and tucked into a floppy hat. Her face was smudged with ash. Anyone passing her in the street wouldn't look twice at her. As she came closer, her eyes widened, and she reached out toward Kestrel. "Are you injured?"

Kestrel looked down at her chest. Her shirt was blood-soaked; her face, sticky with Artie's blood. She crossed her arms tightly. "I'm all right."

"But you are bleeding."

"It's not mine."

Nasrin stepped back. "Whose?"

"It's—" Kestrel swallowed the lump that threatened to choke her. "A man killed Artie." A sob escaped her now that she'd said it out loud.

Nasrin pressed a hand to her chest. Her eyes filled with concern. "I am so sorry, *rais*. Is there anything I can do for you?"

"Maybe later. How did you manage to leave the *Thanos*?" Kestrel wasn't ready to talk about Binns yet. Not while the mention of his name tore her heart open, and not until she was far away from here.

"Happenstance."

Not again, damn it. Did this woman ever give anyone a straight answer? Kestrel took a slow breath, her grief settling into her bones and letting irritation take the fore. She'd just watched her oldest friend bleed his life out on a wooden floor, his world burning around him, and she desperately desired vengeance against the men responsible. She looked at Nasrin and spoke slowly so as not to lose control. "I want to believe you, and I know I'll need your help, so understand that when you offer vague answers to the simplest questions, it warns me you can't be trusted. I can't force you to speak, but I can leave you behind. Take your talk of lost daughters and destiny and tell someone else. I imagine you could earn a coin or two in the pubs with your tale. You'd find a far less demanding audience."

"It is not my wish to confound you, *rais*." Nasrin shrugged, and let her hand fall to her side. "I know you wanted me to stay hidden, but I decided to visit the market for a bit in the morning. I slipped away from the ship in this disguise. While wandering the stalls, I heard the young barmaid who worked for Artemus gossiping that she'd been released from service for the day because the mages commandeered the place, holding a dangerous criminal. Who else could it be but you? I purchased the herbs I needed and found Artemus in his kitchen. I told him to feed you the herbs if he could and I would take care of the rest. I had no idea they intended to kill him." She reached out to take Kestrel's hands in her own. "I am truly sorry."

Kestrel stared at her. The dancer was hiding something, but

not what Kestrel suspected. She feared she'd done wrong. Even though her choice was the only thing that saved them both from being prisoners of the magi. Kestrel squeezed her hands and released them. "You couldn't have helped Artie. And under the circumstances, I'm grateful you didn't obey me. I'd be trapped in that inferno." She slipped to the end of the alley, peering out at the street. More people had gathered, some to throw water at the flames but most gawking at the excitement. Bloody peasants. She'd be willing to lay money they'd been drinking in the pub hours before, and here they stood, gaping at the evening's entertainment.

And there, to her surprise, just past the crowd, stood Menja Lig, and next to him, the man who murdered Binns. They appeared to be arguing, but she couldn't hear them over the cries of the onlookers and the roar of the fire. The man waved his arms in the direction of the burning pub. Lig poked a finger into the man's chest, clearly making some sort of point. The other man rocked back under his assault, but didn't step away. The two were intent on each other. She rather liked seeing Lig not getting his own way for once, but the man opposing him deserved no quarter from her. A thought flashed into her mind like lightning. She could destroy them both from here, dance to awaken the magic and unleash the silver flame. Watch it consume them in a tornado of magical pain. And why not? Revenge for Artie, and freedom for herself all in one go. She straightened and reached out a toe to tap against the ground.

"What are you doing?"

Kestrel spun in a slow whirl, bending her knees and popping up before tapping her toes again. The magic bubbled within her. Too late to save Binns. Too late to save anyone. She raised her arms high, letting the momentum pull her tall. They wanted to know what she could do. She would show them. She would show them all.

A hand fell on her arm, snapping her concentration back to the darkness and smoke. Jerking her dancing to a stop. The first inklings of power faded. "Let me go," she growled.

"*Rais*, we can leave here."

"I don't need to leave here." She flung her elbow up. Nasrin released her, hopping out of the way. "I can kill them. The world is better off without men like them. You know I'm right."

"If you attack the mage while your ability is still raw with anger, he will feel it. Long before you strike him. You will be cut down." Nasrin's eyes were hard. "Others depend on you."

"You mean you?"

"Philip lives."

The words hit her like a fist. McAvery still lived. After Lig's taunting, she hadn't dared hope. "Another reason we should rid the world of those two damnable villains. Lig intends to kill him once they return to court. Assuming he even reaches Pecheta. Lig might just decide to toss him, chains and all, into the ocean." She gripped the dancer's shoulder, the way she would one of her crew. "We can do this, together. You can show me the right steps. No one is looking at us."

"And when you succumb to the power again? I can't carry you by myself all the way to the docks." Nasrin shook her head, and pulled herself free of Kestrel's hand. "Better if we go to the ship now. We can sneak aboard, free your men, and Philip. While Lig is distracted by—" she stopped, her brow furrowing as she searched for the right words. "One you thought safely disposed of."

"Who?"

"The fish that slipped its net. The man who hoped to wear the crown of the Nine Islands, whose ambitions were thwarted by your actions."

A sickening creak moaned from behind Kestrel, followed by an abrupt crash. Sparks exploded from the pub's roof as it gave way, falling into the inferno. Debris flew wildly in every direction, and the crowd scattered, screaming and patting away the stinging ash as it fell on them. The only men who stood their ground were Lig and the murderer. Their argument seemed to have stopped long enough for them to stare at the collapse of the building. Kestrel squinted, trying to make out his face in the distance. It couldn't be. Yet there he stood, his chin jutting out proudly even as the mage dressed him down. The man who killed Binns, who burned the pub and assumed he left her for dead. The fish who slipped its net. "Bloody Grace," she murmured in horror. How had she not seen it before? As if a curtain had been raised, the answer became obvious.

"Jeremie?"

She should have known. Should have recognized him. Former Crown Prince Jeremie, the king's only son. Once in line for
the throne, until his treacherous plans against his father were revealed by Kestrel and her crew. When she saw him last, he'd
been proud and demanding, wearing only the best clothing,
sleeping on only the softest pillows, dining on only the finest
wines and food. Every inch a royal. The thing he wanted most of
all was the one thing he could not have — his father's seat on the
throne. Despite his overindulged nature, he nearly killed Artie in
a misguided attempt to achieve what he desired, and it had taken
what little skill she had with her magic to stop him. She left a
blade wound in his belly, and thought him certainly dying from it.

Wherever he'd been imprisoned hadn't been an easy place.
She wouldn't have believed she would ever forget his arrogant
face, but he looked different now. He carried himself with an
anger that radiated from his very flesh. The softness was gone
from his body, his movements tight and his limbs grown angular
and sharp. The pampered prince had been replaced by a smold-
ering demon. Cack me for an idiot, she thought. Artie knew, at
the end. He tried to make her run, knowing she'd try to kill the
prince if she realized who he was. "You should have told me before," she murmured, though whether she was talking to the
dancer or to the dead man, she wasn't sure herself.

"If you will come with me, I swear I will tell you everything I
know. But the hour grows late."

Now that the pub was reduced to a pile of glowing coals, the
crowd was beginning to disperse. Lig grabbed the former prince
by his arm, and steered him away from the devastation and out of
her sight. When she could see them no longer, she faced Nasrin.
"What do you suggest?" she asked.

"He will lift the holdfast once he is at sea, in order to dispose
of his prisoners. We can catch up to the ship, slip aboard and
take back what is yours."

"Lig will be there." Her hand dropped to her hip, where a
sword should have hung. She felt helpless without some sort of
weapon. "He's been using magic longer than I've been alive.
Against him I'm no more threat than a child kicking a warrior's
shins. He'll gut me before I can take a step in his direction."

Nasrin's eyes were dark with purpose. "You are made of greater stuff, *rais*. I am determined to show you. I had hoped to be well on our way before the prince had your trail firmly detected."

"He's known where I was."

"What do you mean?" Nasrin frowned. "Why did you not tell me before?"

Kestrel wanted to think the dancer was joking, but her face didn't change. "You expected me to say anything to you? You extorted me, you tricked me into thinking I'd remain blind and you didn't bother to warn me that my eyes would look like this," she pointed at her face, "when you finally got 'round to repairing me. You played yourself off as some poor innocent dancer lost in the wilds of the Islands — what would make me think you had even the slightest awareness of Island politics? Not to mention that he's changed his appearance since I saw him last. He looks different enough to have fooled me. I assumed he was just another of the rascals who've been trying to best me for the last year." She threw her hands to the sky. "You blathered on about fish and their nets and never once said anything I could use."

The two women stared at each other, until Nasrin looked away. "I underestimated you, *rais*, and for that I beg your forgiveness. To our fortune, others have also underestimated you. That may prove advantageous."

Kestrel let her head drop back, searching the blackness above for even one familiar star. Smoke from the burning pub was still thick, and impossible to see through. Somewhere up there, in the heavens she couldn't see, were the stars she'd always trusted. They'd been there when she was born, and they'd be there long after she was gone. What sort of adventures had they witnessed? All the nonsense people busied themselves with, none of it meant anything to the stars. But such nonsense still meant something to the people who suffered. She was tired of running, tired of feeling eyes on her back. She could give up and let the Danisobans absorb her, or she could go down fighting. Why not go for the glorious ending, one the stars themselves might even spare a moment to notice? To chase the mage down, take the fight to his doorstep for once, would be an enormously satisfying adventure. Even if she didn't survive the encounter, at least she'd die on her feet, fighting. Kestrel tossed one last look over her shoulder, at Binns' ruined pub. She couldn't let Jeremie get away with what he'd done, nor with what he intended to do.

"Won't we need a vessel?" she asked finally.

"If we hurry, we can take one."

"You want to steal a ship?"

Nasrin shrugged. "You are a pirate, are you not?"

# CHAPTER 20

*How next the powers would use her to work ill*
*On suffering men; we had not long to wait.*
— JOHN MASEFIELD, *The Wanderer*

This late, the harbor should have been deserted, the sailors either abed, keeping deck watches or drinking in rough dockside taverns. Between the islanders rushing back and forth with buckets of water and the Danisobans hurrying to load their waterproof tarpaulins and mysterious boxes of unknown cargo onto the *Thanos*, the harbor seemed as busy as midday. Kestrel and Nasrin huddled in the shadow of a crate that smelled of animal dung. Lig and Jeremie boarded, followed by two Danisoban brothers leading a bound man between them. "Philip," she whispered. McAvery walked under his own power, albeit slowly. Knowing he was alive lifted a weight from her heart. She couldn't save Binns, but maybe she could save everyone else. McAvery's captors shoved him off the end of the gangplank, laughing as he stumbled onto the deck, and one of them made a humorless comment about pirates making prisoners walk off planks. Grabbing his bound arms, they led him to the hatch, and all three disappeared into the lower decks.

"Is the holdfast still in place?" Kestrel whispered.

Lig himself stood on the deck amidships, ordering her men to and fro. Not a one looked happy about it, either. She hadn't caught sight of Shadd. More than likely he'd put up a fight, and ended up locked in the cells belowdecks. She didn't want to assume the worst, not right now. The thought that he and McAvery might be there together, whispering to each other ways to escape, made her smile. Tom was at the wheel, a mage at his side holding a chart under his nose.

"I think the holdfast is released. There is usually an aura from such things, and I cannot see it. Perhaps the mage believes it no longer necessary, thinking you have died in the fire," Nasrin whispered.

"He's a fool if he takes that prince's word on my death."

"Jeremie will have been most convincing. Did he not kill one of Lig's own to get to you? Even if Lig chooses to test him, he believes you dead, and so will appear truthful."

Kestrel shook her head. "I can't help feeling this is a trap."

They'd arrived before Lig did, taking advantage of the excitement to move untroubled through the streets. Unfortunately the increased activity all over the docks had ruined any chance of stealing a small vessel. Plenty of sloops lay anchored close by, but there were simply too many eyes. If she had any hope of freeing her men, Kestrel's best chance was stowing away on her own ship. Which was dependent on finding a chance to slip aboard. She'd considered making Nasrin teach her to dance up some magic she could use to change her look, but the only people getting on and off the ship were Danisobans, and damned few of them. Lig would notice a new brother in his delegation, and if she tried to use an existing brother's face, she'd probably come face to face with her choice at the worst possible second. No, changing her look was a bad idea, for now. She had to find some other way to get aboard and hide in the bilges. Water was always pooling in the depths of a ship, and the mages wouldn't take the chance of wetting their feet.

"I know a pattern that makes the dancer unseen, but it takes time."

"How long?"

"At least a quarter-hour. And it does not mask sound. Oh," Nasrin said. "I believe the point is moot." The last two Danisobans were hustling up the board, as dockhands rushed around releasing mooring lines. A familiar clanking and whining echoed over the voices — the capstan was turning. They were weighing anchor. A breeze rose, blowing from inland toward the water. The sails belled as men loosed them, and the ship moved away from the dock's edge. The wind changed direction sharply. With a sick feeling in the pit of her belly, Kestrel realized Lig was creating the wind. To hell with secrecy, she thought, rising to her feet. I'll have to jump the distance, and hope I can find a weapon.

"Hey, you there!" The cry startled her, but it wasn't directed her way. One of the waiting tow skippers was yelling angrily after the *Thanos*. "It's against the law for you to be leaving Bix Harbor without a tow." Unlike the larger harbors of Pecheta and Eldraga, the Bix dockmaster required that all ships leaving have a tow out to the open water. Whether they needed it or not. Each tow boat was crewed by twenty-four oarmen belowdecks and one skipper in a square wheelhouse, who was in charge of tying on to the ships and guiding the tow out of the harbor. And collecting the charge from the ship's captain. The Bix dockmaster insisted it was necessary due to the cramped nature of Bix' harbor, but everyone knew it was his way of taking home a little extra money at the end of each day.

"*Rais*, they do not appear to be reinstating their holdfast. I have seen no mage reading a course over the ship, and the usual signs are absent. If they are distracted, it may be possible for us to . . ." she stopped, wrinkling her forehead. "What is it called, to sneak aboard?"

"Stow away," Kestrel said. So the barrier was lifted. But the only people freely moving around the *Thanos* were Danisobans. Not many, but enough to make boarding from the dock impossible. There was no way she could walk onto the ship without being seen. If she let the ship leave now, she had no chance of ever catching up again.

The tow skipper was releasing his lines as fast as he could, yelling orders to the men below, who'd probably been sleeping at their posts. He looked to be planning on chasing the *Thanos* down. Kestrel elbowed Nasrin. "There's our ride."

"*Rais*, what do you intend . . ." Nasrin began. Kestrel dragged her to her feet and they ran toward the tow. The skipper in the wheelhouse amidships called out the strokes at the top of his lungs while keeping his eye on the *Thanos*. Oars extended from the open ports, the ones on the seaward side dipping into the water and the ones along the dock pushing away. The stern deck was dark and unattended. Without slowing, Kestrel reached the dock's edge and leaped, pulling Nasrin with her. The dancer yipped in surprise. The tow boat sat a few feet low against the dock, and the fall was startling, but they both landed squarely. Kestrel scrambled to press her body against the wheelhouse wall, and Nasrin did the same.

"You think this little boat can catch up to the *Thanos*?" she asked.

"It can if I help." Kestrel pressed her lips together and blew, a low tone that rattled her back teeth. As the magic tingled through her limbs, she gathered the air against the stern, shaped it into a ball and rolled it, over and over, on the surface of the water, letting it push the boat along. It would have been easier with sails.

The skipper alternately called the strokes to his crew and yelled insults at the *Thanos*, which showed no intention of slowing down. Kestrel increased her volume, and let her body slide down the wall to the deck. Her head was beginning to throb. Nasrin watched her for a few seconds, with questions in her eyes that she didn't seem willing to ask. She extended a hand, rolling it in a circle at the wrist, letting the circling motion move up to her shoulder, her arm resembling a serpent slithering through the water. She repeated the movement on the other side, and finished with a slow turn. Kestrel wanted to watch, but she had to concentrate on her whistling. It was going to be hard enough to catch the *Thanos* as it was.

The oarsmen dipped and dragged their oars faster than she'd ever seen, and the skipper stopped yelling, stomping one foot on the deck to keep the time instead. He must have run out of air himself. She took another breath, her head spinning. Nasrin was still dancing next to her. She could hear the soft shuffles and steps as the dancer moved in her pattern. The tow boat was moving faster now, skipping over the waves with the grace and speed of a tiny sailboat, throwing splashes of water on deck every time it dropped into the swells. Kestrel wished she could see the skipper's face. He'd have to be wondering how his men were managing such a pace. The oarsmen themselves were probably wondering the same thing. She drew another breath and blew again. The tow boat leaped out of the water, and she heard startled cries from under her feet.

"*Rais*." Nasrin's voice was soft. "We are close enough to board. Take my hand."

Kestrel reached up, and let the dancer help her to her feet. She was so dizzy from whistling that her knees were shaking. Laying a hand against the wheelhouse wall, she peeked around the corner. The *Thanos* rose a few feet from the tow boat's bow, and the skipper had walked out to the railing to scream at the escaping ship. No one on the *Thanos* seemed to be paying him any attention. There were no curious faces at the railing, no one peering from the captain's cabin window.

"Hold on to me," Nasrin said, taking Kestrel's hands and placing them around her waist. Kestrel nodded, tightening her arms around the dancer and locking her fingers around her own elbows. The magic the dancer created pulsed around her, as like Kestrel's own as it could be. Nasrin angled both hands palms down, and seemed to push off of the deck, rising into the air and carrying Kestrel with her. Even suspecting what was about to happen, Kestrel started uncomfortably when her feet left the deck, her entire weight hanging from her grip on the dancer. The two women floated past the amazed skipper, who stopped his abuse of the *Thanos* and stared, his mouth open. The tow was already slowing, the distance between it and the larger ship expanding rapidly. Nasrin steered them toward the gunports. The doors were all closed. "I have to keep us in the air. Can you open one of those enough for us to slip inside?"

"If I let go, I'll fall." The wind was rushing past her ears.

"Do not use your hands." Nasrin's voice was calm, soothing.

Of course. Magic. So many years of avoiding the power, fearing anyone realizing what she could do — was she purposely forgetting to try now? Her love and her friends depended on her using every skill she knew to save their skins, and magic could very well be the balance tipper. The time had come for her to treat her magic as a tool, as useful as a sword or a belaying pin. She'd come so far, made so many mistakes learning to control herself. An ordinary pirate would fall. But she was no ordinary pirate.

Kestrel drew a breath, and whistled, forming the tune into a slender shape that slipped beneath the lip of the nearest gunport opening. She couldn't see the rope that pulled it open, but she knew where it must be. Could she do this without sight of it? She closed her eyes, trying to feel the gundeck she knew so well. The rope was where it should be. She sent the magic into the strands, drawing it down to raise the port. She wasn't sure she'd aimed right, but then the port rattled in its casing and rose. Kestrel pulled the rope all the way down and forced the free end to snake out of the opening. Nasrin floated toward it, rising until Kestrel's hands were level with the opening. "Let go of me, and climb inside."

Far below, the ocean churned, dark under the night sky. If she fell, she'd probably break her neck. The gunport was an inch away. She'd swung through the rigging of her ship with less certainty of safety. This was simple. Drawing her left arm even tighter around the dancer, she let go with her right and reached out. And caught the rope. Before she could lose her grip, she released the dancer, and held on to the rope with both hands. She dangled, feeling the toss and drop of her mighty ship, her body rolling against the hull. Nasrin lifted herself high enough to slide inside the square gunport. Kestrel waited for the cry of alarm, but none came. Could their fortune be holding? Had the mages failed to post anyone on the gundeck? Of course they hadn't. They didn't need to. It was doubtful any of them had the first idea how to load and fire a cannon. And they probably didn't trust any of her men to behave themselves anywhere close to black powder.

"Where are the bilges you mean for us to hide in?" Nasrin whispered.

It had been her plan, but now they were here, it seemed wrong. Hiding wasn't her way. She was a pirate. She ran toward the fighting, never away. She reached out a hand, stroking the timbers she knew so well. Whatever happened next, she was aboard her ship. And she was ready to fight for it.

"I've changed my mind," she said. "We should locate the men. We have surprise on our side."

Nasrin didn't argue. It was too dark to see her face clearly, but from her voice, Kestrel almost thought she smiled. "Where will we find them?"

Kestrel tiptoed to the steps and peered up. No one seemed to be near the hatch, and she could hear no footsteps on the deck above. The only sound was the rhythmic creaking of the *Thanos'* decks as the ship plowed through the waves. Looking back at Nasrin, she pressed a finger to her lips, and carefully climbed the steps, her back against the wall.

The deck above was shadowed, but even so she could see

hammocks strung for sleeping. Each one seemed occupied, swaying gently with the ship's roll. No guards stood watch, none that she could see. No mage lurked, either. She took another step, and another. The men in their hammocks rested quietly. It was all strangely quiet. No snoring, no one mumbling to a dream. Were they all dead? She climbed the remaining steps, and tiptoed to the nearest hammock. David DeadEye, with a swipe of ash on one cheek. The man lay still as death, but breathing regularly. She shook him, not enough to wake him but just to disturb his sleep a bit. Instead of puffing and protesting, or turning over, the man didn't react at all. His breathing remained the same, slow and shallow. Kestrel drew back, confused. She moved to the next hammock, where Jaques lay. And the next. Each man slept as soundly as the first.

Nasrin had followed her up the stairs, and stood, gazing at the deck full of sleepers. She crooked a finger at Kestrel, bidding her to come close. "A magical sleep," she said, "Forced on them to keep them controlled for the journey. I could wake them, but it will take time."

Footsteps thudded on the deck above, then down the stairs. Kestrel and Nasrin ducked and ran for the gundeck. Nasrin hopped the steps and disappeared into the shadows between the cannons, but Kestrel pressed her back against the hull and waited just below the plane of the deck. A slender beam of light swept over the room she'd vacated.

"You see? They sleep, Brother." The voice was unfamiliar, probably one of the young mages. "You probably heard some sea bird."

"Indeed," another voice said. "Or one of these cried out from a nightmare." He chuckled. "Perhaps they dream of their deaths."

The beam made one more pass over the roomful of swinging hammocks, then withdrew, leaving the room as dark as before. The footsteps receded.

Kestrel slipped the rest of the way down the stairs, and joined Nasrin. "What will it take to wake my men?" she whispered.

Nasrin shrugged, her face unreadable in the dark. "I cannot be sure. I do not know the specific nature of the Danisoban course that forced them to sleep. I can create a pattern to abolish magic in the entire deck, but as I said, that takes time." She laid a hand on Kestrel's arm. "Have you located Philip?"

"No." She could return to the hammocks, search each one for McAvery, but if she'd been a Danisoban, she would have secured him somewhere else. Somewhere he couldn't accidentally wake from a magical sleep and wander around. Somewhere with a lock on the door. And she was certain they wouldn't have stopped at the lock. He would have a guard set as well. Even if Lig believed her dead, he knew that McAvery was a resourceful man. He wouldn't take chances on the king's Knave escaping.

"He's got to be locked up in the cells," she said. "Shadd, too, I'd guess. And me without my keys."

"A lock should be no hindrance to you."

Kestrel shook her head. "I learned to pick the occasional door lock when I was a child, but I don't have the tools to open iron locks on cell doors."

"I meant your magic. You continue to ignore your heritage, *rais*," Nasrin said, her voice tinged with amusement.

"You say that, but the only heritage I know comes from the alleys of Eldraga." Kestrel's face flushed, and her eyes welled. "I'm still learning how to make this bloody magic useful without killing myself."

"You will learn. Events occurred before your birth, events of which you have no knowledge. Your mother found no opportunity to share with you the information she kept within. I have come to teach you what she could not."

Kestrel sat down on the deck, rubbing the back of her neck. She hardly recalled her parents, she'd been so young when they died. Her mother could have come from anywhere at all, as far as Kestrel knew. Could have been anyone. She sacrificed her life to keep her daughter out of the Danisobans' hands, a forfeit few people in the Nine Islands would offer. She must have known Kestrel was different. The only way she could have known was if she was different herself. Nasrin claimed she could tell Kestrel about her mother, about her own magic. Maybe it was time to stop running from her past, just as she'd decided to stop running from her present and her magic.

"Tell me," she whispered. "Before I change my mind."

Nasrin glanced at the dark stairs. "Your mother was my good

friend. I begged her not to leave the safety of our land, but she insisted you must be born on Eldraga. You see, we knew of your coming long ago. On the day of your mother's affirmation to the sisterhood, the gods revealed to her that her child would be the one for whom we had waited, a child of the sea, the one who would begin the downfall of the Danisobans."

"Downfall of the Danisobans? That's a bit vague," Kestrel said. "I don't understand how you expect me to defeat a whole school of mages when I can hardly create a fire in the palm of my hand."

Nasrin shook her head. "I am not expressing myself well. You will not defeat them personally. There are too many of them for any one person to stand alone. You are the first child born with the fullness of magic within you. You can work their courses without spilling blood."

Kestrel recalled the awful story Lig told about how he'd travelled to Bix. "I always suspected they used the street children somehow. We all sat around at night, telling stories of what happened to the ones who disappeared, but we were only trying to scare each other. None of us wanted to believe the Danisobans spilled blood and took lives to work magic."

"They hide that aspect of their power. As long as it remains only a scary story, no one will rise up to defy them." She stopped, holding both hands down as if telling herself to stop. "You are *giriftana*, the one who can employ all facets of magic. All facets without limitation."

Kestrel wasn't sure she understood. From what she'd seen of magic wielders, once they were trained, there was nothing they couldn't do. She remembered something McAvery had said long ago, that Promises had their own skills but couldn't cross over to others. Was that what Nasrin meant? That she could do everything, after she was trained? Useful, but why would it matter to a nation of magic wielders?

"Ocean water weakens the Danisobans. You already understand magic is born out of the rhythms of life, whether spoken, sung or danced. There are other rhythms, most specifically that of the pounding heart and rushing blood under a man's skin." She sighed, the soft sound heavy with melancholy. "Just as rich men want more gold in their bank chests, those with the ability to work magic are always hoping to achieve greater things. I can lift myself from the ground, but can I fly? I can walk unnoticed in shadow. Can I go about unseen in sunlight? A small group of magic wielders began experimenting in secret, trying to determine if the beat of one's heart could be controlled, in order to create magic. Death resulted. But not every time. Those who did not kill themselves learned that while they could use their own hearts and blood to create magic, they could use someone else's to greater effect and without danger to themselves. The quickly-beating hearts of frightened children produced the mightiest power for their courses. The most accomplished of these was Daniso Ba. If he had been satisfied with merely terrifying children to work his will, perhaps no one would have cared. He was not satisfied. He wanted more power. He wanted to make himself the greatest of all magic wielders."

"He wanted to rule the world," Kestrel murmured, but Nasrin shook her head.

"Not at all. Or not in the way you are thinking. He cared nothing for political strength. He sought something closer to godhood. He hoped to become so powerful that no desire was unattainable, no knowledge inconceivable. His hunger became absolute. One night he abducted a starving street urchin, intending to force the child's heart into a speed and power faster than anyone had ever done. Things went wrong. The human heart is only so strong, and the child was not healthy enough for the strain. His little heart burst. Ba, in a fit of anger, gutted the child before he was quite dead. As the blood flowed over his hands, the course gained incredible power, cast with ease."

A thought flashed through Kestrel's mind, wondering exactly how old this woman might be. Before she could ask, Nasrin continued. "Ba had discovered a new level of working. He began stealing street waifs in the dead of night. He walked a new and dark path. Before long, initiates found their way to his side, others who hoped to learn his secrets. And he welcomed them. Their bloody magic was an abomination, but even then it is hard to say if anyone would have complained, had they known. No one misses a street child."

Kestrel knew that very well. She'd lived that life until she was old enough to work and earn money of her own. So many nights she and her hungry friends slept huddled together in abandoned buildings or unlocked warehouses. So many days of sneaking through the market to steal bread when the baker's back was turned. And always, telling each other tales of what horrors the Danisobans would commit against them, if they let themselves be taken.

Footsteps, muffled through the deck above their heads, creaked along. The two women ducked close to the cannon they crouched behind. Light flashed over the deck hatch. Kestrel held her breath. If the mages came down here searching, she still didn't even have a weapon. The light faded and the footsteps diminished. She let her breath out, her heart thumping at her ribs.

Nasrin continued, her voice softer than before. "One night Ba took a child back to his workshop, as he had been doing for many weeks. Unfortunately for him, this was no street child, but the oldest daughter of a powerful *girifta*. The girl was untrained, unable to defend herself, and so she died screaming. Her terror communicated itself to her mother. The mages did not wield the political power they hold in the Isles, so the furious sisterhood took to the streets, railing against the murder of their *girifta*'s daughter. Soon the ordinary people of the city were roused to action, some for the *girifta*'s cause, others for the mages." Nasrin shook her head. "I can't fathom why anyone would choose the side of such cruelty, but it happened. After a vicious and brutal war of weapons and magic lasting many months, the mages and their followers were nearly overcome, and surrendered in hope of saving their lives. They begged the sisterhood for mercy, but the *girifta* declared they should be put to death. Their crimes were too horrific."

"Obviously something happened to stop their execution?" Kestrel asked.

"Too many of the ordinary people who fought for the *girifta* still had family and friends on the mages' side. Once the fighting ceased, those ordinary people, who greatly outnumbered the magically skilled ones, lost their taste for killing. They threatened to take up arms again if their misguided loved ones were put to death. The *girifta* grudgingly agreed to their exile."

"To the Islands."

"Yes. The *girifta* insisted on a magical limitation to keep the mages from returning, and thus the nature of the mages' blood was altered. The histories say they were fed a substance that caused this change, something that would remain in their blood and be passed through to any children they might conceive, but the recipe for such a substance is locked away in the most secret vaults, and only known by the highest of our order. The result you already know — exposure to salt water leaves them weak as new babes. It was all the *girifia* could do without risking open war again, but she was not happy with the decision, and went to her deathbed warning that the mages would never stay contained."

Of course they wouldn't. Mages as ruthless as the Danisobans would have been patient, waiting for a large enough population before beginning their bloody research again. They'd have focused on repairing the alteration to their blood, or finding a way to use magic in spite of the water. She wondered how many of the Promises taken over the years could have been skilled in some less murderous form of magic.

A low moan rattled the deck under her feet. A higher cry echoed far above, trilling in a way that was eerily similar to the moaning. "The *devwella*," Nasrin said, her voice wondering. "It calls for its own."

Poor little thing, Kestrel thought. I should have chased it away from the start. "It doesn't know I'm here."

"No, no, it is calling to the one in the water. The adult one."

"It's near? That isn't good at all." What might it do, if it feared for the little one's safety? She had no idea how to communicate with it, but she could not risk it sinking her ship either. Kestrel waited until the serpent moaned again, to determine what side of the ship it approached, then walked softly to a closed gunport and pressed it open an inch.

The waves below were black glass, rippling as the ship swept through. But a different ripple swelled and sank in the distance. The high-pitched cry rang over the empty sea. Kestrel didn't dare open the gunport any wider to look up, but she could hear human voices. Frightened voices.

"We have to find McAvery and Shadd," she said, letting the gunport close. "This is the kind of distraction that could serve us well."

"We must also release the *devwella*. It calls to its own. And it does not know you are here. Can you imagine what it is saying?"

As much as she relished the idea of seeing a pack of Daniso-bans flailing in the waves this far from shore, Kestrel knew the mighty serpent in the water wouldn't have any way of knowing there were any people aboard the *Thanos* worth sparing. Unless the little one told it. And quickly. She closed her eyes. *Little one,* she thought, *can you hear me? I'm coming to help you.*

Kestrel waited, but nothing floated into her mind's eye in response. She tried again, this time dispensing with words, instead recalling the lizard hiding on the bookshelf and playing with Shadd's hair on that first night. A comforting image. Again she waited, and again, Still, nothing. Was she too far away?

"What are you doing?" Nasrin glanced toward the stairs to the deck above. "Should I set myself to waking the sleepers?"

"Wait." She didn't know how many mages were on the deck. McAvery and Shadd were locked away somewhere, assuming they weren't already dead and decorating the rigging for the mages' amusement. She didn't have a sword. *Bloody Grace be damned.* Would nothing go right for them?

The lizard's cry warbled through the distance again, and the larger moan answered. If only she could see through the little one's eyes, she'd know the answers she needed. Kestrel looked at Nasrin. "I was trying to make contact with the little *devwella.* I suppose I'm too far away." She snapped her fingers. A bit of ash from the deck popped up in reaction. "How did you speak to me when I was trapped in the inn?"

Nasrin cocked her head. "It is a simple pattern."

"That's not what I want. Would I have to consume the spices? The ones you slipped me in my food?"

"Those were necessary to force your mind open against the Danisoban course. If you only mean to call the little creature, the pattern alone should work well enough." She frowned. "You wish to dance?"

"I wish to dance. Now."

# CHAPTER 21

*And like a never-dying force, the wind*
*Roared till we shouted with it*
— JOHN MASEFIELD, *The Wanderer*

"It is a slow pattern," Nasrin said. She sounded tired and a little impatient. The dance she was teaching Kestrel wasn't merely slow, but excruciatingly so. Kestrel could hardly detect a rhythm to it. Hardly, but the magic was responding. The trouble lay in Kestrel's hurry. She understood what Nasrin said, but her body couldn't help rushing through the movements. Every time she hurried, advanced a movement too soon, the power receded, like a wave rushing back from the shore.

"Stop anticipating what comes next. You must let the magic flow, and thinking so hard only limits your reach. Now slide your hip to the side, and hold the pose for a count of two."

Kestrel bent her knee, pushing her hip out as far as she could. It was a strange position, and she found herself holding her breath, until her heart was pounding and she had to let go.

Nasrin took her hands, forcing Kestrel to look at her. "Think how simple it is to whistle the power to hand. You are trying to force your body to dance the way mine dances. Stop that. Look at me for reference only, but let your body move as it is able."

"This is ridiculous. I'm no dancer." She rubbed her temples, and leaned against a cannon. "I don't understand anything. You said I can do all kinds of magic, but I can't even do this. And even if I could, you're teaching me. I'm not the special one. You are."

"We will train you in our way, but there are facets of magic we must learn from you. The whistling — we cannot do that. And the Danisoban courses, as repellent as they are, if we attempt them without spilling blood, we suffer greatly. Some have even died.

You did not."

"The Eusabians wanted to breed me. If that's your plan, too . . ."

"Not at all. I swear to you, *rais*."

The depwal out at sea called again, waves of sound rumbling through her gut. No way to know, but it seemed closer. Kestrel took a deep breath and released it, letting the tension drain from her. She could do this. She needed to relax, as Nasrin told her, and let it happen. She shook her hands, and bent her head left, then right. "I'll try again."

Nasrin stepped away. She murmured her directions to Kestrel, her voice smooth as velvet in the darkness. As she spoke, Kestrel let herself move. Not watching the dancer, but feeling the slow rhythm in her muscles, allowing herself to move in tiny degrees. As she moved, she noticed the familiar tingle of magic. Instead of the sharp pinpricks she felt when she whistled, or the blistering bubbles from her mistake that left her blinded, this energy rose slowly, a tide of warmth filling the spaces within her. Her cheeks flushed, and Nasrin touched her shoulder.

"Keep your eyes closed. Imagine your lizard friend as you saw it last. Remember how it felt to have the lizard in your mind. Now call to it."

The last time she'd seen it, the little lizard had been curled up on her bookcase, drowsy and well-fed. Its blackish red skin hidden by the shadows between the books, so that only its eyes were clearly visible. She remembered it yawning, its tiny mouth lined with sharp teeth, its long tongue flicking. It had been so funny, playing with the bits of biscuit when she first took it to her cabin. And Shadd's curls . . . she almost laughed out loud at the thought of his startled face when the lizard had pulled at his hair. She couldn't bear the thought of anything happening to it. If there was something she could do to free it, she would. Poor little thing. Her feelings were so strong, reaching out with astral hands to touch the thing she cared for. And she felt a nudge at the corner of her awareness.

*Can you hear me?*

She heard nothing but the creaking of the ship's hull, saw nothing but the darkness behind her own eyelids. Until two red lights glimmered like faraway stars in the darkness, slowly growing clearer and brighter. The lizard's eyes, as she remembered them. Kestrel wanted to laugh out loud, but she didn't dare. They weren't safe yet. *It's me, little one.*

The eyes gazed in the way she'd become accustomed to seeing, watching her, studying her. Kestrel didn't know how long she could maintain the contact. *Can you show me what you see?* she asked, hoping the lizard wasn't locked in a box somewhere. Lig had assured her of its safety, but that meant nothing coming from him.

The eyes faded, replaced by something dark and unyielding. Damn, she should have guessed. It was locked away where it could see nothing. But wait, the darkness moved an inch. It wasn't a wall. It was a robe. A black robe that she knew well.

As she watched, the man wearing the robe walked away. She could see her deck. Through slender bars. The lizard was in a cage, hanging from a hook near her cabin door. Ten or twelve Danisobans were gathered amidships, as far from the railing as they could be. They hadn't been prepared for a sea journey, that was clear. The ship's lanterns were lit from one end of the ship to the other, each one swaying gently with the ship's roll and throwing weirdly lifelike shadows, which gave the illusion of ghostly sailors moving around. Four of her pirates sat against the starboard railing, not bound but clearly unhappy. The mages were probably forcing them to handle the ship as needed, and keeping them quiet under the threat of magical punishment. She wondered if Tom remained at the wheel, or if the ship was being controlled by some magical force alone.

Two men were chained to the mainmast, their drooping heads covered with burlap sacks. One tall and lanky, the other beefy. McAvery and Shadd. As she watched, McAvery let his head tip toward Shadd's, as if he spoke. Shadd's shoulder rose and fell, a subtle movement none of the Danisobans seemed to notice. So they were alive. She hadn't known she could feel such relief. It would have been simpler to free them if they were locked away belowdecks with only had a guard or two to overcome. But there was often water standing on the lower deck where the cells were located, and the mages wouldn't have risked the soaking. At least both men were together in one place, and she didn't have to hunt for them separately.

The lizard looked to the left and up the quarterdeck stairs. Lig and Jeremie stood on the steps, their heads close together as they argued.

Lig pointed at McAvery and Shadd. "We're far enough out to sea. Toss them over, and be done."

"When they'll make such a fine decoration for my palace wall? I hardly think so. Remember you're working for me now."

Lig scowled. "Together, perhaps. Never for. Have a care with my temper, boy. You've already endangered my plans by killing the pirate."

"She was nothing."

"She was everything, you fool. Your desire for petty revenge cheated me out of a simple path to freedom. We searched twenty years for her, and you burn her like a peddler's trash."

Jeremie waved a hand. "Pfft. You didn't need her. You have your depwal. Once it's grown and skinned, you can go where you like."

Lig drew a small blade from his sleeve, and sliced the heel of his left hand. Blood oozed from the wound, pooling in Lig's cupped palm. He muttered something, and flung the blood at Jeremie. It splattered against his face and neck, and Jeremie cried out, brushing at the burned spots.

"Never assume you know what I need." Lig said. "And never assume I won't discard you as I choose."

The former prince stomped down the steps and over to the prisoners. Drawing a foot back, he leveled a hard kick at Shadd's leg. Shadd grunted, throwing his head back blindly and bouncing it off the mast behind him. McAvery started, jerking away. Jeremie turned back to the angry mage. "I'm still keeping these," he said. With that, he marched to the door of the captain's cabin, letting himself in and slamming it behind him.

Another bone-rattling moan sounded from out in the water. Lig turned to stare across the star-dappled ocean in the direction of the sound. He said nothing, but his jaw tightened visibly, and he stalked over to the mage at the wheel, muttering something close to the man's ear.

*Little one, ask the devwella in the ocean not to attack the ship. Tell it you have friends aboard,* Kestrel said. It responded with an eerie wail of its own, the cry soaring over the water. She had to hope it relayed the message. Otherwise it wouldn't matter who won in the coming fight. They'd all drown.

*Are there any weapons lying about?* she asked. The lizard swung its head to and fro, finally landing its gaze on a sword tossed casually against the railing.

*Good, good. Now, there's one last thing,* she said, hoping she sounded reassuring. *Look closely at your cage, especially the lock.* The lizard pressed its snout against the bars, opening its mouth to flick its tongue out. Kestrel tasted the cold tang of iron. The lock was also iron, and functioned with a key. McAvery could probably master the lock with his skills, but she hadn't the first idea how to do it herself. She'd need to unchain him or find the holder of the key.

*Thank you, little one. I'm coming to help.*

She opened her eyes. Nasrin leaned forward and laid her hands on Kestrel's arms. "What have you learned?" she asked, a touch of excitement in her voice.

Kestrel ran a hand over her head. Ash clung to her braids, and her hand came down black with it. She desperately wanted an hour of quiet and a tub full of water. The first thing she'd do when this was all over, assuming she lived. So much had happened, and so much was yet to be done. She told Nasrin what the lizard had shown her. "Lig and Jeremie are at odds," she finished. "That's the best help we're going to get."

One more moan echoed in the night. Closer than it had been. "I told the lizard to ask its friend to hold off. I hope that means the message got through," Kestrel said. "I imagine Lig would love to catch the big one right now, somehow. Save him the trouble of growing mine to adulthood in a lagoon somewhere." She rubbed her temples. "I wish I'd known why he wanted the skins before. I might have sent the little one away right after I found it. I could have returned to Pecheta and reported to the king, who would have recognized the false orders."

"He doesn't seem a man inclined to waiting," Nasrin said. "If he can drive the ship fast enough, he could stay ahead of the *devwella* that pursues us, all the way to some prepared trap. Did you not read the little book you purchased for Artemus?"

It had been a flapbook, a few short tales of the legendary pirate Flingo Naile. Kestrel had glanced at the pages when she bought it, but there hadn't been time to read since then. She remembered Nasrin offering to read it to her, and her blood ran cold.

"There was something important in that book?"

"Flingo Naile, if he actually existed, encountered many wonders in his journeys. Including the *devwellas*. Your anger seemed likely to consume you, and I could not be sure. And the way you cherished the little one . . ."

Of course she'd been angry. She'd been blinded by magic she didn't know how to use, all because she thought Nasrin treated her like a child. She was angry still, but she understood a little better. And they only had each other now.

"There is a story in the book detailing Naile's battle with a Danisoban wearing a suit of such skin. In the story, the mage hopes to trap another *devwella*, but Naile becomes its friend and saves it from doom. The tale is amusing, but with what we understand now, it's clearly something of a prediction. Lig in a suit is a threat to only a few people at a time. Many Danisobans dressed thus could leave the Nine Islands and cause mayhem of a terrifying degree."

Kestrel stared at the dancer, the full implication of her words settling in. Lig figured out a way to leave the islands, to bring the Danisoban war back to the unsuspecting Continent dwellers. And she'd been a part of it. She'd caught the lizard, and they were drawing its kin to them with its cries. How many mages would one creature be able to clothe? She told the lizard to warn its friend away, but would the bigger one listen? The sea creature was close now, and if some magical trap existed, she didn't know where it might be. She had to stop Lig, before they got any further. She had to let the little one out.

Nasrin seemed to know what she was thinking, because she nodded. "Release the *devwella*, free the men above and take the ship back from the Danisobans. What do you have in mind to make this goal succeed?"

"First, we need to lay hands on some Danisoban robes." Kestrel rubbed her eyes. She was so tired. Had it only been a few hours since she'd waked from her magical sleep to watch her best friend die? It seemed like days. "Follow me, and keep low."

They climbed the gundeck stairs to the silent deck above. Hammocks swung peacefully in the dark, all the men in them as quiet as death. Kestrel crept to the darkest corner opposite the stairs, hoping to maneuver herself behind whatever mages had the duty of checking on the men. If any. So far, the only time anyone checked on them had been when the one thought he heard someone cry out. If they believed themselves beyond worry, and sent no sentries down, she'd have to come up with another idea. She pressed herself into the shadows to wait. Nasrin situated herself on the other side. Kestrel could barely see her, but she heard a soft rhythm begin, a shuffling that could have been mistaken for rats if one wasn't listening closely. She wondered what Nasrin was preparing to do, and wished she had enough understanding of her own magic to bring it to bear so easily. She reminded herself that she'd someday be trained to do what the dancer could, if they survived the night. She would survive. She had to, for Binns. For her mother. For everyone who'd ever been victimized by the power-hungry Danisobans.

Footsteps thudded on the stairs. Kestrel ducked low as a warm light glimmered and grew. Two mages came clumping down. Their hoods were drawn, but she was sure neither man was Lig. He would never take on such a menial task. Kestrel looked across at Nasrin, who nodded. She was ready.

The two men stopped at the bottom of the stairs. "They're asleep," said one, turning to ascend again.

"Wait," said the other. "Master Lig insisted we walk all the way and back."

The first one made a low, grumbling noise in his throat, as if walking the length of the deck was a backbreaking chore. "Fine," he said. "You do it. I want to get back and see the fishing."

The fishing? So whatever trap Lig laid had to be nearby. Their time drew short.

"Give me the lantern, then," he said. The first mage stepped down from the lowest stair, holding out the lantern. Kestrel jumped at his back, snaking her arm around his neck and pulling her elbow tight against his throat. He let go of the lantern. Clawed at her arm. Struggled to free himself. He couldn't cry out, but his whimpers sounded as loud as shouts in her ears. He overbalanced. The two of them toppled backward. His weight nearly knocked her loose, but she managed to hang on. His heel thumped against the deck. Kestrel arched her back, trying to pull

tighter. When would the man pass out? Her arm began to trem-
ble under the strain, until suddenly the mage collapsed against
her. She let go, pushing him away and scrambling to her feet.

The other fellow had caught the lantern, but Nasrin stood in
front of him, her palm inches from his face. He stared, wide-
eyed, at a light flickering from her hand. She popped her palm
forward, connecting with the bridge of his nose, and he crumpled. Nasrin grabbed the lantern as he fell.

"Take his robe off," Kestrel whispered. She bent to her own
man, stripping his robe from him and throwing it over her shoulders. She lifted him by the arms and dragged him across the deck
to a small coil of heavy twine used for repairing fallen hammocks,
and tied him securely. Nasrin joined her with the smaller man.
"He will not wake for some time," she said. "We must hurry."

"Mine won't be out long. I'm going to free the lizard. I want
you to wake my men."

"If I cannot—"

Kestrel smiled. "I know you can. And when they're awake, tell
them to grab anything they can use as a weapon, and come
abovedeck. It's going to take all we have."

Nasrin turned away, then looked back. "What will you do if
they see through your deception?"

What indeed? Kestrel didn't answer, because she couldn't
know until she was tested. The robes stank of unwashed bodies
and old food. Within the sleeves she discovered tiny pockets,
holding coins, bits of charcoal, a short, sharp blade and a small
roll of bandage wrapping. Kestrel raised her hood, and climbed
to the main deck.

The air smelled sweet off the water. After so long in the lower
decks, Kestrel couldn't help breathing deep. The mages had
hung a lantern every few feet, lighting the deck as if it was
adorned for a celebration. The night watch usually lit two or
three lanterns at most, just enough to keep from running into the
water barrel and tipping it over. As she'd seen through the lizard's eyes, the mages were gathered together as far from the railing as they could stand.

McAvery and Shadd hadn't moved since the kick, and for all
she knew, they'd fallen asleep. The cage holding her lizard hung
from a hook near the quarterdeck steps, and as she glanced that

way, the lizard looked at her. It flicked its tongue. She couldn't
see Lig at all. Jeremie must have recovered from his tantrum and
left the captain's cabin. He leaned over the quarterdeck railing,
staring into the night. Kestrel slid her feet over the deck, moving
toward the discarded sword the lizard had shown her. She bent
down, watching the mages, and wrapped her fingers around the
hilt.

"Get away from the edge! You'll get wet!" One of the mages
waved at her, half-panicked, as if her proximity would somehow
affect him. She rose quickly, easing the sword as far into her
sleeve as she could, and holding the exposed blade end against
her robe to hide it.

"What were you thinking?" The mage who'd called to her laid
a hand on her elbow, drawing her toward the group. "You could
have been splashed. Or fallen over. Besides, the course is starting. They need us all to catch and hold the depwal." Kestrel let
herself be led. As long as no one knew her, she might be able to
learn more.

The magi were all standing now, their heads close together as
they spoke. "If you use *korbera*, the net will spark fire. Master
Lig will set us on fire if we burn that creature's skin."

"No, no, you're thinking of *korbuna*. *Korbera* is cold."

They blathered on for some time, arguing about the intrica-
cies of their course, and Kestrel listened close. After a few minutes, she realized that they were attempting to create a net of pure
magic energy. They planned to catch the depwal in much the
same way bozorgi fishermen cast rope nets. That's why they
needed her ship, she thought. There were very few vessels big
enough to haul such a huge creature, and the king wouldn't question Lig retrieving the *Thanos* if there was evidence Kestrel was a
traitor. She had to give him credit. Lig would have made an exceptional pirate.

"Hey, you," one of the mages poked Kestrel in the ribs.
"Take this drawing and compare it to the bait in the cage. I need
to know the ratio between the wing bones and the height of the
ridges along its tail." Kestrel hesitated, not sure how to respond,
and the others laughed. "Scared of the sting?"

"It has a stinger?" she asked, peering at the drawing. Lig had
mentioned that, as had the scroll describing the lizard. But she'd

carried the lizard against her skin, with no ill effects. Only the slightest tingle when they first touched.

"The skin stings if you touch it with your bare skin," the mage laughed. "So, careful with your measurements, right?" They turned back in to the huddle, shutting her out.

Perfect. A chance to free the lizard, with a reason for being near it. Bloody Grace was watching over her. The goddess rarely bothered, so Kestrel couldn't waste the opportunity. Pulling her hood as far out as it would go, she walked to the cage. Now that her back was to the rest, and no one was watching, she let the sword slide out of her sleeve, and moved it to hang from her belt. It poked out strangely, so she hooked the blade behind her knee. It affected her stride, forcing her to walk more slowly than she liked, but the alternative would have left her unarmed. Taking the charcoal from her voluminous sleeve, she folded the drawing in half and leaned in close to the lizard's cage, letting her bare hand rest at the bottom. The lizard shuffled over to her, leaning its head against her skin.

"I miss you, too, little one." She rubbed its jaw with her knuckle. "Do you know who has the key to this thing?"

A vision appeared in her mind's eye. A man, white hair and a black robe. Menja Lig. Wonderful. The key was probably in his pocket, or hung on a lanyard around his neck, where she couldn't get at it while Lig still breathed. McAvery was chained, and even if she could free him, he had no tools to pick the lock on the lizard's cage.

But she did. The tiny blade from her robe. She slid it out, and tried to fit it into the lock. The blade was too wide. Putting it back, she huffed a frustrated breath. How could she do this? She had only seconds before the magi noticed she wasn't doing any measuring. It was a lock, a simple one, since it was designed to keep small animals in cages. She could untie knots and pull ropes with her power — could she turn a lock mechanism, too? She blew a soft whistle, bringing the power to bear on the keyhole. She pushed air in, feeling the shape of the lock and forming the air around it. A little more, until there was no room left. Holding the air steady, she cocked her head to the right and was satisfied with a gentle clunk. She'd done it. "When I step away," she whispered, "slip out of the door and head for the sea. And ask your—" what did lizards call each other? "Your kin. Ask it to swim away with you. As quickly as you can."

It licked at her knuckle. Taking up the charcoal, she made up some numbers and scribbled them on the paper.

"What are you doing?" Jeremie was striding across the deck, straight for Kestrel. "No feeding the animal, you."

"I wasn't, sir. Merely taking some measurements." She ducked her head and tried to walk past him, but he grabbed her arm and swung her in front of him.

"Wait! You're a woman." He bent at the knees, trying to peer into her hood. Kestrel turned her head away.

"Yes, sir. I'm very busy."

"Whose ridiculous idea was it to give a woman an education? Lig, was this your doing?" He dragged her toward the quarter-deck steps. Lig popped his head around the topmost slat.

"Keep quiet, Jeremie. We're preparing to build the net."

"I want this woman. You don't need her for your workings, do you?" He licked his lips and leered at her. "She could help me sleep."

"That's no woman, you fool. I brought only male brethren on this trip."

Jeremie shot his free hand to Kestrel's chest, grabbing her breast and squeezing painfully. "I'm never wrong on this kind of question. You have a woman in your midst."

Kestrel let the drawing flutter away. Yanking her elbow loose from his grip, she reached inside her robe to draw her sword. She raised the point and stepped in front of the former prince. He skidded backward, cursing. His hand dropped to the sword at his side. Kestrel swung her blade at his hand. Its edge sliced flesh. Blood sprayed.

"Damned magician!" he roared. "You'll die for this!" He turned his sword side out of her reach, and drew his blade while he spun. Kestrel raised her blade to block his attack. The two of them paced in a circle, staring at each other, waiting for the right moment to strike.

"What's happening?" Lig stopped halfway down the steps, and he seemed happy to remain there. Kestrel shot a whistle to the lizard. It needed to run, now, before anyone decided to se-cure the cage somewhere else. It nudged the unlocked door with its snout, forcing the door to swing open. The lizard scampered free, romping across the deck as other mages swarmed to catch it. It ran to the railing, slipping past grasping hands as if they weren't there at all.

"Don't touch! It stings like acid!" Cries rang through the mob. Two mages came at the lizard, edging slowly from two directions toward the danger of the rail. Just as they were close enough to grab, the lizard spread its wings, shrieking. One mage recoiled, but the other was too close to the side. He lost his balance, slipped over the edge and fell, screaming, to the black water far below.

"Catch it!" Lig yelled. The lizard threw itself backward over the railing, escaping into the water below.

Kestrel shook the hood loose, letting it fall away from her face. Jeremie frowned, then stared. His sword arm dropped a fraction. Kestrel took advantage of the weakness. She drove toward him. He raised to a block just in time. Her blade sliced another wound higher on his arm. Blood dripped on the deck. Jeremie didn't notice.

"I killed you," he said, his voice disbelieving.

"And I've come from the grave for my vengeance." She grinned and launched at him, chopping with every ounce of her strength. He blocked left, right. She spun, aiming low. Her swing caught him just above his knee. Blood sprayed from the wound. He toppled to the deck with a grunt. Kestrel pressed her sword's point into his belly. "Yield," she said.

"Kestrel!" Pirates boiled up from the hatch, armed with swords and cooking ladles, whatever they could lay hands on. Danisobans ran to and fro, some trying to stay out of the way of the battle long enough to build magical attacks, others merely running from angry pirates. One robed mage swept his hands in front of him. A bolt of silver lightning erupted, striking one of her men. As he fell, two other pirates grabbed the mage and tossed him overboard. More flashes of silver lit the deck, amid cries of pain. Nasrin emerged from behind the crowd. She began a dance. Sharp turns, hard stomps. Kestrel looked back down to her enemy.

"I'm giving you the chance you didn't give my friend," she said. If she wanted to remain the king's Privateer, she'd lock Jeremie up, deliver him to his father again. For Binns' sake, she hoped he wouldn't surrender. She wanted to give him the death he deserved.

He grinned at her. "Never," he said. All the answer she needed. Kestrel moved the sword point to his neck, and flexed her arm to drive his sentence home.

As she moved, Jeremie rolled away. Once clear, he leaped to his feet and attacked. Kestrel blocked his thrusts, but he seemed to find new energy. He swung overhead, came down hard. His strike nearly knocked Kestrel's sword out of her hand. She backed away, not taking her eyes off Jeremie. He lunged at her again.

Kestrel hopped backward. Out of the corner of her eye, she saw Nasrin dancing, her body gliding across the wood like a silk flag caught in the wind. The dancer reached her lovely arms out, gesturing toward the mages who crowded around. One rose off his feet, flailing and shrieking as he was carried over the railing and dropped. Nasrin shouted a loud ululation, the sound a battle cry. And Kestrel remembered her own unseen weapon.

She whirled away from her attacker. Side to side she stepped, and a stomp. A whirl again to the other side. She moved in rhythms she'd denied herself, avoiding Jeremie's attacks. The more she tried, the easier it seemed. So smooth, so simple, so graceful. It almost made her laugh.

The magic rose, tickling under her skin, burning with promise. Bubbling heat filled her, shone like the sun from behind her eyes. She surged toward her enemy, letting the heat lead the way. Jeremie stepped back as she drove forward. The light solidified into molten silver, liquid anger that boiled within her. This time it didn't boil over. She maintained control. Kestrel danced another step, two. Getting closer to Jeremie. She could melt him like a confection on the hottest summer day, until he was nothing but a stain on the deck.

"Mercy!" he said.

"You beg for mercy? From me?" Her voice echoed in her head. "I, who was forced to watch as you murdered my friend?" She let a ray of the silver light flow from the tip of one finger, pointing it like a stiletto until it scraped against his bare cheek. He howled in pain. "You weren't fit to clean the pots in his kitchen. You deserve nothing." She opened her fingers wide, prepared to blast him from her deck.

"I can testify to the mage's crimes." He raised his chin as he dropped his sword to his side. "I surrender and live, you defeat Menja Lig. I know you hate him."

Was it enough? Could she even trust him that far? He betrayed his own father, and now the mage. He'd turn on her, too. But the king would want to deal with his son. Kestrel allowed the silver fire to recede.

In that instant, Jeremie snapped forward. He raked at her with his blade. In reflex, she thrust forward, impaling him on her sword. They stood, face to face, his blood pumping over her hand and hilt, her sword clean through his belly and out his back. An eternity later, his eyes darkened. His body slackened. The dead weight forced her to let go of her weapon as he sank to the deck.

# CHAPTER 22

*Then the wrack tattered and the stars appeared,*
*Millions of stars that seemed to speak in fire*
—JOHN MASEFIELD, *The Wanderer*

Nasrin held a wailing mage above a yardarm, letting him drop and rise in the air as she continued to dance. Kestrel's men battled hand-to-hand with the mages around them. David DeadEye and Hudee took hold of one mage, carrying him to the railing together to fling him overboard. The mages were casting their own courses at her men, blood spattering everywhere. Her men bore the marks of the magical attacks, blood streaming down one's face, another's chest burned and his shirt in rags. One pirate cried out, and fell, clutching his head in agony, and rolled away from the fight. Jaques had found his way to the chained men, and was working to free them. Shadd bellowed for his freedom, and Kestrel laughed. Her quartermaster hated to miss a good fight.

Menja Lig stood on the quarterdeck above the main deck. He cried out in the sibilant Danisoban language, flinging blood in Nasrin's direction. His magic didn't seem to bother the dancer, but soon he'd find some course strong enough to break through whatever defense she had. He caught sight of Kestrel, his eyes widening. He turned, waved a pattern of arm movements in the directions of the quarterdeck stairs, and retreated to the shadows of the stern. Kestrel bent and retrieved her sword from the dead prince, wiping the blood on her robe, and ran.

Something crashed against the hull of her ship, tilting it sideways in a sickening roll. Kestrel fell against a barrel, slamming her hip hard and grabbing on to keep from falling. A moan roared from below, close enough now to feel through the deck. The creature had arrived. The Danisobans were in no condition to try and capture it, not now, but the creature couldn't know that. She hadn't seen the lizard since it chased a mage over the side, but she hoped it remembered to tell its kin to spare the ship.

She glanced over her shoulder. Six mages remained on their feet, as well as most of her own men. Shadd held a Danisoban in his meaty grip. He looked as if he intended to throw the man as far as he could, whether that meant against the mast or over the side. Jaques worked frantically on McAvery's chains. The burlap sack was gone, and he caught her eye. She'd known he was safe, but seeing his face sent a wave of relief through her body.

Nasrin was spinning, her hair floating in the air. Kestrel imagined she could see the power building around the graceful dancer.

Another strike rocked the ship. A long, leathery tail ridged with hard scales stretched up and over the railing onto the deck, splashing water everywhere and slapping at anyone too close to duck for cover. Danisobans and pirates alike shouted and ran. It slithered away again, the ship swaying under the weight. Kestrel ran for the quarterdeck stairs, wrapping one hand around the railing just as the ship rocked again. She was thrown off balance, but she didn't lose her hold. She scrabbled to her feet and forced herself up the steps. She would destroy Lig, stop him once and for all, even if it killed her. At the top of the steps, she stopped to get her bearings.

Only one lantern swung behind the ship's wheel, sending eerie shadows across the quarterdeck. Lig crouched behind the wheel, and he looked up when she reached the top. Bloody coward thought he could hide? Kestrel ran at him, her sword ready to strike his head from his neck, and slammed into an unseen wall. She staggered to the railing, catching her breath. He'd raised a magical defense. She aimed a heel kick against it, but it was as unmoving as a stone. The only thing that might release it was magic. Kestrel let her sword fall against the railing. It would do her no good against a mage, and it would throw off her balance.

She looked for Nasrin. The dancer was too far away to call for, busy with her own battle. It was up to Kestrel. Nasrin had said she could do anything. Time to try. She took a step to the right, tapping her toe, then turned to the left and tapped again. Sidestep, sidestep, and spin, and repeat, she told herself. She couldn't recall exactly what every step had been from that very first time. It didn't matter. What she had in mind would work. It had to. She reached one arm out, letting her upper body follow it like a ribbon in a breeze. The dance carried her along, a storm of freedom within her, but not once did she dare take her eyes off the mage. His rage at knowing she lived pulsed across the deck. Crouched down, he moved his arms in a pattern, back and forth, and he spoke words she couldn't hear.

The music in her mind filled her with power. She danced to a tune only she could hear. She became light as a feather, warm as the sun, and bursting with purpose. She strode to the invisible wall. Placing a hand against it, she pressed her palm flat and sent a rush of her silver fire against it. Sparks exploded, crackling outward from her hand. The wall creaked, shook, and fractured as if made of real glass. Shards of gleaming magic tumbled away in a burst of silver. Kestrel took a step forward, past where the wall had been. "On your feet, you coward!"

Lig rose, opening his arms wide as if to embrace her. She stopped, stunned at what she saw. Blood and gore covered his chest and face, dripped from his hands. He smiled, showing teeth stained red.

"I should have known you were not so easy to kill."

Kestrel tilted her head, raised a hand and sent a ray of silver fire at the Danisoban's body. He flicked it away as one would a bothersome fly.

"What makes you think you can hurt me?" he asked. A bloody gobbet plopped from one ear. "Perhaps if you and the witch had found each other sooner."

She extended both hands, shooting bolts of fire at him, but he only laughed as the silver sprayed left and right away from him.

As much blood as soaked his clothing, he should have passed out by now. How could he still be standing? She growled, and threw everything she had stored at him, but nothing.

"You broke a wall, but you're not ready to fight me, girl." He let his head fall back. "*Hesh coorrup ken beha ta*!" he shrieked to the sky. The blood on his body began to pool, gathering from random spills into an enormous bubble on his chest. The mass of gore broke loose from him, rising into the dark, and his now-clean body shimmered like glittering starlight. "Someday, if your little dancing witch doesn't kill you," he called, his voice a warble.

The definition of his body faded, becoming ghostly. She could almost see the stars through his chest. "You haven't stopped me."

Kestrel ran at him, reaching out to catch him. Her grasp fell on emptiness. Her heel slid on the befouled deck, sending her skidding to her knees into a pool of fresh blood. And suddenly she realized why Lig hadn't suffered from the loss of blood. It wasn't his.

She'd assumed he was using his own blood to shield himself from her, but so much had been spilled, he should have died. She'd watched Binns die from it; she should have realized earlier that it wasn't Lig's blood at all. She remembered what he'd told her, about the ways Danisobans travel. *We spill the child's blood,* he'd said, *while arranging the entrails into a pleasing pattern and speaking the proper incantation. The gods, in gratitude for our thoughtful sacrifice, transport us to the destination of our choosing.* Apparently an adult's blood was equally useful. Red Tom lay on the deck, his abdomen torn open and his guts arranged before her.

Kestrel stumbled to the railing, gagging with horror. She bent over the edge, her belly heaving with disgust. How many more friends had to die? She leaned back, screaming to the heavens, but got no answer. Letting herself sink to the deck, she stared at Tom's poor mutilated body behind the wheel.

The ship rocked again. The creature continued beating at the hull. At this rate it might sink them. She needed to call to the lizard, ask it to communicate with its huge companion, ask it to stop. Kestrel wiped her face, and bent over the railing again.

A wide, deadly wave of water rolled toward her ship. The creature, coming around for another strike. She whistled, hard and loud, not even trying to make magic, but just whistling. Water splashed from far below, sweeping up the hull nearly high enough to wet her. She whistled again, and this time heard a familiar answering call.

"Tell it to stop!" she howled. She couldn't bear another death. So many times she'd killed men in battle, sent them careening across her deck, their blood spattering the sails. Those deaths had at least mattered. Binns and Tom, their deaths served as tools, nothing more. No better than street children with no one to look out for them. She should have been looking out for her friends.

An image floated into her mind's eye – a huge creature diving deep, swimming away. The mighty beast swept its tail once before vanishing into the dark, and the image faded. The ship's rocking slowed. This night, at least, they would not be sinking. "Thank you," she whispered. If the little lizard heard her, it didn't respond.

"*Rais.*" Nasrin was next to her, kneeling on the deck.

She had a job to do. She struggled to her feet. Broken lanterns and broken men littered her deck. What few mages were left huddled silently together on the deck, staring with terror at the quarterdeck. McAvery finally free of his chains, had found a sword. He used it to keep the Danisobans back, but when he saw them staring, he looked up and caught sight of Kestrel. He took the stairs two at a time, snatching her up in his arms and holding her so tight she feared she'd never breathe again. She didn't fight him. It didn't matter who saw, not now. She twined her hands in his hair, and breathed in the comfort of his nearness. He was alive, and so was she.

# CHAPTER 23

*Among her crew the song spread, man to man,*
*Until the singing rang across the bay*
—JOHN MASEFIELD, *The Wanderer*

Once Lig was gone, four Danisobans remained, abandoned by their leader and all the fight gone out of them. Shadd suggested letting them swim back to Bix, but Nasrin threatened to put him back in his chains if he tossed anyone else into the ocean. They eventually settled on herding the men into a hackney boat with a lantern and a small cask of drinking water to last them a few days.

After the boat was lowered to the water, Shadd yelled, "Ye can either row or create a wind to drive yerselves home. But don't be lookin' back for help. My captain ain't in the mood to help ye."

One man rose shakily to his feet, then thought better of it when the boat rocked under him, and sat down again. "Give us our dead for burial. It's the decent thing to do. And the book you stole."

Shadd turned to Kestrel. She hadn't spared a thought for the book, but of course it must be on the ship. She'd look for it later. Shadd was waiting for her answer, so she shook her head no. He laughed. "Sorry, not happenin'."

The other mages pulled at his robe, but the man went on. "At least give us the prince's body. For his father's sake."

"They're full of demands, for defeated men," McAvery said. He'd stayed next to her since the battle ended, as if he feared losing sight of her again.

She shrugged. "They're used to getting what they want. I think it's time they learned a lesson." Kestrel joined Shadd at the railing, and stared down at the mage wordlessly. The prince would be given no state funeral, no recognition. She wanted his body to sink, to be food for fishes and never to be spoken of again. It was only fair to Binns. Licking her lips, she blew a few notes, sending the hackney boat rocking and making the mages cry out. It appeared to be the incentive they needed. Without another word, the mages picked up the hackney oars and began to row. They were soon lost to sight.

"Kestrel, look," McAvery said, close to her ear. He pointed to the east. Fingers of pink light teased at the horizon. The sun, making its appearance after a long and brutal night. "There's still some work to finish," she murmured back. "We have to see to the dead."

The dead mages and the prince were tossed into the water unceremoniously. But the crew gathered together to bid farewell to Tom. Hudee and DeadEye wrapped Tom in canvas, and Kestrel tucked his beloved books in the wrapping with him. "You'll have all the time in the world to read now, my friend," she said softly. When she stepped away, the men lifted Tom onto a smooth board, and carried it to the railing.

Jaques tried to offer up a prayer to the gods. "No man serves the sea but for knowing his mates were beside him to help stand the watch . . ." He stumbled over the words, and turned stricken eyes to Kestrel. "I don't know who he prayed to," he said.

Kestrel laid a hand on his back. "It doesn't matter, lad. His gods will sort it out." Jaques nodded and finished his words. For a time, the entire crew kept silent, and in the quiet, Kestrel found herself wishing she could have given Binns a funeral like this instead of abandoning his ashes on Bix. He deserved to rest below the waves, but there'd been nothing she could do. She hoped he knew how much she regretted losing him. Peering up into the brightening sky, she smiled, and nodded to the men holding Tom's board. On Kestrel's signal, they tipped it upward, letting Tom slide off into the ocean. He fell through the air until he hit the water, and with a gentle splash, disappeared from view.

Nasrin approached her after the funeral. "*Rais*, there is much we must discuss. I promised to explain how your mother came to be in the islands."

She'd wanted for so long to know about her mother, about what made her special. She looked at the sky. The stars she'd watched were gone now, fallen to the influence of the rising sun. Binns had said a new day always follows, and he was right.

Sometimes that new day meant grief and sorrow, but it was a new day just the same. And there would be one after that. She had a long journey ahead. There was time to hear stories, time to know the truth. She could wait.

Nasrin no longer looked like the young beautiful dancer. She'd let the illusion fall, now that it wasn't necessary. Kestrel found she preferred Nasrin's mature face and silver hair. It was more honest, somehow. "You have the Danisoban book and we should begin your training as soon as possible. Menja Lig will not wait long to come after you."

"Not right now, Nasrin. I need to rest."

Nasrin bowed her head. "Of course, *rais*. When you are ready, send for me."

Kestrel retired to her cabin to change her clothing. The shirt was stiff with dried blood, and she didn't even want to try washing it. She'd never wear it again, not after what it represented to her. She balled it up, opened the window and leaned on the casement to throw it away.

A little snout poked around the edge. Kestrel smiled, and sat back on the bed. "Come in," she said. The lizard tumbled into the room, romping over the tousled bedclothes to rub its face against her hand. Kestrel stroked it gently. "You silly old thing," she murmured. "Why are you back?"

It stared up at her, its eyes wide. In the depths of her mind, she saw a memory of it sitting next to her, snuggled close in the dark. When she'd been blind, it had comforted her. Was it trying to say it was taking care of her, or she of it? It didn't matter really. As long as it wanted to stay, she would let it. She rolled it over, scratching its belly. It purred like a kittle, opening its wings in pleasure. "I've been thinking of a name for you," she admitted. "What about Kourosh?"

The lizard rolled upright, and scampered to its favorite spot on the bookshelf. Tomorrow she would find where Lig left the book, and she would finish reading it properly. There was time. So much time. The horizon was a long way off, and she had nothing holding her in the Islands. Not anymore.

She tossed the ruined shirt into the sea, pulled on a new one and started taking down her damaged braids. Her hair was a filthy mess, and her scalp itched badly. She wasn't a vain woman, but at that moment she would have done almost anything to wash. The pitcher and bowl weren't going to be enough. This time, she needed a real bath. She wandered onto the deck to ask for a tub of water to be brought up.

The light of the early morning sun gilded her ship. Hudee, armed with a mop, swabbed what was left of the blood stains, David swung in the rigging as he checked for loose knots, and the rest were going about their business as usual. Kestrel caught young Hudee's eye. "It's a fine job you're doing here, but could I trouble you to bring me a tub of water for washing, lad?"

He nodded, set the mop to rest against the mast, and vanished below, passing McAvery on his way up carrying two plates of food. He smiled, and the world was lit with gold. "Care for some breakfast? Rumor has it that you haven't eaten since some bitter ale and salted fish yesterday."

"Haven't I?" Had it only been a day? He handed her a plate, loaded with fruit and bread and not so much as a scrap of fish. "Thank you. I am hungry. But right now I'm desperate to wash my hair."

He raised an eyebrow. "That's not what I would have guessed you'd say. I expected you to be storming around, making sure everything was in place for the trip and insisting on starting your training with Nasrin."

Once that would have been true. Once she would have worried about being an outlaw, a true fugitive from the law. Menja Lig still lived, with even more reason to want her dead. She had to assume the king of the Nine Islands no longer considered her an ally. Lig would poison him with the tale of Jeremie's death. And the four she'd sent off in the boat — if they made it home, their tales of her cruelty would spread across the islands like lightning. But today, with the early sun warming her skin, her pirates busy about their jobs, and the man she loved standing a foot away from her, she couldn't order up the energy to be in charge. For once, she would let things go. She would wash her hair and comb it out to dry, and rest, truly rest, on the huge bed in her cabin. She eyed him thoughtfully. His tangled hair wasn't in much better condition than hers. Not that it made him any less desirable in her eyes. "You could use a good scrub, too, I think."

McAvery gazed at Kestrel, and a delicious tingle snaked

through her belly. "Where will I find any hot water, Captain?"

"Follow me," she said, taking his hand and leading him to her door.